OTHER BOOKS BY LUCY KAVALER

The Secret Lives of the Edmonts
A Matter of Degree
Noise, the New Menace
Freezing Point
Mushrooms, Molds, and Miracles
The Astors
The Private World of High Society

*For Young Readers*

Green Magic
The Dangers of Noise
Dangerous Air
Life Battles Cold
Cold Against Disease
The Astors: An American Legend
The Wonders of Fungi
The Artificial World Around Us
The Wonders of Algae

# Heroes & Lovers

# Heroes & Lovers

## Lucy Kavaler

A DUTTON BOOK

DUTTON
Published by the Penguin Group
Penguin Books USA Inc., 375 Hudson Street,
New York, New York 10014, U.S.A.
Penguin Books Ltd, 27 Wrights Lane,
London W8 5TZ, England
Penguin Books Australia Ltd, Ringwood,
Victoria, Australia
Penguin Books Canada Ltd, 10 Alcorn Avenue,
Toronto, Ontario, Canada M4V 3B2
Penguin Books (N.Z.) Ltd, 182–190 Wairau Road,
Auckland 10, New Zealand

Penguin Books Ltd, Registered Offices:
Harmondsworth, Middlesex, England

First published by Dutton, an imprint of Dutton Signet,
a division of Penguin Books USA Inc.
Distributed in Canada by McClelland & Stewart Inc.

First Printing, March, 1995
10  9  8  7  6  5  4  3  2  1

 REGISTERED TRADEMARK—MARCA REGISTRADA

Library of Congress Cataloging-in-Publication Data

Kavaler, Lucy.
    Heroes and lovers / Lucy Kavaler.
        p.   cm.
    ISBN 0–525–93815–X
    I.  Title.
    PS3561.A8684H47   1995
    813'.54—dc20                                                94-34526
                                                                CIP

Printed in the United States of America
Set in Simoncini Garamond
Designed by Leonard Telesca

PUBLISHER'S NOTE
This is a work of fiction. Although real people appear in their natural settings, none of the events depicted in the story really happened and are entirely fictitious. Any actions, motivations, or opinions attributed to or about real people in the book are purely fiction and are presented solely as entertainment.

TO ARTHUR
always my companion on the exciting journey
of exploration that is life


This book is also for my daughter, Andrea, with thanks for the wholehearted enthusiasm and unfailing confidence that keep my spirits high—and for offering me sound critical judgment.

I appreciate the warmth and interest shown by my son, Roger.

My thanks go to my sister, Anne Estrin Maurer, for encouragement, moral support, and a listening ear through the crises of the years.

And I remember Anne Craver, the long gone, long dead friend of my childhood, and think of the days when we shared the imaginative force that has led me to this book.

# Heroes & Lovers

# Chapter One

I HAVE ALWAYS BEEN FASCINATED by older men. A father complex, people say. It is not so, but rather that like Shakespeare's Desdemona dazzled by the Moor, I loved them for the dangers they had passed. Titans of their time. Polar explorers so like the heroes of the golden age that even late in life, they carry the aura.

When with an older man—in love—I can capture for myself the grandeur of my great-grandfather, Byron Tremaine, the most famous explorer of the golden age, imagine him looking out on the ice fields surrounding the South Pole. The Antarctic in that golden or heroic age is my obsession.

Ronald Graham, the man I am in love with now, is the foremost polar explorer living today. Just thinking of his achievements serves me as an aphrodisiac. He has led expeditions to the polar regions, overwintering in the most desolate parts of the Antarctic ice cap, filling in blank spaces on the map. He is tall, and his still powerful build is well displayed in the leather jackets and tight blue jeans he usually wears. His face is ruddy, weather-beaten, lined, and there is a small scar on his forehead, barely perceptible most of the time, but turning red when he is excited. He has a slight limp, an occupational hazard, the result of a kneecap broken by a fall into a crevasse. Part of a finger has been lost to frostbite. I think I can read the record of his courage on his face and body.

When Ronald takes me in his arms and with such skill caresses me, the acts of bravery, the many women he has known—none of it is lost. It is as if all the exploits he has performed, the loves he has possessed before me still cling to him. He knows how to please, makes me feel cared for, protected.

We are in a manner connected, as Ronald is the grandson of Horace Graham, Byron Tremaine's closest friend, business manager, second-in-command on his expeditions, and finally, executor of his papers. I might have met him sooner, but he had been away on a journey of exploration each time my father took me to the Graham house to relive the Tremaine legend with Ronald's father.

Byron Tremaine epitomized the golden era of exploration. On his first voyage to the Antarctic as a junior member of a Swedish expedition, he leaped into the icy polar waters to rescue a seaman swept overboard in a gale. By 1904 he was leading an expedition of his own to Greenland, where he made a scientific reputation on the basis of revolutionary fossil discoveries. His place in history was secured by his successful assault on the South Pole in 1915–1916.

The son of a United States senator, Byron Tremaine had been imbued with the need to distinguish himself, and every moment of his life was fully documented. I immersed myself in his diaries and journals, read the letters stored in the archives at the Center for Polar History, spoke with the descendants of members of his expeditions. And so, quite naturally I have become Byron Tremaine's historian. I give lectures on his expeditions, using slides made from his own photographs, ending with the incomparable pictures of an icy wasteland, broken only by the figures of the men on their skis, facing the flags marking the location of the South Pole itself. When that photograph with its stark drama is thrown on the screen, there is invariably a gasp from the audience.

It is such pleasure for me to share my knowledge of my great-grandfather that I will speak to any group that expresses interest—a small club, a junior college that can pay little more than my expenses. My refusal to insist on large fees dismays my friend Aimee Peters, a partner in the lecture bureau that arranges my bookings. But royalties from Byron's writings still trickle in, and I make an adequate living as a portrait artist. I have a skill—the ability to make my subjects look appealing. Most of my clients are pretty mothers with pretty children.

Now that my parents are dead, I live by myself in the house on Gramercy Park that once belonged to Byron Tremaine. The last close relative, my great-aunt Susan, has moved to a nursing home. But I am seldom alone. I have a profession. I have a lover, and I have all the people who visit me to learn about Byron Tremaine. Authors of projected biographies, writers on polar exploration, journalists preparing anniversary articles come to me for information and photographs. I welcome them all. Or did. Until I received the letter from Steven Avery requesting an appointment.

Of course I knew the name. Who does not? The host of the immensely popular weekly television exposé show "Avery Tells All," he opens each program by declaring his aim to improve society by revealing hypocrisy and sham. But who is really the hypocrite? He achieved his fame by finding perhaps a single discreditable act and using it to throw doubt on an entire life. Even so, it is not possible to dismiss Steven Avery out of hand as a ruthless scandalmonger. Some exposés did set the record straight, reveal a malefactor or a cheat, produce reforms.

Knowing his reputation, I was uneasy, though there was nothing to object to in his letter. He was not seeking to expose Byron Tremaine. How could he? The life of my great-grandfather, dead for some seventy years, has been investigated to the last detail. Two generations of biographers have sifted through the documentary evidence without discovering any discrepancy that would cast doubt on his exploits or character. No, it was exactly that reputation Avery planned to use. Tremaine was not to be the subject of an exposé, Avery's letter insisted. Quite the reverse.

Ronald thought I should talk with Avery. A refusal might be used to reflect on Byron Tremaine or on me as his historian. "He's not to be trusted, Bibi." That is his nickname for me; my name is Beatrix.

As soon as Steven Avery entered the room, I recognized him as the kind of man who always puts me off. I cannot respond to the aggressiveness, the challenge men like that give off.

His frame was large, and he appeared taller and thinner in person than when walking onto the set on camera. He was dressed with a casualness that seemed conscious, almost pretentious—a blazer, sports shirt, gray slacks, all clearly expensive and so well fitting they must have been made to his measure. The clothes were unsuitable for him, I thought; there was nothing else casual about him. Though he could not have been past forty, his face was deeply lined. His looks were striking, I thought, sexy. Sexy. But not for me. I am not attracted to such men. They are not attracted to me.

What the camera did not reveal, though, was the intensity of his manner. Charm lay in the total attention he gave. A technique? Perhaps. But I was affected by that charm, seduced by that interest.

"You're younger than I expected Tremaine's historian to be."

I did not comment; I am twenty-seven, though I do not appear to be that age.

He looked around the room deliberately, as if seeing it as a stage set for his program. The rest of the house has been redone, but the living room is as it was in my great-grandfather's day, with a seal's head affixed to a plate on the wall, a walrus tusk mounted over the door, and virtually every other foot of wall space filled with photographs. I had framed the front page of *The New York Times* bearing the news from New Zealand that Tremaine had conquered the South Pole. Around it are enlargements of the famous Antarctic photographs. The medals he had received from geographic and explorers' societies the world over are mounted and occupy the entire mantelpiece. Replicas of his fossil findings cover every table.

It is too much and I know that, but I like to have this memorabilia around me. Ronald laughs at me, but indulgently; he never criticizes. Medals have been bestowed upon Ronald, too, but they are never displayed. Once I found the Hubbard Medal, the most prestigious award of the National Geographic Society, in the glove compartment of his car.

Avery observed everything without changing expression. "Have you been to the Antarctic, Miss Tremaine?"

"Yes," I replied, not adding that it had been under the auspices of a luxury tour company. Making the most of my name, the directors had paid me to escort a group of tourists to the Antarctic Peninsula.

When I said nothing more, Avery took a tape recorder out of his briefcase, pushed aside the objects on one of the small tables, and sat down across from me. "I'm a great believer in oral history, Miss Tremaine. I tape everyone I talk with. I've done that for years, long before I started this program. Later I played over the tapes of men and women connected in some way with one another and observed how the words of one contradicted the statements of another, added to them, changed their meaning. Someone was lying. Who and for what motive? I was intrigued by this; I simply had to find out where the truth really lay. That's what gave me the idea for 'Avery Tells All.' "

His words were reasonable. It must have been something about the way he spoke that made them ominous. "What is the program to be about, Mr. Avery?"

"Avery. No one calls me 'mister' or uses my first name."

The affectation of a television performer, I thought. "Avery then. Why are you here?"

"I'm just looking for information, Miss Tremaine. But people don't seem to accept that as my motive. They get nervous when I'm around. Do I make you nervous?"

Avery smiled, rather thinly. He was teasing, but I was in no mood to give the bantering answer that was called for. Seeing me unresponsive, he continued: "The program? I'm investigating possibilities for a program on polar exploration. It holds a fascination for us all. Something left over from childhood perhaps. We're all looking for heroes—and then for the evidence that they have clay feet." I began to interject that Byron Tremaine did not have clay feet, but Avery forged on. His intensity drew me to him, despite the sense of unease he inspired.

"Just think. In 1990 a book was published challenging Admiral Byrd's claim of having made the first flight over the North Pole. The author says the plane was not out long enough to have made such a journey and the pilot confided the truth to a companion later. That flight took place in 1926. Going back even further, did Peary or Cook reach the North Pole first? That was in 1909. You might say, who cares? But still today, some long-hidden document turns up and catapults the story onto the front pages of newspapers. Yes, people are still interested.

"But are they interested enough? That's the question I've been asking myself. I need a modern angle for an exposé."

"Why do you come to me then, Avery?"

"I need you, too," he replied. "You know what makes a show exciting, Miss Tremaine? It's the good guy against the bad guy. Point counterpoint. Your great-grandfather is my choice as the good guy for this program. He'll be the true hero versus the false—the nobility of history against the corruption of today."

Why did I feel so apprehensive when I agreed with him? My fascination with the past, with the men I met at the Explorers Club, is based on that belief.

"Aren't you curious to know who the bad guy is? He's someone you've met. He must have come to see you for information about the Tremaine expedition; he couldn't do without it."

Now I knew who it was: Bucky (for Bernard) Sheridan (his father changed the name from Stein, he said quite openly). And he had come to me. I liked Bucky, and in contrast to Avery, felt he liked me. Bucky had a clever idea for a new expedition to the Antarctic. He would reproduce the legendary Tremaine expedition of 1915–1916, following the route carefully marked on the maps my great-grandfather had used.

A master at attracting publicity and followers, he easily formed his party of twenty-two for the Antarctic expedition. The second-in-command, Joseph Harney, was the businessman. And what a businessman he was. He obtained financial backing for the expedition by contracting to show on television the products, featuring the brand names, of each manufacturer who contributed. Skis, boots, tents, freeze-dried food, fuel, furs, parkas—not an item was without its price tag of the promised seconds or minute on television. The august scientific organizations deplored the commercialism, but I found it impossible to condemn Bucky's unabashed acceptance of opportunities. I was also touched by the way he spoke of Harney, the obvious friendship between the men, reminiscent of the relationship of Tremaine and Horace Graham.

The Sheridan expedition had just returned from the Antarctic in triumph. Like my great-grandfather, Bucky had led the journey on skis and on foot. The expedition's crossing of the polar continent was confirmed by highly dramatic videotapes and photographs. A documentary was scheduled for network television, and cover stories had already appeared in the major news magazines.

Avery was right that a program pitting Tremaine and Sheridan against one another would be dramatic in impact. Were ever two men more unlike—Tremaine, the son of a senator, the man of destiny, and

Bucky Sheridan, coming out of nowhere? Tremaine had been handsome in the Greek classic tradition, and Sheridan is the all-American
boy, complete with snub nose, crooked front tooth, lock of blond
hair falling over his forehead, and bright blue eyes in a deeply tanned
face. My great-grandfather had been tall, while Bucky is short, with
a compact, muscular body and a spring to his step. His smile and his
manner are cheerful, engaging. Tremaine went from one success to
the next, whereas Bucky's ventures—before the Antarctic—invariably
failed.

"What makes Bucky Sheridan a bad guy?" I asked Avery. "Just because of the way he got supplies and equipment? He's done something great, shown real courage and fortitude."

Avery smiled again. I was coming to dislike his smiles; they did not
reflect amusement. "Has he? I think that's open to question. What
would you say, Miss Tremaine, if I were to tell you there may be evidence he did nothing of the kind?"

"What is the evidence?"

"I can't tell you that yet. But people come to me, Miss Tremaine,
for one motive or another. Many of the stories they tell me are spu-
rious. That may be the case here; I have to confirm that what I was
told was true. But if I do, Bucky Sheridan deserves to be revealed as
the con artist I think he is."

"And if it doesn't check out?"

Avery gave one of his thin smiles. "Then I'll drop that segment of
the program and look for someone else. I don't concoct phony stories."

I wondered if that could be true, but there was no point in arguing. My great-grandfather was not being threatened.

"Tremaine is the one man whose word and exploits have never
been doubted. Bucky knows that. When he set out to repeat an exploit of the past that everyone would agree was heroic, he immediately thought of Tremaine.

"Tell me about your great-grandfather. Help me to make the viewing
audience see him through your eyes." Avery's voice was softer now, intimate. He was gazing at my face—almost like a lover. I was repelled
by him for using this technique and by myself for responding to him.
Yet I could not resist what he was offering me. It was seductive. He
was giving me the opportunity to make people who never read books

and view history as boring to see my great-grandfather as he himself
and his executor and friend, Horace Graham, had wished him to be
seen by generations to come.

At first Avery's questions were much the same as those I was accustomed to hearing from previous interviewers. But my responses were
not the same. Captured by Avery's attentiveness, I became more flu-
ent, spoke with greater passion, remembered episodes I had never
told any other biographer, events that displayed Tremaine's character
at its best.

Every so often Avery stopped to ask a question, to rephrase what
I had said in such a way as to turn it into the dramatic prose he
would use on his program. As he spoke, I could see Tremaine rise in
all his splendor. Avery had the image and the means to communicate
it. Why then was I still so uneasy?

He changed the focus then, asking—as other journalists had
done—about sex on the expeditions. I find little to say about that. In
the Arctic some of the men made use of the Eskimo women, but according to his own writings and the reports of his expedition members, Tremaine never did. Perhaps that reflects his chivalrous attitude
toward women; he supported suffrage in its early years. Of course
there were no women in the Antarctic, but not a word about deprivation or perversity can be found in the diaries.

Only when my voice began to tire did Avery take his eyes off me,
stand up, and start walking around the room, inspecting the photographs. They cover a range of years, yet Byron's face hardly changed.
He died at forty-seven, when his good looks had barely begun the
slow dissolution of age.

"I'd like to show photographs that have not been used before. Perhaps you could help me with that, Miss Tremaine; there must be
some. What a great number of photographs there are when you think
this was before the period when every person has a camera. It would
seem that Byron Tremaine's family had decided he was going to be
great almost from the time he was born, and subsequently he agreed
with them."

The words had an unpleasant connotation, but he spoke them so
pleasantly that perhaps he did not mean them that way.

He walked over to the mantel and looked at the selection of
framed photographs standing among the medals. There was Byron

with one hand on the shoulder of his son, my grandfather Byron Tremaine II. A striking pose, but my great-aunt Susan had always disliked the picture. That hand on the shoulder, she said, made it look as if Byron were pushing the boy.

"His son?" asked Avery. I nodded. "What happened to him?"

"He was lost in a blizzard on his first journey to the Antarctic. He was only twenty-one, recently married, expecting a child—my father. Byron Tremaine was dead by then."

"Maybe there's something in the story for human interest," remarked Avery, but he did not seem interested.

His attention had been captured by the wedding portrait of Byron and my great-grandmother, Hermine, side by side, elegant in their formal clothes. "She was very pretty, lovely really, so feminine," said Avery, looking at the picture again and then at me, studying my face. "You look like her." He was speaking in a flattering manner, with intent, I suspected, but it is true that I look like my great-grandmother. Everyone speaks of it. We have the same oval face with large gray eyes, a small nose, soft mouth, and blond hair that falls naturally into loose waves. Byron once wrote that she appeared serious, almost somber—until she smiled, and then her whole face lit up. It is the same for me, or so I have been told. My physical build is similar to hers, tiny-waisted and slender. I, too, am viewed as fragile; Ronald is not alone in wishing to protect me.

For all that Avery was being so charming, I sensed he was not charmed by me. The attention he was showing was designed to get from me something he wanted. I was not sure what that could be; it worried me. His eyes met mine, not to make a connection but to catch a flicker of emotion. Yet though he did not attract me, I could tell he was attractive. Other women must think so. He is one of those men whom one cannot help but imagine in the sexual act—something about his build, his flat hips, his long legs. The image was disturbing to me. He would be sexually demanding, I thought. And he could not be trusted, would take advantage sexually, use his strength, his skill to get his way, just as he was seeking to gain advantage emotionally with words.

"What's the family story? A loving couple?" Avery asked the question in an offhand manner, but I suspected he was hoping to pick up a breath of scandal to enliven his account.

I was amused. To add spice to their works, biographers have sought more vigorously for the hint of an illicit affair than for the inside story of his expeditions. In vain. Tremaine's private life was as ideal as his exploits were courageous. His great romance was with the lovely woman he married; her photograph accompanied him everywhere, was placed close to his head in the rudest shelter in the field.

"I've heard of that photograph," said Avery when I finished speaking, "and I'd like to show it on my program. It's part of the Tremaine legend. But my researchers couldn't find it in any of the books about him or in the archives, and I don't see anything here that fits. There's not a picture of her alone."

The photograph had been sent back with Tremaine's body from his final, ill-fated climb up steep, hazardous Mount McKinley in Alaska. "As he could not bear to be parted from it in life, it was buried with him."

I expected Avery to greet that statement with his thin smile, indicating disbelief, but instead he looked serious, almost wistful. "I don't often find stories of happy marriages." He paused. "Certainly not mine. I was married for ten years, Miss Tremaine."

It was hard to imagine this hard man being married for so long. As he seemed to expect an answer from me, I gave the standard cliché: "Some of it was happy, no doubt."

"No doubt? I wouldn't say that. When it reaches the point where you hate each other, your memories get dirtier until you can't remember that there was ever anything good. And at the end, the child—we have a son—becomes a weapon that is used against you."

He had not seemed human to me before. Now I felt he was reaching out to me, as any troubled person might do. Something passed between us, a spark perhaps, not altogether pleasant, but not unpleasant either. This time his dark brown eyes met mine, made contact. What did he say to make me doubt him? What did he do? He listened to my account of my great-grandfather's life with an intensity of interest I had never met before. Avery made me believe he would not dim Byron Tremaine's luster.

Ronald had warned me about Avery, and I was accustomed to relying on his judgment. But the program Avery described—point counterpoint between the true hero and the false—was perfectly valid. And besides, there was this unexpected moment of warmth between us.

Just as I began to speak kindly, to offer comfort in Avery's unhappiness at his broken marriage, I remembered what I had read of it in the many feature articles about him. He had been starting out as a newscaster and the woman he married was older, already established as director of programming at the network. She had launched the program that made his career. After that, he had a highly visible affair with another woman, an account executive at a major public relations agency, who was also useful to him. The divorce had been ugly and scandal-ridden. When he tried to meet my eyes again, I turned away.

As if nothing personal had passed between us, he asked the next question, his manner falsely casual: "Your great-grandparents: Did they sleep together? In the same bedroom, I mean? A loving couple like that. The same bed?"

Of course they had not slept in the same bedroom; none but the very poor did so in those days. A smile was my only response.

"Let's talk a little more about this marriage. The family story is that it was a perfect marriage, you were saying."

The words were bland, not his manner. There was an air of suppressed excitement about Avery. Excitement? It was not really so much as that. Just a hint of something.

"Theirs was one of those very good marriages that have become rare."

"I usually find that these perfect marriages in family legends fall apart when one examines them," he said coolly. "In fact, I'd go one step further, Miss Tremaine. I find that most legends fall apart when one examines them.

"There's the photograph you describe so movingly. Where is that photograph? Missing. How come? You say it was buried with Tremaine. That's a touching explanation. And short of opening the grave, there's no way to prove it wrong. But it seems wrong.

"Maybe that photograph never existed at all. Maybe someone invented the story to enhance the legend."

The challenge was delivered at last, and I was relieved that he was going in the wrong direction, must reach a dead end.

"Invented?" I was on firm ground. "Members of every expedition reported seeing that photograph."

"Or so you've been told. Maybe the men who gave those reports were ordered to do so by Tremaine or Graham. And maybe you believe them because you want to believe them." Was he accusing me of lying? He was too skillful to say so outright.

"Everyone thinks there is nothing new to be learned about a famous person." Avery spoke in an offhand manner, yet his eyes never left my face. "But I probe a little here, a little there, and something comes out. Always."

"But is that something true?" I asked coldly. Avery's manner caused me—usually both timid and tactful—to speak harshly to him. But far from being offended by my question, I could see he was pleased to have obtained a reaction from me.

"My program could not stay on television if it were inaccurate. What I look for is the truth—the hidden truth. Everyone's life has something in it to be concealed. Everyone's."

"Seeking to debunk great men has been a historian's game for quite some years, Avery. You're not the first. No one else has succeeded with Byron Tremaine. And neither will you."

Instead of answering, Avery removed the cassette from the tape recorder. The difficult, demanding interview was over, and I thought I had done well. However, to my dismay, he took another cassette out of his pocket and inserted it into the recorder. I did not like the expression on his face. He was pressing the play button. What could possibly be on the tape to make him look so pleased with himself?

The cassette began to play. The voice was old, terribly, terribly old and shaky. At first I could not even tell the gender, and then I recognized it was a woman. "Poor Hermine. She was so pretty, soft, delicate, that lovely complexion, tiny waist, all the graceful womanly arts. That meant nothing to him; he hardly spoke to her, took her roughly without a word of tenderness when he came to her bed.

"He thought her a simpering doll. 'How can I live with this simpering doll?' He wrote that in his diary. Let her see the page and laughed. She told me after he was dead. 'How can I live with this simpering doll when I know what love between a man and a woman can be?' "

# Chapter Two

*TOOK HER ROUGHLY WITHOUT A word of tenderness?* Why, Byron and Hermine had lived an idyll. Everyone who knew them had recognized how rare and beautiful was their feeling for one another. Their love story belonged to me now. Ronald and I often talked of it when we made love, said our romance descended from theirs.

Avery was leaning back in his chair, apparently relaxed, but missing nothing. Watching me. Watching. That had been the whole point of this performance, I thought—to see how I would respond out of my shock and dismay. I was being drawn into the unreal world of television by one of its brightest stars, a master at manufacturing the facts he wanted to present. There was no ancient woman with private knowledge of an ugly past. Had there been, she would have told her story long ago. I could hardly give credence to the idea that a woman so bitter would have remained silent through decades, waiting for the unlikely advent of a television talk-show host.

A dramatic script is needed to capture the attention of television viewers, and so Avery wrote one. With his network contacts, it was easy for him to find an actress to read her lines convincingly. He did his job well, and she did hers. I have read Byron's diaries and there is no such page as the one described on the cassette. A clever fabrication, as is all the rest. A "simpering doll." Why, the words are unlike any he had ever applied to Hermine. And the cruelty, the callousness attributed to him was completely foreign to his nature; members of his expeditions spoke repeatedly about his many acts of kindness. Yet Avery thought it would make a better program to portray Byron as a brute of a husband who turned the marital act into rape, sneering at his wife the while. There is more inherent drama in that image than in the portrayal of a husband who could not be parted from a treasured photograph of his wife. Then I thought about the last words on the tape, indicating an adultery. A television basic: If the illicit lover does not exist, she has to be created.

In a sense, these accusations are unimportant, having nothing to do with Tremaine's greatness as an explorer, but they make him so much less of a person to be admired that I could not let them pass unchallenged. They denigrate my life's work: If he is made to appear unworthy, I, his historian and apologist, am made to appear unworthy. I had to keep Avery from playing that tape. The dead cannot be libeled, so I could stop him only by proving the falsity of the tape.

"It's such a good script that I assume you wrote it yourself." I do not think I had ever spoken so nastily to anyone before, but he seemed pleased by my anger. "It doesn't even fit the theme for the program you told me about, Avery—point counterpoint, the true hero versus the false."

Avery gave his thin smile. "It may fit; it may not. Nothing's decided yet. I'm still gathering information. You see, Miss Tremaine, in the years since I started this program, I've discovered that once I find one falsehood, one secret in the life of a 'hero,' I find others. The perfect marriage. It doesn't seem like so much of a lie at first, does it? But then I start looking into it and often other facts turn up."

No man is a true hero to Avery. Two exposés are better than one. He would link Tremaine and Sheridan, not contrast them—if he could. He had come with the cassette in his pocket, led me on with questions and false assurances.

Having had enough of him, I got up and walked toward the door, not turning till I stood on the threshold. Avery followed me slowly; there was more he wished to say. Something in his stance made me think he would put out his hand, and I backed away, unwilling to let him touch me. His eyes, so dark a brown they seemed almost black, narrowed; he sensed my reaction and did not like it. Odd, really, when he had been pleased by my anger before. He put out his hand then, not to touch mine, but to give me the cassette.

"Don't you need it?" I asked coldly.

"I have copies. I think you'll want to play it again, let other people hear it."

"Anyone else who would hear it would know what I knew immediately, that it's a fake."

He was smiling and this time his smile seemed to show some real amusement. "I'll be back. We can talk some more about it then." I shook my head. "Oh, you'll see me again, Miss Tremaine. You'll want to find out if I've discovered something new.

"I know what you're thinking. You're going to try to prove me wrong so that I'll change my mind about the tape, about telling of the marriage on my program. You're not the first, you know. But in all the years 'Avery Tells All' has been on television, only one person ever convinced me to give up a program. And that wasn't because I was wrong."

He had changed his tone again. Flirtatious. I was curious, but would not ask him what he meant, and after waiting a minute or so, he went out.

A tape. That was all Avery had to offer. A lying tape. But even away from Avery's overwhelming presence, I could not think how to prove it was a lie. Ronald would know; he never failed me. Aimee, my closest woman friend, has little patience with my dependency on Ronald. "It's the way I was brought up, the way I am," I tell her. "You can change," she invariably replies. But why would I wish to do that when Ronald is here for me?

Ronald listened to my emotional presentation calmly, and I observed he was not as surprised by Avery's trickery as I had been. But then, few things surprise Ronald. He has seen too much of life. The solution seemed simple to him: There are still people living who had known my great-grandparents. Surely I could find a valid witness to record a tape for me. If it were sufficiently moving, Avery might very well build his program around it and abandon his own fraudulent version.

"A witness. Of course. My great-aunt Susan." A girl in her teens when her father had died, she could attest to her parents' devotion. My great-aunt was so genteel that throughout her life she found the notoriety, as she called it, surrounding her father distasteful. She never married, but had changed her name to protect her anonymity. All photographs of her were long since put away, and at her request, I tell those biographers who trouble to ask that she is dead. Even so, I thought she would for once recognize the importance of giving up her privacy and make a tape recording.

"I think you'd better get to your great-aunt before Avery does, Bibi. If he continues his research into the Tremaine family, it won't be long before his trained investigators find her, and she might turn out to be his witness, not ours."

Aunt Susan is so retiring, so sheltered that she could not anticipate Avery's ruthless, unscrupulous behavior, the clever way he might twist her words.

We have a great affection for one another. Aunt Susan helps to fill the void left by my mother's death. I am warmed by her love and upset by her disapproval of my devotion to Byron Tremaine.

"Any man would want you, Beatrix. You should have a life of your own," she insists at every visit.

As if being Byron's historian and Ronald's lover were not a life of my own. I know she means that I should marry and have children, and someday I will do so. But I do not like to think about that now, as it implies that my love affair with Ronald will be over. Of course I know a relationship with an older man has an end. Inevitable, but I cannot bear to think of that.

My aunt is living in a nursing home to the north of the city, and hastily checking the bus schedule, I set off. The home looks like a country inn, set in the midst of green lawns and trees. Aunt Susan is among the frailest of the old old ladies nodding in their wheelchairs, but her skin is still fair and clear, her coloring the pink and white we both inherited from Hermine. It is easy to tell she was lovely when young; there is something about her face that catches at my heart, an elusive resemblance to someone I cannot identify.

She smiled at me, touched my cheek with fingers distorted with arthritis. "Such a pretty girl," she murmured, "like my mother."

I felt I was intruding on her solitude, bringing in the ugliness of the outside world. This was what Avery had forced me to do. And so I told her about the exposé and the cassette, while she listened in silence. As she made an effort to rouse herself, I noticed how bright her eyes were—pearl gray like Hermine's, like mine. Her voice was faint and she paused for breath every few words. "That man from the television program was here."

I was too late. Avery had beaten me. I could hardly bear to hear what he had succeeded in getting her to say. My great-aunt was no match for Avery.'

"He said he was sent by a friend, but I felt something was wrong about him."

"What did he ask you, Aunt Susan?"

"Why, about my parents . . . the hero's home life. Did he love her? What a question. Did he love her?"

Idyllic, everyone had said. Was that what she meant?

"Why didn't you tell him to go away?"

"I . . . liked him."

The reaction surprised me, though I know he is attractive; that is one of his weapons. I hoped my great-aunt had not been influenced by his appearance and attentiveness.

"My mother's photograph . . . what happened to it? And a diary page . . . he wanted to know that, too."

"How did you answer?"

"I talked nonsense, pretended to be senile. He believed me."

I sighed with relief at having underrated my great-aunt. Avery had been no match for her.

"I wish I could have talked with him, Beatrix . . . really talked."

I could not imagine what she meant. "You handled him so well. Why would you want to talk to him?"

"He brought a breath of life into this old place. We all felt it . . . the nurses, too. He cares so much, Beatrix. . . ." He does care, I thought, but that would work to our detriment. My great-aunt clearly did not understand what Avery was up to.

"I have a tape recorder with me, and I'd like to ask you to record your memories of your parents on a cassette, Aunt Susan." Unlike Avery with his actress, I have a witness whose existence can be confirmed.

There was a long pause. "No . . . I couldn't do that."

"Just a few words about their marriage. You're the only one who was actually there, who knows what it was like. I've told you what

Avery means to do with his faked tape. I think we can stop him from using it on his program."

"I didn't tell him, but that diary page. There was one, you know, Beatrix. Oh, yes. I was a child . . . they quarreled . . . my mother screamed . . . yes . . . she screamed at him. She tore out the page." A long pause. "My poor sad mother."

What did my great-aunt mean?

"Did you ever see the page? Do you know what was written on it?"

Aunt Susan shook her head. "I never saw the page, don't know what was on it."

Surely not a simpering doll, nor a hint—no, more than that, almost a declaration—that there was another woman. I must not forget that the real diary page had surely been destroyed long ago. Avery had based his deception on no more than the knowledge that Tremaine always kept a diary.

"Let it go, Beatrix. The dead are dead . . . and their secrets with them."

If Avery does not accept that, how can I? *My poor, sad mother.* She had screamed. Hermine had screamed. Well, why not? The mildest of women will lose control once in a while. I was close to screaming at Avery myself, and I am a most diffident person. They had quarreled. Their daughter had heard them. Well, why not? Couples do quarrel, even happy couples. And children are alarmed at hearing them, jump to the wrong conclusions.

There are many things a wife—particularly one so delicately nurtured as Hermine—might have found offensive in a diary entry. A crude word in his reference to the sexual act would have been insult enough, and Byron was used to being with men, out in the field, away from proper society.

Whatever was the source of the quarrel, they had made up. Byron's love for his wife was proven beyond doubting by the photograph he could not be parted from, the first thing he unpacked when making camp, the last he looked at before going to his sleeping bag at night. Avery had tried to make something of the fact that it was missing. I wondered now that I had never really sought evidence that the photograph was buried with Byron's body. I could not even remember where I heard that. Certainly I had repeated it often enough and no one but Avery ever questioned the statement. Only now did it occur to me that there might be another explanation for the disappearance of the photograph. Perhaps Hermine had taken it as a keepsake in remembrance of Byron's love for her. In that case, Aunt Susan might very well know where it was.

I put my hand on my great-aunt's shoulder; there is practically no flesh covering the bones. "The photograph. The one of your mother that went everywhere with your father. What happened to it?"

Was that a nod? The movement of her head was almost imperceptible. Then she drew up her lips in a half smile, curiously suggestive. "Ask Graham."

"Horace Graham is dead, Aunt Susan."

"Oh, yes." A long pause, then: "The other one . . . that one you're sleeping with . . . he might know. . . . Why don't you sleep with young men, Beatrix?"

I was too shocked to answer. *That one you're sleeping with.* Isolated in a nursing home, how did she find out? My great-aunt had spoken of Ronald almost as if she disliked him, although she hardly knew him. *Why don't you sleep with young men?* How could I answer her? That no young man can be compared with Ronald? That no young man carries so glorious a history? And sexually? I have no complaints. I have gone out with young men, was nearly engaged once. How drab and uninteresting this man turned out to be, thinking his triumphs in business proved his virility, and so must arouse me sexually. Ruining a competitor, acquiring a company for a sum below its value: These were the exploits he viewed as heroic. I would go to the Explorers Club, where I was welcomed because of my great-grandfather, and talk with men whose virility and courage had been proven in ways that counted. An older man. A hero of the Antarctic. That was how it started. In time there was Ronald.

*That one you're sleeping with . . . he might know.* Does Ronald know something of major importance that he has hidden from me? I could not believe it. Could I not believe it? Much as I love him and am convinced he loves me, he is of another generation, thinks women need protection. I had always liked that. But now I wondered if protecting me meant hiding an unpleasant truth. The thought made me uncomfortable, and angry, too. I had never been angry with Ronald before.

As soon as I reached home, I called Ronald. He came immediately. I took that as a matter of course. Older men have the time. Except when lecturing on his polar explorations, Ronald is free for me. He is writing his autobiography, but will readily put it aside if I call. I never ask if his wife objects. She is his third wife: Inconstancy has been his style ("before I loved you," he told me).

*That one you're sleeping with . . . he might know.* "What do you know, Ronald? What have you hidden from me?"

"Avery is already poisoning the air. You mustn't let him come between us, Bibi."

Ronald was right about Avery's malign influence, but I could tell he knew something. "What do I know? Very little really—that Byron and Hermine did not have quite so idyllic a marriage as they both insisted throughout their lives. And that my grandfather was himself in love with Hermine."

My father had described Horace Graham as grave, austere. The belief was that he never recovered from the early tragic death in childbirth of his wife, Ronald's grandmother. Yet now I was told of an illicit love so well concealed that all my research had given me no hint.

"It was one of those idealized, unconsummated passions people had in those days. Even though my grandfather never touched Hermine, he felt guilty, Bibi, just for wanting her, perhaps for making her want him. His one bold gesture was to take her photograph after Byron's death."

"So you do know what happened to the photograph."

"I saw it on my grandfather's desk when I was a child. Though many years have passed, I remember Hermine's face. So pretty, and her smile was of the most incredible sweetness. Like yours. It's not surprising first Byron and then my grandfather fell in love with her. Or I with you.

"One day—I was a boy then, about ten, clumsy—I knocked the picture off the desk. Before I could bend down to pick it up, my grandfather did so himself. 'I loved her,' he said. I think he had forgotten I was a boy. 'I loved. I had no right. She was another man's wife. My friend's wife. Now that my life has passed, I think what a waste. I loved her desperately and . . . well . . . she loved me as well. And Byron did not love her; he could not, could not help it. How can one help loving and not loving?' That was my grandfather. He couldn't blame Byron for anything.

"My grandfather was one of those men who attach themselves to a hero, someone with the force of personality they lack. He admired Byron to a degree you can hardly imagine. His friend's wife. Even after Byron was dead, my grandfather could not take her.

"Now that it's out, I can tell you that I've never believed in the perfect marriage. Not just because of what my grandfather said, but because Byron saved practically every letter that was ever sent him, except for hers."

"I always thought that was because they were too intimate for him to share. Why didn't you tell me what you knew, Ronald? Why did you let me go on thinking and telling people that my great-grandparents had an ideal marriage?"

"I didn't have enough evidence to destroy a legend that three people maintained throughout their lives, a legend that brought you such happiness.

"You glow when you're happy. It's so winning. I want to keep you that way. If you're looking for exposés, Avery is your man, not I." He paused and stroked my head, smoothing my wavy hair. "There's something else, too. Why are you with me? A pretty woman with such loving ways—you should be thinking about marriage. Why aren't you with a young man? You can't say this is the usual thing."

"You're an unusual man. I don't want anyone but you."

He smiled a little sadly. "I sometimes think you look for Byron in me. We've lived much the same kind of life. Believing in his perfect romance makes ours seem more perfect to you. I never wanted you to think he might have treated Hermine coldly, been unhappy in the marriage. I felt it would affect your feeling for me, subtly, of course, but even that would be intolerable."

I could not remain angry with Ronald. "I love you for yourself, not because of Byron Tremaine." Yet it is also true that I do treasure whatever of Byron Tremaine I find in him.

Without saying anything further, he took my hand, running his finger over the palm. An old-fashioned gesture, but charming. Troubled by what Ronald had told me, I had not been thinking of making love. Ronald never insists, but somehow knows how to make me want him.

Practiced. He led me into what had once been Hermine's bedroom, the room where she had lain with Byron Tremaine.

Ronald was skillful in undressing me, despite having lost part of a finger to frostbite. The edge of the joint remaining is strangely smooth, but otherwise his hands are dry, hard, reddened from years of cold exposure. The skin is rough, but his hands touched my breasts, my body so gently. Tenderness, such tenderness. And he spoke of how beautiful I was and how he loved me. Love talk. For an instant, I remembered Byron; surely he had caressed Hermine's graceful body in just that way, told her how beautiful she was and that he loved her.

Then when Ronald kissed my throat, all thought of Byron disappeared and I was with Ronald and only Ronald, and I whispered his name, spoke of my love for him.

Naked, Ronald looks younger, though the many scars on his body are like a map of the hazards he endured. I find these evidences of a lifetime of courage arousing. When we make love, I am unaware of his age. His experience—yes, that I recognize, that I like. His touch, for all its gentleness, is exciting, dizzying. Forward and back, around and around, rising to a climax together. His timing is never off. Practiced.

Afterward, when we were dressed again, I remembered the photograph. "Byron treasured Hermine's picture, kept it with him always, Ronald. No matter what your grandfather believed, that's hardly the action of a man out of love with his wife."

"People are complex. Byron may have loved her at some times, not at others."

"Avery is insinuating that the photograph never existed. I told him it was in the grave with Tremaine, but he didn't believe me. If only we could find it and bring it to him. I'd have to admit I was misinformed about the picture's being buried, but I don't think he'd make too much of that. What he wants is to show the photograph on his program. It would make the love story between Byron and Hermine more poignant, more real."

"My grandfather put the picture away after that day I spoke of and I never saw it again. But I think I can guess where to look."

"Why didn't you ever do so?" But I had never thought to look for it either.

"I believe the photograph is stored in the garage on the grounds of my grandfather's house. And while it certainly seems that the diary page must have been torn up and thrown away by Hermine long ago, if it has survived, that's where it would be, too. Let's drive there right now."

The old Graham house in Rhinebeck is a white elephant, much too large to be managed without a staff of servants. I went there occasionally with Ronald, but only to make love. We never looked into the garage, which is similarly oversized, converted from the old carriage house and horse stables. After Tremaine's death, Horace Graham reviewed the papers, documents, and photographs, and arranged for them to be stored at the Center for Polar History in Washington, D.C. It is generally believed that the archives contain the entire Tremaine legacy. But that is not quite true. While most of Byron's writings are stirring, with lines quoted by politicians and memorized by schoolchildren, there are papers that Graham, careful of Byron's reputation, held back, as being repetitious, trivial, or boring. Even so, Graham had not been able to bring himself to throw anything away, but packed cartons and stacked them in the garage.

My father had been given a key, which in time came to me; and when I first became Byron Tremaine's historian, I went to the garage several times to sort through the boxes. I unpacked one after the other before conceding that Graham's assessment was correct.

"Perhaps I became discouraged too soon," I remarked to Ronald as we came into the driveway, and I felt hopeful that the photograph I sought was in one of the many cartons remaining.

When we entered the garage, I was struck anew by its vast size and dimness. The light coming from the few bulbs hanging from the beams made it appear more, rather than less, dark. Standing there in the gloom, I imagined Horace coming to the garage to open the box where he had placed the photograph, to look at the face of his lost love. He had loved, and to recast the customary cliché, had loved more wisely than too well.

Ronald took down a box at random. A cloud of dust scattered as he placed it on the floor and cut the string. "You go through that box and I'll do the one on the top of the next stack."

I sat down on the floor with the box in front of me and lifted out the papers with gentle fingers. The ones on top were dry, and crumbled as I touched them. The ink had faded into illegibility on a few more, but I was able to read most of the rest.

It was as I had found before: These were papers dealing with the trivialities of a man's life—complaints about a shirt torn by the laundry, bills from haberdashers, manuals on dog handling. I finished that box and put the papers back as best I could. "Nothing here."

"Nothing in my box either."

And so we went on, one box after the next, after the next. Every so often I saw a folded piece of paper that looked like a diary page, but when I read the writing, it turned out to be something else. A photograph would fill me with hope. Invariably it turned out to be a picture of my great-grandfather with a minor, long-forgotten figure of the day.

My legs were stiff and my back ached. The floor was of concrete and cold. I stood up, stretched, and walked over to Ronald, sitting on the floor nearby, with a box between his legs, displaying no sign of discomfort. He was not as neat as I; pieces of paper, envelopes, and bits of string lay all around him. One of the envelopes had English stamps on it, and as I bent down to look more closely, I saw that it bore the words PERSONAL URGENT. With shaking hands, I opened the envelope. Empty. What personal message had it contained? I turned it over and looked for the name and address of the sender. The envelope was dirty and smudged, the ink faded, so that I could barely make out what looked like "Limbug" and then "8   Chess   Co   ndon." Considering the stamps, "ndon" was undoubtedly London, but the rest of the address was not so easily deciphered. Despite the missing letters, I thought there was something familiar about both the name and the address, but before I could figure out what it was, Ronald cried out, his voice loud in excitement: "Beatrix. Look what I've found."

He jumped to his feet, holding out an object carefully wrapped in a faded red silk scarf with a monogram in black: HG. Dropping the envelope, I took the package, and with trembling fingers pulled back the soft fabric.

The fabled photograph. The photograph that Byron had carried with him to the most desolate parts of the earth, the photograph that had been his inspiration.

Hermine's pretty face with its heartwarming smile looked up at me, brightening and warming the cold, cavernous garage. That smile gave new life to my great-grandparents' romance, and I was certain that Ronald's instinct about their unhappiness had been wrong, that the quarrel my great-aunt remembered was of no lasting significance. My earlier doubts faded in the mood captured by a long-dead photographer. Hermine had been so lovely, with such delicacy of feature, such melting eyes. Though she was a married woman, she still looked a girl, virginal.

Avery had asked for photographs never published before. He would use this one, I knew, and throw away the tape.

The frame was loose at the top and I thought that the glue holding it together must have disintegrated over time. But when I looked more carefully, I saw that the frame had been made in such a way as to come apart on purpose. I pulled the loose piece very gently, and lifted off the top. I took out the photograph. It seemed oddly thick, so I turned it over. And when I did, I saw another photograph glued to the back.

A woman. The print was discolored with age, faded, the shiny surface creased and smudged, as if from much handling. Nothing detracted from the dramatic quality that captured the heart. The subject of the picture had not been carefully posed, but caught in action, in the midst of life. I stood there in the gloom, the picture in my hand, trying to understand the meaning of what I was seeing, already aware that the peaceful world I had inhabited was suddenly and irrevocably altered.

Even in the damaged reproduction, I could see that the woman was beautiful. More than that. What leaped from the picture was a vitality and eagerness so strong, so strong, that still today, generations later, they filled the room. Across all the years, I felt the tremendous sense of well-being and joy displayed in the faded image in that long-lost photograph. The woman's arms were outstretched, reaching, reaching. For what? For whom?

# Chapter Three

SHE SAW THE SEXUAL ACT as the matching of equals, two tigers mating. She never tested this belief by checking a zoology text to learn how tigers actually do mate; this is the way it must be. The matching of equals. The first time Viola saw that clearly was when she was lying in Byron Tremaine's arms, caught in the intensity of her passion for him, his passion for her. The matching of equals. Later, it became the philosophy that ruled her life.

Marriage repelled her. From girlhood on, she had not liked what she saw of it. Her mother was as intelligent as her father, yet she deferred to his opinions. Anything he wanted was done: The soles of his shoes had to be polished, his suits sent to Paris to be cleaned. His tone when he referred to "my wife" was the tone he used to refer to "my house." Viola did not like the way her brother-in-law, Bertram, treated her older sister, Evelyn, either. He doted on Evelyn, indulged her, bought her gifts, behaved as if she were a treasured, fragile object that could break. And Evelyn lived up to his image of her, did indeed seem more frail, less of a presence than formerly. Nor did she raise the smallest objection when their father accorded Bertram control of her inheritance from their grandparents.

Once Viola had observed these attitudes in her own family, she saw the same pattern of power elsewhere. Why were so many wives so docile? What did these women win for accepting a subservient position? The girls who had been her classmates at the Spence School devoted their energies to being gowned by Worth and the other great Parisian designers, selecting the menus for the dinner parties, devising seating arrangements. To turn one's life over to a man: How could any woman of spirit agree to that?

Viola. Every action of her life was a rebellion against what was expected of her as the daughter of the prominent Lambert family in the first years of the twentieth century. With a fortune made in iron ore three generations earlier, the Lamberts were in the inner circle of society. They had been disapproving, baffled by everything Viola wanted to do. College, for example. What possible use could higher education be to a woman whose future lay in marriage to one or another of New York's leading citizens? Viola did not see it that way; her father had to flatly order her to attend the Junior Cotillion at Sherry's, and she was moody and unhappy about her own debutante ball at the Waldorf-Astoria. In truth, she was hungry for men, but not for these men—these men of the great society families who were brought to meet her. She found their conversation stultifying, the flirtation rites absurd.

Seeing Viola at home, caged and restless, her parents finally yielded about college. They were surprised, but if anything pleased, by her selection of Oberlin College in Ohio. No one in their circle had ever heard of it, so Mrs. Lambert thought to present it as a sort of finishing school. Viewing college as no more than a way to pass the time before marriage, she was not sufficiently interested to discover that Viola settled on Oberlin because it had been the first coeducational college in the country.

It was at Oberlin that a professor known to the students for his dullness spoke the sentences that set Viola's life on a course few women followed. "The history of the earth is written in fossils as if in a book." Professor Johnson's voice was a monotone. "Barely a fraction has been found. Countless fossils must still exist, hidden in parts of the world that are desolate, hostile, and distant from civilization. As man explores the farthest northern and southern regions of the globe, what relics of prehistory will be discovered? Perhaps one of you will make these discoveries."

Viola wanted to leap up, to shout. She had never heard so exciting a concept. To her amazement, the other students in the class looked bored; some were sleeping. From then on until she graduated, she spent every free hour working with Professor Johnson in his laboratory, ignoring the efforts of the male students to gain her attention. Required to accompany her parents on society's vacation route to London, the Swiss Alps, Paris, and Newport, she thought only about voyages of discovery.

Engrossed in his research, pleased to have so brilliant a student to share it with, Professor Johnson was unworldly enough to recommend Viola for a place on the expedition about to set off for the Far North under the leadership of a dynamic young explorer, Byron Tremaine. He thought she could be of service to Mr. Tremaine, he told her, not seeing the double entendre.

For the rest of his life, Byron remembered how he had felt when Viola walked into his office for the first time on an early summer's day in 1904. Dazzled, he had been wondering why she came to him, how he could arrange to see her again. Then she smiled and held out her letter of introduction. And he knew she was his. Her college professor was recommending her for a place on the expedition to the Arctic, suggesting that she could help classify the fossils brought back to the base camp. Byron had hardly been able to believe his luck.

To see her once was to remember her forever. Viola looked like no one else, was never compared to anyone else. The color of her hair was a rich russet brown with strands of pure copper that gleamed brightly. Her eyes were a very clear, deep blue, with just the faintest hint of violet, deep set beneath dark lines of eyebrow. Her complexion was vivid, fair, translucent; the blood coursing through the veins seemed almost too close to the surface, giving a brilliance to cheeks and lips. Even when corseted, her figure did not take on hourglass proportions; rather, she had an elongated line, a body ready to take action, quick and strong.

There was something riveting about her. She would come into a room and all eyes would turn to her. Taller than most other people, it was not her height or even her beauty that commanded attention so much as her vitality, an energy that filled a room. Viola. The excitement she communicated.

In later years, when Viola looked back on the time spent in Greenland, her passion for Byron Tremaine and the excitement of scientific discovery were inextricably linked. The fossil findings had been anticipated. Not Tremaine. The leader of the expedition—who could expect him to pay attention to so junior a member of his party?

Byron Tremaine looked the part of an explorer, she thought. His presence was overwhelming. Unlike other men, he was clean-shaven, so that the ruddiness of his complexion, weathered by wind and cold, was all the more striking. It contrasted with the shiny blond of his hair, worn rather long, with sideburns. His eyes were an odd shade of green, very dark, the darkness of evergreen needles with flecks of black. It was a strong face, a leader's face, defined.

Destiny was a word invariably applied to Byron Tremaine. The lure of exploration had captured him when he was little more than a boy, and as he grew older, he saw it as his path to greatness, believed he was building his reputation with this expedition to the Arctic. Horace Graham, his closest friend, was chosen to serve as his lieutenant. Slender, with thinning brown hair and steel-rimmed spectacles, Horace did not fit the classic image of the explorer. Nonetheless, he had gone to the Antarctic with the Swede Nordenskjöld because Tremaine had joined the expedition, and once there, proved his ability in the field.

Byron thought it would be best to have Horace explain Viola's duties to her. Certain a relationship with her was to come, he did not want to jeopardize it by rushing, perhaps frightening her. She was so young. He would pick his time. "You mean she's actually supposed to do something. Not just exist?" Horace had taken one look at Viola and decided that fossil identification was merely a pretext. "Why, Byron," he had said, "she looks like a picture painted with colors that are too bright." Horace gave no hint of his opinion when he explained to Viola that she was to set up a laboratory at the base camp on Disko Island, the largest of the tiny islands lying just off Greenland itself. There she would in time be studying the geological specimens the men would bring back from their field trips across Greenland in the spring and summer of 1905. She was to give him a list of whatever she needed. Tremaine was taking her work seriously; the thought filled her with pleasure.

When Horace saw the sensible list of equipment and chemicals Viola had drawn up, he was impressed. And troubled. He had believed a girl who went away from her parents' protection to a college with male students knew exactly what she was here to do. But now, it occurred to him that she had no idea of what surely must happen. She viewed Tremaine as a leader, out of reach, did not yet see him as a man, a lover. That would come, thought Horace. He felt he should warn her, but knew he could not. Byron would never forgive him. "I hope you'll think of me as your friend" was as much as he could say. She smiled so winningly that he could hardly stand it. Were he not a married man and Byron's friend, who could say he would be any better able to resist her?

Viola departed for Greenland with the Tremaine expedition, having deceived her parents as to her destination. Knowing they would lock her up rather than permit her to go, she had fabricated a visit to a college friend to cover her departure. However, an enterprising reporter in Indian Harbour, Labrador, caught sight of her, and used the new wireless equipment to telegraph the Associated Press about the one girl on an all-men's expedition to the Arctic. So much for the deception. Viola's father used his influence to force her to return, but by then the expedition had steamed across Baffin Bay, out of reach.

Upon arriving at Disko Island, Tremaine hired native Eskimos to help build the base camp and carry supplies across the narrow strip of sapphire blue water to Greenland. A makeshift camp of a few primitive huts and a shelter for the supplies was put up on the coast. A tent was brought along for Viola and she was told to accompany the group. By then Byron wanted her nearby all the time. The excuse for bringing her on these trips (that is, the excuse given her; a leader needed to make no explanations for his men) was that she was quickly learning the Inuit language from the Eskimos and was helpful in communicating with them. None of the others knew more than a few words. Viola accepted the excuse, though she did wish Byron were not always so businesslike. That was foolish, of course. Her acceptance on the expedition was due to Professor Johnson's introduction only, she was certain. This was a professional relationship, different from the normal social interplay between a man and a woman.

The Eskimos had their own huts, and Viola often visited them to practice speaking Inuit and to watch the women at their work of softening, cutting, and then sewing the animal skins together. Every part of an animal had its use: Viola soon was given a waterproof jacket made from seal intestines. The other members of the expedition seldom ventured into the Eskimo compound, complaining contemptuously of the dirt and bad smell. Nonetheless, sometimes when Viola was out of view within the hut, one of the men would come to the door, beckoning, and a woman would immediately put down her ivory needle and without a word go out to him. Once she thought it was Tremaine and was amazed by the violence of her reaction. With relief, she realized it was not he.

Greenland. Viola had never imagined the incredible beauty of the shoreline, broken by huge fjords. If only she were able to dress like the men, she could have climbed the nearby cliffs, though they were higher than those she had achieved when on vacation with her parents in the Swiss Alps. She had abandoned her corset and cut off the hems of her skirts, but they still hampered her movements.

Byron or Horace walked with her along beaches covered with shells and bits of granite and gneiss rock. The other men, though, seemed to avoid her. This came as a surprise. Men, whether in the social world of New York or at Oberlin, had invariably sought ways of catching her alone. These men, however, had a disconcerting way of disappearing the moment Byron came into sight. It never entered Viola's mind that they viewed her as Byron's—"property" was how they put it to themselves—and were afraid of angering him by being too obviously attentive. At least Horace was willing to spend time with her; they had become fast friends. He described what exploration meant to him, to Tremaine. "Standing where no man has ever stood before, Viola—a sense of power comes over you. Of wonder. It is the greatest experience of your life." Women were barred from such experience, Viola thought, but she was close to it, might someday be closer still.

They spoke of Byron then and Horace again felt misgivings. "Be careful," he told her.

"Of what?"

Of what indeed? His best friend. Horace wished the autumn and winter were over and they were safely away crossing the great ice sheet. Safely? Who would be safe as they traversed Greenland? Not they certainly. Only Viola.

To hide his discomfort, he spoke of the journey they would be taking in the spring, of climbing up the steep, crevasse-broken ice walls at the margin of the ice sheet. Their journey would take them inland to the region where mountains and valleys become all but indistinguishable, both buried under the thickness of the ice. The goal was to reach the remote outpost of Angmagssalik on the northeastern coast following a route no one else had ever taken before.

Viola listened to the plans with avid interest. She was not envious of the men . . . then. Being a full member of an expedition was satisfaction enough.

Byron had ordered one of the Eskimos, Anaukaq, to build a shed next to her hut. With his help, Viola set up a laboratory of a sort, with a microscope, glass slides, Bunsen burners, and chemical reagents and preservatives.

The weather was far from hospitable as the autumn advanced, changing from one hour to the next, from bright sunshine to lowering clouds and snowfall, from balmy breezes to icy, sleet-bearing winds. By November it was no longer possible to navigate the waters, and the expedition settled in to overwinter at the base camp. The men repaired the sledges, the tents, the equipment they would take with them on the trail. Byron passed hours studying the maps, reading the journals of earlier explorers, preparing for the journey ahead. But his mind wandered; now that the frantic rush of getting the supplies onto Greenland was over, he could wait no longer for Viola.

She was taken by surprise by the passion that sprang up then between them. Not he. From the moment he had looked into her deep blue eyes, he had known that what did happen had to happen. From the moment they had set up the base camp, he had been waiting for their time to come.

Late one afternoon Byron called her to him. He wanted to see her in his hut. Surely the man who brought the message was smirking; she could not imagine why. Well, she could imagine why, but must not allow herself to think that way. This was a professional relationship; she had known that from the start, and must not be deflected by his attractiveness.

The timbered hut was dark and silent, its double walls lined with heavy blankets. "Take off your jacket." His voice was throaty. He had thought to make it appear that she would be too hot in the layers of clothing needed out of doors, but the inflection of his voice made his words suggestive. So young. Had she recognized what he really meant? Her eyes had narrowed just a trifle and then widened. She took off the waterproof jacket and heavy sweater, and in the dimness her blouse was so white, and whiter still the skin of her throat and neck. White, but glowing. Yes, her mouth was trembling, but he was not sure whether she were frightened.

Then she gazed at him across the room intently, meeting his eyes. A moment. Then she smiled and held out her arms. Reaching. Reaching. For him. During all the years of his life, Byron would picture that gesture. Later Corbett, the expedition photographer, had captured that look, the arms reaching out. The photographer had been in love with Viola; he recalled being jealous of the man. But that photograph. He had never been able to part with it. Reaching.

What came back to Viola in later years was the way he had looked at her, and she had known how much he wanted her, how much she wanted him. Who was the more driven? What came back to Viola was her excitement when he took off his sweater and in the dim light of the gas lamp, his shirt was so white, and then, naked, his skin. She had never seen a man's body. His chest was broad, covered with blond hair, his arms and shoulders powerful. His body was heavily muscled all the way down, the ridge of bone at the pelvis prominent, and beneath it the parts of the male body that she had only imagined. Impossible for her to resist.

She had never touched a man before, but she put out her hand and stroked him, first his chest, then his abdomen, and lower down. He kissed her, putting his tongue between her lips, and she opened her mouth to him. His eyes were open, dark green, blazing. The air was chill in the hut, but it was excitement rather than cold that made her shiver when he took off her clothes, pushed her down. Not gently. She knew how their bodies must come together, had read in scientific texts what it is that men and women do. The books had not described the excitement, the heat at the groin, the desperation.

They lay on the floor, on the Eskimo blanket. Rough wool, harsh to the bare skin. Byron turned on his side and looked at her breasts rising and falling so fast, panting. But did she know what was to happen? He felt a sudden qualm. Was he taking her virginity? There was no certainty at all that she was a virgin. Could a virgin give off an air of such sensuality? He put his hand between her legs, pushing them apart, and she opened them to him so naturally. And he thought with a mingling of emotions, relief and regret, that she must know what she was doing, what she must yet do when making love with a man. At his touch, he could feel the wetness begin.

It turned out that she was a virgin after all. He had hurt her; well, he must have hurt her, forcing his way inside her body. Later he saw the blood on her legs, on the Eskimo blanket, mixed with his semen; he had withdrawn at the last, fearing to impregnate her. But she had given no sign of feeling the pain, had clutched him to her more and more tightly. Surely her cry at the last was of rapture, pure joy.

Her hand on him. Sweetness and desire.

A virgin. He had put his mark on her. No other man would dare to touch her; he had claimed her. "Now you are truly mine." She thought it charming . . . then.

"A man and a woman making love are like two tigers mating," she told him. "The matching of equals." She said that, too. He thought it charming . . . then.

Years afterward, he told her nastily that he had been shocked by her touching him. Nice women did not behave like this. She had deceived her parents. Nice women did not lie. That was later, when he wanted to hurt her. Then he had rejoiced in her behavior, in her lie.

All that winter, at any moment, on any pretext, they would come together in his hut or hers, or anywhere the mood seized them. They had made love in the snow on one of the rare days when the air was clear and still. He put snow in her mouth; she passed it back, half-melted, teasing.

What had she not said on those cold winter nights of the Greenland expedition? What had she not done? When he would say she was his, she would look into his brilliant green eyes and reply that he was hers. He did not disagree. Not then. Love. They spoke of love. Never of marriage. Freedom.

Here, on the stormy, foggy seacoast, there were no conventions, no rules. Being overwhelmed by sexual desire, yielding to it was natural.

Only in time, she discovered that no one else thought it was natural. No one. Until the suffragettes.

The men called her his whore. But Byron knew it was not quite as he put it in later years when he threw it in her face to cause her pain. Viola. All that fire and vitality. Who among the men had not wanted her, had not been at least half in love with her? He had seen it—the looks of envy, resentment at his using his position as leader to make her his. When they called her his whore, it was to pretend he possessed only her body.

The bloodstains on the blanket covering the floor of Byron's hut never came out. No one noticed them, except for Horace. Nothing escaped him. In any event, it was not long before she told him. This girl alone with no one to protect her: She would ruin her life. His concern for her led him to speak to Byron about the risk of pregnancy. Byron had not been offended. Viola did not know how to protect herself, but he was taking precautions.

Horace did not blame Tremaine for having her. She had put herself in a situation where seduction or rape was inevitable. But he could tell she did not see it that way. A grand passion, she said. Fortunately, thought Horace, Byron was at heart conventional; once away from Greenland he would remember his place in the world. They would marry, of course. Horace told her that. Viola did not see it as of course at all.

Horace's words reminded Viola of her mother, longing to plan a future that must include marriage. It gave her a pang; her mother meant well. But what could she know of love like Viola's for Byron, like his for her? Mrs. Lambert had made do with the hollowness of a proper, loveless marriage.

Horace had left a wife at home, and was often worrying that she was short of money, worrying that she might be ill. There was no hint of passion in his voice. A burden. That was how he saw his wife, thought Viola, taking this as one more indication of the fact that marriage and love were curiously separate.

At last, the winter night drew to its end, and every day the minutes of sunshine increased. Little by little, bands of color began to run over the sky, like paint across a canvas. In March, Byron and the men who were to accompany him on the field trip set off, led by the best of the Eskimo guides. Viola watched them go, desolate at the thought of being so long without Byron.

Life at the base camp was dull after the field party departed. Five of the men were left behind to work with the Eskimos in making repairs on the huts and sledges damaged by the winter storms, and to take weather and astronomical observations. The men clearly expected Viola to prepare the meals now that the cooks were off on the trail, but she knew no more about cooking than they did and would do no more than her share. The men muttered about her unwomanly behavior. Even so, almost as soon as Byron was gone, each of them tried to begin a flirtation. Wanting only Byron, she took no pleasure in their attention.

Viola had her own plan—she would spend the spring and summer exploring Disko Island and the waters around it, seeking unusual organisms, both plant and animal, and fossils of life forms now extinct. The specimens she gathered would be added to those the men were to bring back from the main island.

Plants were beginning to bud, and in a few more weeks, the Eskimos told her, the bleak island would be brilliant with wildflowers. Exploration was impossible in skirts, so she asked the slimmest of the men for trousers and a pair of waterproof boots with leather thongs laced to the knees.

Next, she needed a boat. Anaukaq, not showing his surprise at the strange request, taught her how to handle a sealskin kayak. Soon she was able to wield a paddle with a double blade for speed, a single blade for steering and pushing ice floes away. When she spoke with Anaukaq of her intention of going off in the kayak on her own, he did not think it his place to dissuade her. Instead, he gave her a kayak jacket with a waist that could be fitted over the cockpit rim to make paddler and boat a single unit and a net to drag behind the boat.

Properly outfitted, she was on her own at last. Paddling through the choppy waters, she was happy for the first time since Byron had left, and happier still when she returned to camp that evening and discovered the wealth of miniscule plants and animals captured in the meshes of the net. From then on, she went out every day, disregarding the weather, treacherous even in the summer. Sometimes she traveled around the island for some distance, then steered the kayak close to the land. Stopping to unfasten the jacket holding her in place, she jumped out and dragged the boat ashore, continuing her explorations on foot. As she traversed the island, it became apparent to her that the maps of Disko were inadequate; many of the landmarks she was observing were not indicated. Taking out her compass, calculating distances, she drew up new maps. Upon his return, Byron would be pleased and surprised at how much she had accomplished in his absence.

Each night, Viola told the men of her discoveries. They were becoming increasingly uneasy about her daily explorations. Each of them in turn offered to accompany her. She always refused. They let it pass. After all, she was Byron's woman, his responsibility, not theirs.

Any one of them would be only a burden, she thought, preferring to be alone, with no one telling her what to do, demanding that she dress and behave as men thought a woman should. Viola felt she was adequately prepared for emergency with her knife, compass, chocolate, and flask of water in a caribou skin bag.

Over time her search for specimens led her farther afield, and a curious fact about her findings emerged. Many were out of place. Mollusk shells were lying far from the coastline, evidence that much of the island must have been under water in centuries or millenia gone by.

The summer passed, and the Iceland poppy and saxifrage lost their flowers, the leaves dried on the willow, birch, ash, sedge, and cotton grass, leaving the island desolate and barren. The days grew shorter, the temperature fell, rain turned to sleet, and winds blew fiercely. Soon she would have to give up her adventures, but each morning she would think, not yet. Viola understood the hold that exploration had on Tremaine, on Graham, and on the others in the field party; she was seized by it, too.

The clouds were dark, lowering, obscuring the sun one morning when she left her hut. For just a moment she hesitated, wondering whether to stay in camp, but her desire to go out was too great. Should the weather worsen, she would turn back immediately, and the kayak could cut through the water so rapidly that she was sure of getting back to camp in time. She had been out for about an hour when the wind began to blow in gusts. As she tried to turn the kayak, however, it did not respond, and she was alarmed to see a crosscurrent spinning under the boat. Though she paddled as hard as she could, the craft, caught in the currents, whirled around and around. Around and around. She became dizzy and nauseous from the incessant motion. The kayak was being swept back toward shore. Rocks protruded from the water and at any moment the kayak would be smashed against them. The image of Byron flashed through her mind. She could not die here, not after having found so great a love. But what was she to do? At that instant, the kayak swung all the way over and lay on its side. Struggling to keep her head above water, she all but panicked at the realization that the Eskimo jacket was tying her to the boat. Terror—and then she remembered Anaukaq doing this very thing to show off for her. He had turned the little boat way over on its side and then righted it, laughing all the while. Paddling as she had seen him do and swinging her weight sharply to one side, Viola was stunned with relief when the kayak rolled over and was right side up again. The Eskimo jacket had saved her. And then the boat was out of the whirlpool. The brilliant blue water beyond was calm, and she paddled in toward the shore, easily avoiding the rocks.

Unfastening herself from the boat, she climbed out and waded ashore, dragged the kayak as far from the water as she could, and started up the steep slope leading inland. She had just reached the summit when an autumn blizzard struck so suddenly as to knock her down. Viola wanted to lie flat on the ground and let the snow-laden wind gust over her head; then she realized that a blizzard could go on for all the rest of that day and that night and the next day. If she stayed where she was, she would die. Keeping her head down, she took out the caribou skin bag carried on her back, found the compass, and calculated the direction to the base camp, miles away. Then she began to creep forward, a few inches at a time. At first the ground beneath her was rough, rocky, tore her jacket and the borrowed trousers. But gradually, the surface became covered with snow and it was easier to crawl. In some places, the wind was less fierce and she was able to rise to a crouching position and walk, using a stick broken from one of the trees as a cane. Each time she thought the worst was over, the storm rose to new heights and the winds battered her to the ground again. Lying there on the frozen earth, she thought once more of Byron, of lying in his arms, feeling his breath on her face, his kisses on her throat just where the pulse beat. She would not let this be the end, must survive to look into his dark green eyes, put her lips to his smooth-shaven face, feel the silky blondness of his body hair.

Exhausted, she tried to get up, once, twice. And now she was on her feet, staggering forward. She looked at the compass, but it had shattered when she fell. How could she find her way without a compass? And then, looking around, she realized that this was the very area she had mapped when the weather was fine a few weeks earlier. The ground ahead was sloping upward. A mountain? She would never be able to climb it in this wind. No, remember the map she had drawn; this was no more than a hill. Once over it, the camp would be straight ahead. What she needed to do was turn all the way around and set off in the direction opposite to the coast. And in that moment, she felt a doubt. What if she were wrong? What if the map had been of a different place? She would have to take that chance. There was no other.

Bending down to avoid the full force of the wind, she began a crouching walk. Her face was cold and wet; water had seeped into her boots and she feared frostbite. If only she could rest. But people died who stopped to rest in the cold. Remembering the map she had drawn, she started pulling herself up the hillside, facing into the wind, hanging on to every bush, shrub, or rock along the way. Her feet, her legs to the knees, were so numb that she could no longer feel them. And then she was at the top of the hill, and starting down. A gust of wind blew her against the trunk of a pine tree, and she threw her arms around it in an embrace. In that strange gray-white world where she could see no more than a few feet away, it seemed as if she were embracing Byron's body. All at once, she stepped back, recognizing the tree. That had been a landmark; the base camp was directly behind it.

As Viola stumbled into camp at the end of her strength, she saw dim figures looming in the falling snow. Were there not too many people? And the noise. The quiet she had grown accustomed to was broken by the shouts of the Eskimos, the barking of the dogs, the screech of sledge runners. Byron Tremaine. Come back from the ice sheet. To her. She never forgot their reunion. Nor did he. She was holding out her arms to him. As in the photograph. He had taken it with him on the trail. It had become creased; he would ask Corbett for another print. Every night he had looked at the photograph and it seemed to him she was with him in the tent. Reaching for him, as she was now. Smiling in the way that caught at his heart, speaking his name in her low throbbing voice. Mine, he thought, all mine. "I feared you were dead." His voice was choked, he was close to tears.

The field party had returned that morning just as the blizzard struck, to find Viola absent and the men at the base camp frantic. Byron was enraged that they had been so thoughtless as to allow Viola to go out alone in a kayak—as if anyone could forbid her anything. This was no time for recriminations. Byron rapidly organized a search party, but it had soon been forced back to camp. The wind was blowing at gale force, pushing the men to the ground. How could a woman survive that ferocity? It was almost certain she must die in the fury of the storm. Byron had imagined Viola's lovely body dashed to the ground, broken. And now, here she was, in his arms.

Viola was triumphant. What man could have done better? For the first time the thought came to her that she was ready to go on a field trip herself. She was shivering. Her knees buckled then, and the men rushed over, but Byron waved them away and carried her into the nearest hut. There he removed her mittens and saw the signs of frostbite on her fingers. Unbuttoning his jacket and shirt, he put her hands inside against his skin. It felt hot, burning, and the pain of returning sensation was agonizing. But what did it matter when they were together? He took off her clothing, frozen outside, wet inside, and tenderly wrapped her in blankets.

By the following day she was sufficiently recovered to want him. They had been apart for all the summer months, and she felt again the desperate sexual hunger he could arouse in her. When he kissed her, she felt his lips were blistered by the punishing cold of Greenland. His face was red, cut, and bruised by the polar winds. But when he was undressed, the bare skin of his body was still so white, so white. As on the first time, she ran her hand over the blond body hair. And making love was as it had been that first time. Perhaps better. Because by now she knew what it was that she liked and could show him how to please her. "Put your hand on me here. No. Here. Just like this." She lay on top of him, pressing her hips against him. In her joy, she never thought that this was not the proper way for a woman to act.

Afterward they quarreled. She told him—honestly, why not?—about all she had done in his absence. There had been this one episode of danger, but she had handled it well. Far more important was all she had accomplished in drawing maps and finding samples of primitive organisms on the island. Byron ignored the maps and the scientific specimens. "How could you be so careless of yourself? It's my body, too, now." *His body.* The concept was unpleasant to her.

She would have continued the quarrel had he not caressed her, kissed her tenderly, whispered into her ear, "I could not bear it if anything happened to you, Viola. I love you too much." She had never heard anything so beautiful. And so they made it up . . . that time.

Viola's explorations were not referred to again, but she noticed that the maps she had made superseded the earlier ones. Swept up in her renewed passion for Byron, she did not notice for a time his lack of interest in her scientific research. The specimens gathered in the moraines at the foot of the glaciers, in the permafrost, on the rocky nunataks, in the waters off Disko were stacked on tables in the laboratory. Cleaning the mud off the rocks and shells and viewing them through a magnifying glass, mounting the tiniest specimens on slides to view under her microscope—she felt the lure of the unknown, the excitement of the explorer. Notebooks were filled with observations and drawings. Sometimes she was so engrossed she was slow to come when Byron sent for her.

Byron was surprised and annoyed by her absorption in her studies. It was intolerable to be told that she would not come to his hut because she was identifying a fossil. She could not really be taking her role as expedition scientist seriously.

As the winter months passed, Viola made the scientific discovery that was to change her life and Byron's. In the beginning she hardly dared believe what she was seeing. The organisms that had existed in an Arctic of millennia past had become trapped by the Greenland ice sheet. The granite, gneiss, volcanic rock, ice-veined meteorites, sandstones, and shales contained the imprints of forms of life that could have existed only in a warm, temperate climate. Viola began to write articles for the major scientific journals, presenting her view of a prehistoric Greenland very different from the cold, hostile island of today.

Going from her laboratory to Byron's bed, Viola was completely happy. Making love and doing her work was the perfect way to spend a life. Men had that life as a matter of course, she knew; women could but rarely achieve it. Even now, she was quarreling with Byron over the time spent at the microscope or writing.

Coming into the laboratory and seeing the rapt face she lifted from the microscope gave Byron a pang. Sometimes it seemed to him she was as intent and joyous as when they were making love.

She was so lovely, such a pleasure to touch, to be with; only her obsession with the ancient organisms detracted. Byron thought it ridiculous really. He no longer told her that, however; the only time she was unresponsive to his lovemaking was when he made his opinion too obvious. Viola, a girl fresh out of school, was probably making discoveries that had been made repeatedly before. They were new only to her. He must ask valid scientists to review her writings, so as not to be made to appear a fool himself. His would be the name appearing on the scientific papers, not that it was likely her research would be good enough to be submitted for publication.

Viola found it extremely odd for Byron to be so irritable about her excitement over the fossils. After all, that was why he had taken her on the Greenland expedition. Yet he demanded that she stop work whenever he wanted her, became almost abusive when she refused. She wanted him, too, loved him passionately, but surely he should be able to understand the significance of the work she was doing. They began to quarrel about his determination to dominate her, quarrel and make up. It was not serious. In Greenland. When they made love, their differences disappeared. Soon they would be leaving Greenland; the realization gave a greater intensity to their lovemaking.

Out of no more than curiosity, certain that her scientific work must be amateurish, Byron read through her notebooks. Idly, carelessly at first. And then, all at once, he saw the significance of the theory being presented. Why, it would make him famous.

When they lay together during those last nights in the Arctic, Byron told her of his plan. The Antarctic, an unknown continent, bound in ice, was still to be conquered. He would be first at the South Pole and make great scientific discoveries along the way. They would be at the Pole and make the discoveries together, she amended, her eyes shining with eagerness. She had proved herself in Greenland, would stand beside him on the ice plateau that stretched out brilliant and gleaming in the never-ending Antarctic sunshine. Yes, said Byron, as she embraced him, she would go with him.

"Do you promise?"

"Yes. I promise." She must realize that he was only making love talk, Byron thought. Surely she was aware that a woman could not survive on the Antarctic ice cap. But why say that now when Viola was lying naked in his arms? Love talk.

A promise. He would not renege on a promise. The matching of equals. His body was pressing heavily upon her, his mouth was close against her ear—she never dreamed he did not mean his promise.

# Chapter Four

Two weeks later they lay on the floor of his office and she thought it was as it had been on the floor of the hut in Greenland. Skin against skin. The feel of him against her, the whole length of his body. Viola knew Byron better now, loved him no less for being aware that he made her wanting him a weapon in the competition he waged with her. Two weeks since arriving at New York Harbor and she was desperate with desire for him. As he was for her.

They lay on the floor of his office and for the first time he realized what he had done to her in bringing her back into a hornets' nest of gossip and ill-feeling. Foreseeable—had he looked ahead as he should have done. What was to become of her? His strong, bold girl. She was indifferent to the gossip, refused to concede its effect on her future. Byron was overwhelmed by the guilt he had not felt in Greenland. He had been inexcusably careless in taking advantage of the passionate nature she could not control. Why else would a woman, well bred, of good family, come to his hut? Let him take off her clothes, put his hands on her body? He had never forced her. Never even asked her. He had merely looked at her and she had reached out for him, touched him intimately. But she was a virgin. What had she known? Understood of what she was doing? Only he had known. He was the man, responsible.

Holding her in his arms, sated, but still caught by her desirability, he put what he was thinking into words. "I shouldn't have done it."

"Done what?"

"Taken you in Greenland. Taken you now. No. I shouldn't have done it."

"I." . . . "I." . . . Surely it was "we." They had made love as equals. She sat up shivering in the cold room as the perspiration from his body dried on her bare skin.

As he saw it, there was only one course for him to follow. Marry her. Yet he hesitated. Sexual desire was not enough of a reason to marry. Not for a man like him, meant to make his mark in the world. He needed a helpmeet, someone to stand behind him, greet him with a smile and a kiss when he returned from expeditions. And here was Viola with all her fire and dash. It would not do. Well, not unless she changed. And, of course, she would. After yielding her virginity to him, she must be grateful.

The Lambert family would feel the same way. They had disapproved of his taking Viola to Greenland, but that was past, and now only marriage to him would rescue her reputation. Why, the Lamberts would be invaluable to him. They and their friends and business connections could back future expeditions. Now that he had reached this conclusion, he felt better. Had it been any other woman, he would have arranged to see her father to make a formal request for her hand, but he knew Viola would be offended if he did not ask her first.

Byron waited until he was in his suit again and had helped Viola lace her corset. That was evidence of her having changed already, he thought. In Greenland, she had said she would never wear a corset again. Her dress, too, was fashionably cut, with tiny buttons all the way down the back. She would no longer put on her clothes herself without his help; at home he assumed there was a maid. Now he was ready to speak. Marriage.

Viola recoiled. He was stunned. Recoil? From marriage with him?

"Marriage!" she exclaimed, her voice filled with shock, almost with outrage. It might have been her mother, not her lover speaking, she thought with distaste.

"My poor girl," her mother had said, "don't you know what you've done to your future? What kind of man will have you now?"

"I don't want a man who couldn't accept me as I am."

"As you are? How are you? What are you? But a well-brought-up girl of good family who has unfortunately behaved so foolishly as to wreck her reputation. There is only one way out of this and that is for you and Mr. Tremaine to marry. Mr. Lambert and I had aimed higher for you, but we must be practical now."

Viola had been unable to answer what seemed to her to be supreme illogic. And now she was discovering that Byron felt exactly as her parents did. Certainly Byron was the only person she wanted, but wanting and wanting to marry were not the same thing at all.

It was clear from his tone that he thought he was conferring a favor. But what could she think? How could she marry him? They were lovers. As lovers, they would still make love as equals. She had been told about sex in marriage . . . at the man's command. When he wished it. His right. His legal, unalterable right. Even in Greenland, he had been astonished, angry about her refusing him her body when she was engaged in important scientific work. But the fact was that she was able to refuse him. What if she were a wife? Then were he to tell her to leave the specimen on the slide without a preservative so that it would be worthless by the time she returned, she would have to go with him.

As a lover, she could still be his companion, accompany him on his journeys of exploration. He had promised her the Antarctic as a lover, surely not as a husband. All possibility of adventure, of scientific discovery, must end with marriage. She would be a tamed woman, staying at home, while all the excitement of life went on elsewhere. From the bitterness of their quarrels she knew that Byron would dominate a wife, make her a doll-like creature. There was no joy in that.

He was waiting for her answer. She knew women were supposed to thank a man for such an offer, and so she thanked him. "But I don't want to get married."

He flushed and then turned white. "Just like that? You refuse? You must be out of your mind. How can you be so foolish? What other man would make you the offer after having had you?"

"Had me? You have never had me."

"Don't be naive. That's what it's called, Viola. That's what it is. Have you any idea how people are talking about you? The gossip is vicious; you'll never live it down. You'd better accept what I offer. Because I can tell you I will not be so generous again."

She had run at him then, wanting to strike him, but he had caught her arms and held her. So close to him that she could not look away. She saw then that his eyes were suspiciously shiny, and realized she had hurt him.

"I thought you loved me," he said, his voice very soft. Was it trembling? "I love you, Viola. Don't you love me?"

And she almost melted, only she remembered then that this was the bait, the bait men held out to capture women. She would not be captured. "Why do we need to be married, Byron? We're lovers. I want us to go on being lovers. I'm afraid of what marriage will do to me, to us."

"Every other woman in the world wants to be married. And you know better. You're making a terrible mistake, Viola. And by the time you realize that, it will be too late."

"Too late?"

"What if I marry somebody else? How will you feel about another woman's body in my bed?"

But he would never marry. Not when he was breathing hard, and, in a moment, starting to take off her clothes again, unfastening the long row of buttons, unlacing the corset. They made love. And as she stroked the blond hair on his chest, she thought that he was accepting her view, accepting that they could remain lovers. Yes, it was as it had been in Greenland, as it would always be—so long as she did not marry him.

How careless she was of herself, of her name. In the Arctic, the men had called her his whore. He repeated that to hurt her, but also to make her recognize what she was doing. That name would follow her everywhere in view of the fact that she refused to marry him— and how that rankled. He never doubted that she must continue as his lover and people would find out as they always did and ruin what was left of her reputation. Not much was left, certainly. It was not his concern. He had made his offer and she had made her choice. As she would not be his wife, he did not need to take care of her. That realization should have lifted his heart, yet somehow it was heavier than before.

But after that day, on the many occasions when they met to make love, it was not Greenland anymore. She came to see that he could not forgive her. He was rougher, insistent on getting what he wanted, not waiting for her response. Not always. But often enough. On those occasions, he would not call it making love, but something cruder.

Whatever he said, whatever he did, she had guaranteed herself her freedom. Now she had to find a way to use it.

# Chapter Five

PEARY WOULD TAKE HER TO the North Pole. Or so she had thought. She had the Greenland experience to recommend her, and he was said to be predisposed to women. But Peary did not know what to make of Viola, an unmarried woman, claiming to be a scientist. He could not imagine what she wanted, decided she must be making a sexual overture. It turned out to be very embarrassing.

Had she been able to claim credit for her theory about the prehistoric climate, the situation might have been different. The research papers she had written were accepted by the most prestigious publications in the field and her hypothesis was already gaining attention from leading scientists. But the articles were signed by Byron, with only a footnote to acknowledge any participation by her. Byron was the one invited to speak to scientific organizations and university-based paleontologists. She accepted this. Not until she joined the suffragettes did she chafe at the injustice of his having the credit and taking it as his right.

"When will you learn, Viola?" Byron asked a few days after Peary's rejection. She had not told him, but there it was—explorers' circles were small. "Who'll take you seriously? Who would take the chance of having you on an expedition?"

"You did."

But he had done it for the wrong reason—because he wanted her and this was the way to have her. He never imagined that anything she could do would be useful. Her discoveries and interpretation of the fossil evidence had been unforeseen. So had been falling in love with her.

"Except for me."

She wondered how she would get through the time of waiting for Byron to launch his next expedition. For a short while after her return from the primitive living conditions of Greenland, she took pleasure in the comfort of her home. There was always a footman waiting should she have packages to carry or need the protection of an umbrella. Every evening a hot bath was fragrant and steaming in the marble bathtub. After the dried beans and ill-cooked reindeer meat and cod fillets in Greenland, it was agreeable to be served salads made with tender greens and delicately seasoned fish and poultry. The pleasure soon wore off and she began to wonder what she was doing in the huge house on Fifth Avenue and Fifty-fourth Street, its lawn and garden enclosed by an iron fence, protected by a gatekeeper. She felt troubled by the very grandeur of the mansion, the marble entrance hall ringed with columns and statues, the forty-five rooms with antique furniture and works of art. All this was cared for by servants so well trained that it seemed the house was cleaned without human intervention. Mrs. Lambert's social secretary dealt with invitations and seating arrangements.

Viola had been unable to resist her mother's insistence on her resuming the corset abandoned in Greenland. A waist laced to eighteen inches was standard for any young woman. Mrs. Lambert at fifty could still lace to twenty and a half.

The New York society life that her mother and sister enjoyed bored Viola. Evelyn now lived in a house that was almost a duplicate of the Lamberts' just a few blocks farther north on Fifth Avenue, at Sixty-third Street. Viola's lack of interest in balls was viewed as an oddity. She subscribed to the scientific journals—Viola's hobby, her mother said indulgently.

In view of the unfavorable gossip, it took all Mrs. Lambert's skill to gain invitations for Viola from members of the old New York families, invitations to events that were irksome to her. Could she really be expected to spend the rest of her life with the kind of man considered suitable, a man who spoke to her of nothing but trivialities?

Neither her mother nor sister was oblivious to what Viola was feeling. They were appalled that Byron Tremaine had not asked her to marry him. What kind of a man would take a twenty-year-old girl to the Arctic with an all-male expedition? Not that Mrs. Lambert believed for a minute the rumors about what had passed between them. Viola was too well brought up. But her mere presence on the expedition had given rise to gossip that could only be stilled by marriage. As Mr. Tremaine would not do the gentlemanly thing, someone else would have to take his place. There was no question that a husband for Viola could be found at any time. After all, she was a beautiful young woman, and it was common knowledge that Mr. Lambert was able to assure a son-in-law an excellent position in one of the many companies he controlled. Still, the Lamberts were sadly aware they could no longer pick and choose among the eligible bachelors.

Viola had gone so far as to claim that Mr. Tremaine had indeed proposed marriage and she had refused. Mrs. Lambert and Evelyn did not believe it. Aside from the fact that she needed to marry him to repair her reputation, anyone could see that Viola was in love with him. Her face lit up at the mention of his name. If he had asked her, it was not possible that she had refused. And every time Mrs. Lambert went out to pay calls on the women in her social circle, she would return home to find that Viola was gone. Visiting a school friend, she would say afterward, her face flushed. As if it were not obvious she had slipped out for a meeting with Mr. Tremaine. Innocent of course, but people were talking. What was needed was time, time for Viola to get over him, as she surely would now that she was attending the balls and dinners where she was presented with nice young men. The right young men.

Unfortunately, from her mother's viewpoint, it was proving impossible to avoid Byron, whose exploits in the Arctic made him the social lion of the 1906 fall season. Viola was never his dinner partner; hostesses knew better than to antagonize the Lamberts, but the gossip was so widespread that there was invariably a gasp as the music started and Byron precipitately excused himself from the table and went to ask Viola to dance.

When he took Viola's hand to lead her to the dance floor and put his arm around her waist, a tremor, barely visible, but clear to her watching mother, swept over her body. A very faint flush could be seen, not so much on her cheeks, which were always bright, but rising faintly over her neck and breasts, partly exposed in the low-cut ball gown. Her mother's best efforts to keep her from Byron had reduced the occasions for making love, but they were lovers still.

It was strange to see Viola like this, thought Byron, with the body he knew so well drawn in tightly at the waist to push up the breasts and accentuate the hips, as was the fashion. But her figure was too long-waisted, too slender to be formed into an hourglass shape. Her body was the same as it had been in Greenland and yet different. He could not get used to it.

She appeared to be of a different breed from the rest of her family. Mrs. Lambert had also been a beauty. (That was how she had captured her rich and socially prominent husband, it was said. Meanly.) But she bore no resemblance to Viola, being small, fragile, blond, pink and white. Viola had inherited her father's height and strong features, but not his stiff bearing or cold manner. Even Evelyn, lovely as she was, seemed a pallid version of her sister.

As they danced, Viola was thinking that he was close, so close that she was aware of his naked body under his evening dress. His gloved hand caressed her bare shoulder and she trembled. The contact lasted only a few minutes; as soon as the first dance ended, her brother-in-law or her father was there to claim her. After that came the succession of young men, the eligible bachelors being encouraged by her family and theirs.

Viola sustained herself by following the plans for the Tremaine Antarctic expedition, pleased that Horace, efficient as ever, had made contact with Major Pond's lecture bureau, viewed as the best for having arranged Peary's successful tour. All explorers needed to go on the road like this in order to raise sufficient funds for an expedition, considering how high prices were in 1906.

Once he had started on his lecture tours, Byron was rarely in New York. Viola had never felt so alone. Her friends now were the girls she had known at Miss Clara Spence's school, girls who had gone to the Dodsworth dancing classes with her, been debutantes, attended the Junior Assemblies. Some had married, but all were concerned with their social lives, clothes, and jewels. What could she have to say to people like that?

She longed for Byron, was desperate for the sexual release she had come to take as a matter of course. What did all these other single girls do with their sexual yearnings? She hinted the question, but they did not seem to grasp what she was talking about. Were they pretending, behaving as well-bred girls were supposed to do, or were they really ignorant of sexual matters, waiting for the secrets to be revealed on the wedding night? Remembering how she had put her hand on Byron's body, the feel of the coarse blond hair at the groin, Viola came to believe that she alone among women was driven by sexual desire.

The only way out of what she viewed as a meaningless existence, she decided, was to get a job. With her scientific background, she would surely find employment. Byron was in New York on one of his visits between lectures; intent on making love with her, he did not take her quest seriously. "Who would hire a woman? For what?" He said it idly, not even thinking he was being cruel. Intent on making love with him, she let it pass.

The next night, she informed her mother of her plan and was dismayed to be greeted with an indulgent smile. "Why, every girl thinks of a career. I remember I had the idea of training as a schoolteacher. Imagine that! I'd have worn plain black gabardine skirts, probably rather shiny in the seat, and white shirtwaists, have my hair pulled back in a bun." Mrs. Lambert patted the blond hair piled elaborately on top of her head. "I might have been an old maid myself. Men don't like women who work.

"Yes. I'd have had nothing. Instead of all this." She waved her hand, soft and white, at the oil painting of poplars by that French artist, Monet, who was having such a vogue. Everything in the sitting room was perfect, from the Aubusson rug to the frescoed ceiling. The walls and chairs were covered with a beige flowered silk that was replaced every two years so it never looked dirty. The desk and end tables were inlaid with three different kinds of exotic wood. She gazed with satisfaction at the portrait by Carolus Duran showing her in rose chiffon and diamonds, with Viola and Evelyn as children beside her. Centered on the mantel top was a clock, one of the very few of its kind to have survived into the twentieth century. The clock had been made during the French Revolution according to revolutionary theory, with the day divided into ten hours, not twelve.

"My father put an end to it. And quite rightly."

In an abrupt change of mood, Mrs. Lambert said briskly, "You can't take a job right now in any event, Viola. We're to leave for Paris next week to see the design collections. Appointments have been made with Worth and Pingat and Poiret."

"I'll just have to miss that, Mother."

Miss the Paris showings, the private sessions with the great designers—Mrs. Lambert had never imagined that the woman lived who could resist them. Viola had developed her own style in dress, favoring velvet or gleaming satin in russet tones that brought out the highlights of her hair. Many of the women this season were wearing pale "Alice" blue, named after Alice Roosevelt Longworth, the president's daughter, but Viola selected blue of the deepest hue tinged with violet, blue to match her eyes. Her gowns were cut into a deep vee to reveal her long, slender neck and beautiful throat, and her arms were always bare. It had seemed that clothes represented Viola's one suitable interest.

Hastily Mrs. Lambert offered another lure. "We could go on to Switzerland from there and you could ski."

Viola wavered for a moment; the Lamberts had taken winter vacations in the Swiss Alps, where the ski instructors had tried to keep Viola on the beginner slopes, as befitted a girl. She would have none of it. Her daring and natural ability soon took her to the most dangerous slopes, where few of the boys ventured. The thin clear cold air, the speed of her rush down the mountain exhilarated her. But she must not allow herself to be distracted.

"Not now, Mother. I can't spare the time."

Mrs. Lambert gave way gracefully. After all, there was no possibility of Viola's finding a job. The only positions available were for women of quite another social class, to be typists, clerks, waitresses, salespeople.

Viola's search for employment proved as unsuccessful as both her mother and Byron predicted. Interviews were easily obtained on the strength of her name; the Lamberts were known for their philanthropies. When she asked for employment, however, the directors of laboratories were simply baffled. A job as a scientist—what would women think of next?

In the end it was Byron after all who led her, unwittingly on his part, to her goal. He told her he had sent the fossil finds from Greenland and their (he said "their") interpretations of them to the American Museum of Natural History. By means of so major a contribution, he hoped to win over Morris Carter Jerrold, president of the museum, who had given Peary and other explorers major financial support.

Listening to Byron, Viola suddenly saw what this could mean to her.

"Once the scientists at the museum have a chance to study the specimens themselves, they'll recognize how important the new theory really is," declared Byron.

He was taken aback by Viola's reaction. She asked him which of the curators at the museum had received the fossils, declaring her intention of calling the very next day to ask for a position there. Byron was not sure he liked the way Viola was using him for her own ends.

She could see he was annoyed, but this was an opportunity, perhaps the only one she would have, and she must make the most of it. Viola had been inside the museum immediately upon her return from Greenland, lured by the reconstructed skeleton of an enormous brontosaurus which had been put on display in the new Hall of Fossil Reptiles. That had been her only visit; the museum's location on the West Side of Manhattan put it completely out of the way of any other place she might be.

The next morning she presented herself to Averell Ruskin, the curator of the Department of Geology and Invertebrate Paleontology. While waiting to see him, her confidence wavered. If her name had not been mentioned in connection with the Greenland fossils—as was entirely likely—Dr. Ruskin would not even consider her. Viola learned, to her pleasure, that he had attended one of Byron's lectures and recalled that she had been mentioned as a helper. This was recommendation enough for him to offer her a position. It was the drudge job in the departmental laboratory, but she was elated at becoming a part of the foremost paleontological center in the United States.

She feared a bitter quarrel with her parents, but they received her news impassively. Viola's tremendous vitality could not be contained by those activities that were sufficient for other women; the house all but shook under the force of her personality. As they saw it, the museum would soon pall and she would be ready to take up a normal life as wife and mother.

On the morning she was to start work, still barely able to believe in her good fortune, Viola stood on the pavement, looking up at the huge Romanesque-style building that housed the American Museum of Natural History. Constructed in the 1870s, when the Arsenal in Central Park became inadequate for the museum's growing collections, it was a castle of red brick and granite, with wings, towers, and balconies; statues jutted out from the pointed roof. For a moment, she hesitated, knowing how hard it would be to gain acceptance by the male scientists who would be her colleagues. Then she reminded herself that she had done important work in Greenland and would do so here.

Standing in the doorway of the laboratory on that first morning, she immediately became aware of an atmosphere. The men had been joking—about her—she could tell. Her presence in their laboratory seemed something to ridicule. Refusing to reveal any sign of discomfort, she walked into the room. And when the men saw her, the joking stopped, and they stared openly at her tall figure, striking in the white laboratory coat she had been given. Waves of coppery hair escaped from the chignon, and her widely spaced violet blue eyes were shining. When Viola entered a room, it was hers. The men gaped at her, but made space at one of the long laboratory tables and began giving her tasks.

Other women worked in the museum, it was true, but they were there for such duties as taking dictation for letters, directing visitors, on occasion answering the telephone. Though hers was the lowliest job in the laboratory, Viola took pride in knowing that never before had a woman been considered for a position that required a scientific education.

It did not take her long to realize that she would not be able to perform her duties restricted by the corset her mother demanded. She could not bend down to pick things up, and was out of breath when going from one end of the laboratory to the other. And so each morning she removed her stays, undoing the lacing with some difficulty in the lavatory at the museum, and put them back on with even more difficulty before going home. The only way she could contrive to do this was to wear shirtwaists with buttons down the front instead of dresses with long rows of fasteners concealed in intricate tucks down the back. Her mother shuddered at this choice of clothing, but supposed it was all part of going to work and would be abandoned when the job came to an end. Did the men notice that she was uncorseted? Viola was aware of them ogling her, trying to discern her figure beneath the straight lines of the white coat, to catch a glimpse of the hand-embroidered pattern at the ankle of her rose-colored silk stockings. She had grown accustomed to receiving this kind of attention from the men she met socially, but it seemed different in a professional setting. Obviously, there was nothing to do but ignore it, and in time she succeeded in doing so.

Although the duties assigned her were elementary, Viola observed everything that was going on in the laboratory. Here she could gain the knowledge that would stand her in good stead in the Antarctic. The senior scientists were amused by Viola's questions about the taxonomy of the fossils she was required to list in the catalog. The first time she discovered an organism assigned to the wrong genus, she showed it to the scientist who had done the work and told him what she thought the proper classification should be. After studying her data carefully, he conceded she was right. He was very nice about it and thanked her, but there was a certain coolness in the way he treated her from then on. Over time, as she found further errors, the other scientists began to talk about her intuition. It troubled her that no one mentioned her intelligence and understanding.

Coming home from the laboratory each night, Viola stepped back into a world she had almost forgotten during the workday and would have preferred to escape. Even Viola, however, knew that she could not oppose her parents by refusing the social life that was so important to them. The transition from laboratory to ballroom was painful to her. The upstairs maid dressed her on most occasions, but for the most important events, her mother's personal maid was pressed into service. Mrs. Lambert had begun to speak of the need, the *need* for Viola to have her own maid.

Viola would return from a ball at two o'clock in the morning to find a maid trained to show no sign of weariness waiting up to prepare her for bed. Then four hours later she would rise and be made ready to go to the laboratory. The coachman also was waiting, fully uniformed, with carriage and horses, to bring her across town to the great museum building in the west; her father had purchased a Packard motorcar, but it was for his exclusive use. (No young woman of good family would be allowed to travel unaccompanied by taxi, let alone by electric trolley car, horse-drawn bus, or even the new, fashionable subway.)

Viola was unhappy about inconveniencing so many people, but Mrs. Lambert dismissed her objections; these were servants and of course they must do whatever was required by a member of the family.

The scientists in the museum thought they understood what had brought her to the laboratory. As a daughter of the wealthy Lambert family, she must be acting on whim. The job could be no more than an unusual way of passing time while waiting for her broken heart to mend. Byron Tremaine had thrown her over. Everyone knew that.

# Chapter Six

A BEAUTIFUL YOUNG WOMAN WITH a bad reputation. Single. Working outside the home. The scientists in the laboratory found it unsettling. They brushed against her as she placed the slides under the microscope or the flasks on the Bunsen burner, and were clearly startled and excited by touching her uncorseted body.

It should not have been hard to refuse them. They were not brutes, had no intention of forcing her. But it was hard, hard, when she wanted a man so badly.

Her mother sighed each time another woman in their circle became engaged. It was becoming evident that the men she was paired with at social events did not treat her quite as they did the young girls who were unquestionably chaste. Hardly an evening passed without one or another of these men suggesting that they leave the ballroom, go out into the garden to be alone. To be alone ... with a man, that is. In the garden, in the dark where no one could see. That was she wanted, too. But not with one of these boring, superficial men.

Even Byron's manner toward her had changed since she had refused to marry him. In Greenland, the rules of ordinary life did not apply, and he came close to seeing her as an equal. Taken. That was what he thought now. He was taking her. Each time he returned from a lecture tour, she would receive a note, telling her to come to see him—and where. Not asking. Telling her. She recognized the difference.

As she continued to work at the museum, a rumor arose that she was a suffragette, following the example of Eileen Lincoln, the secretary to Curator Ruskin. Everyone in the department knew that Mr. Lincoln had left her for another woman. Her manner of speech was cultured and she had obviously come down in the world, living in a furnished room far downtown. Travel to the museum took her two hours each way, starting with a walk to Washington Square Park to pick up the Fifth Avenue coach at its terminal, then a change to an electric trolley, and then another lengthy walk. She was so thin that it was not possible to tell whether she was corseted. A mass of black hair fell in tangled ringlets to her shoulders, and she had a small, rather pinched face.

Well past thirty, she possessed an unmistakable sexual quality and Viola sometimes saw her leaving the museum on the arm of one of the men in the laboratory, leaning toward him with an air of intimacy. Over time a sort of friendship with Viola developed, and they talked at quiet moments during the day, addressed one another by first name. Eventually Eileen spoke about suffrage, saying it was the most important thing in her life. Viola felt remote from the movement. Of course women should have the vote, but that was not her cause. Would having the vote get her to the polar regions? Obtain for her a decent position in a laboratory? Obviously not. But she could not say that to a fanatic like Eileen.

One summer evening when Viola was leaving the museum building, she saw Eileen shaking her fist at the figure of a man retreating down the steps.

"That's my husband. He won't divorce me, says he wants me back." Eileen spoke as if this were an insult.

Viola could not understand why Eileen would refuse when the man was repentant and her life was clearly so very hard. As if guessing what Viola was thinking, Eileen laughed. "You've heard that story about his leaving me, Viola. A man's story. Not one of them can believe the truth.

"George didn't leave me for another woman, Viola. He didn't have a lover; there isn't that much red blood in him. But there is in me. Well, it turned out that George had been tipping my maid to spy on me. So he walked in on my lover and me in bed in an out-of-the-way hotel, told me to put on my clothes and come home. I didn't know what else to do, so I went with him."

Eileen turned away then, walked down the museum steps, crossed Central Park West, and sat down on a bench. The Lambert carriage was waiting at the curb, but Viola signaled the coachman away and followed Eileen.

"What did your husband do after he found out about you?"

"He never referred to the episode again. From then on, he was polite to me in front of others, but when we were alone, he refused to speak to me, beyond asking where his foulard tie had been placed or complaining that the laundress put too much starch in his shirts. Still, at night, sometimes, he would come to my room, to my bed and make love. His right, to satisfy his need." Only a suffragette could talk that openly about sex, thought Viola.

"I could not think what to do," Eileen continued. "If I left him, he would give me nothing. And how would I live? For a long, long time, I wasn't strong enough to walk out." She paused. "And then I found the strength."

It was obvious she was thinking of the suffrage movement. By now Viola knew that with Eileen, everything came to that.

"What happened to your . . . lover?"

"I got tired of him. He wasn't good enough at sex—not better than my husband—different, but no better."

"But didn't you love him?"

"Love? Nice, but unnecessary. I did in time discover that sex could really be as thrilling as I had imagined it. Now . . . I have sex any time I want it."

Viola had never before heard of casual sexual experience for a woman. A great passion, such as hers for Byron, was a different matter, and even that was frowned upon by almost everyone. But Eileen, it appeared, dared to have sex like a man.

"I think you know what I'm talking about, Viola. I catch you looking at the men in the laboratory when they're brushing by you, putting their hands on your arm casually, it might seem, while you work. Those men are attractive, aren't they? Some of them are good in bed; others start out being clumsy. Until I teach them what a woman likes."

Viola thought of Byron, smiling as she showed him what she liked when they were making love, disapproving afterward.

"Sex on a regular basis is what you don't have, Viola. Oh, you have sex; I know that. I don't need to read in the newspapers that Byron Tremaine is in New York. I just need to see your face when you walk into the museum. The glow. I recognize it. Your skin. Your eyes.

"But he's here so little, and the rest of the time, what do you do? I know that, too. You go without."

Eileen thought love was unnecessary. Not to her—Viola had lain with the man she loved, the man she desired, on the floor or outside on the permafrost on blankets or animal skins, or in his office in New York. But to go without. That had become a part of her life, too.

In the days following, Viola looked at the men she worked with in a new way. Which of them had Eileen considered good in bed? Could it have been Dr. Ruskin?

Except for the day he hired her, Dr. Ruskin had paid scant attention to Viola. She was surprised, therefore, when late one afternoon, he summoned her to his office to talk over some laboratory matters. Dr. Ruskin was one of the great names in paleontology, and even the senior scientists were in awe of him.

He closed the office door with undue care, it seemed to Viola. All at once the thought struck her that he had something other than scientific work in mind. Then he cleared his throat and turned to her, nervous, expectant. Common sense told her she should find an excuse and leave, but how could she walk out on a man of this caliber? And what if she were misreading the signs? A man of his age—fifty at least—could not be interested in her.

"I've been watching you ever since you came here, Miss Lambert." His voice was throaty. She was not misreading the signs and could not help feeling flattered that this man, this very great scientist, found her attractive.

Viola looked at him, really looked at him for the first time. Though not good-looking, there was something appealing about his lined face, his tired eyes. His body was heavy, but not fat. She wondered what he would look like naked.

Without speaking, he put out his hand and ran his fingers through the gleaming russet strands of her hair. As he came to the pins forming the chignon, he pulled them out, let down her hair, and gasped.

If she did not immediately extricate herself from this situation with whatever grace she could summon, it would be too late. But she could not force herself to move.

The afternoon light was fading; he did not turn up the lamps. The situation was both repugnant and enticing to her. She must get up and go. But she wanted ... she could not believe it ... she wanted to take his hand and have him stroke her hair where it fell over her shoulders, her breasts. She willed herself to think of Byron. But Byron seemed to have nothing to do with the scene being played out in this dimly lit office. She had done without and could bear it no longer.

Not helping him, but not resisting either, she let him take off her laboratory coat, unfasten the buttons of her shirtwaist, and lie down with her on the couch. He did not undress her fully, or himself, removing just what was necessary. He opened his trousers, and then his drawers, pushed his male organ through the openings, lifted her skirt and petticoat, and pulled down her lace-trimmed silken underwear. It gave a furtiveness to the act they were performing, a furtiveness she had not expected. Oddly, that was degrading and exciting at the same time. They had passed the point where she could have refused him, but must go on. She could not help herself; she was desperate with a sexual hunger to feel the weight of his body, the pressure, the looked-for release from tension. Pent up. So long pent up.

And it turned out to be nothing like the act with Byron, the way she felt lying in Byron's arms. Dr. Ruskin was nervous, rushing himself, not waiting for her. She wished he would not be nervous, rushing, that he would caress her slowly, gently, bring her to a peak of excitement. Instead the act was completed in minutes. He did not use a contraceptive—she had learned about such things from Byron—but withdrew just before his climax.

Dr. Ruskin stood up, looked down at his open trousers, his male organ, now small and limp, and hastily closed the buttons to conceal himself, embarrassed. She arose as well, feeling wet with his sweat, uncomfortable. There was no way of getting to a sink to wash, so she put her underwear back on, fastened her blouse.

"Are you all right?" he asked. She nodded. Then, in so soft a voice she could barely hear him, he said, "I didn't make you do it. You wanted it, too."

And there was something so pitiful in his having had to say these words that Viola felt sorry for him. What could she answer but yes, she had wanted it, too? She had not wanted it to be like this, but she had wanted him. No force had been used; she could not blame him for being subject to the same sexual hunger that drove her.

"Oh, Viola," he said, and sat down, putting his head in his hands. It seemed only natural for her to pat his shoulder, almost as if to comfort him. He reached up and covered her hand with his, and they remained like that in the gloom for a long time. At last she left. What had she done? Eileen had spoken of women having sex as casually as men did. That seemed only fair. Why then did she feel so bad?

The next morning she was apprehensive about facing Dr. Ruskin, and when the coachman had driven off, she stood at the foot of the steps to the museum, unable to force herself to climb them and go inside. She crossed the street, went into Central Park, and sought out the most deserted walks. There she would be safe from annoyance. At last she realized she owed it to Dr. Ruskin, to the museum, to go back and do her assigned tasks.

As soon as she appeared in the laboratory, however, he called her to him and with a look made up in equal parts of pride and shame, told her that from now on she was promoted to performing experiments independently. She knew herself capable of doing more advanced work, but there was something blatant about this, as if, she thought with dismay, he were paying for her sexual services.

"It's not necessary, Dr. Ruskin," she said. "I'm perfectly willing to continue with my job as it is."

"Ah, but I am not willing to let you."

Viola walked into the laboratory to begin her new duties. Dr. Gentry, the scientist who supervised her work, was cordial, suspiciously so, and after explaining what she was to do, quickly handed her an engraved invitation to the luncheon soon to be held in the Loubat Hall of Archaeology for the visiting members of the Seventh International Congress of Zoology. She had never before been included in any museum event.

As she set up the experiment, she was miserably aware that all the men knew. The men had known in Greenland, too, but there she had been free of social restrictions, there she had been passionately in love. She was not going to be able to remain here.

At day's end, she waited until all the other scientists had left before gathering together the few things in the laboratory that were hers. There was no need to resign. Dr. Ruskin would know why she was leaving. So would everyone else.

She stood there looking at the long tables stacked with boxes of slides, tweezers, scissors, vials of preservative solutions, Bunsen burners, flasks, petri dishes, microscopes, and magnifying glasses. It was over. Advancement from a drudge job in a laboratory, she now saw, had been predicated upon her becoming the curator's mistress. Perhaps even the drudge job itself.

Leaving the laboratory for the last time, she started down the nearest corridor, almost running in the vastness of the museum building through one exhibit hall after another. What had these elaborate installations to do with her? With life, for that matter? Were the birds perched on the branches, the bears on the plaster rocks in the glass cabinets, anything more than a mockery of life created by the taxidermists' art? Now she had reached the exhibit of invertebrate fossils. She had contributed to it. But who would ever know? The reports issued by the museum each year gave the names of all those who had made finds and brought them to the museum collections. Not her name. Not now. Not ever.

She ran on. In her distraught mood, she had not followed her usual route to the exits and did not know this part of the museum. At last she realized she was lost and wearily sank down to the cold marble floor. And it was there that a watchman found her, helped her up, and led her back through the halls. The birds. The black bears. The paleontological displays. Finally, the exit.

She stood on the stone steps and could not think where she might go or what she might do, and it seemed there was no place in the world for her as she was, for her as she wanted to be.

In later years she was to say that at the lowest moment of her life, she found the suffragettes. Or rather, they found her.

# Chapter Seven

"I've been asked to recruit you."

Eileen was waiting on the steps when Viola left the museum. Dazed and heartsick, she did not immediately grasp what was meant. "Surely you know the movement I give my life to, Viola." Suffrage of course. "Come home with me now."

She did not wish to listen to Eileen's exhortations, but saw no way to refuse, and ordered the coachman to drive to the unfashionable Greenwich Village address. Viola's spirits sank further when the carriage stopped in front of a dilapidated Georgian house that must have been elegant in the 1870s. By now the concrete was pitted and the stone angel over the front door was missing a wing. Eileen's room was no larger than one of the wardrobes holding Viola's clothes, and the furniture, an odd collection of styles and periods, had been purchased at bargain prices, she was told, in the auction rooms on University Place and the lower-grade Jefferson Market on Sixth Avenue.

"I have nothing to offer you, Viola," said Eileen as soon as they were seated. "I can't even boil water for tea here."

"Where do you take your meals then?"

"I board with the family on the first floor. They have a kitchen, the only one in the building. Their apartment is more expensive, of course. I get this room for twelve dollars a month; I lived on Minetta Place for seven dollars, but that's a real slum."

This then was what independence had gotten Eileen ... *but I can have sex any time I want it.*

"You belong in the suffrage movement, Viola. Going to Greenland and getting a job as a scientist in a laboratory have made you a legend of a sort."

Eileen had captured her interest, flattered her, but she must make her position clear. "I'm not interested in politics, Eileen. I'm a scientist." Even as she spoke, she knew her career as a scientist was over.

"The suffrage movement isn't just about politics; it's about a way of life. A way that you want. Equality."

Equality. A mating of tigers. Thinking of Dr. Ruskin's embrace and its aftermath, she wished she could believe suffrage would make a difference.

"Let's go, Viola," said Eileen abruptly. "I asked you to come tonight because there's a gathering of the National American Woman Suffrage Association. The hall is on MacDougal Street. I guess your coachman has never heard of it, but I'll give him directions."

The meeting was already under way when they arrived, and the large hall was packed. At first glance, Viola was struck by the shabbiness of the women's attire. When she took a second look, however, she realized that what she had taken for shabbiness was not that at all. Rather, the women had adopted a style of dress quite different from that viewed as fashionable in the early winter of 1907. Rigorous corseting, full-busted bodices, tight trailing skirts, and high, stiff neckbands had been abandoned in favor of flowing tunics with graceful folds falling from the shoulders. Instead of being piled in a pompadour and padded, hair was worn long, reaching the shoulders. What impressed Viola the most was how comfortable the suffragettes seemed to be. Who could have imagined a woman's clothing being comfortable?

As she began to distinguish individuals in what had seemed an amorphous group, Viola recognized Marguerite Van Allyn, wife of one of New York's leading financiers and a close friend of Viola's sister, Evelyn. Unlike the others, Marguerite might have posed for a fashion plate in *Dress* magazine—a three-quarter-length coat of Robespierre cut over a hand-embroidered velvet vest with wide lapels and a pleated blouse of shaded taffeta. Viola was amazed that the suffrage movement could attract a woman belonging to the inner circle of society, and even more amazed when Marguerite greeted her, say-ing, "if Eileen Lincoln hadn't brought you here tonight, Viola, I was getting ready to recruit you myself."

It would have been discourteous to say she did not intend to join the movement, so she merely smiled. Then Eileen announced Viola's name and the suffragettes gathered around her in excitement. Viola had never received this kind of admiration from women. Men usually took notice of her, made excuses to talk with her, to brush against her as if by accident. She had grown accustomed to that, but women were usually wary. The suffragettes, however, took pride in her, told her that what she had done reflected well on their sex. Until this mo-ment Viola had faced nothing but disapproval for her rebellion against the conventions of society, for her ambition and determina-tion. The man she loved desperately sought to transform her into a dutiful wife. She stood alone, believed she would always stand alone.

Going home after the meeting, Viola was lost in thoughts of what the suffragettes had shown her. For the first time, she saw her life in its larger context. Only a few hours had passed since she walked out of the museum, feeling the deepest despair. Now she understood that her job in the laboratory was important not just to her but to women in general. Her spirits lifted as she realized that she could go back to the museum, should go back. Dr. Ruskin had offered her an oppor-tunity. Forget his motive.

Secure in this knowledge, she was able to tolerate the knowing looks the scientists gave her when she reappeared in the laboratory the following morning. She faltered only when Dr. Ruskin came out of his office and greeted her with obvious warmth, putting his hand on her arm. Everyone was watching, while pretending not to watch. It took an effort of will to look him in the face; she could not forgive herself for having been so desperate as to accept him. Whatever Eileen said or did, sex without love was not for her. Dr. Ruskin sensed her withdrawal and hastily returned to his office.

After some weeks, it was as if they had never been intimate. As for suffrage, Viola kept going back to the meetings, pleased that the women there thought so well of her, but bored by the information being pressed upon her. Eileen and the others were convinced that once she really knew the history of the suffrage movement, she would be fired with enthusiasm. They talked of how far they had come from the Friends meeting in 1848 where Lucretia Mott and Elizabeth Cady Stanton had spoken for the rights of women as well as slaves. Viola was amazed to hear that Wyoming granted suffrage back in 1869. She had not known that women were able to vote anywhere, and now it appeared that Colorado, Idaho, and Utah had also granted the right prior to 1900, and passage appeared imminent in eight other western states. The American Woman Suffrage Association called for a constitutional amendment every year and maintained a congressional committee in Washington, but suffrage had been brought to a vote in the Senate only once, never in the House of Representatives.

The suffragettes saw all things as related to the major issue of the vote—jobs, salaries, control of money, respect, equality in marriage, in sexual activity. Were all these matters related to the vote?

And then one day, at a meeting no different from the others, without knowing how it had happened, Viola saw the suffragettes' dream. And it was her dream. To stand on the Antarctic ice plateau in the January sunshine. To gain acceptance as a scientist. To be an equal partner in marriage.

Yet even after she had joined the association, she often felt out of sympathy with Eileen and the other women. The stand on prohibition of alcohol was hindering all their efforts. It had aroused the implacable enmity and well-funded opposition of the powerful liquor and brewery industries. And the suffragettes' position made no sense to Viola—an organization committed to greater freedom should not seek to create new restrictions.

Few of those in the movement agreed. Alcohol consumption was but one of the many ways in which men abused women. Indeed, men were responsible for all the suffering and injustice endured by women. Eileen certainly insisted this was true, pointing to her husband's actions as evidence. Viola did not agree. She thought Eileen was too unforgiving, showed no comprehension that her husband had been hurt and jealous. In their focus on a goal, many of the women wished to have as little as possible to do with men. But Viola had not become a suffragette to do without men.

Gradually she became aware that after the meeting, when they went, as the custom was, to the Three Steps Down cafeteria on Eighth Street, some of the women paired off, giving each other the rapt attention usually accorded lovers. Occasionally, a hand would rest on her knee under the table. Eileen, who missed nothing, re-marked coolly: "Just refuse if you don't want it. These are not men; they won't force you."

Returning home after a meeting, Viola often found her mother waiting up to plead with her to give up the association with the suf-frage movement and agree to marry one of the men in their social cir-cle.

"You're a woman yourself, Mamma. Can't you see what suffrage would do for us?"

"You're naive, Viola. Women benefit more by being cared for than by being treated as if they were no different from men. We are dif-ferent. We bear the children. We need the support of men. Look what happens to those unfortunate girls who have babies without husbands."

"Isadora Duncan has done it."

"She is not a member of society, Viola; she's a celebrated dancer and doesn't have to care about convention."

"Marguerite Van Allyn is a suffragette."

"She can afford to be. She accepted a husband first, a fine man of whom her parents approved. That's all I'm asking you to do, Viola. After you're married, you can engage in whatever activities you wish." Her mother left unspoken the obvious, *If your husband allows you to do so.*

"Let men keep the vote, Viola. To give up all we have . . . for what? To elect one politician or another? To cast your vote to go to war? To raise—what are they called?—tariffs? Not having the vote is a small enough price to pay."

It was as if her mother belonged to another era, not to 1907, with its advanced thinking.

Viola continued to attend the suffrage meetings, and one evening was deeply stirred by a group of visitors from England, where the militancy was greater than in the United States. Viola's imagination was fired by the accounts of marches to Parliament Square, of dem-onstrations and battles with the police in which clothes were ripped off down to the petticoat. What struck Viola most forcefully about these women was their exaltation. The visitors took particular notice of Viola, as people always did, and urged her to join them in London.

She returned home, filled with excitement, unaware that her time in the suffrage movement was running out. Mr. Lambert thought he had been patient long enough, too long, really. Give women the vote and who knew what foolishness they would get up to. Just consider their opposition to alcohol. What right did they have to tell him not to take his port or brandy after dinner?

He had been inexcusably lax in allowing his wife to persuade him to wait for Viola to see reason. When did a headstrong girl like that ever see reason? She had to be made to see it. Even quiet little Evelyn was speaking favorably of the suffragettes—Viola's influence no doubt. Of course, his son-in-law had put a stop to that. If Viola were married, her husband would keep her in line. As it was, an unmarried girl was her father's responsibility. Fortunately, he had control of Viola's inheritance from his parents until she turned forty, and could cut off the small quarterly allowance paid her from the trust fund. He could put her out on the street for that matter, if she refused to quit the suffrage movement. Her job was unsuitable for a member of his family. If she did not resign voluntarily, a word to Jerrold, the museum president, would be sufficient.

Presented with this ultimatum, Viola gave way. She would be acting in opposition to her father's wishes soon enough. Byron Tremaine was scheduled to complete his lecture tour and return to New York to organize his expedition. Before long she would be leaving with him for the south polar continent. Parental consent? She had not asked for it when setting off for Greenland and would not do so now.

But when Byron called her to him, it was to announce that he was postponing the Antarctic expedition and was on another course altogether. Arnold Plumley, publisher of the *New York Daily Star,* was having the newspaper sponsor the ascent of Mount McKinley, the highest peak in North America. Journalists and photographers would accompany Tremaine to the lower slopes of the mountain and wait there to record his descent from the peak. The fame attendant on the Alaska Range exploit was essential to his future—to their future, he hastily amended. Raising money for the south polar expedition was harder than had been anticipated. Graham was trying to found a Tremaine Antarctic Club on the order of Peary's Arctic Club, with members pledging several thousand dollars apiece, but had met with indifferent success so far.

It was true that British explorers were racing for the South Pole:

Ernest Shackleton was in the Antarctic right now, and Richard Everett Sharpe, who had failed in 1904, was no doubt weighing a second attempt. Byron would have liked to be the first at the Pole, but was convinced that whatever other explorers achieved, his was to be the expedition studied in textbooks for generations to come. As the first American to raise the flag over the South Pole, he would win the honor for his country, as well as renown for the greatest program of research ever carried out in Antarctica. Byron had gained a reputation as a scientist in the Arctic and meant to build on it.

"Won't Mr. Jerrold give you backing?" asked Viola. The Greenland fossils had been contributed to the Museum of Natural History collection for that very purpose.

Jerrold was proving elusive, however. Nothing but the Arctic attracted him now. He had assigned museum funds to somebody named Quackenbush, who had been lucky enough to find mammoth remains in Alaska. Plumley was a godsend.

Viola was horrified. The Mount McKinley expedition that would deflect Byron from the Antarctic for years meant nothing to her. It should mean nothing to him. Reaching the highest peak in the hemisphere was an exploit, a sporting event, not an expedition for a serious explorer.

She turned on him. "You're convincing yourself that this . . . trip . . . is really a preamble to Antarctica. Is it? Or are you just using it as an excuse?"

"An excuse for what?"

"For not having the nerve to plan, organize, supply, and lead an expedition to the Antarctic." She paused for a moment, and went on. "Perhaps for being afraid to be out on the ice cap for months on end with no one but yourself to rely on."

Afraid? How dared she suggest it? "Afraid when Mount McKinley towers twenty thousand feet above sea level, half of it covered with snow year around? A climb is dangerous beyond belief; life dangles on the end of a rope held by a companion slithering on icy rock over an abyss."

This sponsored ascent of Mount McKinley was a prelude to the great expedition to the Antarctic. But had his relief when Plumley came to him with the offer been due to the realization that the more hazardous journey must be postponed? Certainly no one else saw an assault on McKinley as anything other than an act of courage. But no one else was comparing it to the prolonged heroism required in Antarctica—the journey back from the Pole as desperate as the journey toward the goal, the awesome responsibility for the lives of so many men. He knew the difference, but it was insupportable for Viola to throw it in his face.

Byron stood up, came around to the front of the desk where she was standing, grasped her shoulders, and shook her—anything to stop her from saying more. She backed away and, as he relaxed his grip, pushed him with all her strength until he lost his balance and fell over the large burgundy leather armchair. He struggled to his feet and came toward her, reached out, and seized her. He was breathing hard. So was she.

And then, as he pressed against her, she could feel the change in him. The change in her. And was disarmed. He released her and, shuddering, she embraced him. Tight against him, she was not sure whether she was still fighting him or making love.

She did not desire him; he was letting her down. She desired him. Driven. She could not wait; surely, he could not wait. He reached down, put his hand beneath the skirt of her dress to her petticoat, her underwear, could not stop to undo the intricate corset lacing or unfasten the long line of tiny buttons down the back of her dress. Barely a minute passed before he had thrown his suit coat to the floor, opened his trouser buttons, and seated himself in the large armchair. He pulled her down on his lap, and oh, why did he not take her to lie with him on the couch, but then in another minute, the discomfort did not matter.

She lifted her hips to enable him to take off her skirt; the skirt was tight, so tight that the fabric tore with the strain. His hands at her hips, he pulled her down, down, onto him. She was aware of his harsh, heavy breathing, of her own. And every breath was a struggle against the imprisoning corset she had not taken time to remove when he telephoned her to come to him. She was gasping; her heart was pounding desperately in her constricted chest. He did not notice, holding her to him more tightly, moving his hips, as she was moving hers. To steady herself, she put her hands on his shoulders, feeling his shirt dripping with his sweat. The sensation of his big body beneath hers, inside hers on the leather chair. She bent to kiss him, and he bit at her lips, put his tongue inside her mouth, moving it, in and out, out and in as he was moving, in and out, out and in. Oh no. It was too fast. And then it was not too fast.

He brushed her hair away, put his lips close to her ear; his voice was low, throaty, hoarse, almost harsh. "Viola. You are mine." Those words: he spoke them during the act of love. Always. And always, even as she felt his breath warm against her ear, as he stroked her hair, something in her recoiled at the word. "Mine." His.

How beautiful she was, his high-spirited girl, he thought; she claimed to belong to no man. Just words. She was his. However she fought against it. He was sure of that.

"Say it. Say it."

When he was holding her in his arms, their bodies tight against each other, she would say it, anything now to keep him there. But in the next moment from deep inside her would come a flicker of resistance.

Then it was over and she stood up without looking at him, picked up her petticoat and underwear, and put them on her hot, wet body. *You are mine. Mine.* How could she have repeated it like an automaton? Like his automaton? How was it that she yielded in this way again and yet again? She had refused marriage so as not to give him this dominance over her and then she handed it to him each time they were together.

She rearranged her clothes as best she could. Her lips felt bruised; she licked them, tasting blood. Byron left marks upon her; sometimes she thought the act of love was not fully over until they disappeared.

Byron buttoned his trousers slowly, carefully, looking at her all the while. His eyes were filled with a warmth she did not quite trust. "Why don't you marry me, Viola," he whispered, reaching out, taking her hand. "That's what I want, what you really want.

"Come to me. What else in your life compares with this?"

What else in her life? Looking at him, feeling his hand, strong, hard, slightly moist, she wondered if he might not be right after all.

"It's time, Viola. You've played at being a suffragette. Your parents put an end to that. You had a minor job in a laboratory. Even if your father let you keep it, you wouldn't have gone anywhere with it."

At his words, a sense of outrage seized her. *Played at being a suffragette,* at being a scientist in the museum, and before that on the

Greenland expedition. But these were not games. They were the most important things in her life. Except for him.

All at once, conscious of the pull he exerted, she was afraid she would give way. It would be so easy to marry him. And so hard not to. If she remained at home, she would have to marry. And if she married, it should be Byron, even knowing that he would never allow his wife to go to the Antarctic.

She thought then of his life. Byron's life. He could do anything with it, had the whole world of exploration open to him. And he asked her to accept that her life held nothing. Nothing but him. Marriage with him. Only a part of his life, his rich full life, but the whole of hers. What he was offering her was whatever was left over from that life, a position in the background, loved perhaps, desired certainly. Had she not learned better from the suffragettes?

The first time he proposed, she had known marriage to him meant renouncing her ambitions. That was no less true now. No matter that he procrastinated, the expedition to the Antarctic must eventually take place. He would take her with him, because he recognized her worth.

There was only one thing for her to do. She would have to leave home, return only when Byron was ready to mount his Antarctic expedition. England—she could go there, as the visiting suffragettes had urged, and join the militant movement. Whatever was achieved in England must have an influence on American politics as well. And she would be far away from Byron. Pulling her hand away from his roughly, she moved out of his reach.

Everything he had said was true, thought Byron, but evidently she did not see it that way. Were he not to apologize, he would lose her. Hard though it was for him, he sought to conciliate. "I didn't mean to make suffrage sound like a game, Viola. I'm in favor of it. I'll say so for the record in my next newspaper interview."

Why was it so hard to hate him when it would have been so much easier to leave if she did? He was so close to her that she could feel the heat of his body, smell the odors of sweat and lovemaking.

There was still a possibility that she was wrong in her belief, still one question to put to him: "Will you take me to the Antarctic with you, Byron?"

"I've told you I will." The reply was ambiguous, accurate as far as it went. He would certainly lose her were he to destroy her hopes for Antarctica.

Viola could not leave it at that. "But as your wife? Would you . . . allow . . . your wife, the mother or future mother of your children, to go to the Antarctic, to stand beside you in the gale-force winds on the ice plateau?"

That was not a reasonable question. Byron was convinced that once they were married, she would be content as other women were. He could hardly say that, however, and though he was ready to do almost anything to hold her, it was dishonorable to tell a blatant lie. And so he remained silent.

There was a long pause. Her mouth was trembling and he thought she would give way, but instead she settled her Gibson girl straw hat on her head, not troubling to smooth down the cloud of russet hair with its copper highlights. Byron followed her to the door.

"Viola, doesn't it mean anything to you that I've asked you to marry me . . . twice?"

She must never make love with him again. He weakened her. His very desirability, her passion for him, weakened her. Nothing less than the Antarctic expedition would bring her back to him.

"Ask me once more when we're in Antarctica, Byron. Ask me then."

His face flushed, and when he spoke, his voice was harsh. "I'll be married long before then, Viola. And you won't like it a bit."

"Neither will you."

But as she walked out of the building, holding her torn skirt together carefully, her heart ached. Only an hour before they had been making love; her clothes were still damp. England was so very far away.

That evening she told her mother of her plans. After a lengthy silence, "Oh, Viola. I've done my best to save you from the results of your willfulness and carelessness. Your father and I have put up with so much from you. More than any other parents would have. We took you back after that insane trip to Greenland, with everyone we knew whispering about you. And in all the time since." Mrs. Lambert thought bitterly that gossip about Viola's relationship with Byron Tremaine had never died down. Worse still, one of Mrs. Lambert's friends in all kindness let her know of rumors that there had been "goings-on" at the museum. If Viola kept on in this way, she would be the first member of her family to be dropped from the *Social Register*. "I've always tried to tell myself that this wildness in you was Byron Tremaine's fault. He imparted all these ideas when you were too young to know what was going on. But you're not a girl anymore; you know what you're doing.

"Why, Viola, everyone says the suffragettes believe in free love. They'll think that's why you're going. You'll disgrace us."

"I cannot bear to stay here." Viola was thinking of the conflict with Byron, but her mother did not take it that way.

"Can't bear? Well then, go. But you do know we cannot accept this action." The anger in her mother's voice, well modulated even now, shook Viola. "No other mother could have achieved what I did in getting you back onto the best invitation lists, arranging for you to meet eligible men. And this is my reward."

How was she to reply? "I know how hard you've tried, but I don't fit into the world of society, Mama."

"This is the last straw. If you go to England, you're going out of our lives."

This could not be happening. "You can't mean it."

"I don't want to, but I do."

With tears spilling over, Viola went to her mother then and tried to embrace her. Mrs. Lambert, trembling, leaned into the embrace for a moment and then slipped away and left the room. On the threshold, she turned and looked back with such regret expressed on her face that Viola almost weakened. Perhaps she had been too hard to live with, too hard to understand. Still, her mother was being unreasonable by demanding she give up everything that mattered to her. This could not be a real breach. They were mother and daughter until death. Sooner or later, they must make it up.

Her father was equally horrified by her plans, and informed her he would foil them by having her allowance cut off. He saw it as his duty to save her from her own foolishness. Someday she would be grateful.

So she was not to go after all. It had not occurred to her that her father would withhold this fraction of her own money. Her own. She would never have thought of that before the suffragettes.

In a mood of despair she went to visit Evelyn—another victim of male domination, she thought bitterly. "The sad thing is, Evie, that it would take so little money to make England possible for me. But there's no one I can ask."

"Isn't there? I can think of someone."

"You mean . . . you? But Bertram wouldn't like it, and Evie, you have to admit you're not a fighter."

"Oh, you're the fighter. I admire you for doing things I wouldn't dare to. But I have my ways, too." At that moment, Viola noticed an envelope lying on the small bois de rose table beside the sofa. "Yes. It's for you. Take it."

Viola's hands were shaking as she opened the envelope and saw the dollar bills inside. "Count the money. Is it enough?" Added to the savings from the pittance she had been paid at the museum—less than the stockroom boys—she saw that it would allow her passage by ocean liner, with a little over to start her life in England. "Does Bertram know?"

Evelyn shook her head. "I'm so absentminded, Viola, that it's impossible for me to keep track of every dollar I spend. It just goes out of my head, and when Bertram asks me where this sum or that went, I can't remember. A small amount of money like this . . . he'll never notice it. Just one thing—don't write me from England, Viola. The footman brings Bertram the mail first and he wouldn't like it."

Viola looked at Evelyn, elegant in the flawlessly fitted at-home dress made to order for her in Paris and the everyday pearls around her slender neck, and thought how deprived was her life.

"How can you stand your life?"

"What do you mean, Viola? I have a wonderful life."

Viola had never spoken openly to Evelyn about her marriage, but if there were ever to be a time, it was now.

"I mean the way he treats you."

"But he treats me very well."

"You know what I'm saying, Evelyn. He treats you like a pet when you're an intelligent woman."

"Oh, Viola, that's not what marriage is about. I wouldn't change places with Bertram for anything. He has so many worries about business and the people working for him and the state of the economy. Why, sometimes he's so tired at night he doesn't want to go to a dinner party."

It seemed to Viola that Evelyn was completely missing the point. "But he gives the orders . . . and for the most part, you follow them."

"Oh, sometimes I get annoyed with him and think he's wrong. But I can usually find a way to get around him, as I have today. Every man has his faults. The main thing is that he takes care of me, Viola. I like being taken care of and protected. Bertram loves me and I love him. That makes me happy. Most married women would tell you the same thing."

Viola was stunned. Her affair with Byron Tremaine had shown her that one could love a man who sought to dominate. But to be happy about that? She had not believed it possible. Perhaps she had been wrong in assuming that the married women she observed were miserable. Had she been naive in her appraisal of marriage?

"But Evie, do you think it's right for the husband to dominate, for the man alone to have the right to vote, the right to succeed in a profession of his choosing?"

"Oh, you're beginning to make your suffragette speech. But do I think it's right? No, I don't. That's why I support you in your suffrage activity. It's not for me. But for you . . . yes, I can see that you can't bring yourself to take orders from a man. So go on and fight for women's rights. I'll tell you, though, that I don't believe the suffrage movement will ever succeed. This is the way the world has been run all through history. You can't change the world."

"Oh, yes, I can."

# Chapter Eight

"WHY DID HE KILL HIMSELF?

"What could have led him to such a desperate act, Beatrix?"

And we had been getting along so well—or so it had seemed. I was lecturing about Byron Tremaine that afternoon at a college in southern New Jersey, and to my surprise Avery was in the audience. I did not know how he heard of the lecture; there had certainly been little publicity. And so I had been flattered. Foolishly, I now saw. After all, I know what the man is, how little he is to be trusted. But today, coming in so quietly, listening attentively, speaking to me with respect, he had been able to make me forget what he had done before. Technique. How could I have forgotten?

He waited for me after the lecture, until the departure of the last of the little group that inevitably surrounds a speaker with questions and comments. "You're a good lecturer," he said. Flattery is a time-worn practice, but the praise was pleasant to hear. "When you're talking about Byron Tremaine, you catch fire. Your eyes shine and the tone of your voice is so moving. You made everyone in the room care about him. That's a very unusual trait. Maybe I'll put you on my program."

Were I more at ease with him, I would have responded with some sort of joke. I am said to have a dry sense of humor, but in his presence, nothing came to mind, and I shook my head in negation. I thought he appeared disappointed, though that hardly seemed possible, as his suggestion could not have been seriously made. My personality is not flamboyant enough for a program like his. After a somewhat awkward moment, he suggested that we have coffee together in the cafeteria of the student commons building. Still pleased that he had attended my lecture, I accepted, and only then realized that any conversation with him was dangerous. What if he were to challenge me to refute the tape describing Byron's harshness to Hermine? I could not refute it. There really had been a diary page, fought over, torn out, and a photograph that bore a secret message. Until I found the photograph, I had been convinced I would be able to prove the happiness of the marriage so conclusively as to show the tape for the fraud it was.

I sat beside Avery in the cafeteria, deserted at this hour, drinking watered coffee, dreading what was sure to come. Contrary to my expectations, Avery did not mention the tape and instead spoke amusingly and at length about the celebrities who appeared on his program. He moved his chair closer, smiling as if he found me interesting as a person, not merely as a source of information. Relieved that he was not asking about Byron, I was willing to revise my judgment of him, almost to be charmed. I began to be relaxed—well, to some degree. It is not possible to be fully relaxed in his presence. He carries an air of tension with him always, an integral part of his personality, curiously winning. As the minutes passed, it seemed to me that without the tape recorder between us, he spoke with greater warmth. I was drawn to him, uneasily, and felt he was drawn to me.

"I live alone now with my dogs," he told me, something suggestive in his manner, and this time I was able to make the small joke that they must be Dobermans, and there was something suggestive in mine as well.

"Why did he kill himself?"

Just like that and when we were talking in such friendly fashion, perhaps even flirting a little.

"What are you talking about?" My hand shook so that the coffee in my cup spilled into the saucer. He watched me, his eyes narrowing.

"You heard me."

"You can't be talking about Byron Tremaine." I was sufficiently angry to find the courage to face him down.

"Come on, Beatrix, I've heard the rumor; there must be something to it."

How could I have deluded myself for so much as a moment about Avery? The appearance of friendship was a ploy.

"He fell to his death while mountain climbing. Everyone knows that."

"Fell? Or leaped? I'm told he leaped."

"If there were something to it, you wouldn't call it a rumor. What are you trying to do, Avery?"

"I'm trying to get at the truth as I always do," he remarked blandly.

Byron's death while on his second expedition to Mount McKinley in Alaska is too well documented to question. It was an accident, a tragic, heroic accident. "Members of the climbing party reported that in pulling a falling companion to safety, Byron lost his balance and fell himself. A hero's death," I said softly, moved as I always was by his selfless action. It fitted the man, I explained to Avery with some passion; Tremaine had first come to public attention by saving a drowning companion on the Swedish Antarctic expedition.

"You speak so touchingly, Beatrix, that I'd like to think you're right. But I've read the newspapers on microfilm for the day after his death, and they don't ring true. The survivors contradict one another. My researchers found there were hints of suicide from the very beginning; I can't just dismiss them."

"How is it I never heard about those hints?"

"Maybe you didn't want to find out anything that would change your image of the hero."

Now I thought of the way to answer him: "Do you have a tape recording of these rumors?"

I was half joking, but he took me seriously. "Oh, so you're beginning to see that tape recordings are valuable when seeking the truth. I don't have one now, but I probably will in time."

"I suppose you want to play it on your program."

"No. As a matter of fact I don't. Suicides don't build ratings for television shows. The public doesn't like them. Neither do I. But they tell something about a person. How can a hero lack the courage to go on living? I told you once that you find one fact about a man, one fact that doesn't fit the picture, and before you know it there are a hundred facts. We have the story of the happy marriage. That wasn't true. We have the story of the adored photograph. That doesn't exist. Now we have the story of the hero's death. I say that's false as well."

"Are you trying to make a connection? You can hardly suggest that a less than perfect marriage—which you also haven't proven—is enough to make a man commit suicide."

"You made the connection. Not I. But there was another woman. I'm positive of that." It was just a guess; only Ronald and I had seen the photograph. Even that did not prove anything. "And I say he did commit suicide," Avery concluded firmly.

I must not allow him to see he had upset me. "You say. You say. But even you admit it's just rumor. You don't know anything." What was there about Avery that made me, usually timid and retiring, so aggressive? The suggestion of suicide was absurd. Byron had been at the peak of his fame for almost a decade, an acknowledged hero. As the first explorer to reach the South Pole, he received constant adulation. I thought of the photograph of Byron with his hand on his son's shoulder. A son who bore his name. This was a man who was fulfilled.

Biographers and journalists had looked for disappointments in his life to set against his successes. They complained that he had lived a charmed life, not thinking, they would joke, that his biographers needed contrasts to bring drama to their accounts.

"There was no reason for him to commit suicide, Avery. He was famous, admired, successful at everything he did."

"Not everything."

I realized how careless I had been to give Avery such an opening, knowing as I do that there was one failure in Byron's life. He ran for Congress in the early 1920s and was defeated. The race was close, and Byron's opponent had been hard-pressed to find anything damaging to say about him. But when a candidate fears to lose an election, he will try anything. The charge was that Tremaine had turned against woman's suffrage. That was absurd on the face of it. Tremaine backed suffrage long before it had become politically expedient to do so. He was quoted in newspapers to that effect. Among his private papers—along with the letters from Shackleton and Sharpe, two presidents of the United States, governors, the Explorers Club board, the leaders of the Geographical Society—he had kept letters from a suffragette thanking him for his support. But his opponent's charges, "dirty tricks" they are called today, were sufficient to lose him the support of the Woman's party.

However unfairly lost, he must have felt the election defeat. But it was nothing to commit suicide over. Nor would suicide have been his response, whatever the circumstances. Byron lived for history. A good death was intrinsic to his character, never the coward's act.

"Why are you doing this, Avery? Do you think you'll shock me into revealing some dark secret? I thought he was going to be your 'good guy.' "

"I hope he is, Miss Tremaine. I hope he is." This time he addressed me formally; the hint of attraction between us was gone. "I want him to be. That's the program plan I've drawn up. The network management likes it. But I can't go in front of millions of viewers without knowing all there is to know about each person I talk about. I'll repeat what I said before: I'm only trying to get at the truth. You say he's a hero and that he couldn't have committed suicide. Prove it to me. You've got all the information about him. You and Ronald Graham." He frowned at the mention of Graham, though he had no reason to dislike him. "Ask your explorer friend why Tremaine didn't pull anyone else down with him. Aren't climbers roped together?"

I stood up and carried my coffee cup to the conveyer belt for dirty dishes. The brightly lit commons room seemed darker now, dingy; for the first time I noticed the crumpled napkins on the floor. I walked back to the table and picked up the carousel of slides and my lecture notes. Nothing Avery said or did was as it seemed. I wondered that I could even for a moment have believed he came to hear my lecture, that I could even for a moment have been pleased by it.

I walked to the door; Avery followed me. "Wait a minute. I know you don't have a car." A guess? Many people who live in the heart of New York do not keep a car. But he seemed so certain that I was shaken by his omniscience. "I'll drive you home."

"I came by bus and I can go back the same way."

"Are you afraid you'll talk too much alone in a car with me?"

"I have nothing to talk to you about, Avery."

"Maybe you're just afraid to be alone in a car with me." There was the distorted flirtatiousness and suggestiveness I so disliked. Avery waited for my response like a singer waiting for the aria to be cheered, and when there was no applause, went on: "Do you want to know what I think, Beatrix? I think you'll appear on my program when the time comes."

I saw no need to answer. He would find out in time that I would neither meet with him again nor appear on his program. I put on my coat, turning away from his effort to help, not wanting him to touch me. Picking up my box of slides, I walked rapidly to the door and all the way to the bus stop. When I looked back, Avery was standing in the doorway of the commons building, an expression that might have been dismay on his face.

*Prove that Tremaine did not commit suicide.* I was deeply troubled. A man falls to his death while mountain climbing on one of the steepest, iciest slopes in the world. Did he fall or did he jump? Avery's charge would be hard to disprove.

When I returned home and called Ronald to me, however, he did not agree. "Avery records every person he interviews. If there isn't a tape, it means he couldn't find anyone to back the rumor."

Avery's last question still troubled me. I repeated it to Ronald.

"Climbers are supposed to be roped together, Bibi. So are men crossing an icy plateau broken with crevasses. But that doesn't mean people always do as they should. Being roped to another man hampers your mobility. I've been out lots of times when it's seemed just too much bother to fix the line.

"When you're on the trail, you do a lot of things you shouldn't. One time I was out alone and it was getting late and the motor sledge stalled. I had given the instructions myself that anyone in trouble should send up a flare and wait for rescue. Instead, I took off my mittens to fix the engine. I was lucky. I only lost part of a finger; I could have lost the whole hand. You can't make any mistakes in polar regions."

I stroked Ronald's hand. "I can never get over how much your life resembles Byron's. At least you didn't make his last great mistake. If you had, we'd have missed one another."

He did not change expression, yet I sensed an undercurrent, realized I had been tactless in underscoring the age difference. I was not speaking unkindly; I favor older men.

"I can prove that Byron actually did reach out to grasp another man and fell in the effort, Bibi."

"How can you do that? I would think the newspaper reports of his death would have been enough, but Avery denies them."

"I have something better than newspaper reports, Bibi. I can provide an eyewitness, someone who made the climb with Tremaine, saw him reach down and grab the other man and then fall himself."

"I wouldn't think anyone who was on that expedition would still be alive. It all happened in 1925."

"There is one survivor; he's in his nineties now, but I talked with him just a couple of months ago and his mind was perfectly clear. This is one man Avery will never be able to find."

"How is that possible?"

"Well, he's not your most sterling character. He was a member of my first expedition, no good in some ways—he stole things out of our kit bags while we slept. But though he was older than any of the rest of us, he was strong on the trail, pulled me out of a crevasse one time. I hadn't been roped that day, Bibi. My kneecap was broken and I thought it was all over, and then I looked up and there was that old crook—Tim O'Brien, his name was then—leaning down."

"I can never get over how casually you speak of the many times your life has been in danger." Ronald smiled then. When he smiles he looks so young, and wanting to please him, I told him so.

"O'Brien was in jail years ago, for armed robbery," Ronald continued, "and when he came out, he changed his name and disappeared. But he sends me a card from time to time when he needs a handout. The name is invariably different, but he knows I'll recognize his writing. A man who's put his life on the line for you always has a hold on you. He's in an old sailors' home now, not that he was ever at sea. But he stole the papers off a sailor he met in a bar one time and lives in relative comfort as Joe Pulaskie."

"Where's the home for old sailors?"

"It's in Westchester, a nice drive on a beautiful day. We'll have fun."

Ronald and I have good times together, but "fun" is not the word I would use to describe them. "Fun" is the kind of thing to have with someone like devil-may-care Bucky Sheridan, whom Avery has selected as his "bad guy."

I had expected Pulaskie to be wizened and sly, befitting the life he had led. Instead, he was big, stout, only a little stooped, and his face was so open, his eyes so clear, that it was hard to believe he was in this pleasant place because he had stolen another man's identity.

"This is Byron Tremaine's great-granddaughter."

Pulaskie greeted me warmly, looked from Ronald to me and back again. "And something else besides." This was a whispered aside that I could not help but hear; he all but poked Ronald in the ribs. Ronald looked at me a little uneasily, but actually I was relieved the old man was still so keenly observant.

For at least an hour, I listened fascinated as Pulaskie and Ronald reminisced about the expeditions of the past, about the risks they had taken and gotten away with, about this man who had been afraid and that one who was brave, and above all, the good times, yes the good times they had known.

In the midst of the reminiscences, Ronald remarked without any particular change in tone, "As I remember it, you were on Byron Tremaine's last expedition to Mount McKinley. Why don't you tell Beatrix about it; she'll be interested." Pulaskie was relaxed and expansive by then; it struck me that in his own way, Ronald was as skilled a questioner as Avery.

"I'll never forget that climb. Eight days it took us going up that mountain. Terrible days, chopping steps in the ice. And cold enough to freeze your nuts off. Oh, pardon me, miss. It was too early in the season. There was still a lot of snow in the foothills, ice in the streams we had to cross. 'Hazardous conditions' was how they said it—them meteorologist fellows. And the days still so short."

Relief flooded over me. Hazardous conditions. An accident was not only possible, but probable. I would not interrupt him now, but have him repeat this afterward. My tape recorder was in my handbag.

"Didn't anyone try to get him to postpone the climb?"

"You could never tell Captain Tremaine nothing. When he got it in his head to do something, he done it."

"But weren't you afraid to go?"

"Not with him; he went to the South Pole and back without losing a man. Captain Tremaine was a great climber. All six of us he picked for that climb knew what we was doing. And then, the money was good. Mr. Graham—your grandfather, I mean—was in charge there, and you could count on him to pay top dollar."

"What kind of mood was Tremaine in during the climb?"

"What do you mean?"

"Was he cheerful?"

"Captain Tremaine was never what you'd call cheerful, not like you"—he turned to Ronald—"kidding around drinking beer with the boys at night." For the first time, I could almost see Ronald as he must have been before I knew him. Heroic, yet kidding around and drinking beer. "Captain Tremaine'd be writing in his book or mooning over that photograph of his."

*Mooning* over whom? I was remembering the picture of the unknown woman pasted to the back of Hermine's portrait.

"Did he act the way he always did? Or did he seem preoccupied, gloomy?"

"He was like he always was, honey. All he thought about, all he talked about was the next day's climb."

"Was the climb going badly?"

"It was hard, but we was doing okay, right up to the end. That morning we was tired, but raring to go at the same time. Thought we could get to the top by afternoon. It was too windy on the peak to camp for the night, so we figured to stay maybe half an hour, take some pictures, and start down before dark. Well, you don't want to hear about that, honey."

"Yes, I do. I want to hear it from you, because you were there. You told the newspaper reporters you saw Tremaine grab at McConnachy, the man who was falling, and lose his balance. Exactly how did it happen? Wasn't he roped to you?"

"No, he wasn't on the rope just then. Captain Tremaine sometimes went on a little way ahead of the rest of us. He'd done McKinley before, you see, thought he'd spot a landmark and show us the way."

"So McConnachy climbed up after him and lost his footing."

"That's what we said. Just that."

I felt the first faint hint of uneasiness. "What do you mean, that's what you said? Isn't that what happened?"

Pulaskie stopped for a while and thought. "It all happened so fast, miss. One minute he was there on the rock and the next he was hurtling down through space, down, crash. I'll never forget the sounds of the rocks breaking as he went down. We thought it might start an avalanche. We was that scared."

"But what about McConnachy? Tremaine did get him back up on the rock. He told the newspaper reporters how he had started to fall. And you did, too. That's what both of you told the newspaper reporters."

"Well, you see, miss, it's more what the newspaper reporters told us than we told them. They kept asking Mac and me—we was the closest to him, you see—if Tremaine hadn't died doing something heroic like saving one of us. Mac was quicker than me. He spoke right up, said yes, he was the one to fall; he owed his life to Tremaine. They asked how I had felt seeing the fall and rescue. So I told them. And once it was in all the papers, we couldn't go back on it, could we?"

"It was a long time ago, Joe," said Ronald. "It's hard to remember that far back."

Pulaskie looked at my crestfallen face and then back at Ronald, and with hardly a minute's hesitation replied: "Why, that's right, Mr. Graham. My memory goes back on me these days. Past ninety, you know. Now that I think of it, seems to me I remember Mac slipping off the ledge. The rocks was covered with sheet ice. Yeah, Captain Tremaine grabbed for him. That's the way it was. Later when we climbed down to pick up the body, there was a scrap from the sleeve of Mac's jacket in Captain Tremaine's hand." He was smiling, the sly smile I had imagined before I met him.

I wondered what Ronald was thinking; the lines around his eyes and mouth seemed a little deeper, but he gave no indication of how he felt. He looked at me keenly, then away, and I realized he was leaving it up to me. If I wanted to take what Pulaskie was offering, he would not object. I wish I could say I was not tempted. Any means, well, almost any means of stopping Avery appeared reasonable, well, almost reasonable. Were he in my place, Avery would certainly not have hesitated, for all his claims of seeking truth.

"Joe, who else have you told? I mean who else knows about the newspaper reporters?"

"I never told nobody nothing."

"What about McConnachy?"

"Maybe he talked, but who'd believe him? He was usually drunk. It don't matter no more. Mac had the most terrible temper and got killed in a barroom brawl."

"And the others?"

"None of them is still alive. Few men have my constitution; I haven't had a cold since 1948. But they was too far away. Only me and Mac was close to Captain Tremaine."

"Don't look so bereft, Bibi," Ronald said as we returned to the car. "It's disappointing to find out Tremaine didn't die a hero's death, but don't make it into more than it is."

Ronald was right, of course. Pulaskie's revelations did not make the death a suicide. It had to be an accident. *He was just like he always was.* Pulaskie had said that, too. Nothing could alter the fact that Tremaine was indeed a hero. Of that, I was perfectly certain. And so I must win in the end, and force Avery to withdraw his accusations.

The insidious nature of what Avery had done, though, was to cause me to consider whether I had been overconfident in my role as family historian. Did I really know all about Byron Tremaine? Might there be sides to him that I had missed altogether, gaps that still needed to be filled in? I had the first faint glimmerings that the complete story of my great-grandfather's life was still to be told.

# *Chapter Nine*

I DID NOT KNOW HER name, her history, how she came to meet Tremaine, or when. I did not know where she had lived, or whether she was single or married, childless or a mother, a lover or a friend. But one thing I did know—I knew what the lost woman of the photograph looked like. Beautiful, vital, reaching out. Once seen, impossible to forget. Someone must have made note of her. Perhaps she was lost because no one ever searched for her. Certainly I had never done so before Avery came to me with his insinuations about an illicit romance.

"Where should I begin to look?" I asked Ronald as we drove down the highway, away from the failed interview with Joe Pulaskie, only to be stunned by his response: "Can't you put Tremaine out of your mind for once? I get tired of sharing my bed with him."

Ronald had always encouraged me to speak of Byron Tremaine. The sudden change in attitude alarmed me. I did not want Ronald's feeling for me to alter in any way. He was speaking of Tremaine as of a sexual rival, but a dead man cannot be a rival. No, I did not understand Ronald.

"There's no one else in your bed."

He smiled at my obvious sincerity, put his hand on my knee caressingly, and the moment passed. It was he who brought up my great-grandfather again. "There must be something in Byron's writings, some hint that was missed in the past because there was no reason to suspect a great love. It would be worth checking every mention of a woman."

"But why wouldn't he have described her in glowing terms, Ronald? I'm convinced the romance took place before his marriage, and he kept the photograph because he had loved that woman more than he did his wife. After all, he didn't meet Hermine until he was nearly thirty. Tremaine was so upright it's impossible to imagine him being unfaithful." And then remembering that Ronald was unfaithful to his wife, and I the cause, hastily added that times had been different then.

He smiled wryly. "Yes, customs were very different then. He hid the woman's photograph, which does seem to point to something illicit. Even if he hadn't been married, an affair would have cast a shadow on his moral character, and financial backers are conservative men."

As soon as Ronald left me at home, I began leafing through Tremaine's diaries. Considering Byron's exceptional good looks and charm, there had been remarkably few women in his life before Hermine. Everything was much as I remembered it, beginning with the casual flirtations of a young man coming to maturity before the turn of the century. Later he paid attention to one woman or another without appearing to care much about any of them. He had become engaged to a Vanderbilt heiress, but her family thought their wealth could buy them a title and insisted she break it off. He professed himself relieved, and I could not find the smallest indication of a thwarted love. After that, there was no one until he met Hermine. His word picture of her was written with such warmth that their happiness together seemed assured.

I did know of one woman who had played a part, albeit a minor one, in his explorations, accompanying the expedition to Greenland as what we would now call a science intern. She was listed on the roster as Miss V. Lambert, but despite her gender, she received only brief scattered mentions in Byron's diary and in the writings of the expedition members. According to Byron's account, she had done the routine laboratory observations of the fossils brought back from the field. These were the fossils that led Byron to develop a new theory, revolutionary at that time, of prehistoric climatic conditions and

the emergence of life in the Northern Hemisphere. Always generous,
Byron had added a footnote to the published reports thanking
V. Lambert for her assistance, which from the evidence of the diaries
had been quite rudimentary.

The presence of a woman on Byron's expedition to Greenland had
aroused interest on the part of the early biographers, who hoped to
make much of it. Passion in the snow or some such theme. But there
was no hint of passion in the snow or anywhere else. Byron wrote
that he had accepted Miss Lambert—he never gave her first
name—on the expedition as a courtesy to a college professor. She
was not mentioned in the diary again. Her name did not appear on
the list for any of Tremaine's subsequent expeditions; he had never
taken her with him again.

Determined to follow every clue, however unpromising, I then remembered a rather puzzling reference to her in one of Byron's letters.
I had noticed it when making selections for a new edition of his collected writings, but had not given it much thought. Pulling the volume from the shelf, I turned to that letter. Writing to his father,
Byron commented that the newspapers were devoting considerable
space to the one girl on the all-male expedition to Greenland. Miss
Lambert had been oblivious to the implications. It fitted her
philosophy—she was very young, thought men and women were
equal. He did not argue the point with her.

Men and women were equal. Only then did I suspect a connection
between Miss Lambert and the suffragette who had a correspondence with Byron in 1907, thirteen years before the suffrage amendment to the Constitution was passed. She had thanked him for his
support of the movement, proof of the falsity of the antisuffrage accusation that had cost Byron his election to Congress. Could this suffragette have been the woman who had accompanied Byron to
Greenland? The letters were by no means personal, made no reference to a shared past, yet now it struck me as odd that they were un-
signed. The envelopes had not been retained, so there was no clue as
to name and address.

In one or two of the letters, photocopied from the originals, the
suffragette made mention of being an American in London. When I
read them before, that had been of no more than passing interest to
me. Now, however, I remembered the British stamps on the envelope

marked PERSONAL URGENT that I had found on the day Ronald and I were searching the cartons in the garage of the old Graham house. I had dropped the envelope in the greater excitement of discovering the photograph. Now we must go back and find it.

However, when I telephoned Ronald, he put me off. He would be busy the following day and we must postpone the trip to the one after. I was surprised, having grown accustomed to his immediate response. Unreasonable, of course.

He was silent on the drive to his grandfather's house in Rhinebeck; however, I was absorbed in telling him my conjectures about Miss Lambert and the letter from England, and did not think to ask why. When we arrived in the driveway, he touched my hand in the way he had. The scar on his forehead showed red. I had been burning with impatience to find the envelope, but now I wanted Ronald more. He likes to make love to me in that house, his boyhood home. And it is when we come together there that I can best see him as he was in the great days of the expeditions. There is no one else in our bed.

When we made love, his tenderness overwhelmed me. This was what I sought in older men, what I found. But none so tender as he. His touch was gentle and yet firm, his strength controlled. There was no hint of the moment of hesitation I had observed toward the end of my earlier romances with the men I knew at the Explorers Club.

Afterward we went to the garage to begin our search at the point where we had abandoned it on our previous visit. As we started walking between the rows of cartons, my sense of anticipation increased and I was breathing hard as if I had been running. Ronald pressed my arm and I drew comfort from his warmth. The envelope was in full view, lying where I had dropped it on the floor beside the open box. Ronald lifted down a couple of cartons for us to sit on while we studied it.

The postmark had faded so I could read nothing beyond the date—1907—and the writing was barely legible. Ronald and I tried to puzzle it out. I found an 8 in the address and a word that began "Chess" and another "Co." As before, I had a sense of knowing what the address must be, and then all at once I grasped the association that had eluded me. This must be 88 Chessham Court, famed as a center of suffragette activity in the first decade of the century. The address itself had become a synonym for suffrage. The sender's name looked to be "Limbug" or "Linbat"—close enough to Lambert to convince me I had been right.

"I recognize the handwriting, Ronald. It's the same as in the letters from the suffragette."

What can have been so personal? So urgent? The letter that might have revealed the cause was missing.

"You've made a great discovery," said Ronald. "Why, you're just glowing with it."

But my excitement ebbed as I realized that I had solved one mystery, but the most important one—the identity of the woman in the photograph—eluded me. The correspondence from a suffragette—from V. Lambert—had been completely lacking in the passion a woman would have revealed to her lover. I remembered the creased picture made unforgettable by the radiance of the face and vibrancy of the gesture.

"I don't see how Miss Lambert could have been Byron's lost love, Ronald."

"It doesn't seem so," he agreed. "The woman in the photograph was hardly the type to have been a scientist at that time, and I can't imagine her going on a polar expedition. Had Miss Lambert been attractive, one or another of the men would surely have sought her as a sex partner, but apparently no one did. Byron wrote quite openly of liaisons with Eskimo women, but never mentioned her in this context."

"I'm afraid V. Lambert was probably plain, dull, and sexless, a far cry from the vibrant woman in the photograph," I said ruefully. Now it seemed likely to me, and to Ronald when I suggested it, that the PERSONAL URGENT appeal stemmed from her life as a militant suffragette, perhaps a call for Byron's help to gain her release from prison, her return to the United States.

"I'd like to know how Byron responded to her, Bibi. He wasn't the kind of man to ignore a former expedition member in trouble. I think the answers to our questions about Miss Lambert lie in England, Bibi. Why don't you go there? It shouldn't be too hard to learn if V. Lambert actually lived in the suffragette center on Chessham Court. The British keep historic houses like that untouched; documents, pictures, letters will be there. Miss Lambert is the only lead to a part of Byron's life we know nothing about. Tracking her down might bring you to the woman of the photograph."

I was caught up in the excitement of flying to London with Ronald. He stroked the waves of my hair, then moved his fingers inside my blouse. I shivered, very conscious of my body, of his body. We would be together in England. Lovers.

"I wish I could go with you, Bibi."

"What do you mean? Of course, you'll go with me."

"When you smile at me, I think I could go anywhere with you. But it's not possible now." The knee that had been broken in the Antarctic all those years ago had to be rebuilt surgically. He had been unable to accompany me to Rhinebeck the previous day because he had been having X rays and tests; the surgery was scheduled for the following week. His limp was more pronounced, and I had noticed that, but as I knew he hated admitting a disability to me, asked no questions. Now I realized that he had changed his style of lovemaking recently. I had not thought it significant, as he was frequently seeking ways to enhance our pleasure in one another. Now I realized he was also favoring his knee.

"We can put off the trip, Ronald. I don't want to go without you. Not there. Not anywhere."

"I don't want you to go anywhere without me, but you have to do it now, Bibi."

How could he say that when he knew how much I depended on him? "I couldn't handle the search all by myself in London, Ronald. I'm just not up to it."

"I think you are. This business with my knee will keep me laid up for weeks, and you don't have the time to wait. If there is anything to be discovered in London, you'd better get to it before Avery decides to put his researchers onto Miss Lambert. He must know she was on the Greenland expedition; that's hardly a secret. He hasn't taken her seriously yet because he has no evidence.

"You have it. Only you have the envelope with its frantic appeal and the photograph with its secret pasted to the back. You've got the edge, Bibi, and you have to make the most of it."

I could imagine what Avery would do if he turned up this kind of information about V. Lambert and Byron. He would use it to create a scandal.

"You'll come back and tell me everything you've learned, and soon I'll be well again and it'll be just the way it always was. But for now, you can go alone."

With Ronald holding my hand, looking into my eyes, I felt strong. At the same time, I had an image of myself sitting disconsolately in a dimly lit, ill-heated hotel room, trying to will myself to venture out.

Ronald appeared to think the matter settled, because he stood up and said it was time to go. I was eager to leave this dismal room and go out into the sunshine. But as I despise disorder, I picked up the box that had contained the envelope so as to restore it to the top of the stack. The box was heavier than I expected it to be and a whole mess of papers fell out before Ronald could come to my aid. Annoyed at having created more rather than less derangement, I started replacing the papers in the box. The odd name printed on one envelope caught my eye: From the Society of Men Who Love Dogs. Not knowing the mores of the time, I wondered if the double entendre had been conscious or innocent. The envelope contained a folded sheet of heavy, cream-colored stationery. I unfolded the paper, half expecting to find a lubricious message. But there was nothing about men, dogs, or lovers of either. Instead, I saw my great-grandfather's letterhead and the salutation, "Dear Horace." The letter gave a brief account of Byron's plans to return to Mount McKinley. I was surprised Horace Graham had not sent it to the archives, and surmised that the mismatched envelope had confused him.

Just then I noticed the writing on the back of the page.

"Thank God no word of that 1915–1916 all-women's expedition to the South Pole ever got out! I still fear that it may."

# Chapter Ten

"WHATEVER HAPPENS, STAY ON YOUR feet. If anyone pushes or kicks you, hang on to my arm. Once you go down, you'll be trampled."

Viola had been in London for exactly two hours. She was not quite certain how it had happened that she was standing before Hollowran Prison in the midst of a crowd of shouting women surrounded by hostile police. Upon arriving from Southampton, she had been met at Paddington Station by a large, disheveled woman wearing a man's overcoat with the fabric raveling at elbows and cuffs and shiny in the seat.

"Got a letter about you from a friend in New York." At least that was what Viola thought the odd woman said, but the words were mumbled and in a lower-class dialect unfamiliar to Viola. "Thought I might miss you in the crush here, but you're not easy to miss. Anyway, I hoped it was you." She said something more, apparently her name.

The train journey from Southampton would have been easy had Viola not been so tired from the sea journey. In the past, she was known to be a good sailor, even in the rough, choppy seas around Greenland, but on the big, luxurious *Kaiser Wilhelm,* she had been seasick throughout the trip. It was the first time her body had let her down, the first time she was looking forward to being taken to a room to rest and give her uneasy stomach a chance to settle down.

Instead, to her dismay, the woman had declared—as if giving the best possible news—that they could still arrive at Hollowran Prison in time to greet Lesley Penner on her release. Lesley Penner. Why, this then must be Carla Brent. They were two of the most prominent figures in the British suffrage movement, as famous as Emmeline Pankhurst and her daughters. Penner had founded the militant Women's Social and Political Union, the WSPU.

They were certainly in luck with Viola, Carla was thinking. An explorer who had been the only woman on an expedition to Greenland, a scientist on the staff of the American Museum of Natural History, and a member of a well-known family. It had seemed too good to be true. The English suffragettes intended to make the most of the American visitor. Were she ever so mousy, they would have her speaking at rallies and political meetings. But Viola. Tall, beautiful, with a low, thrilling voice—she was irresistible.

"These your bags?"

Viola nodded, and in a moment they were stored in the station cloakroom, and she was following Carla to the underground and then climbing down seemingly endless flights of stairs to the tube where newly electrified trains went great distances at incredible speed. There were three changes of train before they reached the station closest to Pentonville and the prison. There, Carla hailed a horse-drawn hansom cab to take them the rest of the way to Hollowran. She swore at the expense but said there was not time enough for them to cover that distance on foot. Viola's offer to pay was accepted with alacrity.

When Viola saw the women massed in front of the prison, holding up placards—Votes for Women and Welcome Brave Lesley—the first thrill of excitement went through her. On her first day in London, she was already a part of the militant English suffrage movement. A horse neighed, and she looked up into the face of a mounted policeman. She had always thought of policemen as being there to ensure her own safety, but the hostility on the man's face quickly changed her attitude. "Coppers don't scare me," muttered Carla. "I scare them. But horses can kill you." Taking Viola's arm, Carla pulled her deeper into the crowd of women. Despite the menace surrounding them, the atmosphere was festive, as the women were excitedly reciting Lesley's exploits. She had chained herself to the gate of the residence of Sir Henry Campbell Chancellor, the prime minister, and had the satisfaction of shouting to him that he must stand for votes for women before the police broke the chain and dragged her away. In the course of serving her prison sentence, she had gone on a hunger and thirst strike.

"There she is!" The shout went up, followed by cheers. "Lesley! Lesley! Votes for women!" Taller than most of the other women in the crowd, Viola was able to see a small, painfully thin woman standing in the doorway, with a wardress on each side. She raised her arm and waved, then walked unsteadily forward by herself. Within seconds she was grasped and lifted to the shoulders of the women at the front. They marched away from the prison and the crowd formed a procession behind them. Carla seized one of Viola's arms and a stranger grasped the other and they walked three abreast in harmony.

The sense of triumph, of exultation, around her was so strong that Viola no longer felt tired. She began to long for the opportunity to perform an exploit herself. Someday soon, she promised herself, she would be the one being greeted with banners.

The procession marched under gray skies through the streets of London. As the afternoon hours passed, Viola became increasingly aware of the thin misting rain dampening her hair as her ostrich-plumed hat became waterlogged. The velvet band along the bottom of her box-pleated wool cheviot skirt was covered with mud. Her mother had been horrified by the report in *Dress* magazine that some women were wearing short walking skirts two inches from the ground, but Viola was already wondering where to find a dressmaker to shorten hers. She must purchase rubberized boots as soon as possible; her high-laced shoes with their two-inch curved heels were sodden.

Every so often the procession halted and Viola looked over the heads of the women in front of her to see Lesley being lowered to the ground and given a few sips from a bottle of water or lime juice. Each time Lesley doubled over with cramps, and then stood up and raised her arms in triumph. Then she would again be lifted to the women's shoulders and they would go on.

Viola heard cheers and also jeers as they went by. The jeers made her aware, as had the hostility of the mounted policeman, that they were fighting a war. Some of the jeering voices were female, probably members of the newly formed Women's Anti-Suffrage Society.

"Where are we going, Carla?"

"Home, so Lesley can put her feet up. Tomorrow she'll be at an open-air meeting in Ravenscourt Park. She'll have enough of her voice back after the thirst strike to lay it on them."

Home? All at once it occurred to Viola that she had nowhere to go, but Carla immediately announced she was to stay at their flat. Eighty-eight Chessham Court. Why, that was one of the centers of the suffrage movement, famous even in New York.

Carla grinned. "Wait till Lesley gets a look at you. Just our luck to have room for you now. Edna, the other girl living with us, moved out yesterday. In prison once for three days and already running home to Mamma.

"It's share and share alike, Viola. I figured coming from America and all, you'd be able to put up your part of the rent. It's eighteen shillings a week, you see, because there's six of us. And, of course, food's extra."

The procession marched down Pentonville Road, around the Kings Cross, and eventually onto Tottenham Court Road, avoiding with some difficulty the motorcars, motor omnibuses, electrified trams, and horse-drawn carriages on the congested streets. Then the marchers turned off the main thoroughfare and went through a maze of streets so narrow there was barely room for the women carrying Lesley to pass. At last they stopped in front of a four-story building with a short flight of broken stone steps leading to the front door. The exterior walls and the stone curlicues and cornice framing the door and windows were so darkened with soot that it was not possible to tell what color they might once have been. Lesley was set down then, and the crowd of women dispersed.

It clearly did not occur to Carla that an introduction was called for, and so Viola, trained to proper social protocol, introduced herself. Lesley looked up then and greeted Viola with a surprising warmth. Her voice was hoarse, unused, and she spoke thickly, as if her tongue were too large for her mouth. She stood up shakily, clutching at Carla, and slowly mounted the steps into the house. Although there was a window fanlight, the front hall was almost totally dark, and Viola was barely able to make out the first steps of the steep circular stairs. Lesley had to stop every few minutes and cling to the banister, doubled over with cramps. Even so, she appeared unconcerned by the pain; an air of joyousness emanated from her.

"We've got the top three floors," said Carla as they slowly mounted the stairs, stopping on the third-floor landing.

As soon as Carla opened the door facing them, an overpowering smell of rancid lard greeted Viola. She swallowed hard to avoid vomiting. Having expected only women, she was startled to observe three men sitting at an oilcloth-covered table pushed against the wall, with newspaper-wrapped packets of fish and chips in front of them. Visitors no doubt, come to form a welcoming party, Viola thought as they leaped to their feet, embraced and congratulated Lesley, helped her off with her coat, and settled her on the couch. Carla, too, had taken off her man's overcoat, revealing that she was wearing trousers. In London. Trousers. Viola had borrowed them in Greenland but had not imagined doing so anywhere else. Skirts, long and trailing, must be worn, even for horseback riding, bicycling, and tennis.

One of the men ran upstairs and returned with a knit blanket to cover Lesley. These men certainly knew how to make themselves at home. All at once, they became aware of Viola, and were silent, staring at her in wonder. Her regal bearing and her bright coppery hair stood out, startling in the dim, dingy room.

Carla laughed at their obvious interest in Viola. "Here's our new flatmate, boys. Show her you're glad to see her."

But if the men were delighted, Viola was stunned. Flatmates. Boys. Wilbert, Jeremy. James. He was the handsome one, good-looking in the British style, blond and fair-skinned with blue eyes. Her flatmates. She had never imagined such a thing, not as a permanent arrangement. The men were looking at her with the combination of wonder and admiration she had grown so accustomed to at home that she hardly noticed it. At home, though, she was constantly guarded. With a thrill of excitement, she realized that no one was watching over her, acting as her chaperone. As in Greenland, she was in control of her body.

Only there was nothing she wanted to do with it, no one she wanted to make love with. Byron. No one else would do. She had put three thousand miles between them, and still he had been with her every night on board the ocean liner, the last image in her mind before she went to sleep, the first when she awoke. It could not go on like that. She must get over him. But not by taking on one of these men.

Where was the bathroom? The idea of sharing a bathroom with men was oddly repellent. Even in Greenland, a separate outdoor privy had been dug for her, protected by a small shed. This one, she discovered a few minutes later, was far from clean. She retched. Newspaper cut into squares served for toilet paper; a sliver of gritty gray soap lay on the edge of the sink, and a wet and dirty piece of cloth attached to a string above was all she could find to dry her hands. At home she had a bathroom to herself, all of marble, with an oriental rug on the floor and a painting by Millet on the wall, with gold fixtures at the basin, and warmed fluffy towels replaced after every using. A sudden rush of homesickness came over her. Oh, what was the matter with her? The primitive conditions in Greenland had borne no resemblance to the luxury of her home and she had accepted them gladly as a necessary part of belonging to a major expedition. And here she was a part of one of the most important movements of the century.

When she came back to the parlor, Carla was in the kitchen making tea for Lesley. No door separated the two rooms and Viola could clearly see the heavily grease-encrusted stove and the rusty kettle atop the burner. The men were not waiting for tea, but had resumed eating fish and chips with their fingers and drinking beer out of thick mugs. A twist of newspaper was pushed over to Viola and she opened it and, though no one seemed to care, the habit of politeness made her take a few chips, a bite of fish. The food stuck in her throat in a big lump and would not go down; she began to feel unwell. The march today had taken its toll, coming so soon after the long sea journey.

Rising abruptly, Carla wiped the grease off her mouth on the back of her hand and put her coat back on. "Give me your cloakroom ticket, Viola, and some money—I'm flat out—and I'll go down to the train station and grab your bags."

Viola was too weary to refuse the favor, but was surprised none of the men offered go to in Carla's place. Then she realized she would have to stop thinking that way; men and women were equals here.

"I'll show you where to sleep. You'll have the bedroom on the top floor, next to Lesley's," said one of the men. Wilbert, she thought it was. He seemed different from the others, was the only one wearing a shirt, tie, and suit coat instead of a sweater. Even though the shirt was carefully darned and the jacket threadbare, they were clearly well made. What struck Viola most forcibly though was his manner of speech: educated, Oxonian.

She badly wanted a bath, but there had been no tub in the bathroom and she did not like to ask what the others did.

"I'll get you a hot water bottle to take to bed with you and I'll fill the pitcher as well." Viola followed Wilbert into the kitchen and waited while the kettle boiled. What could this kind of a man be doing here? "I'm the solicitor," he told her. "My father is a judge and is so enraged by my representing the suffragettes that I find it easier to live here than at home. In his eyes, a woman has no rights at all, belongs to her father first, and her husband second, and lacking them, a brother. The idea of votes for women arouses nothing but a sneer. How could I not take on the suffrage movement?"

At his words, Viola saw the vision again, the vision that had propelled her to the suffragettes in London. She would be at the center of the activity, militant, performing exploits requiring the greatest courage and fortitude. The exaltation created in her by this vision enabled her to overcome her exhaustion and follow Wilbert up another steep flight of uncarpeted stairs. Wilbert opened the door of a tiny boxlike room filled to overflowing, though it contained only a small chest of drawers covered with a lace doily, a straight wooden chair, and a bed covered by a chenille spread of indeterminate color. Everything in the room, from the walls to the curtains and furniture, was dark with soot, the residue of the soft coal burned in England. For the first time in her life, she understood that unending labor by virtual armies of servants had been required to achieve the spotlessness of the great London houses she had visited with her parents.

Wilbert put the pitcher of hot water on the chest of drawers, and Viola realized that what she had thought was a cachepot for a plant was actually a basin. This was where she was to wash. He lit a small gas lamp, remarking that they used candles whenever possible; gas was expensive. "Well, good night," said Wilbert. He put his hand on her shoulder as a farewell gesture, and she had the fleeting thought that he was suggesting something. When she did not respond, he quickly went out. She was probably only imagining a sexual invitation because of all she had heard about the suffragettes. There was no reason to assume that just because men lived in the house, they engaged in sexual activity.

She was shivering in the dank, cold room. An unfamiliar object in the corner was a gas meter, she decided, but no heat came from it and there seemed to be no way to turn it on. Nonetheless, she stripped off her clothing and washed in a small amount of hot water poured into the basin. The water was hard and unpleasant for her delicate, translucent skin; she wished for her face-massaging cream and then dismissed the thought as trivial. Carla had not yet returned with the valises, so she had no choice but to put her clothes back on.

When she took off the spread, an unpleasant odor rose from the opened bed. Little bits of food stuck to the thick maroon blanket. The sheets had not been changed since Edna had run home to Mamma. They were gray, with streaks of mud, and there were clear indications that the sex act had been performed, apparently more than once. Viola remembered her mother saying the movement was for lower-class people, and she had replied that suffrage allowed for no social classes. Still, the thought of changing the bed when she was so exhausted was daunting. Homesick, she wanted her mother. For a moment she had forgotten that they were estranged.

She made her way down the stairs and found Carla just coming home with the valises. They could be unpacked in the morning. All she needed now were sheets. Sheets? They possessed only the ones that were on the beds. The wash would be done the next day.

Upstairs once more, trembling with tiredness and distaste, Viola put the bedspread back on the bed and lay down on top of it fully dressed, ready to cry. And yet how could she cry over a dirty bed when she had come to perform acts of heroism? She must remember how crude and rough the life in the Greenland camp had been. But all that came to her was a vision of the frozen tundra. White. Clean. Suffrage was an adventure, too; its discomforts were unimportant. Just before she fell asleep, it came to her that she had not given a thought to Byron for hours. She was getting over him, after all, just as she had planned in coming to England. Encouraged by the thought of not thinking about him, she fell asleep.

She was awakened during the night by the sound of thumping

coming from the room next to hers; that was Lesley's, she recalled. Then there was a very soft laugh, an exclamation—she knew what that meant, unmistakable—two voices speaking very softly. Women's voices. She sat straight up in bed, a shudder of repulsion came over her, and she rapidly controlled it as unworthy. Certainly she had been aware that many lesbians were attracted by the movement, and she firmly believed that any woman, any person for that matter, had the right to seek any kind of sexual fulfillment. But she had not dreamed of sexual activity taking place just a few feet away, with only a thin wall for separation.

Oh, she could not bear it. The sounds of love after all were not so different. Byron. She was seized with a hunger so acute it was not to be endured. She pressed her hands there where his hand had been, where his body had been. Years later she told him she thought of him whenever she brought herself sexual release. He had flushed. With pleasure? With shock?

After she had finished, he was gone, and she was alone in the cold, dirty room, and the sounds of love were coming from the women who shared the flat with her. *I hoped it was you. Wait till Lesley gets a look at you.* Now she wondered if it would be possible for her to remain here. She had not joined the movement to be with women.

The next morning, awakening early, Viola came downstairs and found one of the men—Jeremy—in the kitchen making tea. She had never before seen a man working in a kitchen, could not even imagine Byron doing so.

"How'd you sleep? Girls too noisy?"

Viola was too startled by his coming right out with so suggestive a statement to answer.

"You have to figure they'd be having a little reunion." He poured tea into a mug and handed it to her.

"What gets you up so early?" she asked.

"I ain't been to bed yet. There was a night meeting of some bigwig politicians and a couple of the girls were there with placards and banners. I went to give protection. Me and Carla. The two of us—we're like a bleeding army. You should see Carla at a demonstration, takes three policemen to hold her down. One of the girls was arrested—Wilbert'll have to go in the morning—that's Muriel; she's crazy, hit a policeman with a dog leash."

Viola thought of the incongruity of finding a man like this in the suffrage movement; he was more out of place than Wilbert. But it turned out he had his reasons, too.

"Me mum was killed in a suffrage demonstration," he told her, between noisy gulps of tea. "Me dad said 'Stupid old cow, getting in with them loony suffragettes.' But he was crying."

Over the next few days Viola came to see that everyone had a story to explain being in the movement. No, not quite everyone. James alone had none. As far as Viola could tell, he was there for the freedom and unconventionality of the life, or more simply perhaps, for free love. All three men were attractive, each in his own way, but none of them was as clean as the people she had known before. Wilbert would have his shirt washed before a court appearance; otherwise the cuffs and collar were slightly gray. As for James, there was no denying that the smell of his body was always pleasant, faintly sweaty, reminding her of Byron after they had made love. Every so often James would bathe and wash his hair until it gleamed golden, put on his one good suit, and go out, returning the following day or the one after that.

Though she had not believed it possible at first, she gradually became less aware of cleanliness and the lack of it in her flatmates. Not in herself. The others viewed her insistence on a daily bath as an eccentricity, considering that it required her to boil enough water to fill the high metal tub in the kitchen.

It did not take long for Viola to become active in the English suffragette movement. Her history was known, admired, envied. The main article in the current issue of *Votes for Women* was devoted to her achievements.

Within days the WSPU leadership had arranged for her to speak at open-air meetings in Ravenscourt Park and on Hyde Park Corner. The railroad took her to smaller towns where candidates favorable to suffrage were standing for Parliament in by-elections. Viola was an impressive speaker; her voice with its deep undercurrent of excitement had the power to thrill. She was conspicuous in any crowd, with her height, her strong slender build, her good looks. The dampness made her hair curl, and the strands of copper were striking in the London gloom. In no group had her vitality and high energy been more appreciated, more needed. Certain that no one in the suffrage movement gave a thought to social position, she was disappointed to learn that her prominent family was repeatedly mentioned in efforts to attract other young women of similar class and position.

Viola's suffragette activities were carefully scheduled around her work in the fossil department at the Natural History Museum in Kensington, where she had been hired on the strength of a letter from Dr. Ruskin to the curator. Such employment was essential, as the money given her by Evelyn and her paltry savings were not sufficient to maintain her. The attitude toward women scientists was even more uncompromising than in the United States. She was given the simplest record-keeping tasks and occasionally asked to prepare a specimen of a microscopic fossil or help paint preservatives on ancient bones.

The scientists at the museum were puzzled by her presence, unable to understand what could have happened to drive a beautiful woman, obviously of good family—they could recognize proper speech, even if it were American—to come to England and go to work. A man was in the picture somewhere. Certainly they could not ask her; no Englishman would speak of anything so personal to a stranger. Indeed, they hardly spoke to her, and it would have surprised her to know that they were quite as affected by her vitality as the American scientists had been.

The suffragettes saw her connection with the British Natural History Museum as a step forward for women. "Don't tell them you're a member of the WSPU," Lesley cautioned her. "If the men at the museum know you're a militant suffragette, you'll be pushed out the door so fast you won't have time to put your hat on. Any time you leave the museum to join a demonstration or travel somewhere for us, say you're sick."

Lesley saw how valuable Viola was to the movement and feared she would not stay with them, that she would be taken away by a man. Viola insisted she would return to Byron Tremaine only to go to Antarctica with him. But in that case why was she writing to him? There was little privacy in the flat; Lesley saw the address on the envelopes and knew that letters came from America as well. There was something about the way Viola spoke his name that troubled Lesley, too. No, Viola was not a woman for women.

Certainly many of the women took men lovers instead of or in addition to women, and Viola discovered she was no longer in the minority, an oddity, in desiring sexual experience without a husband. Marriage and domination had no place in their lives. They all read *Free Woman,* the new newspaper, exciting in its emphasis on sex, sex for the free woman.

The living arrangement that had so startled Viola was not uncommon, she learned. The police and the public at large thought of suffrage as a woman's movement; the presence of men served as camouflage as well as protection.

But safety was not the only reason Carla and Lesley shared their flat with the three men. It soon became apparent that Carla and Lesley were by no means opposed to having sex with the men as well as one another. In fact, they shared the men between them, playing no favorites. And as far as Viola could tell, the men went off to bed with nothing at all settled and waited to see who if anyone appeared. Everyone was clearly waiting to see how Viola would fit into this circle. They did not press her; it was as if they thought the time would come naturally.

Of the three men, it was James who was waiting for her most eagerly. She would come to him, he thought. Women always did. She would not approve of him. Unlike Wilbert and Jeremy, he had no steady work, preferring to take a temporary job when he ran out of money. Any kind of a job. His handwriting was good enough for him to find employment copying out business letters. His accent, although hardly Eton or Cambridge, was public school and a lesser university and quite suitable for answering telephones, which most businesses had installed by now. He augmented his income with the gifts he received for acting as escort to a number of well-to-do women. One passed his name along to the next.

Oh, yes, Viola would disapprove of him. But it would not matter. Lesley disapproved of him, and hardly a week went by that she did not come to his bed. "Oh, Jamie," she would say in her ruined voice. He could imagine Viola, "Oh, Jamie," in that low, thrilling tone with the little throb. "Oh, Jamie." She would come to him in time.

Viola was drawn to his good looks, his cheerfulness and easygoing ways. He was committed to no cause but his own pleasure, and what a relief that was in this earnest group. She was drawn to him, but her emotions were still centered around Byron Tremaine. She had come to England not only to join the more militant movement, but also to break the hold Byron had on her. And yet, she lay in bed each night, longing for his body, for the relief that making love with him would bring.

She would have liked to attribute the continual exhaustion she felt these days to her sexual deprivation. She, who had thrived in the harsh conditions in Greenland, now could not tolerate the cheap, greasy food, the lumpy bed, the lack of heat. Several times, in the midst of a giving a speech, standing in front of the Parliament building holding the suffrage banner, she suddenly, unaccountably became dizzy and nauseous. It embarrassed her. Why, Lesley, who had barely recovered from her prison hunger strike, was leading demonstrations, holding outdoor rallies, throwing rocks at windows.

Viola's work seemed too much for her, too, and no job could have been easier. There was no time to be ill, as she was to travel with Carla and Lesley to Staffordshire. Mrs. Pankhurst herself had asked for their help in exhorting the women making nails and chains to strike against the conditions of their labor. They received a mere five shillings a week for spending eight to ten hours a day at the forge. The work was heavy, unpleasant, with small holes burned in their clothing by the sparks. Union regulations did not allow women advancement to higher positions, so a new union, more favorable to women, must be formed.

Viola visited the workers in their dark, cold huts, and when she saw rats scurrying under the stove, had to dash into the repulsive outdoor privy to vomit. Feeling a little better then, she forced herself to go to the rally and make a speech.

The following morning she fainted on the train going back to London. It was only for a moment, and when she returned to herself, it was to see Lesley and Carla smiling at her. Smiling when she felt so sick. And then she knew and was filled with dismay. How could she be having a child now? Yes, she had thought to have a child—but not yet. There would be time enough for a baby after she had gone to the Antarctic.

And then a little shiver of delight went through her. Byron. It was his child. And all the love she had ever felt for him returned to her and she thought she could not wait to see him, feel his arms around her, know he shared her joy. The child of their passion, of their love. In that moment she forgot why she had left him.

"We figured for weeks now that you had something in the oven," said Lesley in her direct, sometimes crude manner. "The way you've been sick in the morning and drooping like a lily by evening. Oh, yes. I could spot it. The way you look—you sort of glow like you could see through your skin. And then, you don't want to have anything to do with the boys. They talk about it."

Viola would have liked to hide. How could she have been such a fool as to remain oblivious when everyone else recognized what was happening to her?

"This is great, Viola. Don't be scared; we'll help you. It'll be like it's our baby. When I think what this will mean to the suffrage movement." Carla was triumphant. "Yeah, I know Isadora Duncan had a baby without getting a husband, only she's on the stage. But you . . . you can be an ideal, a model to every woman trapped in a miserable marriage." Carla's vocabulary shifted markedly whenever she was on suffragette topics; she had been taught how to give speeches.

"You'll be our . . . our hero," added Lesley. The suffragettes did not limit the use of that word to men. "A hero of the suffrage movement. A woman having the courage to bear a child openly, unashamed, with the help and support of other women. Only other women. You can do it. You know what I always tell myself when I'm in a dangerous spot? To doubt is to be weakened; to doubt is to fail."

By now Viola was painfully aware that they did not ask her who the father was, did not so much as suggest that a male partner played a part in what had happened. Viola thought over the last time she had made love with Byron. Had he used a contraceptive? Obviously not. Withdrawn before his climax? Obviously not. She had not thought to bring a pessary. When they first became lovers, she had been innocent of such matters. Then he had been careful not to put her at risk, shown her what was needed for safety, later obtained a pessary for her through sources of his own. This last sex act was impulsive. She had been as driven as he. Thinking to escape Byron, she had carried him with her all along. She had said it was over, but wrote him stiff, formal letters to make sure he knew where she was living; he replied with equal formality. Neither thought to give way; neither had been able to break off. Byron's child. And the women talked on and on.

Back in suffragette circles in London, in triumph as it were, Viola was told repeatedly that she was making a grand gesture for woman-kind. A woman's baby. Lesley and Carla were annoyed when Viola went to a physician to have her pregnancy confirmed. Viola did not pretend to be married, and the man was openly contemptuous. An omen of things to come perhaps.

"I can deliver the baby," insisted Carla. "I've helped deliver five of my mum's nine kids. There's nothing to it."

Carla? Why, Carla's hands were seldom clean and she would view it as wasted effort, upper-class prissiness, to put fresh sheets on the bed for the birth.

"Women must care for women," agreed Lesley; but then, observing Viola's distress, she hurriedly added: "You don't have enough experience, Carla. She must have a midwife." It had not occurred to Viola that she would not have a physician at her labor, but obviously no female physician was to be found. She had never known anyone to employ a midwife. But then, she had never known anyone who was a symbol for women everywhere.

When with the suffragettes, Viola was upheld by their conviction, felt strong and bold. The hero of the movement. But at night, lying in her bed alone, with the sounds of lovemaking coming from the neighboring bedrooms, she could not help but think them fools. Not one of them was sufficiently practical to grasp what it meant to bear a child out of wedlock. She was only coming to realize it herself. Where was she to go to bear this baby? How was she to pay for the midwife? And what was she to do with the baby once it was born? She shuddered at the thought of bringing an infant into this flat—dirty, dingy, cold, airless. A crib and layette would be needed immediately. Although unreconciled to Viola's lifestyle, her father still felt some responsibility for her and had arranged a quarterly allowance. It was a fraction of what she had received before going to England and could not possibly cover the cost of all the purchases required. She would lose her position at the museum when her pregnancy became apparent; no other employment could be found while she was nursing, and a wet nurse was out of the question. Later, when she was able to take a job, who would care for the child? Her friends, for all their enthusiasm, were engaged in work and in demonstrations.

There was an alternative, of course—abortion. But that seemed impossible to her when this was Byron's child, a child of love. And even if she were able to bring herself to it, an abortion carried out by her own hand or some back-alley practitioner could damage her irrevocably, and she would not achieve her ambitions with a less than perfect body.

Her parents. She thought of her mother often and regretted the breach. Were she to let her parents know about the baby, they would spring into action. Certainly they would view her behavior as beyond the pale, make her suffer their disapproval. But they would not abandon her. Nor could they allow the shame, the scandal of her pregnancy to touch the Lambert name. They would bring her home, and by hook or by crook, by whatever it took in money or promised professional advancement, they would find her a husband, give the child a name.

A father's name. In those dark hours before the dawn, she realized that was what her child would never have. A bastard. Her child must carry that stigma throughout life. A bastard—who besides the suffragettes would accept that?

She came out of her room each morning, filled with gloomy forebodings, to the praise and cheer which by now were all but insupportable. Going to WSPU headquarters filled her with dread. Her arrival prompted a triumphal reception.

The only person she could bear to be with was James. He alone did not praise the pregnancy. The absurdity of not admitting to a male partner was not lost on him.

"Carla and Lesley behave as if this were the immaculate conception," Viola told him ruefully. "I could laugh at that, if it didn't make me feel like crying."

"Well, it's hard for the girls to see that a man is good for anything. Except on occasion. For protection or in bed."

How beautiful she was, thought James. In bed. That was where he wanted to be with her. He had never made love to a pregnant woman. Yet despite the way she favored him over the other men, she had never come to his bed.

He covered her hand with his own. She observed, with a little amusement, that it was clean. James had taken to bathing regularly these days. Yes, he was waiting for her.

"I like to have a good time, Viola. I want you to have a good time, too, and I worry about you. The suffragettes are making such a fuss over you that maybe you forget what it's going to be like having a kid without a husband."

"I only wish I could forget, James. I lie awake at night worrying about what it will mean to the child."

"The kid needs a name, Viola. How about mine?"

"You can't be serious."

"But I am. We could get married. We don't need to make more of it than it is. We'd have some fun and when it stops being fun, we'll get a divorce or I'll go off somewhere."

It was the strangest of marriage proposals. "What advantage is there for you in this, James?"

He was not offended by the question. "I could tell you a lot of things, Viola, but the truth is I fancy you, I have from the moment I saw you walk in the door. I can be in bed with someone else, and I wish it were you. I even imagine it is you, not that it's easy to imagine with Carla when I'm afraid she's going to break the bed."

He was smiling, always smiling. That was James. He wanted a good time, to have her as a bedmate for however long it lasted. Yet she must be grateful to him. What he was offering was not inconsiderable. A husband. A name for her child.

In that moment, she realized what it was she had to do. Marry James? Appeal to her parents to find her a husband? No husband but Byron was possible. If she turned to anyone, it must be to him. She knew what that would mean. Writing to him of the pregnancy was tantamount to begging him to marry her. And he would. Oh, yes, he would. Byron wanted a son, would envision this child as male. Yes, he would marry her.

She leaned over and kissed James hard on the mouth. Then she stood up and returned to her room, sat on the edge of the bed, and using the top of the dresser as a desk, wrote to Byron, asking him to come to her. She sealed the envelope and addressed it; then, thinking that perhaps a secretary opened his mail, added the words PERSONAL URGENT.

The suffragettes would scorn her, and the marriage be like all the others she had so despised. His tame wife. Under his control. She would never go to the Antarctic.

# Chapter Eleven

WAITING. SHIVERING UNDER THE TARPAULIN, they lay on the roof of the public hall. The fog was dense, a thick layer that covered the light of the moon, the stars, the gas streetlamps. With no buildings recognizable, they might have been anywhere in the world. England in autumn. The inevitable light rain began to fall. Waiting. They would wait for the rest of the night and into the following morning until the crucial meeting began, the meeting where the government officials did not wish to discuss suffrage for women.

Breaking into the cabinet ministers' meeting was dangerous, but the act—if successful—would become legend.

From the moment word of the meeting was leaked by a sympathizer in a government office, the suffragettes began making plans. The prime minister himself was to attend, and the hotly contested issue of male suffrage was on the agenda. The argument was whether all men, not just property owners, should be accorded the vote. The suffragettes meant to broaden the debate and force the cabinet ministers to recognize the rights of women, too.

The meeting was to be held at a public hall in MidValley, a small city some sixty miles to the north of London, in order to avoid the heckling and demonstrations that had become commonplace.

An intricate and daring plan was devised to put a woman into the hall during that meeting. Under the pretext of making repairs, a scaffolding would be erected over the neighboring building. Wilbert was to obtain the necessary work permit. On the night before the meeting, two women would climb the scaffolding to the platform with Jeremy, who would lower them one after the other onto the roof of the public hall. There they planned to remain for all the hours that must pass until morning. Then, after the skylight had been broken, the lighter of the two women would climb down a rope dropped through the shattered glass into the hall.

Stunned by the unheralded appearance, no one was likely to move quickly enough to stop the suffragette from leaping onto the platform, unfurling the Votes for Women banner, and calling on the government officials for support. The dramatic nature of the gesture would give the words more force.

In order for the woman to escape, a way out of the hall must be found in advance of the meeting. That was James's assignment; he was to go to MidValley, ask to see the manager of the public hall, get the building plans in his hands on a pretext, and commit them to memory. James was good at that sort of thing; no guard ever stopped him; he looked as if he belonged wherever he was. The manager would probably invite him to have a pint at the local pub.

Who among the women should perform this exploit? While the suffragettes would of necessity accept help from the men, the break-in to the hall must be done by women if it were to have its greatest impact. Carla was immediately chosen for her strength, great enough to lower a partner through the skylight. Selecting the other woman was harder; there were not many with sufficient strength, agility, and nerve to perform such a feat. One name after another was brought up and discarded. This one was in prison, that one had been beaten by the police.

Listening to the discussion, Viola thought this was the kind of exploit she had come to England to perform. This was the way of life she was renouncing. If only she could take a part in the break-in, she would feel better about deserting the movement. And then she thought that she could do it after all. Past the stage in her pregnancy when she felt ill, she had not yet become heavy. It is said that a baby is never better protected than in the mother's womb. Pregnant factory workers perform heavy duties without ill effects; Chinese peasant women labor in the fields like beasts of burden up to the hour of childbirth.

The suffragettes were stunned by her offer, filled with admiration for her daring. Viola was the ideal person in all ways. Men were disproportionately affected by a woman's appearance. Viola's extraordinary good looks would lend weight to her words and actions.

Only Lesley was troubled, wondered if she should intervene, insist on going herself. But though she maintained her rigorous schedule, she still had not fully recovered from her latest hunger strike. But Viola. This action was dangerous, really dangerous. Should a woman with child be allowed to do this? Then she caught herself. Allow? It was not for one woman to allow or refuse another a desired action.

And so it was that four days later, Viola was accompanying Carla and Jeremy to MidValley. She had been rehearsed in every detail. James reported that the public hall plans revealed the existence of a small window behind the platform, hidden by the back curtain. It was known to be boarded up, so guards would not be posted below. James had removed the boards and broken the lock. Viola would be on the platform in position to rush behind the curtain, get through the window, and make her way down the heavy vines of ivy covering the walls. Carla would by then have climbed down from the roof on the other side and be waiting for her on the ground with a cloak and disguise for the escape.

When night fell, Jeremy assisted first Carla and then Viola up the hastily built, precarious framework of the scaffolding and onto the platform. Carrying the larger of the two knapsacks containing their supplies, Carla went down the rope first. It was not quite long enough to reach the roof, so she jumped the last few feet. Viola then moved to the edge of the platform; it swayed violently and her stomach lurched. She remembered climbing the icy cliffs in the Arctic. This was not so different, she thought, putting her legs over the edge of the platform. The day would come when she could tell her child of the exploit they had performed together.

The rope, held firmly by Jeremy at the top, hung free at the bottom, and each gust of wind made it swing widely from side to side. Looking down, Viola saw the cobblestones of the street far below to one side, the roof on the other. What if the wind blew her off the rope, she thought. And the baby. They both might die. Until this moment, she had been too uplifted by the significance of the action to think about the danger. It was too late to consider that now. *To doubt is to weaken,* Lesley had said. She would not doubt. At last Carla's outstretched arms had encircled her feet, then her legs, and in a few moments she was standing on the roof, breathing hard, trembling from the effort, weak with relief. Jeremy threw down the rope; they would need it again in the morning.

How dark it was, as dark as it had been in Greenland during the midwinter weeks when the sun never rose. And now she was conscious of a sense of elation, akin to what she had felt when she first went to the Arctic. A light rain was falling, so Carla took a tarpaulin out of her knapsack. The two women folded it into a sleeping bag, with one half beneath them, the other over them as a cover. Their hair was soon dripping, their faces wet, but if they pulled the tarpaulin up over their heads, it would not be possible to breathe.

The hours of the night passed so slowly, so slowly, while they waited, shivering, impatient for the morning. What if she were too stiff to move when it came, wondered Viola. If only she could stand up and move around—but she had been warned to stay down. Police patrolled the area at regular intervals, and might notice untoward activity on the roof.

The temperature kept on dropping during the hours of the night, and the tarpaulin gave but little warmth. Viola's teeth chattered uncontrollably. Still, she thought, a cold climate was her natural habitat. She remembered making love with Byron that first spring in Greenland, lying in the snow with him. Damp, cold. Wet, hot. How certain she had been that someday they would be making love again on the great ice barrier leading to the South Pole. That would never happen now. When she came to London, she was convinced she had escaped having to turn her life over to a man. A stomach cramp reminded her she had not escaped at all.

The cold was making her drowsy. For minutes at a time she forgot where she was, whom she was with, what she was to do. Her eyes closed. "Don't go to sleep in the cold; you could die." Whose voice was that? Whose hands were on her shoulders, shaking her? Byron? No, it was Carla's insistent voice. What an irony it would be to have survived the blizzard on Disko Island and succumb to the cold of late October in England. "Talk to me, Carla. Let's keep each other awake." Carla had never spoken about the past. Like many of the suffragettes, she insisted her life began when she joined the movement. Now, at last, here, in the dark, fighting off sleep herself, she began her story.

"I don't think you ever guessed I was married once, Viola." Carla in her man's overcoat, Carla in bed with Lesley more often than with any of the men—no, she had not guessed.

At the time of her marriage, Carla had been living in Harville, a small village about twenty miles outside of Birmingham. "Everyone thought I was a queer duck, being so big and all. They used to say I was like a man and snicker. My mum and dad could hardly wait for me to be married and out of the house. But who was going to marry me? No man ever asked me to go walking or to a church supper. Well, was they surprised when the butcher said he wanted me to marry him. He was bigger than me. I liked that."

Viola expected Carla to embark on a tale of male brutality. It was a frequent theme among the suffragettes, a reason given for hating men. "Bill was a decent bloke, Viola. I never knew no one to treat me so good. But you see, I was working in the textile mill and on the loom next to me there was this girl and she was so pretty and before I knew it, I was in love with her. I shouldn't have married Bill, because I've always been soft on women. I fool around with the boys, but for real love, they're not for me.

"It was a small town, Viola. Pretty soon there was rumors, and Bill heard them. It was awful; he never yelled at me or nothing, just was so sad. I don't know what would've happened if he hadn't gotten sick. A cancer growing in him. I took care of him, but he died in just a couple of months.

"Then people started saying there was something funny about Bill's dying, that I'd put something in his food to kill him, so I could be with my sweetheart. She left town right away, and I got fired from my job, so I had to move back in with my folks. The neighbors used to throw things at our windows at night, nothing hard enough to break them, just things like a rotten lettuce or a bundle of wet rags. My folks prayed over me, prayed I'd take myself off. But with what? No one would give me a job."

Touched by the story, Viola wanted to clasp Carla's hand, but feared it might be misinterpreted and drew away. Carla noticed and smiled a little sadly.

"Well, you can figure what happened next. I seen a poster about a suffragette meeting in Birmingham. I walked all the way, and there was Lesley Penner talking about women like me. I went back to London with her, and we been together ever since."

"Do the others know?"

Carla shook her head. "Only Lesley. None of us has to tell about what we was. Now, you're different—going to Greenland, getting a job in a museum. Those are great things for women. It helps to hear about them. Most of us don't have a story that's anything but rotten."

While Carla had been speaking, the sky was lightening. A cold, gray day had begun. Viola heard the sounds of motorcars and horse-drawn carriages and the voices of the men. The door of the hall opened and shut, opened and shut. In a few minutes the prime minister and his cabinet were to enter the meeting room and the debate would begin.

"It's time to break the skylight," whispered Carla, taking a hammer wrapped in a towel out of the knapsack. "Crawl over there, and when I crack the glass pull it out in pieces. If any broken glass gets on the floor, they'll look up and find us."

As Viola started crawling across the roof, a wave of nausea came over her. Oh, she must not be sick now. Somehow she managed to get to the skylight and carefully pull out the pieces.

Lying prone and looking down through the skylight, she could see the cabinet ministers, dark figures in their black or gray long suit coats. They were greeting one another cheerfully, pleased at having found a meeting place so safe from hecklers. The debate began.

Viola's hair was wet. Mist must be drifting through the open skylight. Soon the men would become aware of it and look for the source.

Carla realized that, too. "We'd better start now. Crouch like I do when you stand up."

Though cold and stiff, Viola peeled off her gloves and the extra layers of clothing that would impede her movements. She had decided to wear only the light jacket with the banner, Votes for Women, rolled up in the righthand pocket, where she could quickly get at it.

She rose to a crouching position and reeled, so dizzy that she had to grasp at Carla's arm.

"What's the matter? You're all right, ain't you?" Carla looked at Viola in dismay. She sighed. "Don't go, Viola. You're not up to it. I'll do it."

But they could not change places. The roof was bare of any projection that could hold the rope's end, and Viola was not able to support Carla's weight. Either Viola went into the meeting hall or the plan failed. She had to be up to it.

"I'm all right. Lying under the tarpaulin for so long made me feel odd."

"Come on," Carla whispered desperately. She was holding the rope firmly and had looped the end around her waist for additional safety. Viola sat on the edge of the skylight and looked down as Carla dropped the coils of rope through the open pane. The descent had not seemed long to her when she studied the building plans. The huge meeting room, somewhat more than two stories high, required a drop of roughly twenty-six feet, nothing really. But why did the uncarpeted floor look so far away as she lowered herself through the skylight?

She could see the government officials below, hear their voices reverberating in the massive hall. In a moment she should be in their midst, on the platform, holding high the banner, clearly proclaiming the right of women to vote. This was her last, her greatest opportunity to make a gesture for suffrage. At this thought, her fear dissipated and her confidence returned.

Her hands were so stiff that she could barely close them around the rope, barely feel the roughness of the sisal against her fingers as she let herself down. She hung a few feet below the skylight, struggling to make her hands obey her. Carla recognized what was happening and decided to end the plan right then and there and bring Viola back up to the roof. She did not dare to call out, but quickly yanked the rope as a signal. At this, Viola's stiffened fingers lost their uncertain grip and she fell. Down, down. It was so fast, so fast. For barely a second, she was aware of the faces of the men staring at her, of the sudden hush that had come over the room, and then she lost consciousness.

When she came to herself, she was at first oblivious of everything but the agonizing pain. She was not even certain where it was coming from. Her arms. That must be it. They were raised in an unnatural position; she must have thrown them up to protect her head as she fell. When she tried to move, she fainted.

Dimly she became aware that people were trying to awaken her. Even dazed and in shock, she knew she did not want to wake up. Ever. Awake she would know that she must lose the baby. Oh, she had known it from the instant she felt Carla tug on the rope.

At last she opened her eyes. A man was kneeling on the floor beside her. He was in his shirtsleeves, and she observed that he had taken off his suit coat and covered her with it. Now he was stroking her forehead with his warm hand. She looked up at him, seeing him as the typical upper-class Englishman. His nose was aquiline, his eyes a clear blue, his lips narrow beneath a well-trimmed mustache. He was not young—his hair was a silvery gray and there were lines around his blue eyes—but he was so well groomed and well cared for that he was still a most handsome man. Then she remembered she had seen him before: Lord Hargreave, the minister who was known for his vehement opposition to suffrage. "Lie still," he was saying softly. "I've called for a doctor to examine you before you go to the hospital. Is there anything I can do for you in the meantime?" How solicitous he was, how concerned, how kind. Yet how implacable an enemy.

Within minutes the doctor was there, and as his skilled hands touched her abdomen, spasms of excruciating pain went through her. Then she was being lifted onto a stretcher, and looking down, she saw her blood-soaked trousers and the pool of blood on the floor.

The hospital physician confirmed the loss coldly; he disapproved of a pregnant single woman and thought it as well she had miscarried. The doctor who set her broken arm was kinder and sat by her bedside for more than an hour, trying to convince her of the errors of the suffrage movement, pointing out that none of this would have happened had she followed the course nature had planned and acted as a woman should. What he thought of her did not matter. Nothing mattered anymore now that the baby was lost.

Two police inspectors came to question her. From the way they spoke, it was apparent that Carla had escaped. Viola claimed to have acted on her own and refused to be shaken from this obviously fictional account. It was the least she could do. She had failed everyone: her unborn child, Byron, suffrage.

And none of the suffragettes blamed her. When they visited her in the hospital, they praised her effort, ignored her failure. Knowing how little they could afford the train fare, Viola had been touched. If only she had not pulled on the rope, Carla kept saying, everything would have been different. Viola was by no means sure of that. She had not been up to the exploit, should not have insisted on it. Nothing seemed worth doing after so great a failure; she could not even imagine how she was to pick up her life again. Not only her body, but her mind felt empty. At Lesley's insistence, she wrote to the curator of fossils at the Natural History Museum explaining that she had been run over by one of those new motorcars that were endangering pedestrians on all major thoroughfares.

She was still weak, and her arm was immobilized in a sling when she left the hospital, but she could not pay to stay longer. Her quarterly allowance was not due, and she would not accept help from the WSPU after letting them down so badly.

Upon her return to London, she was charged with unlawful entry and sentenced to six months in prison. However, to her surprise, she learned the sentence was suspended. When Wilbert, who was representing her, looked into the matter, he learned that someone of influence had intervened. Sir George Arnold Comstock, Lord Hargreave. He was still taking care of her.

Viola went back to her job at the museum, needing the money too badly to wait until she was stronger. Fortunately, the left and not the right arm was broken, so she could do her work. News of her exploit had reached even the inner recesses of the museum, and her excuse of a motor vehicle accident was discounted. However, absorbed in the Paleozoic era, the curator viewed current events as unimportant in the grand scheme of life and did not challenge her. In truth, he was glad to have her back. Not that her work was of any significance, but he had missed her during her absence. Something about her quite altered the atmosphere in the laboratory. The other scientists spoke of it, too.

At home after work, she remained in her room for hours, thinking that the baby had never been more real to her than now. Sitting in the straight wooden chair, lying awake at night in the dank chilly bed, she would imagine a child with Byron's face, with Byron's flair.

Whenever she came downstairs, James greeted her with particular warmth, making it clear that he would like to comfort her, knew how to comfort her. She was not ready for comfort.

Carla, Lesley, and the other WSPU leaders had put MidValley behind them and were planning huge demonstrations. They wanted Viola to join them; having an arm in a sling should not keep her from the platform at a rally. Viola did not respond. For the first time in her life, she was lethargic, unable to recover from the loss of the baby, the failure of the exploit, from Byron's continuing silence. A letter from him should have arrived well before this in answer to her urgent appeal. It ought not to matter; the desperate need was past. Byron did not know that, however. Why did she find it so painful to learn he did not love her? She had left him; anyone would agree this was what she deserved.

When the letter from Byron finally came, she held the envelope in her hand, unwilling to open it. Of course she knew what it must say. The tardiness of his response proved his indifference. When she finally opened the letter, however, she found it to be kind, exuberant. He was elated that there was to be a child, a boy to be at his side in the Antarctic. And she would be at his side, too, as his wife. (He did not mention Antarctica here.) Her letter had arrived when he was midway in his lecture tour and was not forwarded to him. As soon as he read it, he had booked passage to England on an ocean liner. Soon he would be with her. She was not to worry about anything anymore.

A newspaper clipping from the *Cheyenne World News* dropped out of the envelope, and she wondered why Byron had enclosed it. Wyoming had been the first place in the country to grant women the vote, and Byron was asked for his views on suffrage when interviewed following his lecture there. He had expressed a strong conviction in its rightness and inevitability. This was something he did for her, though they had quarreled and she had left him.

Only she could hardly bear to read of his joy in the baby. Too late ... too late from the moment she had volunteered for the break-in. No, it was not too late even now. She wanted him, needed him as badly as when she had written the letter. Only he could comfort her for the loss of their child. Only he would be the father of their future children. Everything was still possible. She could make him understand why she had embarked on that ill-fated exploit. They would go on together, linked more closely than they ever had been in the past.

Desperate to be with Viola, Byron found the ocean voyage, and then the train trip from Southampton, tedious almost beyond endurance. He had been angry with her, had gone so far as to ask Victoria Cahill, a Vanderbilt cousin, to marry him. But two weeks away from Miss Cahill, he could not think why he had wanted her. Viola was ever desirable—however insufferable her behavior, however unreasonable her ambitions. He wanted to embrace her slender body, so supple and strong, hold her long, tapering fingers. And where would she not put her hands and her body? He told her she shocked him by the way she made love. And she did. But life was so dull without her. That voice. The throb, the way she gasped his name in ecstasy.

She had insisted she would belong to no man and fled all the way to England to prove her point. And all she had proved was that she belonged to him. She was carrying his child. His child. This was what she was meant for, not marching through the mud of London at the head of a procession of spinsters, not looking through a microscope in a primitive laboratory in the farthest South. From now on, he would take care of her, see to it that she had the very best of everything. And his son must in time be his lieutenant—no, more than that, his companion—on his expeditions. And in his home, in his bed, waiting for his return from his voyages would be Viola. His. Forever.

Her letter had a tone of desperation; he knew Viola well enough to realize what it must have cost her to ask him to come to her rescue.

As soon as he arrived in London, he stopped at Brown's Hotel only long enough to bathe and change his clothes before hailing a horse-drawn hansom cab to take him to Viola. The driver became stalled in a mass of carriages and motorcars caught in the maze of small streets off what was clearly the seedier side of Tottenham Court Road. Too impatient to wait, Byron got out and sent the cab away. He would telephone for another when he left with Viola. As Byron and his friends obtained each new device as soon as it became available, he already took the telephone for granted.

As last he found himself on Chessham Court, but he had still to find the address. Buoyed by the anticipation of being with Viola, Byron mounted the steps of one house and then the next to study the number plate. Each time he had to wipe off the dirt with his handkerchief in order to make out the inscribed figures. When he finally reached the sought-after 88, he observed with some surprise that the door was not only locked, but barred. He lifted the door knocker and let it fall, listening to the dull thud. After a minute a male voice ordered him to identify himself. The name was apparently recognized, because the door was opened by a tall blond man wearing a sweater frayed at the elbows.

Looking glum, the man led Byron through the front hall and up a rickety staircase. The balustrade was broken in several places, and Byron put his hand on the wall to steady himself. The surface was damp, with patches of mildew. They stopped on one of the landings and, as his companion took out a key, Byron read the nameplate on the closed door in front of him: James Armour. This was the address Viola had given. Could she be living with this handsome, shabby stranger? Byron felt as if a knife were turning deep inside him.

He hesitated on the threshold, half afraid to enter the flat and have his suspicions confirmed. Still, he could not leave without knowing. And as soon as he was inside the room, Viola was rushing toward him, calling his name with such joy that his doubts vanished.

Byron was here, she thought, dizzy at seeing him again. He all but glittered in the ill-lit room. And as always when Byron was near her, she was aware of no one but him. Everyone else, everything else, disappeared. At that moment it seemed the bad times disappeared, too.

They were together in an instant, embracing. Not noticing the broken arm in the sling, he crushed it against his chest. Viola was faint with pain at the pressure, but would not move away. He was holding her and his mouth was against hers, and she was shaken by the force of his physical presence. In a little while, they would be lying naked in one another's arms.

He drew back just enough to be able to whisper to her: "Why did you leave me?"

She could not imagine that she had willfully left him, could barely remember why she had done so, what she had been so angry about. What would her life be without him? When she had told him of the baby, asked him to come to her, she thought she had done so out of despair and necessity, seeing it as the end of the kind of life she valued. How could she have been so sure? Perhaps a marriage with him would bring her happiness. Perhaps she had been too determined to convince herself that it would not.

The sounds of movement, a throat clearing, a crumpling newspaper interrupted them. Byron drew back and stared at the men and women seated around an oilcloth-covered table, eating fish and chips out of newspaper packets with their hands. Viola saw them all at once as he must be seeing them. Carla, large and ungainly, was at her most disheveled, Jeremy at his grimiest. Wilbert and James appeared shabby, Lesley emaciated. These were her friends; she cared for them, and dismissed the wish that they looked more respectable. The contrast between them and Byron was stunning. He was so fit, so cared for. She watched as he took off his hat and overcoat, looked about for a place to put them, clearly thought none was clean enough, and continued to hold them. Observing the perfect white of his shirt cuffs, Viola thought it had been a long time since she had seen a man so well dressed. She knew how this room must look to Byron, this room that would have appeared dirty even if they cleaned the soot off every surface each morning—and busy with suffrage activities, they did not.

Viola made the introductions and Byron thought she stumbled over James Armour's name. And his doubts returned. The people sitting around the table were not pleased to see him. He sensed an undercurrent of resentment. Probably it had to do with his having gotten Viola with child.

He looked at Viola more carefully now. In the first moments he had been too stunned to take in the significance of the sling that held her arm. Were it not for her pregnancy, he might have thought the injury had occurred in the course of one of the militant actions the British suffragettes were known to perform. But a pregnant woman would not show herself on the street, let alone take part in a demonstration. There must be another explanation. Then he thought how ill she looked, pale, haggard, with hollows under her cheekbones. Surely by this stage—he knew the time of conception to the hour—the pregnancy would be apparent. But her skirt was fitted tightly over the abdomen and there was not the slightest swelling. The truth struck him all at once. This was not a pregnant woman. She had lied to bring him to her. A woman's trick. Even Viola was not above resorting to it. He was touched. She had spoken so fiercely, so uncompromisingly. And then, she had not been able to do without him. These people meant nothing to her, even if they did share living quarters. She had rushed into his arms, kissed him with real passion. How could he be angry at her wanting him so much? The lie did not seem at all like something Viola would have done, but how can one ever know what a woman would or would not have done?

"Is there someplace we can go to be alone?"

She nodded and without a word led him out onto the landing and up another flight of stairs to a tiny, bitterly cold, boxlike room. At least it was cleaner than the parlor, he thought, putting down his hat and coat at last, waiting for her to sit down. She took a place on the edge of the bed and motioned him to the only chair.

He was here in her room, where she had so often dreamed of him, longed for him. The room was quite altered by his presence. Wherever he was, she was at home. In Greenland they had lain on the floor of the hut, on his camp bed, in the snow, and she had known there was nowhere else she wanted to be, no one else she wanted to be with. In New York, their passion had all but foundered, yet when she had called him to her in London, he had come. In a moment she would tell him about the loss of the baby. It would be painful, but they would be sharing the pain.

This room, he thought, this dreadful little room in which he felt he might suffocate, was her bedroom. That group downstairs had known where she was taking him and had not so much as changed expression. Perhaps it was not unusual for a man to follow Viola to her bedroom.

"What's wrong? Why are you frowning?"

"How can you ask? You bring me all the way to London and I find that man downstairs, his name's on the doorplate. He's living with you."

"James? Oh, all the suffragettes do that for safety, Byron. The police don't bother us so much if the flat's in a man's name."

"And the rest of those people?"

"We're all sharing the flat."

"All. You mean men and women together?" He remembered what he had heard about suffragettes and free love. Would Viola do anything like that? With all three of them? They were in Viola's flat. In Viola's bed? And was she now going to say that is what all the suffragettes do? He felt positively ill with jealousy.

"Byron, don't look like that. The way they live. It surprised me, too, when I first got here. But I've become accustomed to it now. I have a room here and pay one-sixth of the rent, but that's all I do. I don't sleep with any of them. Not James. Not anyone.

"Do you think I would have written to you if I were living in what people used to call sin with someone else?"

*Used to call sin.* She had lived that way with him, and he had not been able to make her see the necessity of marrying him.

"Try to understand, Byron. These people—they're not interested in living well themselves. Nothing makes any difference but improving the position of women."

"The men, too?"

"Yes. Many men believe it's unjust for women to be denied the right to vote."

"Oh, yes, the vote."

She pulled her hand away. "Don't talk scornfully about suffrage."

He sighed; how hard it was to avoid an argument with Viola. The scorn he displayed was not for suffrage, but for the way women were going about getting it, with demonstrations and violence and prison terms. "I'm in favor of suffrage," he replied. "I'm on the record to that effect."

"Yes. You sent me the clipping." The thought of his speaking out so strongly for suffrage softened her mood, and she took his hand again and pressed it.

Byron realized then that in the dismay at the way she was living, the jealousy aroused by the blond man, he had not spoken of the letter, of the pregnancy she had claimed to bring him to her. It was an awkward topic, considering the joy he had expressed over the child—but one that must be raised. Circling her wrist with his fingers, he felt how thin it was. She had written to him because she needed him. If she had lied about the pregnancy, it only meant she needed him more. He wondered that he could have doubted her when she was looking at him so tenderly, putting out her hand for him to take, and of course he was taking it.

"I have something to tell you, Byron."

"I know you do."

"You know. What do you know?"

He stood up and came over to the bed and sat beside her. She rested her head against his chest.

"It's obvious even to a man that you're not pregnant, Viola. Were you ever?"

"Was I ever?" She sat straight up and repeated his words stupidly, unable to grasp what he was driving at.

Byron was smiling indulgently. "You wouldn't be the first woman to say that, Viola."

"Why would I say that if it weren't so?"

"I thought perhaps you loved me enough to do that."

The words were disarming, but struck her disagreeably for all that. He thought her capable of using the oldest, cheapest trick to force him to come to her. "I was pregnant when I wrote to you. I lost the baby." And then she could not help but weep.

"Don't cry, Viola. Come home with me. That's where you belong. You'll be safe with me. I know what you need, what you want. We have to be together. All those days and nights in Greenland: I can't forget them. I know you can't."

He put his arms around her and drew her closer to him, carefully now, mindful of the sling. He had seen newspaper photographs of suffrage demonstrations; more than a little violence took place. Viola had probably been weak after losing the baby, but had insisted on going. Poor foolish girl. It was time he took her out of all this.

"How was your arm injured?"

Now that he was actually here, she was less certain of his reaction than when she had imagined it beforehand. "It happened during a break-in of a public hall in MidValley." The meeting was of the utmost importance, offered an unparalleled opportunity to make a gesture for suffrage. "If I hadn't fallen, everything would have been all right."

"Fallen? From where?"

The truth was worse than anything he could possibly have imagined. Pregnant with his child and hanging from a rope twenty-six feet up. Viola was bold, daring, but this was sheer insanity. The suffragettes had made her do it. They thought only about suffrage. In its name, they were ready to sacrifice his Viola, had sacrificed his baby. His heart went out to her and he put his arms around her gently, stroking her hair.

"You really got in over your head here, Viola. Without me, without your parents to advise you. Improving the position of women. So that's the way your so-called friends chose to improve it. With theatrics, making a pregnant woman dangle from a rope's end. I suppose they thought it would be dramatic, that the newspapers would write it up and everyone would be impressed. What can they have said to make you do it, Viola? Did they threaten you?

"I will ruin them, see that they all go to prison for long terms. I have relatives here who have influence and there's a Lord Hargreave in the cabinet who knows my father and is a backer of polar expeditions."

Viola was appalled at the turn this was taking. She could not let him blame the suffragettes. "You can't do that, Byron."

"Why not? I've just told you that I can."

"Because I insisted on being the one to break in to the hall. They didn't want me to." The tug on the rope that had broken her hold was intended to pull her to safety.

He recoiled from her. "But why? Why would you do that?"

"How can I make you see the way it was? I've told you how important breaking into this meeting was to us. And so few of the women have the strength and the agility to take it on."

"Even so, why you?"

"I had written to you to come to me and I knew that when you did I would have to go home with you and give up being a suffragette."

"Have to go home? You talk as if it were punishment."

"No. No. But I wanted to make that one last great gesture for the suffrage movement, to do something that would count."

"Count for what? What could count for more than bearing my child? Your body. It was not yours alone to risk in any way you chose, for any cause you chose. You were carrying a child, Viola. My son. What can have possessed you? How careless you were of your body, of my baby. It is not surprising that you fell. What would have been surprising would have been for you to succeed. Did you ask yourself if you had the right to take that risk? Did you ask my permission?"

He was breathing hard and his face was flushed; she could see him clenching and unclenching his fists. His voice was quiet, as if he could hardly bear to speak the words aloud. And how could she answer him? Her grief at the loss and regret at the action matched his. All the time she had lain in the hospital, all the days and nights that had passed since, she had asked herself how she could have been so careless of the child she was carrying.

But his permission? She needed no one's permission for what she did. Right or wrong. It was her body still, not his possession. The exploit, obviously too dangerous when viewed in retrospect, had mattered so much and to so many people. Haltingly she repeated this to Byron.

Her words served only to enrage him further. "Are you trying to justify your action? Did you even think of the baby? Or did you just forget all about it?"

She had thought about the baby. But not enough. That had been apparent to her from the moment she had slipped from the rope.

"My God, Viola, the fact is that you made a crazy gesture that no sensible person would have even considered. A handful of people with an ax to grind—spinsters, lesbians, misfits, hangers-on looking for free love—influenced you unduly. Suffrage will come. Everybody knows that. But it will come in good time, through normal legal channels, not through dramatic break-ins and heckling of legislators."

Oh, she did not want to quarrel with him; he was upset, of course he was upset, and with cause. But this was intolerable. "Some of us don't want to wait that long, Byron. And those misfits, as you call them, are my friends."

With a great effort, he controlled himself. What was done was over; it was not in his character to recriminate. "Perhaps in later years when we look back, we'll say that suffrage was your wild oats." He was trying for a lighter touch.

She did not know if she liked that much better.

"Let's move on from this, Viola. From now on, you'll be mine. My wife. And I'll be there to take care of you and see that nothing like this ever happens to you again."

"How will you prevent it?" The question was almost flippant, but her voice was cold.

"You'll be my wife."

That was it. The simple answer. My wife. My. My. He put his arms around her, but this time it was she who recoiled. When she sent for him, she had believed she was willing to yield to his domination. How could she ever have thought she would be able to live like that? "I'll always be what I am, Byron. I can't become another person. Your wife. Nothing else."

"Nothing else? Viola, every other woman in the world has that as her life's ambition. To be the wife of a man whom she loves and who loves her and looks after her."

"Not every other woman. Not the suffragettes. Not the women who want to be scientists or follow some other profession. Suffrage is not my wild oats, Byron. You can't dismiss it."

"You asked me to come, Viola. I am what I am, too. You knew that when you wrote the letter."

"I was wrong to ask you to come, Byron." Had she really said that? But the words were out and he was looking at her, stricken.

"Be careful, Viola." He was speaking now in a harsh sibilant whisper. "Do you know what you're saying?"

She knew what she was saying—that she would not give up control of her body, her life, to any man. "Not even to you. I love you, but I can't live the life you pick out for me. It was a mistake to think I could."

"A mistake? A mistake that would have been very useful to you if you had not wantonly destroyed the baby. You acted like any other unmarried mother, like a shopgirl looking for a way out, ready to do anything to give your baby a name. I canceled my next lecture tour, called off meetings with potential backers, turned my life upside down to come to you, offer you everything I have. And now, all you can say is you made a mistake. What was I? A backup in case you didn't succeed in getting rid of the baby? That was what you intended all along, wasn't it? Having a baby wouldn't fit into your life. You never wanted it. That's the real reason you took part in the break-in."

Viola gasped. Once they started quarreling, it seemed there was no end to the hurtful things they would say to one another.

Even as he had spoken, Byron recognized the cruelty of his words. She had not known her letter to him was delayed. Perhaps she gave up hope of his helping her and decided on the rash action as the only way out.

"It's not true, Byron. I wanted the baby. Because it was ours, your child and mine." She remembered the doctor telling her unkindly what she already knew. "You're wrong to think I don't blame myself for what happened. Look at me. Can't you see how I suffer? I lie awake night after night tormenting myself."

He walked over to the window and looked out, trying to calm himself. The loss was hers, too; he must not forget that. They loved each other after all. Surely they could make it up. Somehow he must find the way to do that. At last he was able to turn to her and speak in what was almost a normal voice.

"Perhaps you do," he said slowly. "Perhaps you don't mean everything you've told me. I've heard it said that women often act strangely after a miscarriage." If only she would accept this, they could go on as before.

There was something dismissive, demeaning about this interpretation of her behavior, but she realized he was throwing her a lifeline, offering her a last chance. He must love her very much to be willing to go so far. Should she take his offer? All she needed to do was reassure him, agree that she was behaving like a woman, irrationally, and he would take her with him. And she wanted that desperately. She looked at him, filling the dismal room with brightness. No one else could move her as he did; making love meant making love with him. Was it really impossible for her to say those few words and go on with him?

He sensed her weakening. "Come with me, Viola. Forget what I said in anger. There will be other children. We'll put all this behind us."

All this—her wild oats, the folly of her action, the loss of the baby—had nothing to do with the rightness of the cause. Even knowing she was losing him forever, she could not repudiate that. "I can't."

"Of course you can. You love me. It's perfectly obvious that you do. I'm supporting suffrage. That should be enough for you. Only stubbornness makes you keep refusing. Give way, Viola. For once in your life, give way."

But it would not be for once in her life.

"I have to be a part of the fight myself, Byron. It's what I believe in. Equality."

"Principles are not much company when you're alone in bed." He thought of James Armour, of the other men downstairs, and his jealousy took over. "That is if you are alone in bed. Maybe free love is the principle you most believe in, the one you can't bring yourself to give up."

"Don't talk to me like that. You know it's not true."

"How can I know that? I can't know anything for certain." It seemed to him now that all the while he had been repeating *my* baby, *my* child, he had been trying to convince himself. The doubt had been growing. James Armour's name on the door. James Armour's baby in her body? The thought was maddening and he could not stop himself from saying savagely, "I can't even know whether the baby was mine. Maybe when it came down to it you thought I'd be a better choice for a husband than one of those brutes downstairs."

He would stop at nothing in his desire to hurt her, to debase her. Trembling with rage, she raised the uninjured arm to strike him and then stopped in midblow, remembering what happened when they had quarreled in New York. She knew better than to start an act of violence with him that might yet end in a sexual encounter.

"No. You can't be sure. You have only my word for it—the word of a woman who needs permission to act, who must be taken care of. But what gives you the right to be sure of anything about me? You don't have me in your power. I am not locked away, your wife whom no man would dare to touch, as secure as if you had fastened a medieval chastity belt around my hips."

They were both angry, livid, breathing hard, and when he put his hands on her, she broke away with all her strength. For a moment, it seemed that he would overpower her, but at the last, he let her go. He felt spent. The quarrel had taken over and led him to make accusations he only half believed. Yet he could not take them back.

"I dread the life you're going to have after I leave you here, Viola." She shuddered. *I dread the life I'm going to have after I leave you, Viola,* he was thinking.

He picked up his coat and put it on very slowly; then his hat was in his hand. She hesitated. For all the anger and bitterness, there was still a magnetic pull between them. Should she stop him from going even now? Would she regret it for all the years ahead if she did not? Perhaps. But to give up the dream of suffrage? Of equality? This dream was not just hers; it belonged to all women. She could make her life count for so much more than it ever could were she the wife of Byron Tremaine. But never to be together again as lovers—how could she bear it? Still, she did not speak.

The door closed behind him. He was gone. The time had come for her to return to active and daring life as a suffragette. *I dread the life you're going to have.* She shuddered again. How could she bear it?

The door to her room opened and she looked up, wondering who had climbed the stairs to be with her.

James was standing in the doorway. Smiling.

# *Chapter Twelve*

HOLLOWRAN. AGAIN. THE HEAVY DOORS closed behind her, and in a moment, the world outside in all its beauty became irrelevant, all but forgotten. Destruction of property and obstruction of justice were the charges. Viola had led the march from Hyde Park Corner to Exeter Hall, where the cabinet ministers were meeting, taken a hammer from her bag, and broken a window. The police invaded the demonstration, knocked her down, kicked her. She managed to get up, kicked back, hit the policeman nearest her with her fist. Harmlessly. He laughed and put her in handcuffs.

Three months in Hollowran. Wilbert did his best, but was not able to get the sentence reduced. She knew what being in prison meant, had been through it all before. But knowing did not help. This was always a bad moment when the enormity of what she had done, of what she would have to do, swept over her.

It began simply enough with basic questions, which she answered tonelessly—name, age, religion—and declared that she was able to read and write, but not to sew. No one believed that; what woman did not know how to sew? It was viewed as an effort to malinger, and during her last sentence she was set to making men's shirts.

Two wardresses, one on either side of her, were watching her every movement. After her first prison experience, Viola marveled that any woman could accept work degrading both to prisoner and keeper.

Lesley viewed her question as naive. "How many jobs are available to women?" Many of the wardresses despised suffragettes, treated them roughly, declared there was something more "natural" about crimes committed by regular criminals.

One of the wardresses indicated that Viola should unbutton her dress down the front and pull up her embroidered pale cream–colored silk chiffon chemise. A man walked up to her; she could identify him as a physician by his stethoscope rather than by any manner of professionalism. He stared openly, lewdly, at Viola's bare breasts, poked for rather long with his fingers before applying the stethoscope.

The cursory examination of heart and lungs over, she knew the further steps that were to be taken before confinement to a cell. She was required to take off all her clothes right then and there. To refuse was pointless; she would only be stripped by the wardresses. And no one would care.

Each item of clothing was handed to a wardress, who rolled it up and threw it carelessly on a shelf. Viola stood naked, aware of the eyes on her, steeling herself for the body search. Unimportant really, but singularly unpleasant. Those hands, women's hands, but large, hard, rough, with dirt under the fingernails, going over her body, inside, pushing her into this position or that, passing through her body hair, through the hair on her head. Slowly. It was over, and she was handed a chemise so short it did not quite cover the pubic area, and led down the corridor, barefoot, to the bath. The tub was filthy, the water slimy and filled with dirt and foul-smelling scum. It was common knowledge in the prison that half a dozen or more women, some with contagious skin diseases, bathed in the same water before it was changed. When Viola came out of the tepid water, shivering involuntarily, she was offered a rag to dry herself with.

By now it would be a relief to put on anything to keep her warm, even the ugly, much-worn prison clothing, starting with coarse cotton drawers and chemise. The stays were so large that even after she had laced them as tightly as the cords allowed, they slipped down past her slender hips and fell on the floor; the wardress shrugged and put them aside. The petticoat was not much smaller, but the extra fabric could be wrapped around the waist and fastened with fraying tapes. The dress was a drab dark brown, with white arrows painted down the back. As she pulled it on over her head, a faint, unpleasant smell emanated from the fabric. It had not been cleaned since the last prisoner wore it. Buttons were broken or missing, and bits of the bulky chemise stuck out through each gap. A wardress then gave her a small cap, once white, but clearly worn, and two pieces of cotton fabric. The first time she was imprisoned, she had no idea what to do with them and the wardresses had laughed. Now she knew that one was to be tied around her waist to make an apron and the other used as a handkerchief. The clothes were not fresh now, and she knew she would have none to change into for a week, possibly longer.

The socks were of heavy black wool with red stripes around the legs. Lacking garters, they fell around her ankles and feet. On a shelf to the side were rows of clumsy, heavy-soled shoes, unmatched. She picked up one after the other, uncertain which two to select, as none were remotely close in size to Viola's narrow, high-arched feet.

Now she was ready to receive her issue of sheets, a Bible, a hymn book, a religious tract, and a book, curiously unsuited to the surroundings: *A Healthy Home and How to Keep It.* The wardress kissed the Bible before handing it to Viola. "Read it, my girl," she whispered. "It is not too late to change your ways." Many of the women who took up the unpleasant wardress profession were religious, and justified their harshness to the suffragettes on the grounds of a sinful life.

The wardress led Viola down the corridor, past rows of cells, and finally unlocked a door studded with black pegs. A spy hole ensured that she could be observed at any time. She walked inside the cell carefully, fearing to stumble and turn an ankle in the faint flickering light of the gas jet attached high up on the wall. Night had fallen by then, but she knew from experience the cell would be no brighter at high noon. The barred windowpane was so heavily encrusted with dust that no daylight could get through.

Becoming accustomed to the dimness, she was able to guess the size of the cell as roughly five feet in width, seven in length. A mattress and blankets were rolled up against the longer wall, alongside a stack of boards. The wardress, with unexpected kindness, helped her to set up a small platform of the boards so as to lift the mattress a couple of inches off the floor. Viola sat down on the makeshift bed; a wooden stool was hanging on a nail, but there was no floor space for it once the mattress was unrolled. Fearing the gas flame would go out before she had gotten her bearings, Viola quickly located the little shelf holding an assortment of supplies. There lay a comb lacking most of its teeth, a hard-bristled brush for her hair, and a card giving the list of prison rules and an evening prayer. Neither could be read, though, in the dim light. Next to these lay a wooden spoon, a saltcellar, and a tin cup for the gruel of oatmeal and water which the prisoners called "skilly." Well, the utensils were of little importance, as she intended a hunger strike and was determined to add a thirst strike this time.

Without wishing her good night, the wardress left, and Viola heard the key turn in the lock. No matter how she prepared herself, and how little she wished the company of the wardress, it was terrible to be locked in . . . alone.

Viola made up the bed, thinking that only straw could make mattress and pillow so hard and lumpy. The sheets were of a rough muslin, laundered, but wrinkled and gray; the blankets had evidently not been cleaned in weeks or months. Many of the women, she knew, caught head lice, but she had been lucky enough to avoid them on her previous prison experiences. She did her best to wash in the tiny washbasin, dried herself with the threadbare towel that soon became too sodden to do any good, and rinsed the food-encrusted wooden spoon. Viola took off the shoes and lay down clothed, as the garments were cleaner than the blanket, which was, in any event, too small and too thin to keep her warm in the frigid room.

She could hear the noises made by the other prisoners settling down for the night, and yet felt utterly alone. That was what prison did. But she was not alone. Other suffragettes were imprisoned too, and there were informants among the prison workers passing out word of what was happening inside the thick, soot-blackened stone walls.

By now the suffragettes must know where she was and what was her sentence. Viola's reputation at this time came close to rivaling those of Lesley and Carla. Everyone had heard of the American—the "beautiful American," as she quickly became known—who came to London to stand with the militant suffragettes. Newspaper reporters repeatedly singled her out when she spoke at rallies, led demonstrations, and heckled politicians. Viola's hunger strike would obviously receive a great deal of attention, and so help the movement.

The hunger strike had proved to be a formidable weapon for the suffragettes to use. The newspapers reported the terrible cycle of starvation and forcible feeding until the public, appalled, cried out for change. And the public knew only one aspect of forcible feeding, the pain and degradation, and was unaware of the lasting harm being done to the body. Some women never recovered fully. Lesley had required surgery on the intestinal tract.

Lying here alone in the dark, Viola began to gather her strength for what lay ahead. There was no point in thinking about it now, building up fears about what horrors her body would endure. Think about something else. And as if she had called him to her, the image of James appeared, and she smiled as he always smiled, as he would be smiling when she came home. Oh, Jamie. Lying on the hard, lumpy mattress, she could imagine she was climbing up the stairs to her room at Chessham Court, with James following close behind her. In the terrible days after she parted from Byron, she had rested in James's smile.

While she was absent, he was almost certainly in bed with Lesley, with Carla, with one or another of his ladies. Happiness was the quality associated with James, never fidelity. The pleasure she took in James's body was enough for her. Her life had moved her beyond passion. Passion was what she had felt for Byron Tremaine; she was glad to be without it.

He would not have understood prison and the need for going to prison, would have expressed scorn and anger for the way of life she had adopted. Alone in this dreadful place, she thought it was as well that old love with Byron was over. Only she wished his face were not so vivid to her. Falling asleep, she was looking into his dark green eyes.

The next morning, awakening to a cold, damp dawn in prison, she recognized the cell as her home and knew she would be allowed to leave it only for hurried trips to the water closet and twice a week for half-hour exercise periods in the yard. Those would be her sole opportunities to be with her fellow prisoners. Talking was forbidden, but they learned to communicate in faint whispers and by passing notes written on the coarse bathroom paper. Returned to their cells, they tapped messages in code.

This morning she accepted the thin oatmeal porridge, small chunk of hard, dry whole-meal bread, and tea without milk or sugar. It was the last meal she would eat. All the food served the prisoners was repulsive—greasy suet pudding, occasionally a potato still hard in the middle, rotting vegetables, and soup which usually had worms floating on top. Were it not for the horror of the forcible feeding, doing without this food would not have been much of a burden.

The warden was uneasy about having so well known a figure in the prison. Who knew what kind of trouble she could bring? He called her to him and advised her that if she agreed to follow the rules, she would be moved into the first division of the prison, where she could wear her own clothes, have food sent in by her friends, and receive mail. But there was no benefit to the movement in serving out her sentence in this manner. There would be not one line about her in the newspapers, one protest in Parliament. She refused the offer with cold courtesy and returned to her cell to begin the hunger and thirst strike.

During the early stage, there were occasional bouts of dizziness and faintness, but dehydration had not yet taken its toll. Then, as day followed day, her entire body became engaged in a struggle for survival. She became too thin to hold up the petticoat, no matter how she tied it around her. The bones at her wrists, ankles, pelvis, and collarbone protruded. Her hands and feet turned an odd dark red, purplish color. Normal body functions came to a halt. Pain was always present, shifting from one part of her body to another, from stomach to back. More troublesome were the palpitations of her heart and the pain in her chest. A loud ringing in her ears was deafening. A foul taste in her mouth became a torment; her tongue was dry and coated, and a bitter phlegm caused her to retch repeatedly. She was so faint and dizzy that she sank to her knees one day during the exercise period, but pretended she had bent down to put her shoe back on. The wardresses must not notice. Prison staff members and prisoners alike marveled at her courage and resolution.

When she applied to Tremaine and then to Peary, it had been in the conviction that she was as capable as any man of enduring a harsh and brutal environment and shortages of food and water. She was proving it here. But occasionally, her hold on reality would slip. Sometimes for periods of—was it a minute or an hour?—she would escape from her body's misery and reach a peak of exaltation over what she was doing for suffrage. At other times, she entered a strange hallucinatory state where she lost all recognition of the prison and believed herself to be somewhere else—back at the house on Chessham Court, sitting at the oilcloth-covered table making plans for another demonstration, James's knee pressing hard against hers. Or she would be at home with her mother, accepting love and rejecting well-meant but irrelevant advice. In the best of her visions, she was looking upon the limitless horizon in Greenland. And in this dreamlike state, she could believe that everything was still all right and in a moment she would be lying naked with Byron, skin to skin, touching, touching.

Coming to full consciousness after these fantasies, she remembered how they had quarreled and would never make love together again and felt desolate. Only for a moment. As soon as her mind was clear, she occupied herself by making plans for the WSPU, selecting future targets. It had become a joke, bitter but a joke nonetheless, that prison was helpful to the movement by providing suffragettes with time for devising plots.

Each morning she expected to be taken out of her cell for forcible feeding, but time passed and the wardress brought her meals and took them away untouched without a word. Did she dare to hope the barbarous custom had been abandoned?

Viola had no way of knowing that the warden was being ordered to do nothing and wait for her to give up in despair and weakness. The pages of the newspapers were filled with articles about the disgrace of forcible feeding. The prison authorities did not want to see reports of mistreatment of the beautiful American. Mistreatment? The warden thought this attitude woolly-headed and foolish. Feeding a person who would otherwise starve to death was sensible. If he did not order forcible feeding for this woman, he could not order it for any other hunger striker, and the whole situation would be out of control. The body cannot tolerate complete dehydration. No one had yet died of a thirst or hunger strike, but it might happen at any time, and he knew who would be blamed if it did. He could not act, however, against the wishes of his superiors in the prison system.

Not until it appeared that she might die from lack of food or water did he obtain permission to go forward. When Viola again refused to end her strike voluntarily, she was taken to a room large enough to accommodate the wardresses and doctors who would carry out the order. To fight was useless with so many people to hold her down, but that was of no significance. She must resist as a display of determination and courage. Her mouth was forced open, and a steel instrument to separate her clenched jaw inserted, cutting the gums cruelly. A tube was passed down her throat; she coughed it up, and it was put in again. The sensation of the tube going down her throat and esophagus, down to her stomach was both painful and frightening. It was in place. A concoction was poured through a funnel. She felt the lumpy liquid arrive in her stomach and recoiled, sickened. The feeding was complete. Now the tube was withdrawn and the metal clamps holding her jaws apart were released. Her mouth was bruised and already beginning to swell. The hands pressing her down in the chair were hastily withdrawn as she vomited. Some of the food remained in her stomach, a heavy lump. Could she stand up by herself? She had to do so. Hands reached out to help her, the same hands that had held her down; she pushed them away. Head high and back straight, she managed to walk unaided to her cell.

As soon as the door was locked behind her, she fell facedown on the mattress. As she lay there, she heard the faintest of tapping. Words of encouragement were being sent in code by the prisoners on either side of her. After a brief rest, she forced herself to her feet and walked the few steps possible in the tiny boxlike room. Up and down. Up and down. Clutching at the walls that were at no point farther than an arm's length away. And it was all to be lived through again. Twice a day. Every day. Except on Sunday. The torturers went to church that day. Periodically, the feeding was halted for a day or two, as was the practice. But the prisoner was never to know when that would occur. Each time she came into the room for the feeding, she was offered the opportunity to accept food voluntarily and avoid the tube, the funnel, the concoction. She said no, whispered it, because her throat was sore, her voice hoarse.

After a few days, her gums were so sore that blood poured down her chin each time the steel instrument was inserted. A change was decided upon: The tube was put down her nose. Her arms and shoulders bore black-and-blue marks from the pressure of the hands holding her, and her head ached as if a band of steel were constricting it. Stomach cramps doubled her over. She became so white and dizzy that a feeding would be halted while one of the doctors took her pulse and placed a stethoscope against her chest. Her heart was strong; each time, the feeding was ordered to continue.

She would not yield, regardless of the indignity, degradation, and pain. Each day she made a scratch mark on the wall to show her how much time was remaining in her prison sentence and thought how it would be when at last she was freed. Her friends would greet her at the prison door, provide warm drinks, bear her home on their shoulders. It would be as on the day she had arrived in London, the day of Lesley's release.

To her surprise, one morning she was not taken to the room where the feedings were carried out, but instead to the warden's office. The change in procedure worried Viola. What were the prison authorities intending to do to her now? Perhaps they merely meant to perform the feeding in this other place. Sick and dizzy, she was slow to absorb the meaning of the scene in front of her. None of the instruments used in the feedings was in evidence. She was vaguely aware of a gray-haired man too well dressed to be a prison doctor seated beside the warden. Viola swayed and put out her hand to grasp the desk in front of her for support. Then she drew it back; whatever was in store for her, she would show no sign of weakness. There was something familiar about the visitor's face, but she could not remember where she had seen him before. He was addressing the warden; she could not make out the words, but the manner of speech was upper class. She glanced up and into clear blue eyes surrounded by a network of tiny lines. She had looked into those eyes before. It all came back to her then—the day she fell from the rope at the town hall in MidValley and lost her baby. She had lain on the ground while her blood stained the elegant, light gray suit coat placed around her. A hand had stroked her forehead. His hand. Sir George Arnold Comstock, Lord Hargreave. The enemy of suffrage.

"Miss Lambert." He was too correct to put it as a question, but was uncertain that this emaciated, haggard prisoner was the lovely woman he recalled. She was standing before him in a loose brown prison dress, with food stains down the front. Heavy socks drooping

over clumsy shoes made it impossible to observe the shape of her ankles and feet. And her face. The cheekbones were prominent and the
hollows beneath them were deep. The eyelids were so swollen and
reddened that he could hardly make out the deep blue of her eyes,
and there were dark brown smudges underneath. Her mouth was
bruised, the lips broken with cuts. And the hair—he had never forgotten the brilliant coppery streaks—was dry as straw, lusterless, a
dull brown without highlights.

"Lord Hargreave." The low voice with the thrilling throb he remembered was quite gone. The words came out in a hoarse croak.

But of course it was Viola Lambert. The quality that had made her
unforgettable emanated from this wasted body. Why had she been so
foolish as to persist in the misguided course pursued by suffragettes,
women of the lower class too unattractive to do better? From his
viewpoint, however, it was an advantage, giving him a second opportunity to befriend her. "Wardress, bring a cup of warm water. At
once."

Viola waved her hand in a gesture of refusal. She would not break
her thirst strike just because Lord Hargreave wished it. But then, to
her amazement, the warden spoke brusquely: "You are free to go.
Get your clothes."

"Free?"

The warden indicated Lord Hargreave. His influence had saved
her from a prison sentence once before. The cup of water was already being proferred by the wardress, eager now to be helpful. The
cause of suffrage had now been served, and she could accept the cup
and drink. Though she wanted the water desperately, her bruised
throat and esophagus could hardly tolerate its passage. She was afraid
that her stomach would refuse the fluid, as it so often rejected the
contents of the tube, but in a few moments the nausea subsided.

The wardress led her out of the office, to the shelves holding the
prisoners' clothes, and she stood there bewildered at the bundles
jammed together chaotically. Rummaging through them with shaking
hands, she wished she felt better; as it was, she could hardly stay on
her feet. "Just take any one of them," said the wardress impatiently,
but at that moment she caught sight of the filmy cream-colored chemise with the hand-embroidered roses, and pulled out the bundle of
her clothes. They were dusty, wrinkled, and had taken on a musty

odor, but at least they were her own. All her clothes were much too large for her emaciated body, and the shoes were lost; she would have to clump along on the big unmatched prison pair until she got back to Chessham Court. She did not wish to be beholden to Lord Hargreave for bus fare, but her purse had been torn away from her at the demonstration and it was too far to walk.

"I'll bring you to your home, Miss Lambert." It was Lord Hargreave, supporting her with his arm and leading her to his carriage; it was luxurious, much more so than any of the new motorcars. She sank back against the soft leather cushion and raised no objection when he signaled a footman to cover her with a cashmere lap robe and then go to the prison for another cup of water. The carriage moved off and her wretched body recoiled in agony at each bump on the unevenly paved street. Every few minutes Lord Hargreave ordered the driver to stop the horses and allow her to drink. She felt as if the food that had been forced down into her stomach the previous evening were still sitting there, and with each sip, she could taste it in her throat. She opened the carriage door, unable to keep from vomiting. Lord Hargreave held her head, wiped her mouth with his handkerchief.

At last she was able to speak haltingly. "How did you know I was in prison, Lord Hargreave?"

"Articles are in all the newspapers and you are the subject of debate in the Parliament. I must say the need for gestures like the hunger strike utterly eludes me. And what an ordeal to put your body through, Miss Lambert. Your lovely young body."

What a strange way for him to speak. If he had been younger, she would have thought he was courting her. She took another sip of the water. "Why did you have me released, Lord Hargreave? Have you changed your mind about giving women the right to vote?"

"I will never change my mind about that. But I would not have you suffer."

The relief at being out of prison was incalculable, but she regretted that she owed her freedom to a man who was a powerful enemy of the suffrage movement. Lord Hargreave pressed her hand, and out of gratitude, she did not pull away.

It was a long time since he had been so infatuated with a woman as he was with Viola. She had fascinated him the very first time he saw her climbing down the rope to make her illegal entry into the meeting room. A suffragette performing a criminal act. A suffragette, but so different from any he had ever seen before. She was too beautiful, and when she spoke, despite the American accent, he could recognize her social class. To waste that incredible vitality and energy on the suffrage movement seemed to him the height of folly.

"You've done some remarkable things for a woman—going to Greenland, working in the laboratories of two museums." He was well aware that he was telling her what she most wanted to hear.

"How do you know so much about me?"

"I wanted to know." Hargreave did not explain that he had detectives investigate Miss Lambert's history after the episode in MidValley. "Your lifelong ambition has been to make your mark as a scientist, as an explorer. I wonder that you can give it up."

At his words, she remembered the wild excitement she had felt when she examined the prehistoric organisms in the makeshift laboratory in Greenland and understood the vast implications. "I'm not giving anything up. Suffrage is my goal." She spoke as firmly as her broken voice would allow.

How earnest she was. The suffrage movement is so full of words. He did not argue the point and went on. "To be a scientist, an explorer—that is unusual for a man. But for a woman to have the talent is unique. You have it, Miss Lambert, and you should use it." He knew he was being seductive, believed he had found the way she could be seduced.

Viola listened to him spellbound, told him of her plan to go to the Antarctic.

"I am sure you have heard of Richard Everett Sharpe," Lord Hargreave said in a businesslike manner.

Of course she had heard of Captain Sharpe. Everyone in England was talking about him. While Byron was wasting his time, to her mind, climbing Mount McKinley, the Sharpe Antarctic expedition was getting ready to set off and preempt the Pole. Viola's conviction that she would go to Antarctica struck him as charming, though ridiculous, and he realized how much it would mean to her were he to arrange an interview with Sharpe. He did not know the explorer personally. A navy man, put on a training ship at the age of thirteen, Sharpe never went to Oxford or Cambridge. Not the sort of person one would know. But Sharpe no doubt knew of Lord Hargreave and hoped for his financial backing. He might even give it; all Britain would be honored if Sharpe were first at the South Pole. But rather than compromise himself by writing now and asking a favor, he thought to make use of his connection with Sharpe's second-in-command, Lieutenant Ian Crosbie.

"He is distantly related to my wife," Hargreave told Viola. Her heart began to beat more rapidly. "Lieutenant Crosbie is by way of being a hero. He made a name for himself on the journey led by the French explorer, Charcot, and has just returned from the Shackleton expedition that came within one hundred miles of the Pole. I understand that Captain Sharpe was eager to enlist him. I can get in touch with Lieutenant Crosbie, Miss Lambert, asking him to arrange an interview for you with Captain Sharpe." She was captured now, he could tell. It had been an inspiration to think of the Sharpe expedition.

In the midst of her excitement at the prospect of a meeting with the great Captain Sharpe, common sense reasserted itself. Why was Lord Hargreave doing this? And then it occurred to her that he, a vehement and vocal opponent of suffrage, was determined to weaken the movement. Viola was at the height of her reputation and he must want to remove her from London, away from the suffragettes.

Viola was quite wrong in assuming Hargreave's motive was to weaken the movement by taking her from it. Hargreave did not take suffrage that seriously. He wanted Viola for himself, and thought by this means to bind her to him.

Hargreave wished he could remember what his wife had told him about Crosbie. Her maternal aunt, who was Scottish, had known the family. There was something about the man. A nagging memory. Well, no matter. Crosbie would do as he was asked, and that was what mattered. Nothing would come of it. There was not the slightest chance that any sensible Englishman would consider taking a woman along on an expedition to the most hostile and hazardous region in the world. But Viola must be grateful to him for the introduction, pleased that he viewed her ambition seriously. Or gave the appearance of so doing. Hargreave was known for his charm. In time, she must succumb.

"Write to me as soon as you're sufficiently recovered for me to get in touch with Lieutenant Crosbie." She had no need for his calling card. A letter would reach him were it merely addressed to Lord Hargreave, England.

As the carriage drew up to 88 Chessham Court, the front door opened and Carla, Lesley, and James were running down the steps. The prison informant had passed the word of her impending release as soon as Lord Hargreave was seen entering the warden's office. Viola was dimly aware of the carriage driving off while her friends embraced her, cheering. James pressed his mouth on hers, licking her dry and bloodied lips, and then picked her up and carried her inside and up the stairs. She lay on the sofa, covered by two blankets, taking in small amounts of water and tea and describing her prison experiences.

Within the hour, the small living room was filled with women gathering from all over London to express their admiration. Lesley, true to form, had prepared a speaking schedule for her. Viola understood that it did not matter if her throat was still raw and her voice hoarse, if she fell to the platform in a faint. One of the liberal newspapers described her as a "hero" of suffrage, using the form of the word the suffragettes favored.

Later that night, James helped her bathe in the iron tub in the kitchen. When he lifted her out, his touch was caressing, and she remembered how she had longed for love when in her cell. Now she was too dizzy and ill to respond. He did not press her; they would have ample time to make love after she recovered. Maybe tomorrow or the next day, thought James, as always seeing the brightest future.

A letter from the Natural History Museum was waiting for her. This time her imprisonment had received so much attention that even the unworldly curator could not overlook it.

There was also a letter from her sister, Evelyn. Viola was not to answer—the news of her imprisonment had reached New York, and Bertram was disapproving. Nonetheless, Evelyn was sending assurance of her affection and understanding. Their mother, she wrote, had been upset by learning of Viola's suffering—Mr. Lambert, too, had been distressed—and wished her a rapid return to good health. Although her mother had not written to her directly, obviously still objecting to Viola's way of life, the concern expressed gave hope that someday the rift between them would be made up. She thought sadly how much she still missed her mother.

Evelyn had enclosed a clipping in the envelope; it was *The New York Times* report of Byron Tremaine's wedding. The marriage must have been announced in the British newspapers, too, but she had given up reading society news. A reception for three hundred had been held in his father's Washington town house, and President Theodore Roosevelt was among the guests. The Lamberts did not attend. The poor newspaper reproduction could not conceal the prettiness of the bride, the former Hermine Ellin Marwick.

Viola remembered the day Byron had said that when he married, she would not like it a bit. He was wrong. Oh, she felt a pang. How could she not, remembering all that love, all that passion? But it was past.

Now that an interview with Richard Everett Sharpe was assured, Byron had ceased to be her only means of getting to Antarctica.

*Who would take the chance of having you on an expedition?* Byron had asked long ago, and then had answered his own question, *except for me.* He was wrong about that, too.

# Chapter Thirteen

"THANK GOD NO WORD OF that 1915–1916 all-women's expedition to the South Pole ever got out!..."

My hands shook as I reread the letter found in the garage. An all-women's expedition in the second decade of the century, before women had the vote, before women had careers? How could there have been such an expedition without the world's knowing about it? Without my knowing about it? An expedition like this would have been the talk of the Explorers Club for years. Ronald could not accept the cryptic message in the letter from Byron Tremaine to Horace Graham any more than I could. The dates alone give the statement the lie: In 1915–1916 Byron led his legendary expedition to the South Pole.

Perhaps the message had some private meaning known only to the two men, I suggested.

"It certainly is odd for a letter like this to be put in an envelope purporting to come from an organization called the Society of Men Who Love Dogs, Bibi," Ronald agreed. "Maybe it was a joke. You know the kind of thing—someone has envelopes printed up to send to friends to be humorous. I doubt there ever was such a society any more than there was such an expedition."

And yet the history of polar exploration has its dark areas of concealment. In an era before radio and television, events were more easily obscured. Obviously such an expedition never materialized, but perhaps there had been a plan. And at that moment my thoughts turned to V. Lambert, the first woman to be a member of an expedition to the Arctic and subsequently a suffragette. Had a women's Antarctic expedition been conceived, she was the logical person—indeed, the only logical person—to have done so. Now I could see a reason for Byron's dismay. Miss Lambert might have induced him to lend his name or support to her wild idea of an expedition, and its failure would reflect badly on him.

Some record must have existed all along, but lacking a clue, who would have thought to look for it? Until now. The likeliest place to find evidence was among Miss Lambert's memorabilia in the house on Chessham Court. My trip to London assumed an importance great enough for me to overcome my reluctance about going there alone. I postponed my departure for a few days, unwilling to leave before Ronald's surgery was successfully completed. Though Ronald urged me not to wait, I could see he was pleased by my caring so much.

Once in London, my natural timidity reasserted itself and I sat in the hotel room, longing for Ronald, for the comfort of his presence. If he were here, the room, dismal in the morning grayness, would look so different to me. Of course if he were here, I would not be in the room at all (except when we returned to make love), but would be away looking for traces of V. Lambert. Ronald said I am capable of handling this by myself; I have a head start and must make the most of it. In his efforts to find the love interest in Byron's life, Avery might fix on Miss Lambert. After all, there appears to be no other woman. Once on her trail, he might find some reference to the expedition. With his cynicism, Avery would not hesitate to make damaging use of the inference. *I still fear that it may.* Fear. Avery would like that word. Why had Byron used it?

With my own fear of Avery as the spur, I left the sanctuary of Durrants Hotel and made my way to the address on the envelope found among Byron Tremaine's papers. As I approached this destination, my excitement mounted. Here lay the answers to questions buried these seventy years and more.

Eighty-eight Chessham Court. I stood on the sidewalk, staring up at the office building of glass, steel, and concrete towering above me.

This imposing edifice had replaced the four-story building that was the object of my search.

The disappointment was overwhelming. Oh, there were still places to look. Newspapers and magazines published in the early years of the century must contain references to Miss Lambert. But these sources would not contain the secrets of her life, reveal a hidden relationship with Byron Tremaine, a covert plan for a women's expedition. No article would lead me to the reason for the PERSONAL URGENT appeal. Miss Lambert had not been sufficiently famous for her private papers and letters to have been saved when the house was torn down. The mystery would never be solved. To all intents and purposes, I was at a dead end.

Discouraged, I caught a bus to take me back to the hotel. Looking out of the window at the scenes of London going by, I thought I saw Steven Avery walking rapidly down the street. I gave so violent a start that the man sitting next to me looked at me in concern. The bus stopped and I got off without thinking what I would say if I caught up with him. Before I could cross the street, he disappeared into a building. I forced myself to be calm. I had not gotten a good look; it was probably some other man of similar build. My nerves were set on edge by the failure of my journey. I must not imagine Avery was everywhere.

"Miss Tremaine. Beatrix." Bucky Sheridan had come up beside me; at least there was no question that it was he. "You certainly make a dull gray day look bright." I had forgotten how winning was his grin, and felt surprise that I could be quite so glad to see him. Despite my underlying gloom, I greeted him warmly and accepted his suggestion that we go into a nearby coffeehouse.

"The documentary on my Antarctic expedition is being shown on the BBC this week, so my public relations man arranged for me to come over to make some personal appearances," he related with pride. "Bill, my PR man, is terrific. Last time I was here, I stayed at a bed-and-breakfast off Russell Square where they didn't change the sheets for a week, and this time, he's put me in with the beautiful people at the Connaught. I'm endorsing some of the products we used on the expedition. You won't believe what they're paying me. Anyway, he set all this up and now he's getting me on the big television shows."

The mention of television made me think of "Avery Tells All" and I told Bucky I thought I had just seen Avery on the street. "I must have been mistaken."

"No, it could have been Avery all right; he's here, Beatrix, staying at the Connaught, too. We ran into each other in the lobby yesterday."

My anxiety returned, as I thought only Miss Lambert could have taken Avery to London. With the loss of 88 Chessham Court, I had lost my edge. Now he had the advantages of money and a staff.

Bucky, still talking, did not notice my reaction. "He said he'd like to interview me while we're both here. He's thinking of putting me on the program he's doing on Antarctic exploration."

Cheerful Bucky was quite unprepared for Avery's accusations, actual or implied. It is to my interest to have Bucky occupy Avery's time in London and then be the "bad guy" against my great-grandfather's "good guy" on the program. But somehow I do not wish any harm to come to Bucky. I remembered that Avery said he was getting evidence that would prove Bucky a fraud. Real evidence? Or manufactured?

"Bucky, do you think Avery's to be trusted?"

He gave his appealing grin. "Trusted? You don't trust men like Avery, Beatrix. You try to figure out how to keep them from doing you in."

"And do you usually succeed at that?"

"I have so far. I'll talk to him; I don't see that I have any choice. Anyway, I need to find out what he's planning to do on his program; maybe he thinks he has something on me. In that case, I'll prove him wrong. Or . . . I'll show him why something else would make a better program. That's all he cares about." His grin was not so carefree as all that, his innocence not so total.

"Why, Beatrix, you look so serious. I do believe you're worrying about me." And in the most natural way, he took my hand and squeezed it. I usually draw back when someone who is little more than a stranger touches me, but the contact was pleasant. "That's the nicest thing that's happened to me in a long time."

For a moment, I actually forgot how miserable I felt and smiled at him. "That's better; you have the most wonderful smile, Beatrix. What do people call you? People close to you, I mean?" He did not wait for an answer. "Trixie? I like that." I marveled at how quickly and easily he could make me feel we really knew each other; I am usually slow and cautious in making friends. "I've been talking so much that I haven't given you a chance to tell me what brings you to London."

There was such warmth in his manner that I wanted to tell him everything, confess myself at a dead end, ask his advice. I am used to asking for advice; my friend Aimee criticizes me for it. Perhaps in his researches about the Antarctic, Bucky had run across some mention of an all-women's expedition. But even as I began to speak, I remembered that he was going to see Avery, the most adept and devious of interviewers. What if he let something slip? No, the less he knew about me, the better.

"It's mostly a vacation," I told him.

"Are you here alone?"

"Yes, I'm planning to spend most of my time doing research."

"On what?"

"The suffrage movement." That seemed a perfectly safe thing to say.

"It sounds interesting. Isn't there an old feminist hangout around here? On Chessham Court, I think it is."

"How do you know that?"

It seemed to me he hesitated a moment. "Everybody knows that."

His mention of Chessham Court reminded me that I must continue my search, however poor the prospects. I stood up and said I had to go. Bucky looked disappointed, but then recovered rapidly and said he would take me back to my hotel by taxi. He held my hand a little too long when we said good-bye. "I'll call you," he said. "It's not good for you to do research all the time. You'll strain your beautiful eyes."

I found myself smiling as I left him. Ronald called a few minutes after I returned to the room, and once he had reassured me that he was doing well, I told him of the Chessham Court fiasco. "Don't give up too quickly. I still think you'll find something. And, Bibi, try to have some fun when you're there. Go somewhere nice for dinner and take in a play."

Even though I could not imagine going to an elegant restaurant or a theater by myself, just talking with him made me feel more confident.

Wasting no time, I went directly to the British Library to ferret out information about V. Lambert. I decided that a suffragette publication would be most likely to provide me with the details of her life. Every group has its own magazine or newspaper; my great-grandfather's connection with suffrage had merited a great deal of comment in the pages of the *Suffrage Searchlight* in America. That was established only in 1913, but it seemed likely that the British suffragettes would have had an earlier publication.

And in the yellowing, disintegrating pages of the issues of *Votes for Women* published in 1907, I discovered that Viola (now I knew her first name) Lambert's arrival in England was hailed as a coup for the British suffrage movement. A long feature article on the front page of *Votes for Women* was devoted to her. Even allowing for hyperbole, the facts of her life were astounding for a woman in the early years of the century. I was troubled, however, to learn that she was claiming to have made revolutionary fossil discoveries. Clearly, Viola Lambert had not been the most truthful of women. I knew who really made those discoveries—my great-grandfather. The article reported that she was employed as a scientist at the British Natural History Museum. There was no description or accompanying photograph, as the suffragettes opposed the male emphasis on a woman's appearance.

Subsequent issues of *Votes for Women* were filled with accounts of Miss Lambert's bold and daring actions. Her name was linked with those of the famed suffragettes Lesley Penner and Carla Brent; they all lived together at 88 Chessham Court.

My researches next took me to the offices of the staid *London Globe* to study the annual index volumes, starting with 1907. Whenever I found a reference to her name, I went to the newspaper microfilm for that date. Unlike *Votes for Women,* the newspaper articles were written by men and they had no compunction about describing Miss Lambert's appearance. Here for the first time I learned that she was invariably known as "the beautiful American." Beautiful. Again and again. The reporters waxed lyrical. "She is enchanting. Her hair has glints of copper that gleam in the grayness of the long London twilight," wrote one reporter; "her blue eyes are tinged with violet.

And her voice—deep, low, with just a hint of a throb in the lowest register—that could inflame the heart."

I had thought the woman dismissed with an initial for a first name in the diaries and never portrayed in physical terms could not possibly be the beauty of the photograph Byron Tremaine had treasured. Now it seemed Viola Lambert might have been the subject of the photograph after all.

I remembered then that I had been puzzled by something in one of the suffragette's letters to Byron, read before leaving New York. A word had been used that did not seem to belong in this formal correspondence. The woman had been writing about the suffrage movement in London, describing it as militant, violent. And then she had added this phrase: "Suitable for tigers." Tigers. Here was the word that did not fit. Was there not something oddly intimate, sexual even, about it?

I returned to the newspaper files, trying to find a connection with Byron Tremaine. His name was listed in several annual indexes, but only in connection with his expedition to Mount McKinley and his marriage to Hermine; nowhere was there an account of a visit to London. Nor did it seem that Miss Lambert had been in America during this period.

Several of the articles made mention of her family in New York, securely entrenched in society's inner circle. I realized then that I had heard of the Lamberts—money made three generations back in iron ore. The Lambert mansion on Fifth Avenue and Fifty-fourth Street was now an art museum. I had never associated V. Lambert with a wealthy and prominent family. And indeed, the article declared she had been disowned for becoming a suffragette.

The beautiful American had enthralled the liberal British public and enraged the conservatives. It seemed she brought excitement wherever she went. The adjective "heroic" was repeatedly used to describe her. Her vitality and flamboyance carried all before her. Police surrounded any rally where she was the impassioned speaker, were stationed to control the crowds lining the route of the demonstrations. In the small city of MidValley, she had fallen from a rope when climbing down from the roof to break into the town hall where cabinet ministers were meeting. Her injuries were described ambiguously.

The greatest amount of newspaper space was devoted to accounts of her hunger and thirst strike while at Hollowran Prison in the winter of 1909. The hunger strike was then the chief weapon of the suffragettes, and the public was up in arms over the abhorrent practice of forcible feeding. Viola Lambert became the focal point of this reaction, a symbol. The days passed, and Miss Lambert refused steadfastly to abandon the strike. Then came the startling news of her release from prison before the end of her term. The intervention of a prominent person was suspected.

Might that person have been Byron Tremaine, acting in response to her frantic appeal?

I continued my research, and found the final reference of the year to Miss Lambert, dated December 28, 1909. Her name and 88 Chessham Court were cross-referenced and both an article and an editorial had appeared. I scrolled the microfilm to the page listed for the article, and looked in horror at the headline: SUFFRAGETTES PERISH IN BLAZE.

"A fire raged through 88 Chessham Court in the hours before dawn yesterday. The building was occupied by leaders of the suffrage movement. All are believed to have perished. Firemen were still searching for bodies in the smouldering ruins this morning, but no hope of finding anyone alive remains. Tenants of a first floor flat were able to make their escape. From the nature of the blaze and its rapid spread, arson is suspected. The fire was possibly set in revenge for recent acts of arson by the militant suffragettes. (See Editorial on page 22)."

Appalled, I looked down the column to the listing of the dead. As I had feared from the moment I saw the headline, Viola Lambert was among them.

With shaking hands, I scrolled the microfilm to the editorial page. The *Globe* had been a most conservative newspaper, and the editorial was condemnatory. While expressing regret at the loss of life, it declared the suffragettes had brought the fire on themselves by their own rash actions. The editorial expressed the hope that the deaths would serve as a deterrent to other women.

"The house at Chessham Court will not of itself be missed; it was known to be disreputable, disorderly, an affront to decent English women. Suffragettes and their menfriends cohabited there."

# Chapter Fourteen

USUALLY VIOLA SLEPT WELL AFTER making love. Tonight, however, as soon as James had closed his eyes, her thoughts turned to the troubling events of the previous day. It had begun auspiciously. Lord Hargreave had made good his promise and been in touch with Ian Crosbie, second-in-command to Richard Everett Sharpe. An appointment was arranged and the interview took place that very morning. At the outset she was confident; surely Captain Sharpe must agree she was qualified, her body toughened physically by the demonstrations, by the privations of prison.

When she entered the office, she was stunned by the high level of noise and activity, with salesmen coming and going with sample cases, trying to gain attention. Coils of rope, piles of timbers, sledge runners, skis, and pony harnesses had been piled on the oriental rugs. When she looked around, however, it seemed to her that one man dominated the room. Lieutenant Crosbie. He was large, huge really, six feet, six inches, at a guess, broad of shoulders and chest, powerfully muscled. His features were large; the lower part of his face was covered with a beard even blacker than his hair, but his hazel eyes were curiously melting, and beneath the mustache, his mouth was soft. An expression of sweetness was surprising in so heroic a man. Viola was instantly drawn to him, and could tell he felt an attraction as well.

After a moment Viola became aware of Captain Sharpe, seated behind his desk, dark, handsome, intense.

She was lovely, this girl, thought Sharpe, and it was obvious that Crosbie was much taken with her beauty and vitality. He was putting in a word for her, speaking of her participation in Byron Tremaine's Greenland expedition. Sharpe had heard about that; it was quite a story in explorers' circles. Now he realized why Tremaine had taken her along, why Crosbie wanted her now. Sharpe wished to please Crosbie, whom he saw as essential to his conquest of the South Pole. Crosbie had proven his courage on previous expeditions, where he carried injured men on his back across the ice and dragged needed supplies with a shoulder harness. Unfortunately, satisfying Crosbie's sexual urges was not reason enough to take a woman to the Antarctic. Sharpe was consumed with worry over how he would get strong, fit, well-trained men back alive from the South Pole. No, he could not waste his time on Miss Lambert. He was courteous, but brought the interview to conclusion rapidly.

Lieutenant Crosbie accompanied her to the door. "I'm sorry," he said. His voice was deep, pleasant. He put his hand on her arm, a familiar gesture, not proper even with a woman who was a suffragette, but she had been wanting to touch him, too. She felt the warmth of his hand on her skin beneath the wool of the jacket, the thin silk of the blouse. The way he was looking at her was intent but distracted. She knew what that look meant, felt a sudden flash of excitement, was sexually attuned to him. The aura he gave off was one of heroism, sexuality. She was aware of the big body beneath his naval uniform.

In just this way had she been aware of Byron that cold afternoon in Greenland when she saw the whiteness of his skin glimmer in the dim light within the hut, when she put out her hand and touched him. Byron was married now, and sometimes in the morning before she was fully awake, she would imagine that he was making love to his bride in just the way he had with her—passionate, grasping her so that the marks of his fingers showed on her flesh for hours afterward. Only now, standing so close to Lieutenant Crosbie, Byron's image receded.

Out on the street again, her common sense reasserted itself. She would never see Lieutenant Crosbie again. A man like that, so attractive to women, gives off a sexual aura unconsciously.

The exchange with him had briefly taken her mind off the crushing blow of Sharpe's cold rejection. As she walked down Victoria Street to the tube station, Viola thought she had expected too much of the Hargreave intervention.

Upon her return home, she entered into an unpleasant scene with Lesley. During the weeks Viola was in prison, the suffrage leadership had been split by a faction favoring a greater militancy. The legislative measures under discussion were insulting. Particularly offensive was a proposed Conciliation Bill for Women's Suffrage that would give the vote only to women who owned property; most wives would be excluded, because property belonged to husbands. Even this unsatisfactory bill was viewed as too extreme, and was not expected to pass. Violence was the only way to make officials and the public take notice of the suffrage movement—arson.

Only a small number of suffragettes espoused the more extreme course, but a small group was enough to do the damage. To Viola's dismay, Lesley, and under her influence, Carla and Jeremy, were proponents of the new philosophy. Eighty-eight Chessham Court became the center for the new militancy. Two castles in Northumberland had already been put to the torch and a town meeting hall in Manchester burned at midnight.

Viola was appalled. Setting fires was a criminal act carrying heavy prison sentences. Worse yet, fires were impossible to control. Lesley insisted that they burned only uninhabited buildings—government offices after hours, country mansions belonging to members of the nobility and landed gentry known to be in London for the social season. But that did not take into account the watchmen, caretakers, and servants left behind. No one had been killed or injured. Not yet. Day after day, she argued, trying to make Lesley, Carla, and their supporters see the inhumanity of their actions. They refused to listen, uplifted by the attention the suffragettes were receiving.

The arson could not go on, thought Viola. They were sensible women after all. But it was alarming to return home as she did today to find Lesley and two WSPU members studying a city plan, deciding where the next strike should be.

James came in then and smoothed over the quarrel, as no one but he could do. Somehow, nothing ever seemed so desperate when he was there. Lesley put away the city plan; quiet returned to 88 Chessham Court. Viola was able to believe that tomorrow Lesley would agree to abandon her arson plans. With James smiling at her, even the Sharpe rejection did not seem so devastating. She told him about meeting Ian Crosbie, and it seemed to her he looked at her quizzically, as if sensing a rival. But then James saw romance in every encounter.

Sometimes she thought she should end the love affair with Jamie, if indeed love affair it could be called when it was so light, so easy. Her reason for being with him was not worthy: He helped her to put Byron Tremaine out of her mind. The nights they lay together were the only nights she did not think of Byron at the last moment before she went to sleep. James was not an admirable person, she told herself; he had no real commitment to suffrage, lived at Chessham Court because sex was so freely available there. She knew about the rich women he escorted. What was she—a serious person, a scientist, whose previous lover was a hero—what was she doing with him? And then she thought how generously he had offered to give her baby his name.

When he put out his hand, she took it and went up the rickety stairs with him to her box of a room. It was bitterly cold that night, colder indoors than out. They made love with their clothes on, merely removing their shoes, opening this fastening or that, his hand inside her shirtwaist, under her skirt, hers within his trousers. James was so skillful with his caresses, his butterfly kisses on her eyelids, her throat. Experienced. She knew how experienced he was, but who could be possessive of him? She could barely see his features in the darkness of the room, but she knew he was smiling, always smiling. He had a way of laughing a little when he reached his climax. It charmed her. Oh, Jamie.

But afterward, when he had fallen asleep, one hand still resting on her breast, the argument with Lesley reasserted itself. Flames and plumes of black smoke had poured out of the Northumberland castles; she had read the newspaper accounts.

Thinking of those fires, it seemed to Viola she could smell the smoke, the kerosene-soaked rags dropped inside the buildings. Her imagination was so vivid that she started to cough. In a moment she was gasping. This would never do; she must gain control of her emotions.

All at once she realized it was not her imagination, and she sat up in horror, her eyes staring at the wisps of black smoke sifting through the tiny fissures in the walls; the smell of kerosene-soaked rags was real.

"Jamie!" she cried. He slept lightly, always ready to rouse himself for caresses. His hand on her breast tightened, and then, as the smoke reached him, he began to gasp and cough. For just an instant they looked at one another, terror-stricken, and then they leaped out of bed. The floor beneath their stockinged feet was hot; the room was filling with smoke. Viola opened the door a crack and peered out. The hall and stairway were filled with smoke, and little tongues of flame were climbing the steps. Slamming the door shut, she followed James to the window, the only possible escape route. This room was on the fourth floor, but the heavy vines of ivy, growing for two hundred years, might hold their weight.

Almost at the window, she stopped short, all at once aware of the others in the house. What if they were still sleeping? She could not abandon them. James was turning away from the window, too. "You get to Lesley," he said, coughing harder with the effort to speak. "I'll go downstairs and wake the others."

But the stairway was burning. "You can't do it, Jamie."

"I'll get down. I'm always lucky." In the smoke-filled room, Viola could not tell if he was smiling.

The smoke was rising; they were coughing and choking. Viola remembered the water jug on the dresser, hurriedly overturned it on the towels placed on the bed for their lovemaking. Instinctively they covered themselves with the wet towels, dropped to the floor, and crawled to the door. The brass doorknob was glowing by then; James reached up and turned it, wincing, and forced the door open. Unbearable heat and clouds of black smoke assaulted them. Viola watched the soles of his feet as James crept down the hall and disappeared in the smoke blanketing the stairwell.

Pulling a corner of the wet towel over her face, Viola turned toward Lesley's room. Nothing was visible, and she groped her way to where she thought the door must be. It was just a few feet, but the floor was searing her knees and the palms of her hands. At last she crawled through the open doorway, and remembered that Lesley would never stay in a closed room even when she made love. A closed door made her feel she was in prison, she said. The room was filled with smoke, and little fires were licking around the baseboards. Rising to her knees, barely able to breathe, she thought how small Lesley looked lying on the bed, how helpless. Had she been angry with Lesley? That seemed so unimportant now.

Calling Lesley's name, Viola stood beside the bed, grasped the slight, limp body, and shook her. Lesley did not respond. She needed fresh air. The room was so tiny that the window was barely a foot away. Unlike the door, it was tightly closed. Viola tried to open it, but the frame was hot, swollen. With her bare hand, she smashed the windowpane, unaware that the shattered glass was cutting her hand and arm.

Grasping Lesley tightly, she half dragged, half carried her to the window. Clambering onto the windowsill, she looked out. The ground was a long way down, terrifying, but the fire raging behind her was even more horrific. Lesley must regain consciousness so as to put her arms around Viola's neck. She slapped Lesley's face once, then again harder, but there was no reaction. In desperation, Viola took off her belt and fastened Lesley to her back. Then she climbed through the broken pane, ignoring the jagged edges of the glass. The ivy vine was just out of her reach. Somehow she must bend far enough to grasp it without allowing Lesley's weight to cause her to catapult to the ground four stories below.

As her head cleared in the cold air, she became aware of activity below. Of course, someone must have called the fire department, but she dared not wait for the firemen to rescue them. Flames and smoke were bursting through the windows beneath her. The vine, heated by the fire radiating from the house, was painful to clutch when she fastened her hands and then her legs around it and began to climb down through the flames. If only she could breathe properly; her lungs were full of smoke and she felt dizzy. Every movement made her choke and cough more violently. Inert, Lesley's light body had become a heavy weight, dragging her down.

A ladder was being raised against the wall of the house. At last, she thought. Her strength was giving way. Then her heart sank when she discovered that, extended to its greatest length, the ladder was still too far away for her to get her feet onto the top rung.

"Drop her." As if she would do that. Lesley must be saved. What was going on below? The smoke was so thick she could see nothing. "Into the net. Drop her into the net." She should have known the firemen would be equipped with a net. With a feeling of hope, she twisted her legs around the hot vine, reached back and unbuckled the belt attaching Lesley to her back. Then she took hold of Lesley's body, and threw her down, one story, two stories, three. A cry went up. Choking and coughing, Viola was close to losing consciousness herself. Even relieved of the burden of Lesley, Viola knew she would not be able to climb down the few feet separating her from the ladder. She looked about desperately, unwilling to give up even now.

People were shouting, but at first she was too faint to take in the words. The shouts grew louder, until at last she understood. One word, over and over—"Jump!" In her confusion it had not occurred to her that the net could catch her, too. Almost without thought, she let go the vine and in an instant was hurtling through the air, her arms thrown over her head to protect it, as they had been on that day when she fell from the rope in the town hall at MidValley. She was caught by the net, and felt it swaying sickeningly under her, the web biting into her flesh. Hands reached for her and lifted her off the net, carried her across the street and put her down. She had escaped, and the joy and relief at being on the ground were doubled by the knowledge that she had saved Lesley.

The smoke was trapped in her lungs, and every breath was agonizing. As full consciousness returned, she became aware of the pain from the burns she had sustained and the cuts from the broken glass. Her hands and feet were bloodied and blistered and she could see the red angry burns and slashes on her arms. Her shoulders ached from the strain of supporting her own weight and Lesley's on the ivy.

But where was Lesley? She must be nearby. Viola jumped up so as to see better and nearly fell as her leg would not support her weight. The pain in her foot was agonizing. She must have injured it severely in the fire or in the drop into the net. "Let me help you to the ambulance, miss," said a policeman, putting his arm around her for support. "It's just on the next corner."

As the dizziness left her, she observed a woman lying on the ground close by. The woman's foot was uncovered. Whose foot was so tiny and thin? Lesley's foot, and she was so quiet she must still be unconscious.

"I don't need an ambulance. My friend is the one who needs help. How can you let her lie there like that on the ground? Take her to the ambulance. Right away." She was too upset to speak politely to the policeman.

"No point in it, miss," he replied. "She's dead."

"Dead?" That was why Lesley was lying on the sidewalk with her head at an improbable angle. Dead. Was it Viola's fault? Had she killed Lesley when she threw her down?

"She was dead before she ever dropped into the net," the policeman was saying. "A little thing like that. She must have died of the smoke right away."

During that whole fearsome descent, Viola had been carrying a dead body. It was almost like a joke, a bitter, terrible joke.

Now she thought of the others in the house. James had crawled down the stairs to awaken the others; she remembered her last glimpse of the soles of his feet. Had he been in time to save them and himself? Before the fire she had been aware of his weaknesses; now she thought only of what courage he had shown. She turned her head this way and that searching for him.

Pushing the startled policeman out of her way, she managed to stumble across the street, barely aware of the pain in her foot and leg, forgetting that her stockings were in rags and her shoes lost in the house. A barricade blocked her way. "Let me through. I live there." Her throat was so raw from the smoke that her voice was hoarse, rasping.

"No one lives there, miss. Not now," said the policeman.

"But my friends. I must find my friends." She was close to hysteria.

"Get back, miss, this place ain't safe."

"How many people got out?"

"A whole family, miss." They had lived on the ground floor and escaped easily. The suffragettes had taken the upper floors, because of the lower rent.

Seeing her distress, the policeman spoke more kindly. "The firemen are trying to get into the house, miss. If any people are alive in there, they'll be found. You have to get back."

Viola hobbled to the other side of the street; it was getting harder for her to walk. All was confusion around her. The horses that had pulled the fire wagons were tossing their heads and neighing. A crowd had formed behind the police barricade. Although it was not yet daybreak, neighbors had been awakened by the fire bell and come out to see what was happening. Viola peered into the faces around her, but not one of her friends was in view. Her exhaustion was such that she was swaying, ready to fall. She began to shiver uncontrollably, and realized only then how cold it was, a December dawn, and she was barely dressed. All her clothing, down to the petticoats, was torn and singed. A woman in the crowd took off her shawl and put it around Viola's shoulders.

Suddenly she heard someone call her name, and there was Lieutenant Crosbie standing beside her. A feeling of relief—she could not say why—came over her. He put his arms around her, steadied her. She leaned against him, not thinking that he was little more than a stranger.

"What made you come here?"

"I sleep badly," he replied. "I awaken in the last hours before dawn and walk through the city. And I saw the reddened sky to the north where there should be no red, the billows of black smoke, and walked in that direction. All at once, I realized where I was. Near Chessham Court . . . near you."

He had run the last few blocks, filled with fear that he was too late and she was dead and lost to him. He hardly knew her, but the moment he had seen her in Sharpe's office, he had been dazzled. A woman scientist—he imagined she would be plain. Seeing her, he had wondered if she were Lord Hargreave's . . . mistress? Oh, no, he could not bear to think that. Why, she was beautiful. More than beautiful. Vitality radiated from her. It was when he saw the red in the sky that he knew he loved her.

"I was afraid . . . you might be dead." Her face was reddened from the heat, and big black smudges ran down her cheeks, but the glints of copper in her loosened hair were as bright as the flames she had escaped.

They had just met and he had been afraid for her. "Lesley is dead," she said, "Lesley Penner, the suffragette leader. I broke the window and carried her out and down the ivy vine, not knowing she was already dead."

"You did what?" he asked.

She spoke as if her action were natural, the normal thing to do. Ian had never imagined a woman could show such courage, the kind of courage that won men medals. He had arranged the interview with Sharpe merely to please Lord Hargreave. In his heart, he viewed Viola's desire to join the expedition as ludicrous. Now it seemed to him that Viola was the only woman in the world who belonged in the Antarctic.

"Do you think anyone could still be alive in the house?"

"How many are there, Miss Lambert?"

"I'm not sure. Maybe four." There could be more; sometimes visiting suffragettes stayed overnight, sleeping on blankets on the floor.

Across the street, the steam pumps on the fire engines were forcing streams of water through the long hoses. Some of the firemen were hacking at the front door with axes, while others were climbing ladders to attain access through the windows.

"Wait here." Ian pushed his way through the crowd, crossed the street, and went through the police barricade. He was so large, so imposing in his naval lieutenant's uniform, that no one stopped him. As he approached the house, the firemen succeeded in breaking in the door. Taking off his coat, he put it over his head, mounted the steps, and ran into the house.

Lieutenant Crosbie was placing himself in unbelievable danger and Viola was filled with fear for him. What if she lost him, too? Time passed and still he did not come out. Why had he braved the flames? For her?

After so long a time that she was almost certain he must be trapped, Lieutenant Crosbie appeared in the doorway and staggered down the steps, his face blackened by the smoke, his clothing blazing with live sparks. He walked toward her, putting out the little flames with his burned and blistered hands. The relief at seeing him alive was so great she could have fallen.

"It's no use. There's a body on the ground floor, a man I think." Viola's heart sank. What could the body be like that he was not sure?

"I tried to pull him out, but he was too tightly wedged by some boards. The stairs had given way, Miss Lambert."

How many had been trapped on the upper floors? Clearly no one else in the building had escaped. Why did James have to be at home when he might so easily have been off with one of his ladies, nattily dressed in his only good suit with the snowy white shirt he ironed himself and the striped tie from the not quite top-ranked school?

More policemen arrived on the scene, leading dogs on long leashes. The crowd murmured that dogs were trained to sniff out bodies. Crosbie looked at the dogs and recoiled violently, his face contorted. Viola wondered that Lieutenant Crosbie was so moved when he knew none of the people trapped in the house.

Two firemen came out of the burning building, pulling off their helmets, mopping their blackened faces. "That fire was set," one of them was saying. "Everything's in flames. It's a case of arson all right."

"Them suffragettes got more than they bargained for."

Viola shuddered. Arson. The homily that violence breeds violence was proven once again. Chessham Court had been the center of the suffrage movement. Lesley's presence there had made it so. Despite her tragically mistaken espousal of arson, Lesley had symbolized an ideal, fought for suffrage with an energy that became legendary. *To doubt is to be weakened.*

Too dazed by pain and shock to resist any longer, Viola was barely aware of the policemen carrying her to the ambulance. Lieutenant Crosbie wanted to go to the hospital with her, but the attendants would not allow it.

Her feet were even more badly burned than her hands and legs, and one was broken; her ankle was sprained, and the cuts made by the glass required stitching, but as soon as her injuries were treated and bandaged and she had rested for a few hours, she insisted on leaving the hospital. She could manage on the crutches provided her. The doctor urged her to remain overnight, but his manner was cold; he did not think highly of suffragettes.

One of the nurses brought clothing to replace the burned and torn garments she had been wearing. These clothes had belonged to a patient who had died, unknown and unclaimed. The heavy wool skirt was too short for Viola's tall figure, the blouse hung on her slender frame, the coat was too tight under the arms and worn through at the elbows, and she could not get the poorly made shoes over her heavily bandaged feet. Still, at least she was covered decently and was free of the smell of smoke, of burning.

It was only when she was outside, leaning on her crutches on the steps of the hospital, that she realized night had fallen and she had no place to go and not a shilling in the pocket of the ill-fitting coat. All was lost in the fire at Chessham Court. For the first time in her life, no one was waiting for her.

And then in the flickering flame of the streetlight, Viola saw that a man, tall, powerfully built, was walking up and down. Why, someone was waiting for her after all.

Crosbie had been there all day, forgetful of his responsibility to Sharpe, trying to decide what to do when Viola appeared. Did he dare take her to his flat? He had shied away from relationships with women for years. After the last hideous episode. It was safer that way.

As soon as he saw her, his hesitation left him. "Come home with me." His voice was thick with desire and apprehension.

Her answer came swiftly; her voice was firm. "Yes, I will."

Despite his pleasure, Ian was shocked that she did not observe propriety, ask whether he had a wife or lived with a mother. Of course, he had no wife, and his mother would have nothing more to do with him, but Viola was not to know that. There was not even a housekeeper, only a charwoman who came in three mornings a week.

Hailing a motor taxi, he took her to his flat on Clarges Street. Ian had never before been troubled by its ugliness—dark, with small rooms made to seem smaller still by the massive mahogany Victorian furniture and elaborate velvet draperies festooned over the windows. He rented the place furnished and never had the interest to make any changes. It was not as if he invited anyone to his home. But now he feared Miss Lambert would be repelled by it, and he was relieved that, preoccupied, she barely glanced at her surroundings. Ian marveled at the way she brightened the room by her presence, by the brilliance of her coloring. Like a portrait painted by a Renaissance master.

Careful not to alarm her, he quickly told her she was to take his bedroom, his bed, even his nightshirt, and he would lie on the horsehair couch in the parlor. Did she seem a trifle disappointed, or was he reading something into her glance? He was unaccustomed to dealing with women of good family, had for so long taken his pleasure, as it was called, with paid companions. Aware that she was lying in the next room, he did not sleep that night.

In the morning, she said she must go to the headquarters of the Women's Social and Political Union, the WSPU, which was located in a run-down building on the western end of Oxford Street. They would be expecting her, and as she found it hard to walk, even with her crutches, she asked if she could borrow the price of a hansom cab. He would be repaid by the suffragettes; they took up a collection when one of them was in trouble.

It seemed likely they would also find her a place to live, Ian thought gloomily. Had she come with him only because she had nowhere else to go? He had known her for barely a day . . . and he wanted to change his life. But how did she feel? He did not know how to ask her to come back. Bringing her home last night had required his last bit of nerve.

The mood in WSPU headquarters was dark, heavy; it lifted only when Viola hobbled in on her crutches. "We were sure you were dead." The morning newspapers reported that all the suffragettes who made 88 Chessham Court a center for militancy had died in the fire.

Viola had hardly completed the account of her escape from the flames when the door was flung open and, to her amazement, Lord Hargreave walked into the room. His opposition to suffrage was well known; some of the women muttered that he should be put out. As always, his appearance was distinguished and his bearing haughty, but Viola observed that his clothing was not neat. For some reason he had left his home so hurriedly that his valet had not been given time to complete his dressing properly.

"Thank God you're here. I thought you were dead. The newspapers said . . ." Hargreave had been distraught, and hastened to WSPU headquarters in the desperate hope that the newspapers were wrong. Viola had never imagined he could be so affected by what happened to her, and was touched, but a little embarrassed, by the emotion he displayed.

"Viola, now that I've found you again, I don't want to let you go."

The words troubled her, and she tried to pass them off. "I'm not going anywhere, Lord Hargreave. I'm safe."

"George. I would like you to call me George."

Not "Sir George." The suggestion that she use his first name implied a greater intimacy than she liked.

"Come home with me, Viola."

He spoke as if they were alone, she thought; but then, a man like Lord Hargreave was barely aware that people of a lower social class existed.

"I couldn't do that," she replied, startled.

He realized he had not made himself clear. Suffragette though she was, Viola was a well-born young woman, shocked no doubt at the suggestion that she go unaccompanied to the home of an unmarried man, a widower. "I don't mean that in any illicit manner," he said. "I want you to be my wife, Viola. I love you."

But he was an old man. What could he be thinking of? And then she realized she had been inexcusably dense in accepting all he had done for her without thinking why he had done it. He saved her from imprisonment after the failure at MidValley, rescued her from the hunger strike at Hollowran. His motives were not disinterested. Older men did find younger women attractive; that was a truism. Lord Hargreave, too. He had acted on her behalf because he desired her. That was clear enough now. A man of his prominence and social position was accustomed to satisfying his impulses. The only surprising part of it was his willingness to go so far as marriage.

Her response was stiff, formal, but how else was one to speak to a lord of the realm, and one offering his hand in marriage? "It's an honor, George. It means a lot to me that you ask me to be your wife. But marriage is not for me. My life is following a different course."

She was in shock, thought Lord Hargreave. He did not really believe she would reject him when she was calm again. He had been attractive to women for thirty-five years, still looked no more than fifty, he was told. He would give her time to get over the initial shock of the fire.

Soon after he left, word came from a sympathizer in the police department that three bodies, all unidentifiable, had been found so far, but more might be hidden in the rubble. The suffragettes considered the possibilities. Besides Viola and Lesley, Jeremy, Wilbert, James, and a Miss Rolland, come from Manchester to join in a march on Parliament, were known to have been in the house.

"And Carla," added Viola.

But it appeared that everyone else knew Carla was safe, called to a rally in Birmingham some hours before the fire.

Carla arrived in the late afternoon and embraced Viola; they both wept, speaking of their losses. "Let's stay together, Viola. We're the only ones left from Chessham Court. You tried to save Lesley; I'll never forget that. Some friends of mine have a flat on Witherington Road in Islington, and they've been looking for mates. We can move in with them, make another Chessham Court."

Another Chessham Court. But the house there had burned down because of the suffragettes' use of arson. All around her were cries that the deaths must be avenged. "The fire was set. We can't take this lying down! If it's arson they want, we'll give it to them."

Viola stood up painfully, grasping at her crutches. "I can't be a part of it. As long as you're supporting arson, I can't be in the movement."

"But you don't have anyplace to go."

For a moment, she felt lost, purposeless, and then she remembered the previous night when she had seen Lieutenant Crosbie in the glimmer of the flickering gas streetlamps. He seemed to her at that moment as brilliant as the flames. "I have a place to go." She was going to Ian Crosbie.

As he opened the door to her knock, his face lit up: "Viola." He hesitated a moment in case she would object to the familiarity, but she seemed to take it for granted, so he went on. "I am seldom altogether happy, Viola. Even when there is a good event, something in the back of my mind tells me it will go wrong." What could possibly go wrong for him, this man known for his heroic exploits, second only to Captain Sharpe? "But when I opened the door just now and saw you standing there, the feeling that came over me was one of pure joy."

For a moment, she shared that joy. And then, as he went out to pay the hansom cab driver, she thought of all that was gone in the fire, the dead body in her arms, the loss of Lesley and the men of 88 Chessham Court. How could she ever be happy again? But then Ian returned and spoke to her so kindly that she felt comforted. "You did everything you could, Viola. It's not your fault they wouldn't listen when you tried to convince them of the folly of arson. You awakened James Armour. It was his choice to try to save the others instead of escaping through the window. And Miss Penner . . . why, if she had been able to withstand the smoke, you would have saved her." Listening to Ian, Viola thought that, though she would never fully get over these tragedies, she would in time become able to live with them.

A chapter of her life story had come to an end and another chapter had begun.

It seemed only natural to stay with Ian in his flat while the severe injuries she had sustained were healing. He brought the expedition's medical officer to take care of Viola. The doctor told everyone in the Sharpe office where she was staying. Ian did not notice. Viola did not care. She had grown accustomed to the casual living arrangements of the suffragettes. As it was hard for her to travel on crutches, Ian went out to buy her clothing and gave Mrs. Abbot, the charwoman, money for food. Mrs. Abbot provided help grudgingly; she made obvious her disapproval of Viola's unchaperoned presence in the flat.

Unchaperoned. But Ian never put his hand on her, dared not do that. He wondered if he ever could. Night after night, he lay on the sofa, aware of her in the bedroom close by, her body naked beneath the nightgown he had bought her. Awakening in the hours before the dawn, he heard her stirring, breathing, murmuring in her sleep. If he were to go in to her, would she push him away? He must be careful, he thought, not to rush her, not to behave in any way that would frighten her. Above all, he must be sure he was in control of himself. It was better this way. Wait. Above all, he must wait. No matter how much he desired her, he must not touch her.

Instead, they talked through the evenings after Ian returned from Sharpe's office. He was careful then, too, to speak only of his exploits as an explorer, never about the events that had preceded them. Though he was self-deprecating, his life spoke for him. He had been repeatedly commended for bravery, awarded medals by the geographical societies of three countries. Men would have died but for his strength and daring. Heroic. Yes, that was the way his deeds were described. Only he knew them to be no more than the actions of a man desperately trying to prove himself.

His diction was careful, the Scottish accent so slight that most people believed him to have been born in England. He preferred it that way. If he could have wiped out the years in Scotland, he would have done so. He never revealed anything of his childhood or his parents.

When Viola questioned him, he turned the conversation to the Sharpe expedition, now in its final planning stage, described the supplies they would take, the icebreaker, the intended route, the date of departure: early summer. So soon, said Viola. Were they to leave later, they might find themselves in a race to the Pole with Shackleton, who was beginning to organize a new expedition. The dangers of getting up and over the summit of Beardmore Glacier would be greater by far if they had to travel at breakneck speed with a rival explorer at their heels. Shackleton was the only potential competitor, as the formidable Danish explorer, Erik Carlsen, was intent on the Arctic.

Viola was fascinated by every detail, shared Ian's excitement, but with an undercurrent of envy. She, too, was seized by the lure of exploration, and she had been summarily rejected first by Peary, then by Sharpe, because of her gender. She was amazed to discover that Ian favored suffrage, not guessing that he had never given it a thought before, but was ready to take up the cause of equality because that was her cause. Equality. His support wavered, however, when she told him about 88 Chessham Court. This was equality, too. Men and women living together. Living together? What did she mean by living together? The scenes that flashed through his mind were intolerable. Did she sleep with one of the men? With all of them? And explain it by the principle of suffrage? Free love had seemed harmless to him until he thought of Viola in that connection. Surely Viola did not engage in sexual activities with any of those men. Byron Tremaine. He had heard something of that. Shackleton had spoken of it. That was shocking, too. But understandable. She had been so young, Tremaine had taken advantage. No one else.

Sir George Arnold Comstock, Lord Hargreave? Ian had originally thought there must be a sexual connection between them. But she never mentioned Hargreave. There must have been some other reason, family perhaps, for Hargreave to have asked for the letter of introduction to Sharpe.

"Captain Sharpe didn't believe I was responsible for making discoveries in Greenland, for developing the theory to explain them. No one else did either, or ever will."

"I believe it."

"When I think of the fossil record that must be hidden in the Antarctic ice, Ian, I long to be there. Now my only hope is that Byron Tremaine will take me with him."

"He is not your only hope, Viola. I will be leading an Antarctic expedition of my own one day. The Sharpe expedition will reach the South Pole, but that's hardly the end of exploration. Most of the vast continent is uncharted. Generations of explorers will be going there, making discoveries.

"And when I go, Viola, you'll be with me."

The Antarctic would be hers. Her future was written on Ian's face. When she impulsively took his hand in both of hers, there was a slight drawing back. It had been that way all along; he never touched her. In the beginning she thought he was being sensitive, did not wish it to appear that he expected her to pay for his care, so to speak, by making love. But by now she wondered if there were not a simpler explanation. He had taken her in after the fire as a good deed and was not attracted to her sexually. The thought was painful, as she had not felt so attracted to any man in her life, excepting Byron in an earlier time. Each night lying in bed, she was conscious of Ian close by in the parlor. Each time she heard him stirring, she wondered if he would come in to her, was disappointed when he did not. That they would become lovers had seemed inevitable to her. She had misread the situation. It was time to move on.

The day the doctor took off the bandages, she made a tracing of her foot and asked Ian to buy her shoes. He would be repaid for all he had spent on her; she would go directly to the main post office to pick up her quarterly allowance check. Then, as the policy of arson was being abandoned, she would return to suffrage, move into the flat on Witherington Road.

A flat on Witherington Road. With men as well as women, no doubt. How could he let her go? How could he hold her? And then in his desperation at the thought of losing her, he moved toward her and at last seized her in his arms. She had not misread him after all. Only then, for just an instant as he embraced her, she had an instinct of—it could not be—fear. Absurd. It was simply that his size and powerful build were overwhelming. In a moment, he was caressing her gently, stroking her hair. She reached up, touching his face, feeling his black beard and mustache silky in her hand.

He stood up then and drew her into the bedroom. When he took off his clothes, she marveled at his body, at the breadth of his shoulders, his pectoral muscles, the pelvic ridge. She wondered if he meant to undress her, but he made no move, so she took off her dress and undergarments herself, while he watched. When she stood in front of him naked, he gasped. "How beautiful you are." Again, there was a moment of hesitation, and then he took her in his arms, lay down on the bed with her. After waiting so long, she could hardly believe it was happening. She wanted him; there was a rush of heat to the groin. They were both breathing hard, but he moved slowly, carefully, making the most of their excitement, building desire. His hands stroking her body were so big. And so gentle. He spoke to her so softly. His kisses were light, his fingertips touched her breasts. She had never sensed such tenderness.

His style of lovemaking moved her deeply. Perhaps it was that she had never thought a man could be so big, so powerful, yet so sensitive, more thoughtful of her pleasure, it seemed, than his own. It was as though he were moving forward, then stopping himself, and moving back. Waiting. His big body lay on hers lightly; he was supporting his weight on his elbows. She began to make love to him then herself, touching his body in the ways that Byron said nice women did not do. During these weeks in his flat, she had imagined holding all that power within her. And oh, she could not wait. It was time to be done with caresses. Their bodies were moving together in a rhythm that became ever faster, and at the last she cried out. He was silent.

Lying beside him then, she seized his hand, kissed it. He grasped her hand tightly in return and then released it. Even if he kept her with him until he left on the Sharpe expedition, it would not be enough. To return to an empty flat after reaching the South Pole—his triumph would be empty, too. There was only one way to make certain she would be here, waiting for him, and so he spoke the words he had never thought to say. "I want to marry you, Viola," he said hoarsely. "I love you."

Marriage. She had been opposed to it for years. The suffragettes had taught her that you do not have to marry a man because you want him. She had fought off Byron (though she loved him, could not even now say she had not) because the state of marriage had seemed to her to demand subservience. But what was there to fight here? She was being offered marriage by a man who viewed her as an equal. Again, she thought of Byron. Her fossil discoveries had been taken from her, as his right, his due. When will you learn, Viola? he asked after she had been rejected by Peary. He was determined to dominate her sexually, as in all other ways. Ian did not try to dominate her sexually. No. A marriage with Ian would bring her what she had never dreamed could be possessed—mutual respect and the kind of life men have by virtue of their gender. Carla and her other friends among the suffragettes would disapprove, believe she had weakened, yielded to societal pressures. They did not know this marriage would bring her exactly what the suffrage movement sought to achieve for women—a full life, combining love, desire, passion, and the satisfaction of work. Byron? She would forget him. For the first time since the day he had called her to his hut, she realized that she could forget him for more than an hour or a night. She could forget him.

Heroes: Tremaine and Crosbie. In that they were alike, but where Byron was hard, could be cruel, saw sex as a game of domination, Ian was gentle, tender.

Of course she would marry him. It seemed natural, right.

Ian had been so careful when making love with Viola, afraid of losing control of himself and hurting or frightening her. Yet that had gone well. He had not allowed himself to reach a climax, but she had, and her cry was of ecstasy, not pain. Still, he could hardly believe he had won her. What a fraud he was! If she knew all there was to know about him, she would flee.

He remembered with horror how awful it had been. The loss of control. One time, he still shuddered to think of it, he killed his brother's dog. Though conceding it was an act of madness, his brother never forgave him. What came over him? Sometimes even now he could see the dog's dripping muzzle and the red, bloodshot eyes staring at him. He could not remember actually killing the dog. With his bare hands, it was said. And he was just a boy then, fourteen or so. People were afraid of him. Even when he was fourteen, he was more than six feet tall.

He had never overcome his revulsion at dogs. It was not the dogs which revolted him, of course, but what they made him recognize. He was revolted by himself. Ian was relieved by Sharpe's decision to use motorized sledges and Siberian ponies, rather than depend exclusively on dogs. Sharpe actually preferred man-hauling. There Ian, with his great strength, could excel.

After the episode with the dog, a doctor dosed him with laudanum to keep him quiet. After a while, he gave that up, fearing addiction. Worse was to follow.

When he was sixteen, he raped a girl, broke her arm when she struggled. That was another of those times he could not remember. His parents, who were prominent in the town, hushed up the whole thing, paid the girl's family, he believed. But it happened again. The second time his parents committed him to a madhouse. Not what they called it, of course, but what it was. Two years of hell. He was discharged, quiet, determined never to let it happen again, went to the university, was a model student. His size made him an obvious choice for the rugby team. Then he nearly killed a player on the opposing team; his history came out and he was asked to leave the university.

His father pulled strings, obtained a commission for him in the navy, making him promise never to return to Scotland. He could understand, though not forgive, his parents for being ashamed of his madness; he had stood stony faced when his mother wept while saying good-bye. Still, it all worked out better than he would have expected. Away from Scotland and in the navy, no one knew about him. No one need ever know. If only he remained calm. Once he learned about the expeditions to the Antarctic, he knew he had found his way to safety. His size and strength would be valued there. In the Antarctic, he would make up for every wrong he had ever committed. He would prove himself a sane man, a hero.

There was no question that he had done so. Sharpe was waiting for him at Charing Cross Station when he arrived in London after the Shackleton expedition. The offer of the coveted position of second-in-command was made that very day. Later he learned that some of the members of the expedition paid for the opportunity to serve with Sharpe, making contributions of as much as a thousand pounds. Not he. Sharpe was paying him eight pounds a week, three pounds more than the next-ranking man.

For whom had he proven himself if not for Viola? For his parents? They wrote occasionally, but never asked him to return home. His friends of the past? They had broken with him years ago. Everyone he knew now was ignorant of what he had been. As for his history, he concealed it from Sharpe as he had from Shackleton and Charcot. That had seemed reasonable and right to him. But to deceive the woman who would marry him, share his life? That was different. A fraud. A liar. How could he do this? But how could he not? Holding Viola in his arms, he knew he would never be able to bear losing her. Why did he need to tell her? Nearly ten years had passed since the last episode. He was safe now, was he not? The doctor had not been sure. Well, who could be sure of anything?

And the marriage would offer Viola some practical advantages, he told himself. He would arrange to have her receive his pay while he was away on the Sharpe expedition, and should anything happen to him, her widow's pension would amount to some eighty pounds a year. The main thing was that he would make Viola happy during these few months remaining before he left for the Antarctic, and for the rest of his life after his return. Whatever she wanted, she would have. How could Byron Tremaine have been such a fool as to lose her to suffrage? To science? They were an integral part of her life. The vitality that no one else possessed—who could imagine that the so-called womanly existence would content her?

And then he thought, What if there is a child? Did he dare not to warn her? But she asked him hesitantly if he could understand her wish to postpone childbearing until after she had been to the Antarctic. There had been a lost pregnancy, she told him; she could not bear to start again so soon. He was afraid he might cry out in his relief. After the Antarctic. That was far off. He did not need to think about it now.

"Of course, I can accept that. Nothing matters to me but having you"; and then, realizing a suffragette might be offended by that phrasing, he hastily amended it to, "I mean, being with you." Viola was so moved by what she called his generous reaction that he felt guilty. He would use a condom, he assured her. No need, Viola replied; she knew how to protect herself.

Marriage. In view of the imminence of the Sharpe expedition, neither of them wanted to wait. His parents were too old to leave Scotland for the wedding, Ian told her; he did not mention having a brother. Viola thought about her own parents. It was a hard thing to marry without making up with them. Perhaps Evelyn might serve as go-between. But Evelyn responded to Viola's wedding invitation with good wishes and regrets. The phrasing made it obvious that her husband, Bertram, would not allow her to come. Soon afterward, a carefully worded message of congratulations came from her mother. It hardly went so far as reconciliation, but did express approval that Viola was marrying at last. She hoped this meant Viola was through with the foolishness of suffrage. Although she was not due to have access to her inheritance for another fourteen years, her father had generously decided to increase her allowance by a small percentage. Mr. Lambert's health was given as the reason for their refusal to attend the wedding. It seemed an excuse. Yet there was a crack in the wall that had been built up between Viola and her parents.

Two weeks later, with a smiling Captain Sharpe and a disapproving Carla as witnesses, Viola and Ian were married in the Saint Pancras Registry office.

# Chapter Fifteen

VIOLA MARRIED. BYRON COULD HAVE cried out with rage and frustration. She would not marry him. Or anyone, she had insisted. Oh, no, that would destroy her independence. That body against his, her skin radiating heat, the pulse beating wildly in her throat. That strong, slender, passionate body straining in Ian Crosbie's arms, as it had in his.

He even knew the man. That made it worse. They had met when Crosbie, returned from the Charcot expedition, visited the Explorers Club in New York. Not friends: Ian Crosbie was taciturn, kept to himself. But he was brave, no question as to that.

Crosbie's size was what one noticed first. How repugnant this was to Byron now. Those big hands, that big body on Viola, in Viola. That was why she had married Crosbie of course. He knew Viola. She would do anything to satisfy her sexual desires. The ugly pictures in his mind made him feel physically ill. All the ways she had made love with him. Like that first time when she put out her hand and touched him. And she had been a virgin then. Ready to do the gentlemanly thing, he had offered marriage almost immediately upon their return from Greenland. That time she had actually recoiled. The memory rankled still.

The things she had done: She left him to go and live in sin in London. No matter how she cloaked it in suffrage rhetoric, free love had been the lure. Byron could still feel his heart lurch as on the day he knocked on the door to the house on Chessham Court and a handsome blond Englishman stood there looking at him with obvious hostility. Only minutes after that, his doubts left him as her face lit up when she saw him walking into the dingy airless parlor. Only minutes after that, the most bitter of their many quarrels was under way. The things they had said to each other that day. But then, the things he had said to her over the years, the things he had done. Still, she would have driven him mad if he had let her.

Married. One of his friends at the Explorers Club, now in London to join the Sharpe expedition, had been the informant. Knowing that Byron was married himself, his friend had no intention of making him suffer. Yet he did suffer.

He should be glad for Viola, glad she had finally accepted the reality that a woman must have a husband. Instead, with all his heart, he wished Viola misery in her marriage. The black rage engulfing him was against all logic. He had married first. But he had been so hurt by her refusing him, so devastated by the loss of the child, that he hardly knew what he was doing. I will marry and you won't like it a bit. Had he married for no better reason than that? Now it appeared that he was the one who did not like it. He had selected Hermine mainly because she was womanly. He wanted a wife who was womanly. Or so he had thought.

By the time he came to his senses, he was married. He was aware of how rashly he had acted when he lay for the first time with Hermine. His wife. A frightened little girl who averted her eyes when he pulled off his nightshirt. How could he not remember Viola's eyes widening in wonder when she looked at him naked? She had not known a man's body had such . . . *grandeur* . . . that was the word she had used. *Grandeur.* Hermine trembled when he kissed her, lay passively beneath him, so dry, so tight that he did not succeed in penetrating her at all that first night. Eventually he had done so by using a degree of force that was not less brutal because she was so accepting of it. Her mother had told her what she must endure. He had tried to be decent, patted her face, brought a towel and helped her to clean off the blood. What had he done?

Each time he took her, it was not much better. Yielding her body as she knew she must, she could not conceal how she shrank from his touch. Many women, he had heard, lose their frigidity after child-bearing, but giving birth to Susan seemed only to have added to her fears. What had he done?

*Sex between a man and a woman should be like tigers mating.* Odd for Viola to have selected an animal like this when the polar regions were her natural habitat. Had he really made love to her in the snow? It seemed impossible now, as he paced the high-ceilinged drawing room of the elegant town house on Gramercy Park bought ten years before from Stuyvesant Fish. And yet he had. How beautiful she was, her coppery hair brilliant against the white crystals, her blue eyes shining with . . . yes, it was love, not merely desire. She had loved him, he was sure of that, loved him in a violent, tigerish—to use her word—way. Whatever she wanted, she wanted with so great a vigor. She had wanted him then. He could almost hear the throb in her low, thrilling voice when she spoke his name in the act of love. Now she wanted Ian Crosbie.

*Sex between a man and a woman should be like tigers mating.* If he did not analyze that sentence too closely, it made sense, seemed charming. But in truth, it represented the philosophy that led Viola to destroy their lives.

He did not approve of her behavior. Even before England, he had doubted her. There were rumors—the men at the museum laboratory where she worked, even the curator. Her reputation was questionable, and it could not all be due to him.

She accused him of wanting to dominate her. Even his choice of words revealed that, the way he said he "took" her. He could not imagine what she meant. Of course he took her. That was what a man did. He "dominated"—she chose that word, not he—a woman sexually. The man was the larger, the stronger, took the lead in sex as he did in life. Everywhere men were the leaders. Of expeditions, businesses, armies, countries. That was the law of nature. Without his knowing how it happened, the sex act became an act of competition between them. A competition that he won; he was the stronger after all. Won? Not always. Sometimes she could make him melt by the way she made love. No one else could bring as much excitement to the sex act.

More often, though, making love with Viola was a battle, with her biting his neck, raking his back with her nails, or pushing him away, fighting him off. These were the ways she goaded him. Driven almost mad with her perverseness, he would use his greater size and strength to make her do as he wished. And when it was over, it had made no difference. She remained what she was—indomitable, in control, convinced she was his equal. Nothing between them had been changed. She was still independent of him, would do whatever she wanted with her life. The next time they met, the conflict began anew. Were she his wife, he believed, it would be different. A wife had to obey her husband; it was so ordered in the marriage vows.

When he had learned of Viola's pregnancy, he thought she was at last delivered into his hands. Not at all. She had been so determined not to marry him that she miscarried the child she was carrying in an act of folly.

Were she his wife, he would not take her with him to the Antarctic, she declared. It was an absurd idea. As if he could take her with him were she not his wife. The base camp in New Zealand was as far as any woman could go. Yet sometimes when she described her dream, she made it so vivid that he found himself believing—just for a moment—believing she was standing beside him on the ice plateau.

Hermine entered the room then, like a wraith, moving her frail body lightly, with such grace. There was something she wanted to say to him, he supposed, but would wait until he acknowledged her presence. He never lifted a hand to her or spoke to her rudely, and what he did to her in bed was no more than his conjugal right, but she was afraid of him, and he despised himself for being the kind of man a wife might be afraid of.

She would have been happy with someone else. Byron saw how she glowed when talking with Horace Graham. He observed that Horace held her hand a little too long when saying good-bye. Maybe she would not shrink from Horace's touch in bed. But Horace would never put his hand on her; he was much too honorable. Byron wished he could tell his friend to take Hermine. She deserved better.

Seeing him preoccupied, Hermine walked over to the mantel and rearranged the photographs. Here was Byron Tremaine with Theodore Roosevelt, with King Edward VII of England. Her parents could not get over it. Every time they visited, they picked up one photograph after the other, marveling at the inscriptions in one famous hand after the other. Well, it was impressive. What a catch. As soon as he started paying attention to her, they pushed her into an engagement. No, that was unfair. She had felt the same way— overcome, flattered. It was not just his growing reputation as an explorer, but that he was handsome and he charmed her. "You're so pretty," he said, tracing the lines of her face with his finger. She had liked that. Pretty. She knew she was pretty, but had never dreamed she could captivate a man like this. He took as a matter of course a life of adventure she had not even imagined as an only child tutored by a governess, then sent to a school for young ladies, and finally, taken to balls where she met eligible young men. Not one compared to Byron Tremaine. Of course she had been dazzled.

Her father, a vice-president of Altman's department store, spoke every night at the dinner table of retailing and merchandise until she could have died of boredom. Byron Tremaine told her about the Arctic, the icy waters around Greenland, the dangers of crossing the frozen mountains. She was spellbound. The Antarctic was still to be conquered; it was his ambition, more than that, his passion. A place in history would be assured, but that was not the driving force. Rather, it was to go where no one else had gone, to discover an unknown continent. How her friends envied her. Walking into a room with him, on his arm, his choice, made her proud.

Of course she had loved him, would never have married without love. That went without saying. She could love him still. Except for . . . she did not like to think the words, let alone say them. And no time of the day was safe. Even now, midafternoon on a Sunday, he might decide he wanted her. And it was a wife's duty to accept. He said she was too virtuous for her own and his good, rejecting pleasure, an ice maiden, frigid. Oh, if he knew.

Why did she not feel guilty? Horace felt guilty. "I have sinned," he said. "We have sinned," she had corrected him. No, no, she was innocent, frail, a woman, Horace had returned. He had taken advantage; all the blame was his. Byron was his friend, her husband. But Byron treated her as if she were a toy, called her his little doll in seeming kindness, but it was not kind at all. How can a doll be guilty?

That first time Horace had come to her was on a night when Byron was in Boston giving a lecture. Horace knew Byron would be away, he told her later, punishing himself. He had walked through the streets for hours, willing himself not to go to the house on Gramercy Park. And in the end, he had not been able to stay away. It was not late, but in Byron's absence, she had taken off her corset and tight-fitting dress and slipped into a trailing frilly at-home gown. When Byron was present, she remained formally dressed as long as possible.

Horace. He put his hands on her breasts. Her breasts. She never used the word; there were parts of her body she did not name even to herself. But she felt so warm at Horace's touch. How did they find themselves in the bedroom? It looked mysterious in the dim light. Byron always turned up the wick as high as it would go and lit the lamp. Byron took off her nightgown, looked at her, took off his own, insisted that she look at him. Touch him. Call it by dirty names. Her duty, but her flesh revolted.

Horace did not remove her gown, and in the darkness, she was not quite certain what portion of his own clothing he was taking off. But then, he was in bed beside her, his hands up and down her body, inside the loose dress, inside her chiffon underdrawers. Did he pull them down or did she? From habit, she trembled; the act she had learned to dread with Byron was beginning. No, it could not be the same. With Byron, it was brutish, animal-like. That is how men are; a woman must expect that. Instead, there was this softness of touch. Byron bruised her lips with his teeth, but these kisses brushed her mouth with the lightness of a feather. She kissed him, too. How could she not? His voice at her ear, "My dreams are coming true." He did not demand that she touch him, but her hands went down to feel his body. He was wearing his shirt, nothing below.

It could not be the same act. He slipped inside her so easily. That could not be. She knew how much the forcible entry into her body always hurt. But it did not hurt. So easy. Slippery. The warmth, the pressure was pleasant. Loving. "Oh, my." She waited then for him to reach the moment a man had to reach, for the act to be over. For the first time in her life, she did not want it to be over. "Don't hurry," Horace said. "I can wait for you all night." How did she know what he meant? There was nothing in her experience to tell her. But she knew. And it was as if her whole body relaxed, light, yet with a strange tension. "I will wait for you all night." And all at once, as he moved inside her, back and forth, in and out, the sensation she had not known a woman could feel came over her. "My dreams are coming true." Had she spoken this time or had he?

Afterward she wondered whether Byron cared about her. It seemed important now. The next time Byron came to her bed, she tried to respond to him, knowing as she now did that a woman could respond. But it was hopeless; there was no tenderness in the way he handled her body. And yet, there was her picture. The photograph, taken shortly after their marriage, was kept on the small table right next to his armchair, and she saw how often he picked it up. When he was leaving for a trip, he packed the photograph in his hand luggage. That must prove something. Only when she saw his face soften as he looked at her portrait did she feel she was missing some quality of loving he did not express.

"I have sinned." "We have sinned." But then—"My dreams are coming true." Not so. There are dreams that can never come true. They did not talk of confessing to Byron, of divorce, of their being together always. Impossible. Byron was his friend, Horace said, her husband. She knew her duty as his wife and performed it. How then should she feel guilty?

After being with Horace, she sometimes secretly thought of her husband as a brute. It was wrong even to think that way; her husband's conjugal rights empowered him to do as he would. He gave way to his carnal impulses at any time, even during her monthly bleeding or when she was pregnant. Her married friends confided that husbands are celibate at such times. But Byron had no compunction, enjoyed the fact of her pregnancy. "Little mother," he called her. Why was every seemingly affectionate name he gave her belittling? Sometimes, seeing him writing in the diary that would someday be published, she would cringe at the thought he might be describing her in this way.

She cleared her throat and Byron looked up. Now that she had his attention, she must tell him she was pregnant again. For a moment, in Dr. Martin's office, she had thought, What if it is Horace's child? But of course it was not; the dates were wrong. This time she was safe.

This time. When she was carrying Susan, she had not been sure. The whole pregnancy was a torment. She became ill, wasted, thought she would go mad. Periods of great joy alternated with despair. Who had fathered this child? How could this have happened? Anyone who knew her, who knew how strong was her sense of what was right, what was fitting, would have said this could not be. "We have sinned"—but she would not be ashamed of loving Horace.

That was the time, the only time, when she might have forced the issue. Had she been sure Horace had fathered the child, she would have done so. But she had not been sure. In her desperation, she was tempted to tell Horace the child was his . . . without being sure. Horace would have confronted Byron, taken her away. But lacking that certainty, she could not burden Horace with greater guilt than he was already feeling. He suffered enough for loving her. Byron was more than a friend; he was an idol. And so, in the end, she did nothing.

As soon as she saw the child's face, she was sure. But by then it was too late. She could no longer confess to Horace.

Byron did not seem to like the baby. Almost as if he knew. But there was no way he could have known. Perhaps it was just that he was not much interested in a daughter. Horace asked to hold the baby. Almost as if he knew. But, of course, he did not know. No one knew.

She owed Byron a son, but wished she could feel happier about bearing his child. Byron was delighted with her announcement, kissed her with genuine feeling for once; he wanted a son. That would give some purpose to their marriage. She slipped quietly out of the room, and Byron thought she appeared content. He feared, though, that Hermine did not have the strength to withstand another pregnancy and labor; she had nearly died giving birth to Susan.

Viola's body was slender, too, but how different form Hermine's. It was strong, so strong, almost as if the skeleton were forged of steel. Her energy was inexhaustible. He had never seen her tired. Except that time in London. If she had not been so willful, she would have borne a healthy boy already. The memory still hurt. Now she would bear Ian Crosbie a son. Byron made a fist and slammed it down on the small table beside him, knocking down the photograph of Hermine. He felt like crushing beneath his foot the portrait with that other picture behind it. Each time he opened the picture frame, there was Viola, her eyes glowing, eager. Reaching. Reaching. For him. Better not act out of rage and disappointment; he would miss that photograph. He took it with him wherever he went.

Now Plumley was talking of another expedition after Mount McKinley—to the windswept islands of Tierra del Fuego at the southernmost tip of South America. There would be lectures, meetings with explorers to help him make decisions on routes and supplies, and when he was ready, the great expedition to the Antarctic. His life would be full. But there was a hole in it.

The quarrel in England had been final. Or so they had said. Yet even now, married to Hermine, he could not break Viola's hold on him.

He would not lose her, could not lose her, refused to accept that he was never to make love with Viola again. Neither his marriage nor hers could keep them apart forever. She must come back to him. And then he thought of her obsession. The Antarctic. That was still his hold on her. He would never take her there. The risk was too great—for her, for the men he was responsible for. But she was not to know that. So long as she thought there was a chance of his taking her to the Antarctic, she would be back.

# Chapter Sixteen

"YOU COULD HAVE MARRIED ME. Instead you have made the mistake of your life."

About to enter the Parliament building, Lord Hargreave had caught sight of Viola standing there, watching the suffragettes march up and down. It was the first time he had seen her since the day at WSPU headquarters when he had proposed to her, the best offer she would ever have. Thinking Viola needed time to recover from the aftereffects of the fire, Lord Hargreave had stayed away. Not for long as time is measured, but too long, as it turned out. In the moment of shock at reading the marriage notice in the London *Times,* he remembered what his wife had told him about Ian Crosbie.

Lord Hargreave had been rejected, and she knew how hard a blow that must be for him; even so, Viola would not allow him to reprove her. "But you put me in touch with Lieutenant Crosbie yourself."

By God, it was true. He had made the introduction, thinking to bind Viola to him by his seeming support of her ambition.

"I never thought you would marry him." If he had guessed her intention, he would have told her the truth, protected her from committing this act of folly. "What do you know about this man?" Lord Hargreave's face was pale, his lips compressed.

"You told me he was a hero, and that's obviously true. He has medals from the geographical societies. Captain Sharpe would not have made him second-in-command if he were anything less."

But Sharpe probably knew no more about Crosbie than Viola did. "Were Crosbie's parents at the wedding?" he asked.

"They are too old to make the trip from Scotland."

"And his brother? Is he too old as well?"

She did not know Ian had a brother.

"You'll never see his family, Viola. They won't have anything to do with him. Not just his parents. His brother, too; he hates Ian Crosbie. You ask your husband why sometime."

"You're implying something discreditable about his past. I don't believe you."

So much the worse for her. He felt like striking her across that beautiful, unbelieving face, shaking her, forcing her to recognize that she had married an unstable, disturbed man with horrors in his past. And why? Because Crosbie was young, a hero, powerfully built. Hargreave reviewed all he had done for Viola, how he had intervened on her behalf more than once. For nothing, it now appeared. She could not be protected from herself. Turning abruptly to enter the Parliament building, he thought that he would never come to her aid again.

There was no reason to take Lord Hargreave's insinuations seriously, thought Viola, as she caught a bus to take her home to Ian. It was true she had married hastily, but how could she have waited when the departure of the Sharpe expedition was imminent? In the brief time since the marriage, she had come to think more highly of Ian, to feel that, rash or not, she had made the right decision.

Only why did he never mention his brother? When she told him about her past life, Ian listened attentively, but offered no information about himself in return. His diction was good enough to point to a public school and university education, but which public school, which university?

The spiteful words of a rejected suitor must not cause her to doubt her husband. She well knew how easily a breach with a family can arise. In her case, it had been her espousal of suffrage, a cause she believed worth dying for. Ian's family might, for all she knew, have broken with him when he joined the navy. The inadequate pay—less than eight hundred pounds a year—was reason enough for parental disapproval. And brothers were often rivals in one way or another. Surely none of that was important. She thought of Ian and how kind he was. Once or twice he had raised his voice, but in a moment recalled himself, and spoke in his usual soft, well-modulated tone. And the way he made love. So tender, considerate. Byron had been selfish in his lovemaking. The contrast between the two men still moved her.

And yet, she remembered that once when they were in bed together, Ian had grasped her tightly, so roughly that she had cried out. "You're hurting me." He had released her at once, looked stricken. Though she assured him it was nothing, he lost his erection.

That was the only time though. Whenever else they made love, he was careful of his exceptional strength.

Gentle. But not relaxed. When she awoke at night, he would be lying beside her with his eyes open. He must sleep sometimes, but she was never able to catch him at it. There was always an air of tension when he was in a room.

Still, the marriage was everything she had hoped for, a union of equals. Making love as equals. Working together. Ian arranged for her to spend a few hours each day in the Sharpe office with him, helping to check the supplies pouring in from manufacturers in Great Britain and the Continent.

As the weeks passed, Ian's excitement grew. "Sharpe tells me that four men are to make the final assault on the Pole with him. We'll be the first men on earth to set foot on the ice at the South Pole, Viola. The first. Nothing in life can compare to the glory of that moment."

Viola imagined Ian standing on his skis, his handsome face looking toward the Pole, his tall figure dominating the desolate windswept icy terrain. How could she not be glad for him, despite a pang of envy that he could go while she must remain behind? The dream of exploration. Each of them—Viola, Ian, Sharpe, Byron, too—had been seized by it and could never escape its pull. A passion, perhaps more than that—an obsession.

Were it not for leaving Viola, Ian thought, he would be completely happy. His confidence in his ability to perform well on the expedition was absolute. He was at his best in the Antarctic. Nothing he had been before mattered, only his strength and courage. He would distinguish himself so that backers for his own expedition would come easily. And that time, Viola would be with him.

When it came time for the expedition to set off, Viola accompanied the men to Cardiff, Wales, the port of embarkation. Watching the ship depart, she felt dull and empty. Though she had not lived with him for long, Ian had filled her life. She wondered how she would bear his absence. A polar expedition takes two years, with the first summer season devoted to laying depots of food and fuel as far along the route as possible. The assault on the Pole is made the following summer.

Viola determined to make good use of the time Ian was away, so after spending some weeks climbing the Swiss Alps to improve her skills for the Antarctic, she returned to London to the suffragettes. Though a few of the women still talked of avenging Lesley with acts of arson, the catastrophe at Chessham Court had been sobering, and the moderate faction now prevailed.

When Viola walked into WSPU headquarters, the first person she saw was Carla, huge in an oversized sweater and corduroy trousers, and the past swept over her—Hollowran Prison on her first day in London, the shabby flat on Chessham Court, the roof of the town hall in MidValley. The nightmare of the fire came back to her—James crawling down the stairs, oh, Jamie, Lesley's dead weight. In the excitement of her life with Ian, she was for stretches of time able to blank out the horrors of that night. Now her memories overwhelmed her. But in a moment the suffragettes were crowding around her, differences forgotten. They were kind, pitied her for having married and put aside her ambitions. The mood changed when she told them she was yet to go to the Antarctic with Ian. "You'll be a hero!" Carla exclaimed. "Just think what that will mean to suffrage."

Looking around the cold barren room with its rickety chairs and long plank tables, Viola thought it was much like the hall in New York where Eileen had taken her. Only three years ago. Byron was her lover then, and neither of them imagined that could ever end. But it had. She hardly thought about him now.

Suffrage became the passion that sustained her while the Sharpe expedition was in the Antarctic. It was as well; letters from Ian, posted from each port of call, came many weeks after they were written. In the meantime, the newspaper reports kept her abreast of the progress, by steam and sail, of the expedition's ship, the *British Voyager*. All was going smoothly, and then, on a day when Viola was leading a demonstration in the slums of Manchester, huge black headlines on a newspaper placard caught her eye: RACE FOR POLE. In an instant she had dropped the suffrage banner and run to the nearest kiosk to buy the *Guardian,* her heart pounding. The news story, transmitted by the Central News Agency, confirmed the headline. A telegram had greeted the Sharpe expedition upon its arrival in Melbourne, Australia. "Am heading for the South Pole. Carlsen." His original plan to go to the Arctic was secretly changed the previous year when Peary reached the North Pole.

However, Ian's letters mailed from New Zealand, the last stop before Antarctica, were high-spirited and confident. Carlsen's duplicity was outrageous, but the result of the race to the Pole was a certainty. The Danes would still be struggling across the icy wastes while Sharpe and his men were at ninety degrees south latitude, raising the British flag over the Pole.

Reassured, Viola was able to endure the waiting during the months when the expedition was overwintering and cut off from the outside world. At last Ian's letters describing the first summer in Antarctica arrived. He wrote with modesty but obvious pride that the base camp had been established on Ross Island in an inlet of McMurdo Sound, known to earlier explorers as the Skuary, but renamed Cape Crosbie by Sharpe. All had gone well that summer. Sledging parties journeyed out from Cape Crosbie and laid fifteen supply depots along the route to the Pole. Long afterward Viola learned that Ian had neglected to point out the plan was for twenty depots and that the onset of unseasonal blizzards had forced a premature return to winter quarters. Ian mentioned, but only in passing, that the motorized sledges, never before used in polar regions, took three hours to traverse three miles and then broke down, leaving the heavily laden sledges to be drawn by Siberian ponies and dogs. The ponies, though the same breed that earlier explorers had used with success, were not thriving and moved clumsily on the snow.

Ian did say that one of the sledging parties had come upon Carlsen and his men making camp on another part of Ross Island. Studying the map, Viola observed that the location described was somewhat closer to the Pole than Cape Crosbie, but assumed the distance meant nothing in the vastness of the ice sheet.

Reading these letters, Viola was caught up by Ian's exhilaration.

Later she wondered if his letters even then had contained some air of unreality she should have caught, if there had been something not quite right about them. At the time, though, she thought the lack of concern he displayed to be a sign of heroism.

Ian's letters made Viola feel more, rather than less, lonely for him. She missed him constantly, wanted to feel his huge body in her arms, his big hands caressing her, missed the sweetness that had been so lacking in the love affair with Byron Tremaine. Every so often she read about Byron in the newspapers, as he conquered Mount McKinley, explored Tierra del Fuego, fathered a daughter, then a son. The projected journey to the Antarctic was mentioned in every article about him. The British papers reported rather smugly that in the face of the Sharpe expedition, the Americans wanted a hero, too. Viola had found her hero; she did not need Byron anymore.

In the last week of October, spring in the Southern Hemisphere, the Sharpe and Carlsen expeditions disappeared into the interior of the Antarctic continent and the momentous journey to the South Pole was under way. Sharpe intended to attain the Pole by late December so as to allow ample time for a return to Cape Crosbie before the onset of the brutal Antarctic winter caught them unprotected out on the glacier. Then they would overwinter again at the base camp and return to New Zealand in the spring.

Though even the most modern wireless equipment could not reach as far as Antarctica, the transoceanic cables were transmitting meteorological reports of unseasonable, capricious weather in the southernmost portions of New Zealand and South America. Temperatures soared and then plummeted. Warm spells were succeeded by blizzards that blotted out the sun for days on end and winds gusted at a hundred miles an hour or more. The weather in Antarctica was likely to be worse, not better.

Even then, Viola was not really afraid for Ian. It was not her nature to anticipate disaster. The Antarctic held such magic for her that she did not see its hazards clearly.

On a cold, cloudy day in March, fall in Antarctica, the afternoon newspapers carried the first news of the conquest of the Pole. The fabled race between the two expeditions had ended in a draw. Both parties reached the South Pole in December of 1911. Viola ached for Ian in his disappointment.

Within days, however, the initial report was discounted as later cables brought far worse news. Carlsen was declared the winner and the whereabouts of the Sharpe expedition were unknown. By now Viola was afraid, desperately afraid that disaster had befallen the men. The days passed, and though Viola continued to carry out her heavy schedule of suffrage activities, she could neither eat nor sleep as she pictured Ian's body lying frozen on the polar ice cap.

The newspaper accounts of Carlsen's triumph were critical. Driving the dog teams relentlessly, Carlsen took the lead from the start and held it. As the sledge loads grew lighter, the weaker dogs were slaughtered to serve as food for those remaining, and for the men as well. Only twelve of the original fifty-two dogs returned to the base camp on Ross Island. This efficiency aroused more horror than admiration; the British would not behave so. If that was the reason Sharpe lost the race, it was nobler to fail than succeed. The *London Times* reported that the Carlsen expedition had laid 7,500 pounds of food and fuel in the depots; Viola did not think the Sharpe expedition was so generously supplied.

At last the *British Voyager* arrived in New Zealand bringing reassuring news of the Sharpe expedition. The men who were not of the Pole party had been ordered back to Cape Crosbie in early January of 1912, and at that time they were at the summit of Beardmore Glacier, 150 miles from the South Pole. The weather had been horrendous, and the ice surface so treacherous that they had fallen behind schedule, but Captain Sharpe was convinced he could complete the journey to the Pole and arrive back at the base camp before the winter night closed in. No mention of Lieutenant Crosbie was made, but he was, of course, in the Pole party.

No further news of the Sharpe expedition could be expected until the ice broke up and the ship returned the explorers to New Zealand. The months passed and at last it was December, summer in the Southern Hemisphere, then January. There had been ample time for the ship to carry Ian and his companions from the Antarctic continent. Why was there still no word from the Sharpe expedition? In mid-February, when even Viola's customary optimism had failed her, the news reached London: SHARPE AND HIS MEN DEAD AT SOUTH POLE. The full story was on the front pages of all the newspapers. When Captain Sharpe and the three other men making up the Pole party did not return to the base camp, a search party went out after them. Halfway across the Beardmore Glacier, they came upon a tent, and within were the four frozen bodies, and letters and journals were neatly stacked beside each one. The bodies were left in the tent to be preserved in the cold for all time.

Viola stood in front of the newspaper kiosk, with crowds milling around her, tears streaming down her face. Ian. She had lived through these empty years in the certainty of all the years ahead with him. He had come to her on the day of the fire, a day of shock and horror, of the loss of her closest friends. And just when she would have given herself over to despair, he was with her. She had thought he would always be with her.

All at once she had the sense that something in the news report was wrong. In her grief and confusion, at first she could not tell what was puzzling her. And then she knew: "Sharpe and three other men." Three? But there had been four other men. The final assault on the Pole was to be made with five men, including Sharpe . . . and Ian. There must be a mistake. She had not paid attention to the list of names of the men in the doomed polar party, certain that Ian was among them. Now she read through the article again—four names, and Ian Crosbie was not one of them. Further down in the article was another list—of survivors of the Sharpe expedition. There she found Ian's name and could hardly contain her joy. What could have prevented him from making the assault on the Pole? An injury due to accident was most likely, but once he was at home, she would see to it that he received the best medical treatment. He was coming back to her.

The weeks passed and Ian either cabled nor wrote. Fearing he must be ill indeed, Viola contacted naval headquarters, only to receive an evasive answer. The survivors of the Sharpe expedition would be landing at Southampton, then going on to London by train, she was told coldly. She would see Lieutenant Crosbie then. Viola was at Charing Cross Station on the specified date, wondering if Ian would be carried from the train by stretcher. Then she saw him, towering over the others. But her first relief vanished as he came closer. He was thin to the point of emaciation; his shoulders drooped, his hair was unkempt and straggling, his black beard was untrimmed. When she ran to him and threw her arms around him, she felt as if she were holding an inanimate object. His greeting to her was not so much cold as indifferent. Nor did he say good-bye to the other men, indifferent to them as well. What had happened in the Antarctic was enough to alter any man, and she realized how terrible it must be for Ian to come home like this. That was why he had not written, why he appeared prematurely aged. Instead of returning with Captain Sharpe, a hero, he was returning without him, a failure. Or that was how he must be seeing it. Grief for his dead companions and for his lost hopes was reason enough for him to look so broken. He had comforted her before; now she would comfort him, make him look to the future, to the time when they would be going to the Antarctic together.

Ian was silent in the motor taxi driving them to Clarges Street, and when she took his hand, he did not resist, but did not return the pressure.

At last they reached home. He walked in very slowly without looking around, sat down in the nearest chair, and put his head in his hands. Viola was at a loss as to what to do. He neither moved nor spoke. Time passed. When she could not stand the silent misery any longer, she asked him what had happened. "Can't you tell me, Ian?"

At this, he raised his head and nodded. And then, in broken sentences, speaking almost incoherently, he told her that Sharpe had turned him back, refused to allow him to continue with the party going on to the Pole, ordered him to return to the base camp with the last group of men.

Viola stared at Ian's distorted face; she had expected anything but this. Ian went on with his terrible story. "I lied to Sharpe, Viola. And to you. I've been sick. Crazy. The things I've done—as a boy, a young man. I killed a dog. My brother's dog with my bare hands. Hurt . . . no, I won't tell you that. They gave me laudanum. I was in a madhouse. My parents could not bear the shame. They sent me away. To the navy. But nobody in the navy knew. Nobody in England knew. I was so careful that I thought no one would ever find out."

*I lied.* Everything in her resisted that knowledge. Ian was talking wildly about an imagined past because his nerves were shattered by the deaths of Sharpe and the men who had gone to the Pole. It was a temporary nervous collapse. Why, she had lived with Ian, and a husband could not have concealed all this from a wife. She bent over him and put her arms around his thin shoulders. *I lied.* It could not be true.

And yet. Even as she was telling herself it could not be, she was remembering Lord Hargreave's insinuations—the parents who would have nothing more to do with him, the brother who hated him. Until this moment, Ian had never spoken of his early life. *I lied.* She did not want to believe that, but the words rang true. *What do you know about this man?* Lord Hargreave had asked. Nothing. That was her first reaction. And then she thought that she had known everything of importance. A hero, but at the same time so gentle, so kind, loving. The episodes he described had happened long ago. Surely his history was of no significance to her, should have been of no significance to Sharpe. Ian was a hero; his courage and physical strength were all but legendary. Sharpe could not do without him. The tragic outcome of the expedition proved that. Had Sharpe turned Ian back merely because he had somehow learned of periods of madness now safely in the past?

Ian was speaking more clearly now, telling of the desperate march across the ice. Losing time. Always conscious that they must go faster if they were to outrun Carlsen. Just as they approached the summit of the glacier, Sharpe had sent the dog teams back to the base camp. If they went any farther, the weaker dogs would have to be killed one after the other; no officer in the Royal Navy could give such an order. Ian was relieved. He had hated driving a sledge pulled by dogs, being so close to the detestable animals. Viola repressed a shudder. *I killed a dog.* His companions could barely manage to drag the sledges themselves; he was powerful enough to do it easily, had helped the others.

"Sharpe said I had to go back. I couldn't believe it, argued with him. He was exhausted; the other men in the Pole party were exhausted, too, dragging themselves along mile by mile. And so many more to go. But I was still strong, the strongest and in the best condition of them all. Sharpe said yes, I was, but he couldn't depend on me . . . couldn't depend on me. And when I still argued, he said that a man can be strong physically, but weak in other ways. Unfit."

Ian's words called up the image of the men on their skis on the windswept summit of the glacier, exhausted, but driven by their passion to conquer the Pole. And there stood Captain Sharpe, the ambition of his life about to be fulfilled. He would allow no man to stand in his way, and he recognized something in Ian he could not trust.

Somehow in the course of that final desperate march, signs of mental instability, concealed for so long, must have been revealed. Viola believed it now, and pitied Ian as she thought of how he must have suffered on the return journey to the base camp, the days and weeks spent going back in despair over the icy terrain he had traversed so hopefully on the way out, his companions knowing him disgraced. Again she took his hand, and again he did not appear to notice.

After a long pause: "I shouldn't be here, Viola. Because of my weakness, I'm alive, and Sharpe and the rest of the men are lying out there on the glacier, frozen forever. Dead."

# Chapter Seventeen

VIOLA LAMBERT HAD NOT BEEN plain and uninteresting; she had been enchanting. Sexless? The voice with a little throb in it could inflame the heart. She had lived in a house where suffragettes "cohabited" with their men friends. A participant? I have no reason to disbelieve that. But everything else she had done remained a mystery. I would never know what prompted a woman who had written stiff, impersonal letters to Byron Tremaine to make one desperate appeal—PERSONAL URGENT.

After reading about that fiery death, I went back to Durrants Hotel, discouraged. The telephone rang just then. It was Bucky, returned from a three-hour session with a number of executives, suggesting we meet for a drink before his public relations man whisked him off again for television interviews. For no particular reason my mood was lifting as we spoke, and I felt almost cheerful by the time we were seated side by side in a bar not far from the hotel.

I told him about my quest for Viola Lambert. It was on my mind, and there was no reason for concealment now that I knew when she had died. I had been convinced no one but Viola Lambert could have played a part in the all-women's expedition of 1915–1916 cryptically referred to in Byron's letter. But her life had ended in late 1909.

Bucky recognized her name. I had wondered at his knowing 88 Chessham Court had been a suffragette center. Now it appeared he not only was aware of her career in the suffrage movement, but also of her participation in the Tremaine expedition to Greenland.

When I pressed him for details, he was somewhat vague. His grandmother had been a suffragette in London and sometimes spoke about an American woman named Lambert who joined the militant movement there. When he found the name on Tremaine's expedition list, he decided it must be the same person. "Do you think they were lovers in Greenland and continued to see each other afterward, Trixie?"

"I doubt it. I've read my great-grandfather's diaries and he didn't seem to give a damn about her."

"He certainly wouldn't have written about an affair with a female expedition member, Trixie. That sort of thing is frowned on even to-day as sexual harassment. In the early 1900s, it would have been scandalous."

"Even so, I still don't understand why the other members of the expedition to Greenland had so little to say about her in their diaries either. A woman like that. You'd think the men would have fought over her. Instead, no one found her worth more than a mention."

"Oh, I can explain that, Trixie. No one would have dared write about her if Tremaine didn't want them to. Have you ever seen the contracts expedition members had to sign? They couldn't publish anything the leader of the expedition didn't see first and approve."

Now I had the missing fact and everything fell into place.

"I hope Avery hasn't figured that out. He's been making dirty in-sinuations about an illicit affair, and Viola Lambert is the only woman besides Hermine who has an obvious link with Tremaine." I still thought Avery's presence in London must have something to do with her.

"Avery certainly makes us all dance to his tune. What's he trying to do, Trixie? Is he after Tremaine or me?"

"Both of you—provided he can make both of you look bad. Avery says everyone's life has something in it to be concealed. Everyone's."

"Do you think there's something concealed in my life, Trixie?" His voice was as light as ever, his manner untroubled.

Startled by the question, I could only shake my head, while won-dering whether Avery really did have damaging evidence about Bucky. I did not like to think so.

"Well, there is something in my life that could be twisted around. And even if it isn't, I'd rather not have it brought up in front of a television audience of millions."

He was silent then, turning his glass around in his hand, looking more serious than I had ever seen him. "Aren't you going to ask me what it is? Any other woman would."

My friend Aimee can get a man's entire history out of him in fifteen minutes. Not I; it seems too much of an intrusion into another person's privacy.

"Well, I'll tell you. I wouldn't like Avery to get onto my wife."

Wife? One of the women's magazines had included Bucky in a listing of the most eligible bachelors of the year, and he was said to be having an affair with a reasonably well-known actress.

"My wife killed herself."

It seemed impossible that someone married to cheerful Bucky would kill herself.

"She was ... I guess you'd say she was emotionally fragile. She'd attempted suicide a couple of times before when she was in her mid-teens, but I didn't hear about that till later. Her parents ... well, they unloaded her on me. They thought she'd be better off with a husband to look after her. Any husband. Me. We were in college, so they paid the rent for a little apartment off campus, helped with expenses, covered the tuition. My father said if she isn't knocked up, how come they're so generous? But I thought he was against my marrying her because she wasn't Jewish.

"She was calm enough when she was taking her medication, but she kept going off it. Didn't like the way it made her feel, she said. I encouraged her; I didn't like the way it made her feel either. I was twenty years old, Trixie, what did I know? I thought you got married so you could screw every day. We'd be sitting across from each other at dinner, and then I'd hold out my arms and she'd come and jump onto my lap. The times we had. But when she was taking her medication, she wasn't interested, and if we did make love, she'd just lie there like a stick.

"I didn't pay any attention to how depressed she got when she wasn't on the pills."

He broke off at that point, apparently finished, and then he added, "I've been a sucker for anyone with mental problems ever since."

"And you're willing to go on Avery's program?"

"It's worse not to, Trixie. That way, he can say anything without my having a chance to answer back. And he's just interested in the expedition, so I doubt he's found out about my sad little Jenny. No one else has."

I wished I had Bucky's confidence. "He has so many sources at his disposal, Bucky."

"Don't overrate Avery, Trixie. Most people do. They think he's omniscient, has armies of detectives searching out every clue. But he has a program on every week; he couldn't possibly do the kind of research on each one that you're imagining. He's more interested in the one on polar exploration than in most of the others because of you."

"What do you mean?"

"It gives him an excuse to see you. Why do you think he's in London? He asked me if I knew where you were staying, and I said I didn't. I certainly wasn't going to tell him. And he sort of laughed and said he'd find out. I could tell he was interested the first time he said your name."

"You're a romantic, Bucky. He doesn't like me any better than I like him." Avery certainly has no use for the soft-spoken, diffident kind of person I am, and I find him intimidating.

Bucky let it go. He was probably just teasing me and I was missing the point. I am not good at this kind of byplay. Still, at that moment I wondered why Bucky had told me the story about his wife, confided in me as if I were his intimate. It is a heartbreaking story, but I am not his intimate. Now it occurred to me that he had done so to elicit my sympathy, enlist my support so that I would influence Avery. Bucky may not be as open and sincere as he appears. There was his claim of a suffragette grandmother in England. Reasonable enough on the face of it—but now I remembered he had once told me his grandparents came from Poland. And his grandmother would not have been old enough to have been a suffragette in 1907; it must have been a great-grandmother. I thought then how Avery makes one view every person with suspicion. Even Bucky.

When he smiled at me and began to talk amusingly about his meetings with staid, stiff British captains of industry, I was drawn to him again and envied his ability to become cheerful so quickly after reliving the tragedy of his marriage. We were seated side by side on a banquette and after a while his thigh pressed against mine. He had told me I was pretty, admired my eyes, and said he liked my smile, but it was not until this moment that I realized he was attracted to me sexually. I was flattered of course. He took my hand and squeezed it. I found the contact pleasant; nonetheless, I pulled away. Bucky was looking at me in a manner I could not mistake. He is a most appealing person, but I am not free for him. Ronald does not need to ask me for fidelity; I have not wanted to be with anyone else from the time we became lovers. I stood up to go; the parting might have been awkward, but Bucky was never awkward.

A little later that same evening I received a telephone call from Avery, who had of course found out where I was staying and was inviting me to dinner at the Connaught Hotel's grill. Why did I go? Because I was afraid that Avery might be on the track of Viola Lambert? Because Ronald was far away and I was lonely? Because Bucky's story had moved me? Because Avery held a certain fascination for me? Oh, there were many reasons. None good enough.

The evening began innocuously; at least it was as innocuous as so intense a man could make it. My faltering statement that I was in London on vacation was accepted so blandly that I wondered again just how much Avery knew about me, about Viola Lambert. He did mention that he knew Ronald Graham was not with me. As soon as we were seated in the grill, he explained it was essential for him to be in London now, because he was closing a deal with the BBC for a cooperative television production. So much for Bucky's idea that Avery was here because of me. I had never believed it anyway. No, he was not carrying out research for his program on polar exploration; by chance he had encountered Bucky Sheridan in the hotel lobby and arranged an interview. Did I believe him? Was a chance encounter with me also to be put to use? The sense of unease I always felt in Avery's presence returned and I was stiff, wary.

No questions were put to me, however; he spoke mostly of himself, telling of his failed marriage with more emotion than I would have believed him capable of feeling. He seemed moved almost to tears over the son his wife prevented him from seeing. I had viewed him only as a man who inflicted suffering; now it seemed to me that he suffered, too. My misgivings vanished.

For the first time, the exceptional quality of attention he gave did not seem calculated to extract information, but rather to be personal, to reflect an interest in getting closer to me, in making me understand him better. Just me. I felt again that curious mixture of attraction and repulsion he had aroused in me before. Only this time the attraction was the stronger. I was drawn to him by the attention he turned on me, the way he looked at me.

And then I remembered I must not trust him. Men like that—aggressive, demanding—are not charmed by me. There was a motive, and it was easy enough to guess what it must be. In another minute, another hour—whenever he decided I was sufficiently off guard—he would turn the topic to Byron Tremaine and suggest licentiousness, dirty my great-grandfather's reputation. But the minutes passed, an hour, more, and the topic was not raised. I did not trust Avery, but the attraction was there. Growing.

How did what happened come to happen? I have never been able to justify or explain it to myself. Long afterward, I would awaken in the hours before the dawn in a cold sweat of shame.

Up to his room. Willingly. I had not seen it coming. That is to say, I had clearly seen the attentiveness, even flirtatiousness of his manner. But I had recognized that as a part of his technique when first we met and discounted it then and subsequently. This time, though, there was a difference. This time, despite my mistrust and unease, he made me desire him. Before he asked me to his room, I did not think he desired me.

Once he had made the suggestion, he behaved as if acceptance were inevitable. Technique, of course, and, knowing that, I did not have to go with him. And yet I did have to. Was I mesmerized by him? Sometimes I think I must have been. In the elevator I had to hold on to the wall; it seemed my knees would not hold me up for wanting him so. How could I have wanted him so? Men like this—aggressive, demanding—have never appealed to me. I remembered then that when I first met Avery, he had seemed the kind of man one instantly pictures in the sexual act. I had been disturbed by the image then.

He closed the door of the elegantly furnished hotel room behind us and kissed me, his tongue in my mouth, searching, then his teeth against my lips. I forgot what manner of man he was, how he sought to disgrace my great-grandfather, whom I treasured, to disgrace him for no better motive than to produce a television program that would impress an uncaring audience. His hands went down my back, caressing. Not gently. But caressing. He took my arms and put them around his neck and I did not resist, but embraced him, feeling the hardness of the ridge of muscles across his back. My dress fell forward as he pulled down the zipper and then stood away from me to take it off. Later I thought that was the moment when I should have put the dress on again, turned back, left him. But at that time, in that room, the moment had passed. I wanted him. I did not respect him; I did not like him. He stood for the kind of opportunism that I deplore. But I was seized by a sexual hunger. I had to have him. However much I would regret it later. And even at that time, in that room, I knew I would regret it later. I had to have him. And he was so practiced in unfastening the lacy bra, removing the short black slip, the sheer black patterned stockings. "Darling," he said. Just that. He did not seem practiced in saying that. "Darling." His eyes were shining, admiring. Seeing it through his eyes, my body, slight, slender, small-breasted, looked lovely, even voluptuous to me.

I could not wait for him to undress, but reached out and pulled off his jacket, undid the buttons of his shirt, unbuckled his belt. Oh, no, this could not be happening. I had never been so bold. "Avery." There was a throb in my voice when I spoke his name. His body, naked, looked stronger than when it was clothed, thin but powerful. His pectoral muscles and the pelvic ridge stood out. He had a thick mat of dark hair on his chest going down his flat abdomen. The image of Ronald came to me. Oh, I would not think about Ronald now. I put out my hand and stroked Avery's shoulders, his chest, his abdomen. So hard. He drew in his breath sharply, smiled. "Darling." That body. I would feel the strength of that body as he held me in his arms.

And then we were lying on the bed, across the heavily quilted silk brocade bedspread, and the weight of his body was heavy on mine, the bones pressing into me. "Beatrix. Lovely Beatrix. Bibi." And with the use of Ronald's nickname for me, at what should have been the moment of greatest arousal, reality returned. What was I doing here? How could I be lying on my back, on this bed, making love—no, who would call this love?—but having sex with Steven Avery, whom I distrusted?

His hands were caressing my breasts, but now my body recoiled. Yet there was no stopping the act. Not for him. Nor for me. I did not want him. I wanted him. I was awkward, pushed him away at one moment, pulled him to me at the next. Startled, he became clumsy, withdrew his caresses, entered me roughly. He was hurting me. Pain or pleasure. The line between the two is so finely drawn. Now I did put my hands against his chest and tried to push him away, wished the act was over. And in a moment it was. How could I have done it?

The sweat was pouring down his body, matting the hair. My body was wet with his sweat, but not his semen. Before his climax, he had reached over me to the small table by the bed. Protection. Of course. In the most convenient place. How sure he had been that he would need it. I thought of Ronald. His gentleness, tenderness. I had betrayed him. And with a man like this.

I got out of bed, self-conscious about my body now, too slight, too delicate. My dress and underwear lay in a crumpled heap on the rug; I picked them up, held them over me. There was no need for that; Avery did not look at me. I went into the marble bathroom and ran the bath, then remained there for a long time, as if I could wash off the experience along with the sweat. When I came out dressed, I saw that he had put on a shirt and trousers. The shirt was damp. I supposed he, too, had felt uncomfortable naked and wanted to cover himself.

The huge hotel room was part bedroom, part living room, and he had moved to the sofa. Balanced on the edge, he was staring moodily at the floor. I sat down on the bed, as far away from him as possible. We had hardly spoken from the beginning of the sex act to its over-hasty conclusion. Ronald and I whispered love words to one another, but what had Avery and I to say?

Without looking up: "What was that all about?" His voice was flat. "You can't say I forced you." *Forced.* But the word has many definitions. He was experienced, accustomed to getting what he wanted. I was no match for him.

Avery raised his head at last and his eyes were cold. "I thought we were friends."

I was taken aback by the disingenuousness of that claim—as if we had been friends who in the course of events became lovers. We were not friends, but adversaries. If my mood had changed in the course of the sex act, the recoil was natural; the earlier responsiveness had been against nature.

"Friends? Do you think of me as a friend or as a source—one of the best—for your program on polar exploration?" The words were harsh, but my voice was so soft he had to strain to hear me.

He flushed. "Do you think that's why I brought you here tonight?"

"Why else? I'm hardly your type."

"What's my type?"

"Oh, you know, successful women, forceful women. You had to have another reason for . . . asking me."

"Do you think all this"—he pointed to the damp and rumpled bed, the wrinkled brocade bedspread, the crushed pillows fallen onto the rug—"was just intended to seduce you into telling me Tremaine's secrets so I could use them on 'Avery Tells All'?"

I was angry now, too, because what he was saying was what I really did think, and I could not bear to realize I had been so easily manipulated. "Yes. I believe that."

He made an odd choking sound. "If you think that, why did you come?"

How could I explain the overpowering attraction he had held for me?

"All you needed to say was no. Instead it was yes every bit of the way until we were on the bed . . . and even there until the very end. Then you decided you didn't wish to go through with it." The hostility in his voice was chilling.

I wanted to get out of this room and never see him again. But now I was afraid. Turning him against me would only lead him to concoct something reprehensible about Byron Tremaine to use on his program. I thought of the quavering voice of the ancient woman accusing Byron of rape in marriage, hinting at an illicit affair, and later, the rumor of suicide. How much further was he prepared to go?

"Let me give you a piece of advice. Don't get too interested in Bucky Sheridan."

The sudden change of topic startled me. "What does Bucky have to do with any of this?"

"I've gotten the proof I need; I'll be using the Sheridan expedition on my program. You've been seeing him here in London. I suppose you find him attractive. But that doesn't make him innocent."

Avery's tone was nasty. Why, if I did not know how little he really cared about me, I would have thought he was jealous.

"You make insinuations about my great-grandfather who is innocent of any wrongdoing. I assume you're doing the same with Bucky."

"Don't make me out the villain, crucifying the nice guy. Bucky's guilty all right, and it's almost too easy to prove."

"What do you mean?"

"The photographs he claims were taken at the South Pole—they're fakes, Beatrix."

The method used was the oldest and clumsiest of forgery techniques, he continued. An image was created by pasting a part of one picture onto another, photographing that, printing the new negative, airbrushing the lines where the new image had been cut and pasted, photographing it again, and making a final print. Bucky should have taken the trouble to use a computer, Avery remarked. The picture is fed into a special scanner that converts the image into thousands of tiny pixels or dots. A computer operator can move these pixels around to create whatever image is wanted. The method is foolproof; no evidence remains to show that the positions of the dots have been altered. Bucky was overconfident, Avery remarked, counting on the fact that most forgeries are not discovered because no one bothers to look that carefully; people see what they want or expect to see.

"I'd probably have found out sooner or later, because I was studying the records of the Sheridan expedition, but actually Bucky's photographer came to me with the story. People often do that, Beatrix." He paused, and his manner was menacing. "I've something on your great-grandfather, too."

Avery stood up then, towering over me, scowling, and walked over to his carryall, propped against the wall. Bending over, he took out the cassette player and a tape, while I watched him apprehensively. He sat down on the sofa again, put the recorder on the table in front of it, and inserted the cassette.

"I was going to erase this, Beatrix, but I've changed my mind."

There was a meanness in the way he was speaking. He intended to get back at me for the unsatisfactory sex act, for damaging his image of himself as a lover.

Slowly I walked over to the sofa and sat down beside him. He smelled of sweat. I could not control my trembling, waiting for the cassette to begin. But instead of pushing the play button, Avery began to talk: "It's strange, Beatrix. When I first decided to do a program on the fakery of the Sheridan expedition, it seemed quite simple to me. But almost as soon as I started looking into the general topic of polar exploration, I came to see a bigger story. I kept finding evidence that one hero or another concealed the truth or falsified. Peary's journal was locked in a safety deposit box for seventy-six years. The action of a man with nothing to hide? As for Cook, he ended up in jail for fraud. What's his word worth? Now here's Sheridan with his pasted-up photographs."

He was leaning over me, willing me to look him in the face. "I thought that, of them all, Tremaine was the one true hero who could not be doubted. When I told you I saw this program as a point counterpoint, cheats versus the honorable man, that was exactly what I thought. I'm not so sure anymore. It's shaping up into a better story now, more exciting. Maybe everyone has cheated in one way or another. In the end, polar exploration is the biggest confidence game of them all."

"Listen to the tape."

It was a man's voice this time. Ancient, wavering, almost a mumble.

"The Tremaine South Pole expedition? Yeah, I remember. Who could forget that? I was a boy then. Admired him. Worshiped him. We all did. He had a way with him, heroic. We'd do anything for him. The dirtiest work. For a smile. A pat on the back. He knew how to do that." There were long pauses between the sentences, hesitations, coughs, clearing of the throat.

"Drove us all till we dropped. It was that woman making him crazy. Still, never thought I'd learn to hate him. But he used me. Like he used everyone. Needed me for the dogs. And I was scared. Just a boy.

"Then, the things he done. Him and that other one. He covered them up, but I was there, saw what happened. What could I do about it? I was afraid of him then. But he was afraid, too. One day

I saw him on the street. Later, much later, but he knew me; I could tell. First, he started to cross to the other side. Thought better of it. Came up to me. Turned on the charm again. 'How are you, Wally? I remember you so well as a brave boy.' He could turn on the charm all right. He was nervous, though. His eyes slid around. A few weeks later he went off and died on that mountaintop.

"I saw in the papers he had a funeral with all them bigwigs making speeches. But who was sorry to see him go, I ask you?"

# Chapter Eighteen

SHE SAW THE SEXUAL ACT as the matching of equals, two tigers mating. She never tested this belief by checking a zoology text to learn how tigers actually do mate. In one of their quarrels Byron declared meanly that it must be like so many acts in the animal kingdom, the male tiger subduing the female and leaving her battered, bruised, and bleeding.

But was the female tiger defeated? That was the point, she replied, dismissing his claim of superiority. Refusing to concede defeat was how Viola spent her life. And he knew it. The coupling of equals. That was what the suffragettes had taught her. She felt so free when she heard for the first time that sexual fulfillment was a woman's right as well as a man's.

Sometimes Byron could accept her idea of equality in their lovemaking. She would sense it, take the lead when she wished, move on top, caress him, place his hand and pull his body to please her . . . then give over to him.

More often he would remind her nastily that on the Greenland expedition, the men called her his whore, then repeat the snide remarks when she had been seen leaving his cabin. The only woman on the expedition. Of course she fell to its leader. Fair game.

Properly brought up, had she minded the bad name, the crude jokes then? She could not remember. All that came back to her was the passion. Only the passion. From that first time at the base camp on the Arctic coast in 1904. Whenever they came together in all the years thereafter.

When the doctors in London suggested a change of scene, she took Ian home to New York. And there was Byron Tremaine. She had gone to his office on Chambers Street, made the first approach. He threw that in her face, too, claimed she intended them to be lovers again. But she did not intend them to be lovers again, had gone to him only to remind him of his promise to take her with him to the Antarctic. Once she had thought to go with Ian, but that hope was shattered. Ian's collapse meant that only Byron could do it for her.

As soon as they were in the same room, it all began again. The attraction between them took over as it always had. Yet their sexual encounters often ended badly. Viola was offended by his unremitting desire to dominate. Byron could not forgive what she had done in London. And so he would take her, not touching her body with his hands, his lips, or his body in the ways he knew she liked. Rather he would do as he wanted, insist on her doing what he liked. And each time, it surprised him afterward to discover that it made no difference. Were she to have a second chance, she would refuse him again. And still expect him to live up to the promise she thought he had made.

Their love was often acrimonious, harsh, painful, weighed down not only by their differences, but also by the knowledge of the other partner, the legal partner. Nonetheless, they had to come together. Was Byron her weakness? She had no weakness. At least she liked to think so. But, of course, she had. If Ian were as he once had been, she could have withstood Byron. Sometimes she tried to justify the revival of the liaison with him on grounds of sexual hunger alone. Since returning from the Antarctic, Ian seldom wanted to make love. His energies were absorbed in reliving his failure on the Sharpe expedition. Yet when he did turn to her, those were the only times when he was as he had been—strong, tender. And she would think how different was his tenderness from the harshness of her love affair with Byron. If it was love at all. Sometimes she thought that a misnomer. Passion, not love. And the lure of Antarctica.

The saddest part of it was that she still could love Ian and experience guilt at betraying him. Ian was sensitive, knew intuitively when she had been with Byron. Her guilt was greater yet because she spent the most time with him when Ian was sickest. Since their return to New York, she had twice been forced to commit him to Bloomingdale's, the psychopathic hospital in White Plains, to the north of the city. But even when Ian was at home, she was fair game for Byron.

This morning she had awakened with a feeling of heaviness and discouragement that was foreign to her nature. Ian was awake, looking at her, and put his hand on her hip. But he did not wish to make love. She could tell that from the nature of his touch. He was on edge. In a moment he jumped up and began to pace the room as if it were too small to hold him. Fully awake now, she remembered the quarrel with Byron yesterday, bitter, more bitter than usual. They often quarreled. Yet, even as he would speak the most cruel words, he would be locking the door of his office, beginning to undress her. And she, while speaking the most cruel words, would be pulling the curtains shut, returning to unbutton his shirt.

Yesterday, however, had begun well, with a warmth between them. Sometimes he bruised her when they made love, bit her mouth until it bled, but yesterday he had been more gentle than was his custom. She had been taken by surprise when in the aftermath of love, he said coldly, "I would not marry you now, even if you were free, even if I were."

His eyes glittered cruelly. Whenever he spoke of marriage, it was intended to hurt her. To remind her she had ruined her life by marrying someone else, not him. It was not as if they could ever marry. Sometimes they played with the idea, pretending it was possible. But that was only a game during lovemaking. Pillow talk.

"You are not suitable for me, Viola."

The words that were meant to hurt did hurt, despite their irrelevance. Not suitable. He made her see her commitment through his eyes as foolish, willful. What had not been done to her body? She had been knocked down, kicked, been in prison, gone on hunger strikes, on thirst strikes. She had broken the law, and in a country not her own, for a principle: the vote. Ian had understood, loved her more for it; Byron did not want to know.

No, she was not suitable. For a wife . . . but quite suitable as a lover. Her body, restored to health, showed nothing of what had been done to her. It was the body of a lover still, slender, smooth, with high, firm breasts. Her skin was clear, glowing. A few marks, a few scars. Nothing more than one could have gotten in the little accidents of a little life.

"You would never fit yourself into my life."

That was it, of course. He saw his place in history, in biographies, in archives, his courage offered as an example to schoolboys. Of course he would not marry her now were they both free. She did not present the proper image of the adoring wife waiting patiently at home. An activist. A suffragette. The history books would have had to accord her a place.

"You could never fit yourself into my life. Except for this." He pointed to the couch, their clothes crumpled on the floor. *Except for this.*

"No. We can never be more than this to each other, Viola. I have a sweet woman who will bend to me."

Hermine. Viola was thinking that her marriage had been to a hero; what happened to Ian later could not have been foreseen. But Hermine—she could never have been more than she was now. "Sweet . . . and vapid. A simpering doll."

Byron could not conceal his reaction. Viola had touched on the deadness of his marriage as if she were there, sitting between them at dinner, perched on the end of the bed when they made love. He could not help disdaining Hermine, poor Hermine, for not being Viola. Still, the way she sneered at Hermine.

He had believed that were Viola his wife, she would change, be yielding, dutiful as the marital vows decreed. By now he knew better. Just imagine if he were married to Viola—as he had once thought to be, wanted to be—there would be no end to the ways she would torment him. With her ambition. With . . . other men. Even now, perhaps her husband was not his only rival. He remembered that handsome young man in England. The baby. He could never feel quite certain it had been his. Free love. That was a suffragette principle, too.

"How can you live with that simpering doll, Byron, when you know what love between a man and a woman can be?"

And what of that marriage of hers? Psychopath or coward. What did it matter why Sharpe had sent Crosbie back from the assault on the Pole? But a strong, handsome oaf. The image of those big hands on her breasts, that big body bearing her down. He would not think of it. Could not help thinking of it.

"Yes, but she is what I want, Viola. I like a docile, tame pussycat. In bed, too. It may surprise you, but there is a satisfaction in making love, taking rather, a sweetly passive little woman who dutifully spreads her legs under me at my demand and moves so I can invade the most private parts of her body when she is quite dry and unready. It must be painful. If I push hard enough, she bleeds. Yes, there is a kind of satisfaction in that mastery."

"Is mastery better than making love as equals?"

"Two tigers mating." In Greenland he had thought it charming. Now he spoke it as an epithet, then reached out and smoothed her heavy hair as if to hold her down.

"But you would not want docility as the steady diet, Byron. Maybe occasionally. But usually you would want the passion, the hunger, giving and taking, demanding of climax."

Her voice was suggestive, low, with the faintest throb in the deepest register. It was a voice to turn the mind to desire, rapture. He would not be affected by it this time.

"You're wrong, Viola," he said nastily. "This is the occasional—what we have. The other is the regular rule of life."

She thought of the suffragettes. They seemed clean, pure. At that moment he made everything else seem dirty. When she left, she was surprised to observe that he was smiling, not with humor, but as if he had gotten the better of her.

And then today she picked up the newspaper and the advertisement in large bold letters stood out from the page:

> *Men wanted for dangerous journey to the South Polar regions. Only men of courage and the resolution to endure hardship are sought. Scientists with these qualities are also urged to apply. Fame will follow success.*

"What's the matter, Viola? Why do you look like that?"

"Nothing. Just a sudden cramp." He must not guess what she was thinking.

*Men . . . men.* The word seemed to have weight, to crush her, but then she thought that the advertisement was not intended to exclude her. There was no reason to add the word *women* when no other woman would apply for the expedition. Only why had Byron not told her about the advertisement? She had asked about the expedition many times, suggesting he was waiting too long. Carlsen and Sharpe had already reached the South Pole, while he had spent the past seven years on sponsored expeditions to Mount McKinley, Tierra del Fuego, then Greenland again. Wasting time, to her mind. Byron had brushed aside Viola's words. Sharpe's, the romantic expedition, had a tragic conclusion; Carlsen's turned ugly with the eating of the dogs. Sharpe was British, Carlsen, Danish, and the public wanted an American expedition. Theodore Roosevelt had urged one back in 1909, and a committee had been formed to work on it. Now Byron was taking up the challenge, and he had waited only long enough to obtain sufficient funds to carry out an Antarctic expedition on a hitherto undreamed of scale. The advertisement proved the backers had been found and Byron had not so much as given her a hint.

Perhaps he intended the advertisement announcing the expedition to come as a surprise. But Byron was not given to surprises. Jamie might have done something like that. Not Byron. Now she remembered the quarrel of the day before. Instigated by him. Hateful words to drive her from him. Hateful words designed to make her break with him before the expedition.

All these years and she had never doubted. Now she wondered if Byron had been playing with her to keep her with him to make love. His whore. He had bought her with his promise as surely as if he had paid her money.

Forcing herself to be calm, she realized she might be leaping to conclusions. The expedition meant so much to her that she was not thinking rationally. When she came to Byron today, he would explain away the advertisement and his silence. However unkindly he might speak in anger, Byron was an honorable man. She would stand on the polar plateau. Oh yes. Looking out over miles of glittering blue and white ice brilliant as her hopes. And in the golden sun of the Southern Hemisphere, the ice crystals in the air would glisten like diamond dust.

She read the advertisement again and it was all she could do to keep from rushing out of the house right then, locking the door, and, forgetting Ian, running down the street and to the next and the next and all the way to Byron's office, the office where they had made love and quarreled, made love and spoken of his promise to take her with him to the Antarctic.

Ian was watching her; she hurriedly folded the newspaper to another page. In his nervous state, he would not have the patience to go through the paper. Of all days to leave him, this was one of the worst. Ian was restless, never stopping his pacing and muttering, banging his fists and from time to time his head against the wall. She knew that mood. He must be brought back to Bloomingdale's before he advanced to the next stage. Violence.

Today she should be getting in touch with the doctors who had treated him before, arranging for another stay. But that would have to wait until she had seen Byron. So she contrived to get him to take a sleeping pill and then waited impatiently for the maid and laundress to arrive. They were poor girls, willing to work by the hour for the small sums she could pay out of her allowance and Ian's disability settlement from the navy. Luckily this was one of the days they came to her. She had to assure them she would be back before Ian awakened. They were afraid to stay with him by themselves. Several times she had come home to find them gone. They would drift back shamefacedly later, after ascertaining she had returned.

Her life had been given over to Ian. Someone else would have to take her place when she went on the expedition. (*If she went on the expedition.*) Her parents had never offered to help with Ian; she had never asked them to do so. A relationship of sorts had been resumed, but it was stiff, unsatisfying. They had viewed her life in England as immoral; her marriage came too late to counterbalance that shame. Her sister, Evelyn, was sympathetic, but Bertram refused to allow Ian in their home. She would have to call on Ian's family, who had been glad enough to let Viola carry the whole burden. It was time for them to forgive Ian for deeds performed in fits of madness. Viola had decided to write to his brother when the time came, asking for help, promising to resume Ian's care—after the Antarctic.

As soon as he had fallen asleep, she dressed for the visit to Tremaine in the burgundy gabardine suit her mother had ordered made to her measure by Paquin in Paris. A black satin sash buckled at the waist and then draped over the hips, where it was caught in a second chased silver buckle. A crepe de chine black-and-white striped blouse, its rows and rows of tucks edged with Valenciennes lace, was open at the neck, giving an impression of freedom quite belied by the hobble skirt so narrow it was hard to walk. The hem cleared the ground in front just enough to allow a glimpse of her slender ankles in their black stockings with hand-embroidered clocks and black kid shoes with curved heels. A single condor quill, mounted in a pheasant's breast, rose straight up from the small burgundy velvet hat hugging her head. The entire ensemble was a gift from her mother, one of many similar gifts—never anything she really wanted or needed. This was the first time she had worn the expensive suit, the first time she was glad to be so fashionably dressed.

Giving no sign of the uncertainty she felt, she entered the reception room to Byron's office and realized how much had been concealed from her. In just one day the atmosphere had changed. Desks were being brought for two secretaries who had not been there the previous day. Messengers were running in with letters, and the telephone was ringing. It must be that responses to the advertisement were already being received.

As soon as she appeared, conversation stopped while the men stared at her. It was always that way when Viola entered a room—the hut in Greenland, a ballroom in Newport, an office in New York—thought Byron, who was standing in the doorway giving directions to the workers. He marveled that she could look as she did today. Close to thirty and with the Arctic and a hard life behind her, she was quite as beautiful as when she was a young girl. The excitement she communicated—she never lost it. He remembered how he had felt when she first came to his office so long ago. It seemed inevitable that they must become lovers. But the years since then—what she had done to him, what she had done to herself—he had not foreseen any of that.

His heart sank at the thought of the scene ahead of him; he had postponed it as long as he could. That quarrel yesterday. He did not like to think he had brought it about in the hope that it would make Viola realize he was not to be moved. Yet that had been behind every word he had spoken, lashing him on, causing him to flail at her.

Watching Viola walk through the reception room to the inner office, Horace wondered if she would succeed in overriding Byron's objections. Horace had an office of his own, but more often worked at a desk alongside Byron's. As she approached, he had no choice but to rise politely and greet her—coldly. Horace remembered how he had tormented himself over Viola's doomed innocence in Greenland. Those clear violet blue eyes. *Like a picture painted with colors that were too bright.* Who could have guessed? Why, she had known exactly what she was doing, had gone there to do precisely what she had done. Probably she had come to Greenland with a pessary ... whatever a knowing woman used to protect herself. What she had wanted then, still wanted now, to his regret, was Byron.

All that became clear to Horace when he fell in love with Hermine, when he rejected the happiness he could have had. It was the only thing he could do; there was guilt enough in having betrayed Byron's friendship. When Hermine became pregnant with Susan, Horace had even wondered if the child were his. Wishful thinking, because Hermine would have told him. But it could have happened. Yes, there was guilt enough. And if Byron loved Hermine, Horace would not have felt so desolate. But Byron could not love her, because he was besotted with Viola. It was not Byron's fault. Viola had captured him. Horace had been taken with her once himself, remembered that when he returned from Greenland he was unable to keep from thinking of Viola each time he made love to his wife. How ashamed he felt when in less than a year she was dead in childbirth.

For a long time Horace had been able to convince himself that Byron's deeper love was for Hermine, that Viola was only ... well, a woman for sexual pleasure. There was a lovely photograph of Hermine—he would have wished for a copy himself if he could have thought of a way of asking for it—that Byron took with him everywhere. Surely that was an indication of love for a woman. Or so he had thought until Byron in the most natural way showed him the other photograph pasted to the back. Viola. Horace had never been so shocked, devastated really.

Today Viola walked into the office, filled with life and vigor, and he thought of the frail, graceful figure of Hermine. Sometimes it seemed to him that Viola's vitality was draining the strength out of Hermine.

He did not like her, thought Viola; it gave her a chill to feel his ill will. Viola could remember when Horace had liked her. They had been the closest of friends; in Greenland they spent hours together.

She confided the beginning of the romance to Horace, only to learn that Byron had done the same. He had changed toward her when she returned from London and her passion for Byron, his passion for her, flared anew. Disapproving. Well of course a married man and a married woman should not be lovers, but his dislike appeared to be stronger than that, less reasoned.

As soon as Horace left the room, Byron walked over to his desk and stood behind it, his expression blank. It occurred to Viola that all the other times she had been in his office, she had been only dimly aware of the room and its furnishings. Byron had done well for himself. The office paid for by his financial backers was the size of a ballroom, his oak desk as large as a dining table. A huge globe stood beside it, and a map of the Antarctic occupied an entire wall. The other walls were covered by a dark maroon leather, with a tooled gold border of geometric design. On the floor, close to the desk, lay the skin of a massive bear, raising its head, the teeth bared in a savage grin. Armchair legs were carved into the shape of griffins, and a table loaded with surveying instruments, cameras, and a small model of an icebreaker ship was supported by caryatids. The office was so large that the daylight had to be enhanced by electrically wired chandeliers.

Today she saw the photograph of Hermine on his desk. That face. That doll-like face with its sugary smile. That pretty little rosebud mouth and pert nose. This must be the photograph Horace had told her about, the photograph Byron took with him everywhere, placed by his bed. She had not believed Horace, thought he talked out of malice. But here was the picture in the place of honor on the desk. It could not be that he really loved Hermine. Not as he loved Viola. He was as driven in their love affair as she. Byron was a conventional man; this was the way a hero would act toward his wife. Except . . . there had once been a photograph of her that he had treasured. She supposed it was long since lost or thrown away in pique after one of their quarrels.

Now that they were alone together, Byron was thinking if only today were like the other days when she had come to him, filled with the desire to make love. But she was not here for love. The advertisement had brought her.

"I can hardly believe it's here at last, Byron. After waiting so long.

It'll be just as we've always dreamed, the greatest expedition of all to the South Pole." *We,* she had said; she was sure he noticed. Concealing her doubts, she behaved as if her presence on the expedition were a certainty. "Your destiny. And mine."

"Yes, you'll be a part of the expedition, Viola." Her spirits rose, and she felt dizzy with relief. It was as she had known it would be—Byron was an honorable man. And then he went on speaking: "You'll accompany us all the way across the tropics to Port Chalmers far to the south of New Zealand, the final port of embarkation for the Antarctic. You'll set up your laboratory there, just as you did on Disko Island off Greenland, and study the specimens brought back from Antarctica." He was talking rapidly, not allowing her an opportunity to break in, knowing this was not what she wanted or expected.

Viola recalled the premonition of disaster she had felt upon seeing the advertisement. It was as nothing compared to the way she felt now. Turning away so as not to look at him, she thought to sweep from the room. But that could be a mistake. There might yet be something she could say to recall Byron to his honor, convince him to change his mind. "Your promise," she said, keeping her voice level; "you promised to take me to the Antarctic."

Byron did not remember exactly what he had said, but surely there was no promise that she was to go all the way to the Pole.

"You made me believe I would be with you at the Pole."

He could not deny that. Illogical though it was, she was as driven by the promise of exploration as any man. The uncharted regions of the globe held an enticement for her, as for him. The Antarctic. Her dream as well as his. But not her destiny.

No woman could survive on the ice cap. How was it that she could not grasp this undeniable fact? His expedition would journey from Ross Island over the Beardmore Glacier, 820 miles to the Pole, and the same distance back. The endurance of hardy, experienced men would be pushed to the extreme.

"Do you remember Greenland, Byron?" she asked, desperately seeking to make him realize how important she would be to him on the expedition. Now she recalled the moment she had looked at the first of the fossil organisms beneath the microscope and recognized its importance. That was one of the glories of exploration, one of the happiest moments of her life. She had confided it to Byron; he had been offended. He was wary now, thinking she was using the memory of the beginning of their love affair to move him. That was not her intention. "My work created a scientific reputation for you that's helped you get backing for this new expedition."

Byron flushed. Her work. The suffragettes made her feel she had been treated unfairly. It was his work legally. Along with the other expedition members, she had signed the contract agreeing that all writings and scientific observations were the property of the leader. And the contract was hardly unique with him. All expedition leaders followed that practice. In any event, had the fossil discoveries been attributed to a girl—beautiful, with flashing blue eyes and vivid coloring—no one would have believed in them. The finds would have been downgraded, probably ignored.

"You need me, Byron. As a scientist." It was her strongest argument, she thought. There must be fossil evidence to reveal the climate and life forms in Antarctica in aeons past.

Need her? She did have some scientific ability, but so did countless others. He foresaw no difficulty in enlisting paleontologists of stature. She was clearly convinced that enduring Greenland meant she could endure the Antarctic. There was no comparison between the two regions. The Arctic was hazardous, it was true; explorers had died trying to cross the Greenland ice cap. But the region was not usually that dangerous. In the Arctic an expedition leader could rely on Eskimos who understood the terrain and the climate. In the Arctic, there were fish, musk oxen, ermines, lemmings, reindeer, polar wolves and bears. The Antarctic, in contrast, was hostile beyond belief. Always. The smallest mistake and men were dead or driven mad. The terrain was the most treacherous on earth. The extreme cold and brutal winds prohibited the rise of an indigenous population; no land animals could eke out an existence. Seals and penguins were to be found only along the margins of the waters.

She had to be made to understand. "You'd be a burden from beginning to end, Viola. Keeping you alive would endanger the entire party. How could we stake our lives on you? You would be the weak link." He had to conquer the South Pole. It was the goal of his life.

"Going to the Antarctic isn't a sex contest. And I'm strong. My God, Byron, if you knew the physical hardships I lived through for the suffrage movement. The demonstrations and the police brutality.

The horror of Hollowran Prison. Going without food, without water. It made me resolute, hard, able to endure."

Byron flinched. He could not listen to that part of her past without a physical reaction. How dared she bring this up to him now or ever, as if it were a credit to her? Forgetting the consequence—the loss of the child. He thought of the desperate appeal to him that he had answered, only to be refused. Nothing tamed her. From time to time, when they were together in passion, he could put that terrible day in London out of his mind. For a little while. Then it would rise up, taunting, enraging, making him want to do violence upon her, bruise her when they made love. Blind to his emotions, she thought it rough play. And now she would remind him of that, as a reason for giving her what she wanted.

Seeing his face, Viola was brought up short by the realization that she had hurt him.

Sighing, he returned to the present. "Have you stopped to consider what it would be like to be a woman on an all-male expedition in the field? You've never been out in the field, Viola; it's primitive. Where can the men go when they change their clothes? How are they to be out of your sight when they perform their bodily functions? For that matter, where could you possibly go? You just haven't thought this through."

"But I have. There are ways. New Zealand isn't enough, Byron."

"It will have to be enough."

Viola's deep-set violet blue eyes were gleaming, her cheeks were suffused with color. Byron was suddenly aware of the body concealed in the tailored suit with its long, tight skirt. Her body was so different from Hermine's, from those of the women he had known. Uncorseted. Long waisted, with the most gradual of curves. Slender. Almost boyish. But not boyish at all.

Of course she would accept New Zealand, thought Byron. That was the best she could do and she knew it. The vitality . . . the eagerness. Now it was under his control. She would join his expedition in whatever position he offered, sign the contract, obey him as leader. "Take what I'm offering, Viola." As he spoke, he was imagining what it would be like on those long ocean voyages. With Viola. Making love in the narrow bunk, as he had on the journey home from Greenland.

Anger and disappointment swept over her so that she was trembling with emotion. She had mistrusted him, but only now, seeing his impassive face, did she accept the fact that he was not to be moved. New Zealand was his final offer.

Byron could not bear the way Viola was looking at him—as if he had betrayed her. In truth, he was already doing more for her than was wise. Her suffragette history was well known, and a good part of the expedition's backing came from the liquor and brewing industries. They equated suffrage with temperance. How could these women have been so stupid, thought Byron, as to have associated themselves with the Women's Christian Temperance Movement, with the Prohibition party? Temperance had guaranteed the suffragettes the implacable enmity of the powerful liquor industry, which was spending a fortune opposing the movement. Horace had found it hard to gain financial support in the face of Byron's known espousal of the suffrage cause. He still saw the injustice of denying women the vote, but he was not saying so publicly anymore. Taking Viola with him to New Zealand would cause trouble; it was a generous gesture, more generous than she knew.

It seemed to Viola that Byron was smiling in a smug superior manner, and she would have liked to pull at his gleaming blond hair, tear his handsome face apart. *Men wanted . . . men.* Because she had staked everything on being a part of this voyage of exploration, she had gone back to him after that terrible day in London, gone back to him after his marriage and hers, gone back after the most cruel words had been spoken.

Even in her anger, she was so lovely. He would ease her disappointment by making love to her, taking her in all the ways she liked. She never could resist him when he really tried. He put his fingers around her narrow wrist, drawing her to him. "I can feel your pulse racing. You know what you really came for," he whispered in her ear. "We both know."

But it was not what she had come for, and she recoiled at the use he was making of their passion. His arrogance was such that after rejecting her entirely reasonable request to accompany him to the Antarctic, after breaking his promise to her, he remained confident that she would make love with him. She backed away from him, shaking her head.

"You think that by withholding your sexual favors you'll force me to take you to the South Pole?" He was laughing at her now. "Isn't that the woman's way."

"Other women's. Not mine."

"Not Hermine's either. She knows her duty," he said offensively.

She turned away from him, refusing to let him see her despair. "I will go to the Antarctic, Byron. I will."

"The only way you'll ever get to the Antarctic will be to lead an expedition of your own." The idea clearly amused him, so he went on. "Who'd follow a woman leader, Viola? I've got it—Amazons. A band of Amazons."

He was striving for humor, she thought, his kind of humor. She was to picture women in short little tunics running bare-legged across the ice. Byron was not speaking unkindly, but there was nothing intrinsically funny about Amazons. They had been brave women warriors, forerunners of the suffragettes.

"Perhaps we'd meet there on the ice plateau, Viola, dig a shelter, and make love. Remember when we made love in the snow. Struggling to get free of our clothing. Our skins were so hot, melting the snow. Rolling over and over. Your hair looked aflame against the whiteness of the snow."

His body glowing against that whiteness. She remembered the discomfort, the wet, the cold—and then the rapture.

"Your pulse is racing," he whispered again. "No matter what you say, you want me."

It was odd that even now, knowing him as he was, aware of his deceit, his false confidence in his superiority, she could still want him, still think of the ecstasy, not of the pain. She remembered the freedom of England, the sounds of lovemaking, the footsteps on the stairs, James smiling in the doorway. After that had come the tragedy of Ian, the struggle with Byron that had seemed endless, but was coming to an end today. Why not make love with him for one last time? He would remember it on all the nights to come when he was sleeping alone.

Byron moved closer, put his arms around her, and she felt his breath on her neck. Her hat fell off; he pushed it out of the way with his foot. The buttons of his suit coat pressed into the softness of her breasts, his hands moved down her back. He undid the buckle holding the satin sash, pulled off her jacket, unfastened her blouse, the silk-covered buttons resisting his fingers.

Often he was insensitive to what she liked, but today his hands moved softly, seductively. She watched him undress, thinking how handsome he was with his shirt half-buttoned, revealing the breadth of his chest. Putting out her hand then, she ran her fingers down his body until she was touching him as she had on that day long ago when they had been lovers for the first time. Held him in her hand. Hard. And she heard him draw in his breath as he had then, saw his green eyes widen in wonder.

He drew her down on the couch beside him. Like all the furniture in the room, it was large, ornate, with wooden sphinxes as armrests and upholstery made from the skin of a hair seal caught in the Arctic waters. How cold and slippery was the couch, the animal skin beneath her naked body. It reminded Viola of all the cold places she had made love with him. They were so close that she could not tell her panting breathing from his.

Their bodies were wet, slithering on the sealskin. Sweat mingled with the smell of the animal hairs. She moved over on top of him then, caressing him, feeling the smoothness of his skin between her legs, the silkiness of his golden body hair. Then his body was heavy on hers, and she felt the weight against the groin. Harder. Harder. And she wanted him as she had from that first day. Rising to ecstasy. When all at once, his lips were at her ear, murmuring her name, then, "It's my body, too, now. My." At those words all the anger and resentment she felt at his breaking his promise swept over her, and desire vanished. At those words, he felt her stiffen. How many times had he said them to her? Had she ever been his? Even now, lying beneath him, naked, she was resisting. He had thought to deflect her, to win her with his lovemaking. But nothing could change her. She wanted Antarctica. Why could she not accept the life that other women did? But other women were Hermine. He lay more heavily upon her, not resting his weight on his arms, so that she could not pull away from him. When he kissed her, he bit at her lips with his teeth so that he tasted blood, bit at her neck. A moment before she had been wet, warm, ready for him. Now as he opened her legs, he felt her dry, unready.

That would not stop him, she thought, remembering what he had told her of making love to Hermine. Feeling the weight of his body, she wondered what besides the seal he thought he had captured. Still, her body began to move to his rhythm. Faster. Faster. *Yes. Now.*

Oh, he could still arouse her senses. "I can do anything I want with you. And you think you can conquer the Antarctic."

But he could not do anything he wanted with her. And they both knew it.

He believed he had mastered her by this act, thought Viola, asserting his physical dominance, ridiculing her justifiable ambitions. But nothing was changed. She looked up at the walrus tusk mounted on a plaque on the wall, remembered her dream of the Antarctic, and thought of all the reasons she had joined the suffragettes.

The female tiger. Battered and bruised, Byron liked to say. But not defeated, she replied. Never defeated.

# Chapter Nineteen

⁓⁓

DID SHE THINK HIM A fool that he would not know she had drugged him and gone to Tremaine, leaving him in the charge of the servants? Ian stood by the window watching Viola approach the house and thought how surprised she would be to find him awake and ready to confront her. He had not swallowed the drug—the other patients at Bloomingdale's had shown him how to do that without making it evident—and had ordered the servants out of the house. Ian read Tremaine's advertisement in the *Times*. Viola had folded the newspaper so carefully that he guessed there was something she meant to conceal from him. "Men wanted." Except for her, of course. Oh, Tremaine would take her to the Antarctic. And he would be left behind.

Why should he not take her to the Antarctic himself? Beat Tremaine at his own game? In explorer circles in London, everyone had said he would be leading an expedition of his own someday. And then he remembered. So many things were forgotten now, but not the Sharpe expedition, never the Sharpe expedition.

Viola thought he was crazy. Well, perhaps he was, but not so crazy he did not know what she was doing. She would come home, her face flushed, her hair disordered. Sometimes it seemed to him he could perceive the smells of sex, not quite covered by her exotic perfume. When he left on the Sharpe expedition, he had been more of a man than Tremaine could ever be. And then one fatal weakness had undone him. Undone Sharpe as well. Because he could have saved Sharpe.

And now the door opened and here was Viola in some fancy red tailor-made she never wore for him at home. Not that he cared what she wore, but whether she wore it at all. She had been naked. He was sure of it. All those elegant, expensive clothes had been tossed in a heap while she, naked, had lain with his rival on the floor or the couch or wherever the mood struck them. He should tear off her clothes himself and throw her on the floor and take her. But how could he take her when he knew she had been with Tremaine, would be thinking of Tremaine?

"You've been with him." Now he was shouting, and he had not meant to shout. Ian kissed her, hard, the way Tremaine had kissed her; why, her lips were bloody. Did her body bear the marks of the other man's fingers gripping her? There were bruises on her neck. He knew what they were. Love bites. A red haze covered his eyes, blocking out the daylight. That haze had come upon him before and blinded, he had performed frightful acts. Or so he was told afterward. But knowing that, vaguely, but knowing that, he could not stop himself from putting his hands around her neck. All he needed to do was to squeeze a little more tightly and she would never betray him again.

One day, thought Viola, he would kill her. Perhaps today. These manic episodes had happened before—in London and since their return. And she was still alive. But he had not put his hands around her neck before. His hands were so big; he applied a little pressure and her breath was choked off, the light dimmed. In a moment, it would be over.

In desperation she put up her hands to pry his fingers loose. He did not give way, but did not press harder. Her foot went out and kicked him in the ankle. Not very hard. She was half fainting. But it was enough to startle him, and his hands dropped, and in that instant she was out of the room, running to the front door, struggling to get it open fast enough, and dashing down the steps, down the street. His footsteps pounded on the sidewalk; he was running after her. Of course he would catch up with her; he was quick and strong, and her injured throat hurt every time she took a breath. The streets around

Washington Square were quiet today. By an odd chance, no one was out walking—not the policeman on his regular beat, not the old men with the dogs, not the nursemaids with baby carriages. She forced herself to slow her pace, to walk in a natural manner. Hearing his footsteps close behind her, she turned to face him, feigning calm. She was alone with him, must not reveal her fear. Sometimes a show of firmness was all that was needed. Sometimes. Sometimes not.

Ian stopped short, breathing hard. Seizing her arm, he gasped, "You were running away. You'll never get away from me."

But his hold on her arm was loose. She knew him so well; the dangerous mood was passing. If she did not arouse it again, in a moment he would not remember the instinct for violence. "Why have you come out in your shirtsleeves, Ian? It's not warm enough to go without a suit coat."

Ian stood beside her, silent, troubled. She could feel him trembling. "What happened, Viola? What are we doing here?"

"Never mind," she said. "Let's go home." She was spent. Terror is exhausting. And there was no end to it. Periods of quiet, of normal behavior, were succeeded by depression and then by mania. When the fit of violence was over, he would remember only that he had done something wrong. Then he was docile. After the violence.

Ian was tired out, too. As soon as they returned home, he lay down on the sofa, his long legs hanging over the end, and fell heavily asleep.

How many more times would he threaten her life? How many more times before he killed her? During Ian's last stay at Bloomingdale's, the chief doctor warned her: "They always turn on the person closest to them, the one they care about most." He must be brought back to the hospital without delay if signs of violence appeared. She hoped it was the right thing to do. The doctors assured her it was and that Bloomingdale's was the best of institutions. It had even adopted the most modern of all treatments for the mentally ill, psychoanalysis based on the work of Sigmund Freud in Vienna. Still, she knew that Ian was restrained sometimes in a camisole, as they called the canvas garment with closed sleeves, or placed in baths for hours at a time, wrapped in wet sheets, given sedating hypnotic drugs. But sooner or later, whatever treatment had been decreed by the physicians in charge, he was said to be improving. Then he would be depressed, wanting only to go home. With her. The hospital insisted on his remaining longer to calm his nerves with such occupational ther- apy as working in a shop making mattresses and pillows, listening to music in the recreation pavilion, and riding a bicycle around the grounds. Passive at this stage, he would do what was required duti- fully. Eventually, the doctors released him to her care.

Until quite recently mental patients had been thrown into prison, so he was fortunate there was such a place and that they could afford to send him there. Although Viola's inheritance remained in trust un- til she turned forty, Ian's navy disability pay augmented by her allow- ance enabled her to pay the weekly rate of sixteen dollars.

She sighed and went to the telephone to call the doctor to begin the process of committing him to Bloomingdale's. Ian had objected to the installation of the telephone; most people did not have one. It was as if he suspected the use that would be made of it. Looking at Ian sleeping now, she thought that each time he returned from Bloomingdale's, she was hopeful of a normal life. It would be so this time, too. There was still love between them, even though they so sel- dom made physical love. He did not want it. Sometimes she won- dered if he feared the failure on the Sharpe expedition meant he must fail again with her. Viola remembered how heroic he appeared when they first met and he was so close to Sharpe, so close to great- ness.

As soon as she put the telephone receiver back on the hook, Ian sat up and began to mutter. Within minutes, she knew, he would be telling her about the Antarctic debacle. He could not put the Sharpe expedition behind him. Ian relived every moment; he spoke of little else. Over and over. Until she became numbed by hearing him mull over each item of food and clothing, weigh the merits and demerits of each piece of equipment, consider the specifications for the ice- breaker ship, review the strengths and weaknesses of the many breeds of animals.

And how were selections made? Ian noted the differences between the offerings. "Time after time, the wrong choice was made. Most of- ten, the decision was based on cost, with the cheapest winning out. You can manage with supplies of poor quality in some climates, not in Antarctica."

He would stop then and explain to her the dietary deficiencies that ensued because of the poor selection of food. Why had not Sharpe listened to the warnings of scurvy? The clothing had been too heavy and slow-drying, the material for the huts and tents insufficiently waterproofed. The motor sledges were too experimental, too expensive for an expedition with inadequate funding. Sharpe had elected not to wait for the additional backing he could have obtained, being determined to leave by late spring of 1910. That would put him at least a year ahead of Shackleton, who was beginning to organize a new expedition.

Ian knew the total sum available to pay for mounting the expedition, as well as the cost of every item. It was as if he had a balance sheet in his head, the columns clearly drawn.

"The money was short, that was true, yet it could have been better spent."

Finally, he repeated the criteria Sharpe had established for selecting the members of the expedition. If only Sharpe had held to them. Instead, the criteria were waived for sons of backers, for men offering to forgo payment or, worse yet, to invest in the expedition themselves. They had been favored over stronger, more experienced naval officers.

"I had misgivings before we left. But when we finally did set out for the Antarctic, I forgot them, Viola. You cannot imagine the joy we felt; it was almost delirium. The South Pole was nearly within our grasp. Surely the deficiencies of supplies could be overcome."

Then the wireless from Carlsen arrived. A number of expedition members expressed fear about the forthcoming race, displaying, Ian thought, their inherent weakness. Not he. They could best any rival party of explorers. And they would have but for the mistakes, avoidable mistakes, that had been made.

The first summer season, for example, when they traversed the continent laying the depots, Sharpe insisted on turning back too soon. "I volunteered to go forward alone to bring a load of emergency supplies closer to the Pole. I was told not to be foolhardy. Sharpe said he would need me too badly for the final assault on the Pole to allow me to risk my life beforehand."

And then it was the following spring, and they forced their desperate way over the ice cap, up the Beardmore Glacier, agonizing step by agonizing step. But hard and painful though it was, he had been uplifted by the firm conviction that he was to conquer the South Pole with Sharpe. His voice broke as he came to the hour when they reached the summit of the glacier, ready to begin the descent. The sun was hidden that day by a heavy ice shower. They put up a tent, shared their ration of food. Now it was time to say farewell to the men who were not to go on to the Pole. He had pitied them. Though these men had known from the start that they had not been selected for the polar party, it was hard to miss the glory after suffering so much.

Sharpe signaled to him then to come outside the tent. Go back with the other men. The rebuff had been totally unexpected. He was the strongest of them all. Sharpe's right hand. That was the most terrible day of his life. Each time he spoke, the repudiation of him as a man returned with all its pain. Yes. He had been through bad times as a boy and young man. But they were far behind him. Nothing was wrong with him on that final journey across the glacier. He was not mad. No matter what Sharpe thought. Maybe later. But was not the wrong done him on the ice cap enough to drive any man mad?

Each time he told the story, Ian remembered something more, offered additional details on where the expedition went wrong, what could have been done to prevent the ultimate disaster.

The astonishing thing, Viola came to see, was that he was absolutely right. Had the expedition followed the plan he outlined to her now, it need not have come to grief.

He was still talking when the orderlies came to take him to Bloomingdale's. After they were gone, she paced the parlor, thinking it was always dark and airless in that room. With all the money she had coming to her in due course, she could not afford anything better now.

She thought of Byron's office with the oak desk as large as a dining table, the armchairs with legs carved into the shapes of griffins, the marble mantel holding the Hubbard Medal. He had the backers to pay for all the supplies he could possibly need; his expedition was assured. And she was relegated to a minor position. Perhaps she had been deluded as much by herself as by him. His promises to take her to the Antarctic—he spoke them every time they made love. She trusted him, did not suspect his assurances to her were designed to arouse her, were not to be taken seriously after the climax was achieved. Designed to keep her captive. His captive.

A messenger arrived bringing her the contract Byron had drawn up. New Zealand. For all the years they were lovers, they had been locked in competition. *You would never fit yourself into my life.* Byron found that intolerable. Now it seemed to her he had been waiting all these years for the moment to come when he could dominate her life. He thought he had the control, the power, was convinced the competition was over and she had lost. Viola had never envisioned defeat. There must be some way she could stand against him yet.

*The only way you'll ever get to the Antarctic will be to lead an expedition of your own.* The joke had hurt her when he had spoken, but it did not hurt her now. All at once, an idea of such splendor came to her that she was shaken.

Lead an expedition of your own. A taunt? Or a possibility? Byron's words reverberated in her mind. There were other words, too: No woman can survive on the ice cap. But she had never accepted the word of others on what a woman can do. From the time she had been a girl refusing the easy slopes in the Alps, she had been as accomplished on skis as the men, as good a climber with crampons and ice ax.

Night after night she had listened to Ian explaining how an expedition must be mounted, how the dread icy Antarctic continent could be conquered. Over and over. Item by item. Step by step. Of course she could lead an expedition. That no other woman had ever done so before only spurred her on. Unwittingly, Byron had told her what she must do.

She was undefeated still. The greatest competition of their lives was to begin, and she would win it. Byron had thought to sequester her at Port Chalmers in New Zealand. Instead, she would challenge him to a race for the South Pole. It would be a race to rival that of Sharpe and Carlsen. The victor would place the American flag at the Pole. The victor would make the greater scientific discoveries. Why not she?

Who would follow a woman leader, Byron had asked? "A band of Amazons." Another intended joke that was no joke at all. Amazons would accept her leadership on an all-women's expedition to the

Antarctic. The image now dazzled Viola. Amazons on the ice, not in tunics but in fur parkas and high boots, skiing in front of the dog teams up the glacier, down the incline leading to the South Pole. Who would go? Women of great strength and resolution, women like Carla. It had taken three policemen to subdue Carla when she went on the attack.

The messenger was waiting, instructed to carry back the signed contract. "You can go now," she told him. "There is no response."

The next step was the practical one of raising sufficient funds. Somehow she must make her father understand the importance of what she planned to do. If only he would give her access to her inheritance, she would not need too much more. Unlike suffrage, an Antarctic expedition fascinated members of society and it seemed likely that her parents and their friends would be willing to contribute.

Within the hour she was in her parents' home, telling of her plan. Within moments of her arrival, whatever hopes and expectations she had entertained were dashed. "What can you be thinking of, Viola? Spend your money, family money, on a crazy scheme like this! Your grandfather knew what he was doing when he left the money in trust for you and under my control," declared her father, and he called the chauffeur to drive her home. The horses were gone; her father now had a Cadillac and a Packard.

Pacing the floor all night, Viola found the solution. It was so obvious that she wondered why she had even troubled to apply to her disapproving parents. The suffragettes would give the needed financial support, and do so gladly. They were demanding an amendment to the Constitution. Eight thousand suffragettes had demonstrated last year on the eve of President Wilson's inauguration. The crowd had been hostile. Acts of violence ensued and the police offered no protection. The secretary of war called in troops from Fort Meyer to gain control. Undeterred, the suffragettes held more demonstrations, sent deputations to appeal to the president. But nothing had really captured the public imagination. An expedition led by a woman and composed of women, only women—here was the gesture suffrage had been waiting for. A symbol of what women can do. Unconquerable.

The following morning Viola returned to Byron's office. She would have liked to laugh in his face, but instinct told her to keep the plan secret for as long as she could, take him by surprise. Byron was relieved to see her. His disappointment had been acute when the messenger returned without the signed contract. Now he realized she had second thoughts. He would have her with him and all would be as he wished. On his orders, she would remain at Port Chalmers and be waiting for him when he returned in triumph from the South Pole. For him. Crosbie would be thousands of miles away in some madhouse, Hermine would trail like a wraith through the big house on Gramercy Park. Viola would be his alone. He remembered how he had felt on the day he had received her urgent letter from London asking him to come to her. Then he had believed she was delivered into his hands. He was wrong. She refused to accept what she called his domination. Domination—when all he wanted to do was care for her. She would accept it now.

"I'm glad you're coming with me," he said simply.

"I need more time," she replied. "There will be difficulties in making arrangements for Ian. I can't sign the contract until everything is settled."

Something about the way she was speaking troubled Byron, though what she said was reasonable enough. Horace came in then with some order forms and saw that Byron was glowing as he never glowed in Hermine's presence. Horace knew his feelings to be contradictory—he could not bear the thought of Byron's hands on Hermine's body and yet was tormented by the knowledge that they were caressing Viola instead.

Horace did not want her on the expedition, thought Viola, observing his cold, accusatory gaze. He would be pleased when he learned she was not going with them.

Obtaining the support of the suffragettes proved more difficult than Viola had anticipated. She thought to dazzle them with her vision. But the suffragettes proved reluctant. "A grand gesture for suffrage, you say, one that could help speed passage of the amendment. That's true if it succeeds. But what if it doesn't?" remonstrated Ann Alardyce, president of the National American Woman Suffrage Association. She stressed that their funds would at best be limited, while Tremaine had the best of everything.

"If he reaches the Pole ahead of you, Viola, the plan will backfire and the expedition will be used to prove that women are not the equals of men. As a suffragette acting on your own, you can afford to take that risk. As the major suffrage organization, we can't. The suffrage movement would be held up to ridicule for sponsoring you."

The expedition was slipping away from her. There must be something she could say to convince them. And then she knew what it was. The backing by the suffrage movement would be kept a secret. "If . . . we don't succeed"—even saying that seemed absurd to Viola—"then no one will ever know you were involved. The expedition members will be told I am acting independently."

"Even so, the failure of an all-women's expedition would have a detrimental effect, Viola."

"Why should anyone know that? Of course people will be aware of the expedition and its departure for the Antarctic. A few journalists might speculate as to its subsequent fate, but no one will take it seriously.

"The very existence of the all-women's expedition will be forgotten if we do not keep the story alive. Every woman who joins will swear never to speak of the expedition should we fail to reach the Pole. The captain and crew of the ship that brings us to and from the Antarctic will be required to sign such an agreement.

"But if we succeed . . . And we will. Then, and only then, will the all-women's expedition become famous, the suffrage movement get the credit. You can make the most of it."

Fired by her enthusiasm, the suffragettes voted to give their backing, and Viola began to organize the expedition with Eileen Lincoln's help. An advertisement for expedition members was quickly prepared for publication in *Suffrage Searchlight* and the British suffragettes' *Votes for Women* under the heading AMAZONS WANTED.

"Only single women will apply," remarked Eileen. "Husbands will not allow their wives to take part in such an exploit."

Husbands. Not hers. Ian would never have stopped her. In an odd reversal, she was the one going to the Antarctic while he remained behind. He would be discharged from Bloomingdale's before the expedition departed, she thought, and given over to the care of his brother or some other of his relations.

As Viola began to make up lists of supplies, she remembered what Ian had told her. Sharpe had also been short of funds, but his failure,

Ian had insisted, was not due to lack of money but rather to poor selection of supplies. In the gentle sunshine of a spring afternoon in
London, Sharpe had elected to take the wrong boots, the wrong
food, the wrong sledge, the wrong animals. These mistakes led to
death during a blizzard in what passed for summer near the Pole.

Knowing she must not make any mistakes, Viola was sobered by
the awareness of her lack of experience. Ian understood what was
needed, but he was locked away and could not help her now.

On her next visit to Bloomingdale's, Ian came forward to greet her
smiling, and then stopped, an expression of dismay crossing his face.
"You look so bright and excited today." Those words were an accusation. "You're going to the Antarctic, aren't you? That's the reason.
It's Tremaine, I know it. You thought you'd hidden the advertisement, but I saw.

"While I rot here, you'll be with him on his expedition."

"No, I'm not joining the Tremaine expedition, Ian."

He turned away from her. "You're just saying that. You've had me
put away, so you can tell me anything and I can't prove it's false."

When she responded by telling him about the all-women's expedition and the race with Tremaine to the Pole, he was incredulous. She
thought she could tell him anything. The idea was insane. More insane than any he might conceive.

"Believe me, Ian. It's true." She recited the words of the advertisement, told him the suffragettes were to be her financial backers.

At the utter conviction in her voice, he realized she meant it. No
other woman could conceivably lead an expedition, but Viola—he
believed she could do so. Nothing was ever impossible for her.

Then the bitterness of deprivation swept over him as he grasped
what she intended to do with him, understood what her expedition
was to mean for him. *Rot here.* She would go to Antarctica and leave
him behind, incarcerated in Bloomingdale's for the years of her absence. That would be seen as the perfect solution for her mad husband. He would not be able to endure the knowledge of her
abandonment for all those years. There was no alternative to doing
away with himself. Even in a place like this where one was guarded,
suicide was always a possibility.

Viola was looking at him with such love on her face that he was
moved to make an appeal. Of course it was hopeless, but he could

not let her go without that effort. "Get me out of here and take me with you, Viola. I'd take you if it were my expedition."

Her husband. He was not saying that no woman could survive on the ice cap. Instead he accepted her as leader of an expedition; all he wanted was to be there, too. Of course that was impossible; he was not well enough, and even if he were, his presence would destroy the purpose of the expedition. She was glad to have such a good face-saving reason to give him. A gesture for suffrage had to be carried out by women. Only women.

Only women. That was the part of her story Ian did not believe. Perhaps she was right to reject him. He was a sick man; the doctors told him that and it must be true. The psychoanalyst, as this new kind of doctor was called, wanted to know why he tried to hurt Viola and he had only a vague sense of doing so. It was the same kind of feeling he had after the awful business with Gordon's dog and with those girls in Scotland.

Nonetheless, he did remember clearly that not long before, he had been a great polar explorer. Great enough to have saved Sharpe had he only been given the chance.

Now it was all happening again. Viola would die on the glacier, as Sharpe had died, without his help. He could not save her. An inmate in an insane asylum, no one would listen to him.

And at the thought of her lying dead on the ice cap, as Sharpe lay dead, desperation seized him so that he spoke forcefully for the first time. "Get me out of here, Viola. I'll show you how an expedition should be put together. You'll beat Tremaine to the Pole and get home safely if you listen to me. No one else can do it for you. No one."

Did she dare to demand his release from Bloomingdale's? Did she dare not to when he did know more than anyone else about organizing an expedition? Ian was standing straight now, his eyes shining, lifted out of melancholy. Still, she hesitated. "You do understand that, as a man, you can't accompany the expedition."

She was saying that now in Bloomingdale's because she was not certain of his sanity. Once she realized that he was as he once had been, she would change her mind. This was hardly the time to tell her that, so he assured her he did not expect to go to the Antarctic.

All he wanted to do was to help her put the expedition together so that it would succeed.

The doctors demurred, declared Ian not ready for discharge, but Viola was firm, and as most often happened, had her way.

At home, Ian soon discovered that Viola's claim of an all-women's expedition was not false at all. Suffragettes came and went through the parlor that had been turned into an office. They were disturbed by his presence, his obvious involvement in the planning. The women had recognized from the outset that men must help to get the expedition to the Antarctic continent. Ships were powered both by steam and by the wind, and trained seamen were needed to stoke the boiler, unfurl a full mast of sails. This male crew would land the women on the Antarctic ice and then return to winter in New Zealand.

Ian was different. He was in charge of selecting and ordering supplies, behaving as if he were to go to the Antarctic continent. Viola insisted that was not true, but it seemed to the suffragettes that Ian had another view.

Byron wrote to Viola, suggesting that she come to his office to sign the contract; he did not see how she could delay any longer. At the hour named, his office would be deserted. Well, why not? They both knew what usually happened when they were together. Puzzled by Viola's lack of response, he telephoned her. Ian answered. It gave Byron an unpleasant feeling to discover her husband home from Bloomingdale's. He hung up.

The following day Horace came in holding a newspaper. The *Suffrage Searchlight*. Byron read the title. He had never heard of the publication. Viola was the only suffragette he knew. "Did Viola give this to you?"

"No. I have nothing to do with Viola." There was a slight edge to his voice, which Byron ignored. Sometimes he thought Horace was possessive about their friendship, jealous of Viola's position in his life. "My sister is a suffragette of sorts and she showed this to me. Said she thought I'd be interested in an advertisement."

"What are you talking about? Why would you be interested in an advertisement to suffragettes."

"Read it."

AMAZONS WANTED *for the first All-Women's Antarctic Expedi-tion in history. Physical strength, courage, and resolution are*

*needed. Must march, ski, and climb over the most hazardous ter-*
*rain on earth. Will face continual danger. There is risk of death.*
*Success will bring fame and strike a blow for suffrage.*

Completing the message were Viola's name and address.
"My God, Horace. We must stop her!"

# *Chapter Twenty*

AMAZONS WANTED.

Living in a tenement in the slums, bent over a sewing machine in a sweatshop, she was barely aware of the suffragettes. One of the other workers brought in a copy of the *Suffrage Searchlight* and showed it to Araminta (she was going under the name of Jane then for safety's sake). When she read it, for the first time since fleeing to this drab, wearisome life in Chicago, she felt hope. There had to be a better world than the one she knew; perhaps the suffragettes would bring it about. The suffragettes were committed to helping others; that had to mean they would shelter a woman who was a fugitive.

The advertisement promised danger, too, a risk of death. But dying on an expedition was heroic, not like being hunted down and destroyed as if she were a rabid animal. Araminta shuddered. A fugitive. How frightful it sounded. Yet that was what she was. A fugitive—and not from the police. The people she was hiding from had been her friends.

How had she come to this desperate place in her life? She remembered the first time she saw William Carter. An ordinary name for an extraordinary man. Even now, thinking of his deep-set flashing dark eyes beneath their heavy brows could send a chill down her spine. He had drawn her to him from the start, as he drew everyone. She had looked at his hands, long tapering fingers, with dark hairs growing down. What was so seductive about them? And his voice, deep, with a sort of growl.

A minister, he called himself, though he was quick to say he had not been sanctioned by any church. Rather, he established his own religion, wrote his own bible, circulated fliers heralding a new faith, promising to heal the sick with his hands.

By the time Araminta heard of him, the Tribe of the Greater God numbered thousands from the farm states of the Midwest and the rural South, and Reverend Carter was preaching in a magnificent church in Iowa City and traveling to smaller churches in other cities, all built with the money contributed by the members of the Tribe. She was seventeen, and thinking herself trapped on an isolated farm, with exhausted parents wasted in the struggle with the soil. Her schooling ended with the eighth grade, so she could help work the fields and take care of the six younger children. No time for friends, no glamour or excitement. And here he was.

Everything he promised in the fliers came to pass. Were there any in the congregation who were handicapped or sick? A woman limping painfully on crutches was the first down the aisle; Carter put his hands on her head, prayed, took the crutches away, and told her to walk, and she walked. A blind man was led to the pulpit; Carter passed his fingers over the eyes, wiping away what must have been a cataract, and the man shouted in glee that his vision was clear. Miracle healing—Araminta would not have believed had she not seen it with her own eyes.

After the service Carter made his way through the throng of worshipers, handsome in the short black leather jacket and tight trousers that served as his clerical habit. He had noticed her. "I can see true faith shining in your eyes." Then he stroked her head, closing his eyes, as if he could feel her thoughts in his fingers. "Yes," he said. "You are chosen." And she swayed, could have fainted with joy. "Come with me. Take up your membership in the Tribe of the Greater God as you were destined to do from before your birth."

He wanted her to be with him, ordered her to leave home. "But my parents, my little brothers and sisters. They need me." "God needs you more. He will take care of your family if you serve him now." Still she knew they would worry, and having no money, asked

Carter to give her enough for a postcard and stamp. He patted her hand and said God would inform them.

In later years, recalling that scene, she was appalled. Not then. Instead she had gone with Carter into what was the happiest period of her life. He gave her a new name as a symbol of a new beginning—Araminta. What did he not do for her? A house next to the church held a dormitory, and she was assigned a bed.

Araminta had sewn the clothes for her family and knew how to work a sewing machine. She was glad to be useful. Her labor belonged to the Tribe; she was not paid. But she had no need for money. They clothed her and provided her with food. Others who worked in the city for wages contributed half to the Tribe. All for the good of the Greater God.

In the course of his sermons, Carter presented an idealistic code of behavior. The Tribe must be more virtuous than other people. There must be no smoking, no drinking, no drugs, no swearing, no dancing. Dress was to be modest without the corseting that would give the figure a seductive, hourglass shape. Araminta had never possessed a corset or any other undergarment except for drawers made out of flour bags. She must be sure to follow the rules, the members of the Tribe warned her. Not to do so meant punishment. Araminta could tell that some were nervous about this, afraid. She could not imagine why. It was so easy to do as Reverend Carter wished.

Each Sunday after the sermon, after the healing of the sick, came sex: "Who in the congregation has been leading a sinful life? Come forward and the Greater God through me will cleanse you." Each time, half a dozen stood up, waiting their turn to go down the aisle to stand before him and tell what they had done. The sexual acts they described were lascivious, against nature. Sex was performed with dogs, sheep, horses, two men together, two women and a man. One sinner followed the other. Reverend Carter prayed that each of these individuals would find the way back to healthy sex. Then he would call for volunteers, and members of the Tribe would leap up and vie with one another in offers to help. On a few occasions, when the sinner was a young woman and attractive, Carter declared he would bring help himself. Surely, a sexual aberration was most tragic for a woman like that.

After Araminta had been a member of the Tribe for a few weeks,

Reverend Carter sent a message telling her to come to him in the house that had been built for him beside the church. She had never been in a house like his, with a marble floor in the entry hall, thick carpeting in the parlor, ornate mahogany furniture covered with needlepoint, velvet draperies. "Araminta, you must know by now that I have a women's council."

She nodded. There were six on the council; they were the most important women in the Tribe. Araminta envied them.

"I've been watching you since you came to the Tribe, Araminta, and I believe you are worthy of becoming a member of the council."

How could this be? It was beyond her wildest dreams. Was she dreaming now? "Why me?" she asked. "I'm so young and I don't know nothing of the world or . . . nothing."

He smiled. "Your heart knows everything it needs to know. You are pure. Every woman on the council is pure. Every woman on the council is the beloved of God." He paused. "Actively."

"What do you mean, Reverend?"

"William. Willy to you."

"What do you mean . . . Willy?"

He put one long finger on her breast and she gasped. "It means you are chosen to have sex with God through me."

She was moved out of the dormitory and into a house shared by the council women. That first night he came to the house, into the parlor where she was sitting alone. The other women were avoiding her; perhaps they resented a newcomer. He took her hand and led her up the stairs and to her room. Her room. For the first time in her life, she had a room of her own. He put his hand on her head again and smiled. Of course, he must smile if he was feeling her thoughts.

"You are not afraid," he said. "That's because you feel the love of the Greater God."

Afraid? How could she be afraid when she was to have her first experience of sex with this man? His naked body was thin, sinuous, heavily covered with dark hair. He signaled her to kneel in front of him, bury her face in the wiry pubic hair of his groin, told her to pray. And then they were on the bed and he was probing her with his hands, his body. It did hurt, more than she had expected, and she could not help but cry out. He was not angry at that, but smiled, stroked her face, her breasts, her abdomen. Later it was he who cried out. Afterward, he pulled back the blanket and sheet, observed the blood on her thighs and on the bed, and smiled again.

The next day he brought her a dress of flowered voile with flowing sleeves to wear when she came to him and a necklace of bright beads. It seemed to her that the necklace resembled one she had seen in the collection bowl at a Sunday service, but she must have been mistaken.

Willy took her away from the sewing machine and assigned her to the Tribe's office, to work on the account books. Araminta was one of the few women in the Tribe with an eighth-grade education and knew her numbers. A listing was maintained for each member, with figures showing income and contributions week by week. Even in the Tribe, there were some who falsified the amount of income and so contributed less than half. Was it not terrible for people to be so selfish as to keep more than their own share of their earnings rather than provide for their fellows? The money was used for good causes. The Tribe sponsored special schools where prostitutes could be taught a trade, established hospitals to care for the aged. Willy was pained by such evidence of greed. Araminta was to inform him when a contribution was not fully half of all the person's earnings. But how was she to know that? The other council members working in the office shook their heads at her ignorance. The Tribe kept watch; someone was sure to find out and report the correct figures to the office.

To Araminta's surprise, the Tribe was not loved by those who were not members. She had thought that people who behaved with such rectitude and did so many good works would be accepted as the most desirable of citizens. Instead, with increasing frequency, the townspeople broke into the churches and vandalized them, scribbled foul sayings on the walls. On Sundays there were shouted threats directed at Reverend Carter, warning him to get out of town. There will always be individuals who will oppose a great man with a different philosophy. Those belonging to the established religions do not like to see a new faith attract so many followers. It proved necessary to arm some of the strongest men of the Tribe, to have them stand guard at the doors of the church and surround Carter's private residence.

All day, as she worked on the books, Araminta was waiting for the message calling her to the big house to Willy. When he embraced her, she felt as if she were in the embrace of a higher being. He moved his body around hers so smoothly, snakelike she sometimes thought, not meaning it in any sinister way. Willy showed her what he wanted her to do for him—to take his phallus in her mouth. It was so long she thought she would choke and was proud she could keep herself from retching. Once she would have thought it lewdness, but now she did it gladly. He groaned in ecstasy. That was pleasure enough.

But sometimes, at a meal or when all the women happened to be in the parlor, she could not help but think that they also received God's love through Willy. All members of the council were beloved by the Greater God.

"You mustn't mind that I have sex with other women," he told her. "God has more than enough love to give. It would be against his laws to limit myself to just one. You're satisfied, aren't you?"

She agreed, but she did not know what satisfaction meant. When they made love, it was he who reached a climax.

"Of all the women, you're my favorite."

One day another woman joined the council, just sixteen, blond and fragile. Now Araminta saw that the women of the council were friendlier to her, avoiding the newcomer. As the days passed, the other women on the council began to whisper to her. The miracles were false. But the lame walked, the blind saw. The cures were staged, arranged in advance, practiced in private. Araminta must never breathe a word of this or those who told her would be punished. Impossible surely. The women had to be lying.

One day when she was in the office, by accident she opened the file drawer below the one where she stored the books. Nothing was locked, as no one but Willy and the council ever entered the room. Araminta did not hesitate to look through it; Willy told her there were no secrets from her. Newspaper clippings were piled up behind the folders. She took them out. Reverend Pilfers Millions. Forced Contributions Enrich Carter. There were millions of dollars of contributions listed. But this money was not for Carter; it was for the Tribe. Reverend Suspected in Real Estate Swindle. And another. Aged Neglected in Tribe's Horror Hospitals. One foul, false charge and then another. She was filled with rage at the journalists who would stoop to such calumnies against a great and good man. A stack of legal documents occupied the front of the file. Willy was being sued. Lawyers were dishonest, too, she realized with dismay.

The following Sunday Reverend Carter made a stunning pronouncement. The Tribe was to leave the United States and move to the far distant island of Trinidad off the coast of Venezuela and establish an agricultural commune there. This would be the center for the Tribe, a socialistic society in which all worked for the good of others. At its heart would be the church.

"We'll need contributions from each one of you to achieve this utopia. Are you willing to give all you have?"

Who could refuse Reverend Carter, standing there with his eyes flashing, his long, thin arms outstretched? When the bowls for contributions were passed around, arms were stripped of bracelets, watches, wedding bands, pockets were emptied of coins. Araminta had only her necklace to give.

In the end Carter's exhortations produced sufficient contributions to bring fifteen hundred Tribe members to Trinidad. He could have obtained additional funds had it not been necessary for him to leave the United States hurriedly. By now the women on the council knew of threats to arrest and imprison him.

Araminta had expected an island paradise, but the tract of land they were to farm was sandy, barren. The work was hard, harder than on the farm back home, but she was big and strong, happy to be able to do so much for the Tribe, for Willy Carter.

When did the first doubt seep in? Perhaps at the end of her pregnancy. One night she awakened with severe cramps and a violent gush of blood. She screamed, and the other women rushed to her side—all but one, the newest member of the council, the young pretty blond girl. The midwives for the Tribe were unable to stop the bleeding or alleviate the excruciating pain. "Get Willy. He will save my baby." One of the women left the room and returned without him. "He will come in time." Writhing in agony, she waited. At last he was beside her. Relieved, she called on him to perform his miracle healing and save the baby and stop her pain. He put his hands, his magic touch on her abdomen and prayed. An hour later the infant was born. Dead. She knew she must not blame him. Only that was the moment she remembered that the other women in the council had told her the miracle healings were false.

The other women of the council sensed a change, whispered to her of punishment shacks where those who broke the rules were chained, beaten, starved. Children who cried during the sermons were put in the shacks as well. It could not be. Go nearer and hear them shriek. Some of them die. Did she not see the graves? But children do die of illness. Did she not hear shots almost every day? Of course, but that was for hunting. No, if anyone escaped into the surrounding woods, he was hunted down by the armed guards and shot. The number of guards had increased to the size of a small army. No one dared to differ with the Reverend Carter. Any woman, not just the council, could be forced to have sex with him. Forced? Who would not be honored by his touch? But the other women did not feel that way.

Araminta still was not altogether convinced. She saw the guards, heard the screams, could tell that some members of the Tribe were afraid. But not most people. They adored him. There was a glow in their faces when Willy walked by, when he stopped to talk, to put a hand on the shoulder of any man or woman. The members of the Tribe vied for his attention as they always had. Each Sunday his sermons held them spellbound.

A terrible threat was hanging over the commune, he announced one Sunday. Police officers and national guard units from the United States were arriving at Saint Catherine in Trinidad, planning to kidnap him and his followers, torture them to give up their faith, kill any who resisted. The socialistic precepts that ruled the commune were anathema to those who followed only the principles of greed and personal enrichment. Luckily Carter had informants who were giving him warning. The invasion of the commune was planned for the day after tomorrow. He would never be taken alive. It was better to die by one's own hand than by that of one's enemies, nobler to die for the Greater God.

"Will you die with me?" he asked.

"Yes! Yes!" they shouted.

How could this be brought about? The little blond girl spoke at last and revealed the plan. Willy had told her there was poison, enough for all the Tribe. Tonight the guards would fill huge vats with a mixture of the poison with a fruit drink. The members of the Tribe were to pray together; then, starting at high noon, they would line up to drink from the vats and die in a mass suicide. And what a gesture for their cause—the deaths of fifteen hundred heroic people. William Carter and the Tribe for the Greater God would never be forgotten.

With horror, Araminta realized that they would drink the poison. For him. A few might resist the suicide order, but no escape for them was possible either. The compound was watched by armed guards. Those who did not take the poison voluntarily would be forced to do so or be shot. She saw Willy Carter clearly at last.

Did she have to die? Did the Tribe have to die? Everything within her rejected that conclusion. There was one way to stop him. She would have to force her way through the dense woods and down the road to Saint Catherine town to the American consulate and tell what was to happen. Troops could then be sent to stop the mass suicide.

Twenty-four hours—that was all the time remaining. Araminta waited only until Willy called the blond girl to him. Then she took her tools and went into the farthest sugarcane field. The guards did not patrol there. At the end of the field the ground dropped off sharply into a precipice. No one had ever climbed down the rocks into the abyss and up the other side, but that was the only way of leaving the compound unseen. Death in the abyss was preferable to death by poison, and so she started down. Step by step, grabbing at the puny shrubs growing out of the rocks, she climbed, slid, and fell to the bottom, bruised and breathless. It seemed to her that the rocks she dislodged in the descent were making so terrible a din that everyone would hear. But no one came.

The summit of the precipice was at such a distance that she almost lost heart. She would not look up again. Instead, she walked doggedly across the foot of the abyss, a half mile or more to the rock wall she must climb to get out. Deliberately, she stuck her pick in the rock to get a foothold, and began her climb. One step and then another. Coming to a small ledge, she sat down just for a minute to catch her breath. Little time was left before her absence would be discovered and a search party sent out. One step and then another. Strike with the pick, dig it deep, hang on to it, and go up. Her hands were sweating; she rubbed them with dirt and grasped the pick again. She lost sense of time; there was nothing but the effort she was making. And then the brightness around her told her she must be close to the summit. Now she did look up, and right above her head was solid flat ground. With a final desperate push she grasped a clump of weeds, pulled herself over the top, and fell gasping.

Her head was spinning; her stomach churned and she feared to lose consciousness. She could not allow herself a moment's weakness. Dragging herself to her feet, she staggered across the sunlit patch of land and into the dark wooded area beyond. All she knew was that she must keep the abyss at her back. Stumbling over exposed roots and fallen branches, she at last came to a path cleared through the underbrush, and then she was on the paved road leading to the town of Saint Catherine.

Half an hour later she was climbing the steps to the consulate, and then standing before the man at the reception desk who was staring in wonder at her bruised and dirty face and hands, and her hair standing on end. Her dress, torn to tatters, revealed the paucity of undergarments. He could not make any sense of her insistence that police and troops be dispatched to the commune at once. Trying to calm her hysteria, he assured her that police and troops were on the alert to enter the commune the day after tomorrow. Too late, she groaned, wringing her hands. By then the Tribe would all be dead. Mass suicide.

A preposterous story. Still, it would be wise to alert the consul. The two men conferred. The woman must be mad, and indeed she looked mad. But the consul was not quite easy in his mind. Everything about Carter and the Tribe seemed mad. That was why the decision had been taken to deport him and his Tribe. Could Carter have decided on this course of action in desperation? Revenge? Impossible. And yet . . . the consul dared not take the chance that this seemingly crazed woman might be right.

As dawn was breaking the following day, police and troops entered the compound, arrested Carter and his immediate circle of guards, and seized the poison-filled vats that were being placed in front of the church. The members of the Tribe resisted; they wanted to take the poison and gain immortality as the people who died rather than repudiate their faith. They appeared stunned to learn they were not to be tortured, merely put out of Trinidad as soon as passage could be arranged. But when they discovered that the Reverend Carter and his guards had been arrested and were to stand trial, a riot exploded and was quelled with difficulty. The members of the Tribe shouted their loyalty to Carter, looked sorrowfully at the forbidden vats.

The rage of the Tribe then turned on Araminta, who had accompanied the police to the commune. It took six men to wrest her away from the angry Tribe members surrounding her and to pass her through the hostile crowd. Far from being praised for saving their lives, she was cursed, threatened for betraying the Reverend Carter and the Tribe of the Greater God. She was hastily taken back to Saint Catherine and given sanctuary in the consulate until she could be returned to the United States.

Threatening letters were left on the doorstep. Because of her, the commune that was to have been an example for all the world was disbanded. Had they died, they would have been martyrs. Instead, they were being deported, returning home in disgrace. They had given up their families, their jobs, their money and possessions. Now they had nothing. But the defeat was temporary; the Tribe was not finished, the hate letters went on. They had but to wait and William Carter would will himself out of the foul prison cell and return. But so much suffering . . . for him and for them. They would pay her back. Oh yes, they would have their revenge. Araminta was never to be forgiven. Araminta. That had not even been her name. He had named her. What had he not done for her?

AMAZONS WANTED.

She would be safe. No one from the Tribe could find her in Antarctica. There she would make up for the years wasted on Willy Carter's false dream, the years as a fugitive bent over a sewing machine. Strike a blow for suffrage. There must be a better world than the one she knew. Perhaps she could make it happen.

Oh, how sad never to have a man.

That was what people said when they believed her to be out of earshot. They did not like to see her face, grossly distorted by a harelip, drawn all the way up toward her nose. Claireve Dalton could hardly bear to look in a mirror herself. Her efforts at speech were dismissed, as who could decipher the guttural sounds produced by her damaged palate? She had been taught to read and write, could "converse" by writing, but few troubled to do so.

Her parents wanted her to become a nun. As if she could believe that a god who had given her this fearsome deformity yet had wonderful plans for her immortal soul. She went through the motions of religious observance. There was no reason not to pretend. Her mother believed, prayed on her knees each day. For Claireve. She was excused from confession because of her speech handicap. And what sins could she have to confess? A nun. What other life could she have? they asked. It was not as if celibacy were an issue. No man would have her.

No man. So they thought. But how many men possessed her in the kindly dark of the backyard, the open fields? On how many nights was gravel thrown up to her window to wake her, call her out? The first boy had said, when she undressed in the moonlight, "Why, your body is splendid." And it was. Her parents were distressed she was not small and thin, easier to hide away. But if she were small, she would be subject to rape, pathetic. Large, she was any man's equal. Tall, well built, strong. She exercised every part of her body, was in full control of her muscles within and without. But strong as she was, hers was a female body, with full breasts tapering to a narrow waist, made narrower still by the tight corset lacing demanded even of someone like her. And her legs were long and so well muscled that when she wrapped them around a man's hips, he knew, oh he knew, she was there.

That first boy had meant to laugh at her. Later she learned his friends had dared him. In her arms, her legs tight around him, he forgot. In his arms, his weight pressing down on her, she forgot. For the first time in her conscious life, she was oblivious to her deformity.

There was no need for speech in the dark. Her moans of ecstasy were no different perhaps than those of other girls. These men came back. They went with sweet, simpering little girls, pretty for parties, and came back to throw gravel at her window.

Her sisters were guarded; that jewel was to go to the marriage bed untouched. No one worried about hers. Quite right. No marriage bed was ahead. No love. Still, the touch, the skin against skin. That was hers.

But if not a nun, what was she to do? Her parents could not afford to keep her indefinitely, yet who would hire her? She studied the advertisements in the New Orleans newspapers. Nothing. And then one day when she was visiting the city menagerie, she saw a sign posted on the wall of the house of bears: Animal Keepers Wanted. There were no other applicants.

Caring for the bears gave her a kind of satisfaction. They would eat out of her hand, allow her to stroke and brush their fur. The crowds standing in front of the cages did not embarrass her, as their eyes were on the animals, not on her. She felt almost invisible, comfortable in the man's shirt and trousers she had adopted.

It was a tranquil existence, unchanging, until one morning in April she looked up from feeding the bears to see two men standing outside the enclosure talking earnestly. It was a quiet scene just after opening time, and yet she sensed something malign in the atmosphere. Going closer to the fence, she observed a third man just across the way. He was the source of the malignity she sensed. While she stood there, apprehensive, uncertain, the man reached into his jacket pocket, took out a pistol, raised it, pulled the safety catch, and took aim. In that instant Claireve pulled herself up and over the fence and leaped onto the intended victim, knocking him to the ground just as the shot went off.

She lay quietly for a moment and then cautiously lifted her head. The attacker was already at a distance, disappearing into the grove of trees, followed by the second man. The body lying beneath her was moving, trying to pull out from under her weight. She stood up then and held out her hand to help the man rise. The others were out of sight. He brushed the dirt and leaves clinging to his coat and trousers and turned to her, about to speak. Then he stopped short—of course he would stop short at the sight of her. There was no kindly darkness here.

He quickly recovered, saying, "I thank you for my life. My name is Peter Graves. Do you understand me?" She should be used to the condescension, but this time it rankled.

Taking a small notepad and lead pencil stub out of her pocket, Claireve wrote the uncompromising sentences: "If I could not understand, you would have nothing to thank me for. You would be dead."

To her surprise, he flushed. But before he could say anything more, the other man returned. "I lost him, Mr. Graves. He had a head start and I couldn't catch up."

"Never mind, Robert. Luckily I didn't need your protection. This young . . ." He hesitated, and Claireve thought he was not certain of her gender. "This young woman came to my aid."

Robert looked as if he were angry with her. She knew why. Robert had not been pursuing the would-be assassin; his complicity in the murder attempt was obvious to her.

"It will never happen again, sir."

"I think you'd better go, Robert. My secretary will pay you."

When Robert had walked away muttering, Mr. Graves turned to Claireve. "I'm sorry if I offended you. What are you doing here?"

"I take care of the bears," she wrote.

Graves put his hand on her arm. Men never touched her in daylight. "Wait a minute. I just thought of something. I need a bodyguard. How about you?"

He was joking. Claireve had learned how cruelly people make fun of the handicapped, as if they have no feelings. But he went on, apparently serious. She had shown herself to be quick and strong, and women did not serve as bodyguards. "No one would guess why you were with me."

He was a politician, he explained, and at this she recognized his name. Looking at him more carefully, she realized how often she had seen his photograph in the newspapers and on billboards. The most notable figure in Louisiana politics, he was running for election as governor. He was better looking in person. Not a handsome man, but with a particularly winning smile.

"I've made a pledge to clean up the corruption in the government if I'm elected. Many people have a lot to lose and are determined to stop me. Robert suggested the menagerie as a good place to meet my campaign manager, as no one would expect me to be here. Obviously someone got to Robert, paid him off. I need someone I can trust."

He was giving her his famous smile right now. Her lovers took her in the dark; she did not believe they would have smiled had they seen her. Was his smile—a politician's smile—a good enough reason to go with him? "Won't I be better than the bears?"

And so began the strangest part of her life. Graves arranged to have an ex-army officer teach her to shoot, a Japanese master of the martial arts show her how to turn an assailant's strength against himself. She marveled that such people were known to him, realized how hazardous was the life of a candidate.

Soon she was accompanying him everywhere, conservatively dressed in a tailor-made suit of dark gray broadcloth trimmed with black silk soutache, and a shirtwaist of taffeta. A gun was concealed under her arm. No one knew what to make of her. A speechwriter, people were told. And indeed, she was never without her notepad.

Graves learned to understand the sounds she made. Alone among all the people she had known, he looked her full in the face when speaking to her. As if she were like anyone else. It was a politician's trick; she knew why he had chosen her. She was a bodyguard he could trust. Even if her role were discovered, no one could communicate with her well enough to suborn her. And he could travel with her without any risk to his reputation. Knowing all this, Claireve still took pleasure in his treating her as no one else ever had.

The crowds turning out to hear him speak were getting larger. There was talk that after he won the governorship, the next step would be a run for the presidency. The opposition was becoming nastier, threatening. Observant and quick, she was twice able to save his life.

The door between their adjoining hotel rooms was always unlocked so she could reach him quickly in the event of danger. That was the only reason of course, but each night when she went to bed, the gun under her pillow, she imagined Peter Graves opening the door, entering the room. Claireve had never allowed herself to become interested in any man. What was the point? Oh, it was time for her to leave him. He seemed unaware of her body, oblivious of the opportunity being offered.

Only *seemed* unaware, he said on the night he finally opened the door. As soon as she heard his step, she extinguished the lamp on the bedside table. She dared not give herself the pleasure of seeing his body. In the dark her deformity was mercifully concealed. While she lay there filled with hope and fear, he was walking toward the bed, feeling for the lamp. In an instant the room was bright. And in that brilliance she watched him spellbound as he rapidly undressed, dropping his clothes on the floor in his haste. His haste to be with her. Until this moment she had never seen the naked body of a man clearly. Before, her lovers had been no more than dim shadows in the moonlight flickering through the leaves of the trees. His skin was smooth, gleaming with only a light covering of hair across the chest; his hips were narrow, his legs long, with heavy muscles in the thighs.

She could see his arousal, and turned away to bury her face in the pillow. He had not really looked at her yet and she dreaded what must happen—the loss of the desire he had been feeling. No man had ever gazed at her face when making love. He was not doing so either, but was pulling down the covers. She felt more confident now, lying there naked, waiting for him. "Why, your body is splendid."

It was going to be like all the other times, she thought, the man aroused by her body, sufficiently aroused to forget about her face. And then this was not like any other time. Graves sat down on the bed and put his hand on her face, running his fingers over her horribly distorted lip. Worse than an animal's, than the hare it was named after. But he was smiling. He bent down to her and kissed her full on the lips. No one had ever kissed her on the mouth before, and she put out her tongue and licked his lips. And then he lay down beside her, stroking her hair, then her breasts, her abdomen, again and again, slowly, gently, caressing. Passion. She had experienced that. Tenderness, never. Her hands, caressing him in return, were as large as his, as strong. The feel of his skin. He sat up facing her and she lifted her legs to encircle his waist. Angled so, he entered her deeply. She took him on, contracting her muscles around him, relaxing them, again and again. He was whispering in her ear, "My woman, what a woman you are."

At the moment of physical release, did he say he loved her? Or had she only imagined it? Later she was not certain. She had not dared to say she loved him, because he understood the incoherent sounds she could make. Love from a woman so deformed would be grotesque.

Once the climax had passed, she waited for him to leave. That was what every man did once appetite was sated. But he lay beside her, clasping her in his arms. Content, he said. He had never been so content.

At six in the morning, he embraced her, then left the bed and dressed quickly. She watched his body disappear into the dark blue, pin-striped candidate's suit, thinking that tonight perhaps she would see him naked again. It was not until he was fully dressed that she remembered she was his bodyguard. Taking her gun from beneath the pillow, she jumped out of bed. "Let me go out first, make certain it's safe." She was standing in front of him, naked, and he gave his winning politician's smile and waved her back. "No one knows where I've spent the night. Go back to bed and come to get me at eight. I'm supposed to have breakfast with a group from the local chamber of commerce."

He put his arms around her for a moment and kissed her. "Darling," he said. *Darling.* Then he opened the door and went out. She touched her hand to her mouth. In that second, she heard the shot. Grasping the gun and dashing out of the room naked, she saw his body falling. She caught a glimpse of the killer opening the door to the stairway but let him escape. He was not important when Peter Graves was lying there, blood pouring out in a long stream to wet her bare feet. He had kissed her . . . on the mouth. And she had failed him. A bodyguard and besotted with love, she had let him go.

She returned to her parents' home, consumed by grief mingled with guilt, not knowing how to spend the rest of her life. And then she realized that Graves had shown her what to do. He had been a strong supporter of suffrage. In his memory, she would join the movement. The suffragettes were in need of bodyguards, as demonstrations often became riots which the police could not or would not control. No one would care what she looked like.

In time Claireve became known to the police, was all but a legend. Her reputation spread beyond the borders of Louisiana and she was sent wherever militant action was being taken. At a mass demonstration in Washington, she met Viola Crosbie. Afterward the leaders went to the headquarters of the National American Woman Suffrage Association, accompanied as usual by Claireve as protector.

Offended by the way the others avoided looking at the harelip, Viola made a point of speaking to Claireve. This sensitivity touched Claireve. Of course she was immediately aware of Viola's beautifully shaped lips, of her low voice with the little throb in it. But she had gotten past resenting lovely women. They had their lives. She had hers. A man had kissed her; perhaps he had even said he loved her. And since then—Viola would never guess where she went at night. There was almost always someone. The nights were dark everywhere. And men were as hungry as she.

Waiting patiently for the gathering to come to an end, Claireve's

attention was caught by what Viola Crosbie was saying. She was talking passionately about the Antarctic, declaring she would go there
herself as a member of the Tremaine expedition. Now Claireve was
envious. Viola would go to the Antarctic, know the joy of exploration. Not she. No man would consider taking her on an expedition,
despite her great strength and endurance. Beauty should not be the
prerequisite for an explorer, but of course it was. The deformity
ruled her out.

When the list of members of the Tremaine expedition was published some weeks later, Claireve was saddened to see that Viola's
name was not there. Even she could not break into the all-male world
of polar exploration. And then, she read the *Suffrage Searchlight.*

AMAZONS WANTED.

Viola was going to the Antarctic after all. With women. Strong
women. And where could one stronger than Claireve be found? With
Graves dead, she was indifferent to the risks of the journey, believed
she would bring Viola safely to the South Pole and back. She would
rise above the tragic handicap that had ruled her life.

She ranked among the greatest dancers of all time; some critics
placed her above Isadora Duncan. Hers was a new style of dancing,
daring, unconventional, with no set positions, no formal movements.
Freedom. That was what her dances symbolized.

Audiences still went wild; she could bring them to their feet
stamping and cheering (except for those who fled the theater,
shocked by the near nudity and suggestiveness). Her dressing rooms
were filled with orchids; men waited at the stage door, begging to
take her out for an evening, to cover her with jewels and furs. She
had all the trappings of a star.

On the stage she still created the illusion of youth, but in the
bright light of her dressing room, without cosmetics, she looked close
to her thirty-four years. She was as strong as she had ever been, in
perfect physical condition, able to do the most difficult steps and to
carry through a long performance without faltering. Only the sinews
and tendons of her arms and legs were becoming evident, no longer
covered with the smooth flesh of girlhood. In another year or two she
would not wish to appear on stage in abbreviated, filmy costumes.

Evadne. She used only her first name, the one she had been given

for the stage. Rosie was her real name. After her mother died, there
was no one left to remember that. She had come so far from the im-
poverished childhood in Pittsburgh. A father? Her mother had not
known which of her lovers . . . customers, to be honest . . . he was.
She had run . . . well, a house . . . if one could call it such with only
three prostitutes in a tenement railroad flat. At twelve, Rosie became
a woman and schooling was brought to an end. The need for money
was paramount and what else was there for Rosie to do? At her age
she could have found employment bending over a sewing machine in
a sweatshop. Offering sex for money seemed better to her.

She never regretted her past. That was how she found her way.
"Don't never look at the man," her mother advised. "You shouldn't
know how to describe him later. Just give him what he came for.
That's all. What's it to you if he's old or ugly? It's a job like any other.
If you was selling pickles, you wouldn't care what the customers look
like. It ain't any different."

Rosie, always practical, accepted her mother's teaching and gave
good value. "You're beautiful," a customer told her one day. "And
your body. It's a dancer's body. I should know. I used to book dancers for the vaudeville circuit."

"What kind of dancers?"

"Ballet. Well, sort of ballet. The girls do little numbers in the
smaller theaters. It's a tough life, but better than you've got, kid. Take
some ballet lessons. That'll be a start."

He gave her the name and address of a ballet teacher and twenty-
five dollars, more than ten times her usual price.

The teacher was amazed by Rosie's grace, but did not wait long before sending her on. A vaudeville booking agent paid a small fee to
the teacher for supplying pretty young girls, dancers they were called.
No one asked Rosie to dance at the audition, just to turn around and
lift her skirt all the way up to show her legs; after that she was hired.
On stage, she did much the same thing, but in a skimpy sequined
costume that showed much more than her legs.

The vaudeville circuit was a dirty life. It was taken as a matter of
course that the female performers would have sexual relations with
the manager, occasionally with the stagehands as well. Some of the
girls gave up. Rosie had grown up with it. You never look at the man.
Let him do whatever he wants with your body. So long as he gets you

what you want. She learned how to tease a man into a good mood, enticed her way into better bookings.

She began to take ballet lessons and soon learned that at nearly six feet, she was too tall. The formal movements did not appeal to her anyway. The stage manager who had sex with her backstage after the show told her about a new form of dancing just coming into vogue. The dancers performed in bare feet as the ancient Greeks had done; it was the first time she heard there had been ancient Greeks. This style was becoming popular on the vaudeville circuit because bare feet were viewed as erotic.

Soon Rosie auditioned and was hired for the Marla Keats Greek Goddesses. She ran onto the stage, arms outstretched, then leaped, her legs wide, her bare high-arched feet in the air. And her breasts were so firm under the tight bodice. Off the stage, and then on again. And this time she could sense an air of anticipation on the part of the audience. Only a minute on stage, but when she ran into the wings, there was a sudden burst of applause. At the general curtain call, a rose was thrown directly at her feet. She picked it up and held it to her lips. The audience loved it. Fifteen years old and already knowing how to please an audience.

Marla Keats recognized a rival: "Pay her off. I don't want her on the stage tomorrow."

But she had been seen by the journalists for the local newspapers, was mentioned in their columns. "Star quality," they called it. When she was on stage, no one else existed for the audience. That was the kind of energy she projected.

The following day she was taken into Jack Lamotte's company. A male dancer saw the advantage of adding a rising female star. This was not vaudeville anymore, but a legitimate dance company playing in regular theaters. When he had been drinking, Jack was sadistic as a lover, and even sober had a nasty streak, but she never regretted him either. It was he who changed her name to Evadne, taught her to lose the accent of the Pittsburgh slum, to eat with proper table manners, bathe regularly, and wear a corset whenever she was not on stage.

In a couple of years Lamotte's choreography began to seem dull to her. Perhaps classical Greek dancing required more than bare feet. But how was she, whose schooling had come to an end when her mother saw the blood on her underdrawers, to know that? Daring at last to enter the imposing Metropolitan Museum to view the Greek statues, the paintings of the Renaissance artists, she saw what Lamotte had missed—the human body was an ideal to be shown with pride, with joy, with total lack of inhibition. That pride in the human body could be recaptured in the dance. The time had come to leave Lamotte.

Evadne found a backer—and what if he demanded that she perform unconventional sex acts with him?—and founded her own company. The dances she created expressed the freedom of her spirit, of the human spirit, of her joy in movement. The costumes were more daring than any seen before outside the vaudeville or burlesque stage—made of the lightest gauze held together with ropes of silk roses.

How shocked the audiences had been when she first appeared, her nipples showing through the filmy cloth, her hips undulating with unmistakably sexual connotation. Her most sensual dance was performed to the strange, erotic music of a modern composer whose name she could not pronounce—Debussy. Most cheered, but there were always people who walked out angrily. Sometimes the police were called to arrest her and the members of her company for indecent exposure. The first time, she spent a week in jail. After that, she learned better, had a lawyer close at hand. Usually the charges were dropped. Occasionally, she would be jailed for a night. It was in jail that she came to know suffragettes for the first time. To her astonishment, the suffragettes knew about her, admired her as an example of the new, independent woman. "The dance style you've created is symbolic of the freedom women could achieve."

Evadne was made uncomfortable by their respect. It was undeserved. The suffragettes had no comprehension of what it meant to be a performer. Independent? She was no less dependent on the favors of men than she had been when sitting in her threadbare chemise in the parlor of her mother's apartment or lying on a makeshift couch backstage on the vaudeville circuit. Maintaining a dance company and living in the style expected of her required far more money than she could earn by dancing, no matter how successful she became. Gowns must be designed in Paris by Worth and Pingat, and floor-length wraps be of ermine or sable. Her town house was on

Madison Avenue and Thirty-ninth Street, not far from Morgan's mansion. All this was given by one man or another, in return for what she would give back. That was a requisite part of a stellar performer's life.

As she became more famous and achieved greater critical acclaim, the men in her life moved up the social scale. Her great love—or so she had believed him to be—was the scion of a family so wealthy, with so famous a name and such political connections that journalists and photographers followed them everywhere. Gerald was obsessed by her. With other women, he had seldom been able to achieve an erection. Evadne knew how to stroke, caress, press, kiss, and lick his smooth, slim body all over until he was fully aroused. "You make love like a whore," he said to her once. It was a joke; he did not know what she had been. Even with Gerald, she never had an orgasm. A whore did not climax, except by her own hand after the last customer had left.

Evadne was slow to realize that her lover and his friends viewed her as celebrated but not respectable. Gerald never introduced her to his socially prominent mother or the father of whom he was clearly in awe.

Her pregnancy took them both by surprise, as she had long since learned to use a pessary. "Why don't you take care of it," Gerald suggested. "Go to the best doctor you can find; I'll pay for everything." "But I want to have the baby." Gerald did not insist, could not have been nicer, assured her that the child would want for nothing, and did marriage really matter? At his insistence, they made love the day she went into labor.

After the baby, David, was born, however, Gerald was entranced by him. Now he said he wanted to marry her, but his father disapproved, and he was afraid of his father. Gerald objected to her much-heralded return to the stage. It was unsuitable for the mother of his child. But the baby was hers alone, bore her last name, not Gerald's. His doing. They quarreled when she told him she would take David and a wet nurse with her on tour.

Still, she was a performer, and on opening night in Boston, she was happy, knowing the audience spellbound, the baby safe with his nurse in the hotel room. As she left the theater, the men in their evening clothes were waiting at the stage door, seeking to press their cards upon her. Even though she had been angry with Gerald, she missed him already; there could be no one else. She would make it up with him tonight, she thought. With Gerald's wealth, he had a telephone not only in his office, but at his palatial home on Sixty-seventh Street and Fifth Avenue. After she had seen David, she would call and tell Gerald she loved him.

She ran up the two flights of stairs to her rooms in the hotel. The larger, more elegant hotels had elevators, but in conservative Boston dancers were made unwelcome there.

As soon as Evadne opened the door, she knew the hotel room was empty. Nervously, she turned up the gas on the lamp and lit the wick. The crib was empty, the nurse nowhere to be seen. She rushed into the adjoining room, which was her bedroom. Empty as well. Frantic, she raced down the stairs, ran to the front desk, and importuned the night clerk hysterically: "My baby! He's gone!"

The clerk observed her distress in amazement. "Your nurse went out with him a couple of hours ago. Is something wrong?"

"Where did she take him?"

"She didn't say. I thought . . . well, she is the nurse you brought with you." He was looking at her in hostile fashion, thinking the shrillness of her voice might awaken the manager and the other guests. What can you expect when you allow a woman who dances all but naked into your hotel?

Evadne felt faint with horror, grasped the front desk to keep from fálling. Kidnapping. The nurse had been paid to kidnap David. Gerald's vast fortune must be the key, as their relationship was well known. She had heard of babies stolen and held for ransom. "Did anyone leave a telephone message for me when I was at the theater?" The clerk shook his head. Perhaps the demand for money had gone directly to Gerald. She must get in touch with him immediately. His family had limitless financial resources, political connections. They would restore the baby to her.

Barely waiting for the clerk's grudging permission to use the telephone, she put in the call. The telephone rang and rang, but no one answered. How could that be when there were always servants in the house? The only thing to do was to insist that the reluctant clerk telephone the police to report the missing baby. The two weary policemen who responded to the predawn call were not much interested in

Evadne's account, thinking it a performer's ploy to get stories about her in the newspapers.

All through that night and the following days, she waited, losing heart with every passing hour. By the time the letter from Gerald arrived, she was certain David must be dead, and was half-crazed by grief. With overwhelming relief, she learned that David was alive. Then she read on. Alive . . . but lost to her. Gerald's father had arranged everything. The baby had been taken to the family estate and adoption proceedings were initiated.

Gerald regretted hurting her, but his father had been adamant. "He will not allow his grandchild to be brought up by a woman like you, leading an unconventional life, a woman with a disreputable past." Detectives had been hired, he wrote, and had discovered her mother's profession, her own illegitimacy and early life as a common prostitute. The child must be saved from her corrupting influence.

She wrote; her letters were returned unopened. Upon going to the estate, she was stopped by the gatekeeper. She never saw David again.

Despite her misery, perhaps because of it, she was dancing better than ever before. For a long time, it was easy to be on top. Then the struggle to remain there began. The younger dancers in the company were becoming competitors. Better to retire while she was still at her peak, the "legendary" Evadne. But retire—and do what? Other dancers became teachers—Isadora Duncan sought millionaire lovers to help maintain her schools; Vernon and Irene Castle, at the height of their "hesitation waltz" fame, were giving ballroom dancing lessons at the Saint Regis Hotel. But Evadne lacked the patience, the inclination for teaching.

Then one day upon arriving at the theater for a matinee, she observed the suffragette newspaper lying on her dressing room table, folded to display an advertisement: AMAZONS WANTED. One of the younger dancers must have put it there maliciously, a hint that Evadne should be off to the farthest ends of the globe. At first Evadne, angry, crumpled the newspaper to throw it away, but she quickly picked it up again and smoothed it out.

AMAZONS WANTED. The Antarctic. To conquer the South Pole, be acclaimed as one of the foremost explorers of the age—that was something a woman like you could do, something to make a son proud. In that moment Evadne saw a future as glorious as her past in the theater, running across the stage with her bare arms outstretched and her legs wide and the audience on its feet cheering.

And in Hollowran Prison, a friendly wardress smuggled a copy of *Votes for Women* to Carla Brent, serving her sentence for throwing rocks through the windows of Lord Hargreave's London residence.

# Chapter Twenty-one

A THOUSAND MEN RESPONDED TO Byron Tremaine's call for expedition members; three secretaries were hired to assist Horace Graham. Viola's advertisement produced twenty letters.

"But we have Amazons," Eileen remarked cheerfully. And it was true that all the applicants described themselves in that manner—close to six feet in height, well built, and strong. Hardy, athletic, many were mountain climbers, skiers. Not one was married or possessed close family ties, an advantage in that secrecy was demanded.

The newspapers gave the count for the Tremaine expedition: thirty-five explorers, half a dozen scientists, a physician, a photographer, plus a full complement of seamen, carpenters, animal handlers, orderlies, and cooks. The Crosbie expedition could not afford to take even the paltry number of applicants. The suffragettes were doing their best, but the sums made available were meager.

"I think we'll have enough to supply fourteen women," declared Ian. "We can manage with fourteen."

*We*—Viola remembered when she had used the plural to indicate to Byron that she expected to be a part of his expedition. She wondered if Ian gave the word the same meaning. Surely not. Before arranging his release from Bloomingdale's, she had made it perfectly clear that a man could not be a member of an all-women's expedition. And at Bloomingdale's he had assured her that he understood and agreed.

They read through the letters again, seeking to form a well-balanced party of explorers. Some positions would have to be left vacant. There was no possibility of a woman physician; first-aid training by the American Red Cross must suffice. A photographer was essential to the expedition, but where could a woman with that unusual skill be found? Viola had all but given up hope when an application from Marcia O'Toole, a photographer's assistant, came in.

To Viola's amazement, a letter—scrawled in a rather childish handwriting—turned out to be from the famed dancer, Evadne. Once, Viola recalled, she had gone with Byron to see Evadne perform. It was early in the love affair, before she had left him to go to London, but there was already conflict between them. After the dance program, under the spell of Evadne's sexuality, they had forgotten their resentments and made love with a violent passion. And this woman, this beautiful woman, wanted to go to the Antarctic. Viola wondered if the sensual Evadne had given any thought to the enforced celibacy of an all-women's expedition. The great dancer's love affairs were pruriently described in every magazine and newspaper. Viola had some concerns about living without sexual fulfillment for so long herself. And for her, the Antarctic was a dream she was ready to risk her life for. Then she read the letter over and recognized how sincere was Evadne's desire to join the expedition.

Ian and Eileen voted to turn her down. "This is just a way for her to gain attention in the newspapers." They simply could not believe a woman like this, with the world at her feet, would give everything up for the hardships of Antarctica. Viola did not find it hard to believe. Nothing in life could compare to climbing over the great ice barrier and planting the suffragette banner alongside the American flag at the South Pole.

"Remember you've promised to conceal the suffragettes' sponsorship if the expedition doesn't reach the Pole," Eileen cautioned. "You can get away with that so long as the newspapermen don't pay much attention to us. They certainly don't now. But Evadne's presence will change that. What a great story the all-women's expedition is then. Everything will come out, the suffrage backing, everything."

Viola would not dismiss Evadne on those grounds. "No one needs to know who she is. I'll ask her to use another name and announce her plan to retire from the stage at the end of this season and live in seclusion. Afterward, she can take advantage of her newspaper prominence."

Evadne agreed without hesitation, and that left only one place open on the expedition. Saved for Carla Brent. Viola remembered that once they had spent the night side by side, shivering on the roof of the town hall in MidValley. Viola had failed the suffrage movement then; this time she would not fail, and Carla would be by her side on the summer day when they achieved victory at the South Pole.

At last the letter arrived, smuggled out of Hollowran Prison. Carla rejoiced that her term would be completed in time for her to join Viola. "I've gotten word to one of the blokes I live with to book passage to New York for me. I'll make it all the way to the Pole with you. For suffrage. For Lesley."

Even before the membership roster was completed, supplies and equipment were being selected for the expedition. During these months, the change in Ian was all Viola could have hoped. It was as he had promised at Bloomingdale's. Samples were tested and compared and no shoddy workmanship was accepted. Yet there was no waste, as each purchase was weighed against Eileen's daily record of the money on hand, the sums they could yet expect to receive.

Ian's eyes were brighter, his manner more forceful. In bed when he reached for her, his touch was no longer tentative. Now he wanted to make love to her every night. He caressed her with such sweetness, waited for her arousal at each touch, each movement, did not achieve his climax until after hers. Viola could believe that Ian had at last come back to her from the defeat of the Sharpe expedition. Later, when he was sleeping, she held his body in her arms and felt at peace. His mouth was against her neck; in his sleep, he kissed her, murmured her name.

In the morning, though, she remembered how quickly his calm facade could crack and mania seep out. He had nearly killed her. It was not long ago. There was no choice but to consign him to his reluctant brother. Viola was heartsick at the thought of his despair when he would finally be forced to accept that she was to realize the dream of every explorer of the century—the South Pole. And he, who had twice been within a hairbreadth of that achievement, was to be deprived again. Perhaps she should have refused him a part in organizing the expedition. But such summary rejection of his experience would have been an act of greater cruelty. And folly as well.

For the present, occupied with plans for the Crosbie expedition, he appeared oblivious of what was to come. He followed the newspaper reports about Tremaine avidly. A ship, the *Polar King,* had been built to order in Britain at a cost equivalent to one hundred thousand dollars. Constructed of English oak, fir, and Honduras mahogany, the frame was more than two feet thick. The huge, metal-reinforced prow was designed to batter through the heavy pack ice of the waters around the Antarctic continent, and the engine was the most powerful yet developed. Well, why should he not have the best when he had the funds raised by the lecture tour as well as the sponsorship of Plumley's *Daily Star* and of the Tremaine Antarctic Club founded by Horace Graham, with memberships going at five thousand dollars apiece?

Undismayed, Ian went from shipowner to shipowner until he learned of a former sealing ship with the oddly appropriate name of *Explorer.* It was shabby and battered, but still seaworthy. Ian leased it for a pittance, hired a crew of seamen down on their luck.

Every moment Ian could spare was spent poring over maps of the Antarctic. This was the place where Sharpe had gone wrong and been forced to retrace his steps over thirty miles of broken snow. This was the part of the plateau where the ice had appeared solid but turned out to be a thin cover over a chasm and they had barely escaped with their lives. Ian marked the safe places in blue ink, the dangerous in red.

As he worked, he became conscious of a nagging sense of discomfort. The base camp on Ross Island, the route to the South Pole over the Beardmore Glacier—that was the way Sharpe had gone, the way Tremaine was planning to go. Ian thought his careful mapping would be for nothing if it brought Viola together with Tremaine on the ice cap. Though he would be there, too, his presence guaranteed nothing—Viola would find a way to be alone with Tremaine. Had she not done so during all these months in New York?

"I don't think we should follow Sharpe's route to the South Pole," Ian told Viola. "It didn't work for him, so why should it work for us?"

*Us.* This time she let it pass. "Is there another possible route, Ian? Tremaine said there isn't."

"Maybe I know a few things Tremaine doesn't."

Ian would find the shortest and safest way to reach the Pole. Viola trusted him implicitly.

The final order was placed and a warehouse rented. Then in February, with barely half of the supplies in hand, deliveries came to a halt. Viola and Ian were baffled and alarmed. Tremaine had scheduled his departure for the first week in June, and the Crosbie expedition must follow suit soon thereafter. The loading of the *Explorer* had to be well under way by May, or the competition would be over before it began.

What could have gone wrong? A few of the smaller suppliers were induced to provide food and fuel for a higher price than had been agreed to, but the major companies proffered nothing but excuses. At last Ellerby, who headed one of the largest firms, told her the truth. "We've been told not to fill your orders, Mrs. Crosbie."

"By whom?"

"Can't you guess?" For a second, she stared at him, unable to believe. But she could guess. More than that, she knew who was responsible and was sickened by that knowledge.

"How can you agree to this?"

Ellerby was distressed; Mrs. Crosbie was lovely and he admired Lieutenant Crosbie, but what choice was there? "He said he'd cancel all his orders with us if we supply you. And Mrs. Crosbie, his purchases are five times the size of yours."

Viola was often angry with Byron, but never thought him perfidious. Everything that had passed between them seemed dirtied by this action. She remembered how passionately they had loved. They were unable to resist one another even when marriage made it wrong to accede to the sexual pull. She had launched the competition knowing he had the advantage of her in money. That was not enough for him. He meant to guarantee himself the victory by foul means.

Trembling with rage, she hailed a motor taxi to take her to his office. No one tried to stop her as she swept through the reception room. Horace Graham looked up warily; he knew why she was here. Without a word, he left Byron's office.

"How could you do this to me, Byron?"

She would have liked to strike him down. "Underhanded. Unethical." The words were delivered in the low, throbbing voice that always excited him. Byron knew that Viola must find out what he had done, but was unprepared for the vehemence of her attack, nonetheless. Her severe black gabardine tailored suit and white tucked shirtwaist did not diminish her flamboyance. Her cheeks were red and her eyes gleaming as if she had a fever. The coppery hair had escaped from its chignon and was curling around the small feathered toque. The last time she had been in his office he had taken her right there on the couch where he would like to take her now. Somehow he had to make her understand.

"I'm trying to save your life, Viola. I had to do this . . . for your sake. Sharpe and his men perished on the Beardmore Glacier, and it's the only way to the Pole. It rises nine thousand feet above sea level, sheer ice and snow, and I lie awake nights worrying about how to get my men over it. You haven't thought of the unendurable suffering awaiting you and the women you plan to take with you, and in the end, you won't get all the way to the South Pole and back. You might even die—and I couldn't stand that, Viola." There was a catch in his voice; at least in this he was sincere. "And for what? My expedition will reach the Pole first and we'll get all the glory.

"Forget the expedition, Viola. Come to New Zealand with me. Don't you remember how happy we were in Greenland?"

Happy? Because they had been making love? Yes, she remembered being happy. But she also remembered what came later. He had taken over her discoveries, sought to take over her life. And now he thought he had merely to remind her how once he lay on her body on the Eskimo blanket and she would meekly agree to follow him as the least member of his expedition.

"I know why you've threatened the suppliers, Byron. In your heart you know I stand as good a chance as you of conquering the Pole. You're afraid I'll succeed and you'll fail."

"You could never succeed—you and that pack of freaks and misfits you've assembled. Supplies! You'd have been weighted down with cartons of—what is it . . . Lister's towels that you ladies use for your monthly bleeding." Freaks and misfits. Freaks must mean Claireve and her harelip, and misfits refer to Carla in her mannish clothes. And Lister's towels. No man ever referred to a woman's bleeding. Men were supposed to be in ignorance; even among married couples the deception was maintained that he did not notice.

"If you're not afraid, tell the suppliers to fill the orders for the Crosbie expedition, Byron. Let me have my supplies and then we'll see who arrives first at the Pole."

"Give up, Viola; for just this once, listen to reason."

He came around to the front of his desk and stood beside her, putting his face against hers, almost a caress. A sense of outrage overcame her. Intolerable. A paperweight lay on his desk—she picked it up and struck him on the forehead. For a moment she stood there, staring at him, watching the blood trickle down his face. Then she turned and left the office.

Going home by streetcar, she faced the inevitability of defeat. Few manufacturers produced supplies for explorers, and they were controlled by Byron with his large orders. There was no place to turn. He had spoken of Greenland; she would wipe out the memory. And just then, deciding never to think of Greenland, she remembered the Eskimos and the hours spent in their tents watching the women cut and piece together the clothing by hand. Caribou skins, they told her, made the best garments, as the hairs were hollow, creating thousands upon thousands of small insulating air pockets. The women did not begin to make the fur clothing until the winter was almost upon them, yet all was ready by spring. The men, too, were at work, building the sledges, making the harnesses.

Now she remembered that Byron had brought Anaukaq and seven other Eskimos back to New York with him from Greenland, thinking they would add a touch of the exotic to his lectures. It had not worked out. But Anaukaq, showing surprising enterprise, had remained in New York and started a small business to import raw materials from the Arctic and make fur garments, sledges, and other equipment. From time to time Viola had gone to reminisce about the past with Anaukaq and the Eskimo workers.

The Eskimos liked her; Viola was the only member of the Tremaine expedition who had troubled to learn the Inuit language. They would make the things she needed. In time.

Viola arrived home to find Ian standing at the window, waiting for her. She put her arms around him, but he recoiled. "You've been with him. I can smell him on you."

It was true, she realized. Clean-shaven, Byron used soap and a lotion with a subtle lemony scent. Viola started to speak, but Ian cut her off: "You've been telling me I couldn't go with you on the expedition because it's only for women. Oh yes, I've heard you, though I've pretended I didn't. I remember when you first said it in Bloomingdale's and I had to agree in order to get out. But you never told me the true reason for leaving me behind. Suffrage. The Antarctic. They really don't have much to do with it. This was the only way you could think of to be with Byron Tremaine without me and without his wife. On the ice cap. The two of you. Has he been in on it all along?"

"How can I make you believe you're wrong about Byron and me?"

"Take me with you." He had spoken impulsively, and now realized he was going too far and would lose everything. Somehow he knew instinctively how to reassure her. "I'll just go along on the *Explorer* with you. No one can object to that. There'll be other men—the officers, the crew—and I'll go back to New Zealand when they do."

He was certain that by the time they completed the long and arduous ocean voyage, he would have convinced her that the expedition could not succeed without him. The South Pole and the uncharted territories of Antarctica were yet to be his.

Viola thought of all Ian had done for the expedition and recognized the inherent injustice in taking advantage of his experience. That she had told him what was to be did not absolve her. He deserved better. But would he go back to New Zealand with the *Explorer*? He said so now, but she knew how desperately he desired the Pole.

Still, everything in her wanted to postpone his misery. Why not? Months must pass before the ship would break through the pack ice and deposit the women in Antarctica. By then she would have convinced Ian that, as a man, he could not continue with the expedition to the South Pole. Anyway, that was a long way off.

# Chapter Twenty-two

" 'THE THINGS HE DONE. HE covered them up, but I was there, saw what happened. It was that woman making him crazy.' "

I was describing the tape to Ronald, giving no hint that Avery had played it for me on the catastrophic night in London when I was in his room, in his bed.

"A woman again. And this was on his own expedition of 1915–1916, years after Viola Lambert's death."

"The words ring true, as does the emotion behind them," Ronald responded. "Hatred, resentment carried for a lifetime."

They did ring true, even though the tape must be bogus. The person speaking could not have been on the Tremaine expedition, as he claimed. The survivors were honored at the Explorers Club annual dinner until the last one died. A notice in memoriam had been sent out. That was three years ago.

"Could Avery have based his script on something that really happened? Exaggerating it of course."

To my dismay, Ronald did not appear particularly interested. "Maybe you can get a hint of that from Avery when he comes to see you again, Beatrix," was all he said. Nowadays Ronald is less eager to help me in my quest for the secrets of Tremaine's life. He no longer compares us to Byron and Hermine.

The first time Ronald made love to me after my return from London, I thought we were as close as ever in the past. At every moment, with each movement, each gesture, embrace, murmur of love, I was conscious of how different it had been with Avery. As I stroked Ronald's body, still hard, still muscular, it seemed to me that I had returned from a much longer voyage than just across the sea. Recalling Avery, I could have wept at Ronald's tenderness. Recalling Avery, did I somehow give myself away?

Always before, after making love, we took a particular joy in lying in one another's arms, speaking of our feelings. This time it did not happen that way. Ronald sat up abruptly, then left the bed and put his clothes back on, not looking at me. He knew without my telling him—how could I have told him?—that something had taken place in London. That it had been with Avery did not occur to him, I thought. How could it?

"Beatrix?" *Beatrix.* He was not calling me Bibi anymore. His expression was questioning, but he said nothing beyond my name, with that rising inflection. It made me uneasy, and I thought Ronald had never made me uneasy; he stood for security. I had to answer. Not the unspoken question, but another. "I'm glad we're together again, Ronald. I missed you in London." It was true, so true, but sounded false. How could it not?

Did he hesitate before he answered? "Yes," he said, "of course."

I am not sure what I expected—a jealous scene perhaps; but he said nothing more, just picked up his leather jacket and went out.

After that day, when we made love, it was good, but I was not comfortable with Ronald in the way I had always been before. The question he did not ask outright was between us. Had it been any man other than Avery, I think I would have told Ronald. It had been an episode, happening only once because I was lonely and he was far away. He would have been angry, jealous, yet he could have understood and forgiven. But how could I speak of what had passed between Avery and me? A man Ronald had warned me against at the outset? The mood that overwhelmed me in London, the sexual hunger Avery had aroused, seems incomprehensible to me now. All I want is for Ronald and me to be as we had been before.

*When he comes to see you again.* I had fled London the morning after being with Avery, but I did not think he would let me escape so easily. His program means far more to him than any incident in his personal life, and I am still his best source of information about Byron Tremaine. But the days passed with no word from him. And then he appeared quite unexpectedly at the annual Explorers Club dinner. He was unexpected because the attendance is strictly limited to explorers and their nearest of kin. As Byron Tremaine's direct descendant, I am welcome there.

I should have known that even the staid Explorers Club was unable to turn away so influential a television personality.

Avery arrived late, and I was already seated at one of the best tables, close to the dais where Ronald was placed, as befits the leading polar explorer of the day, his wife, elegantly gowned, beside him. Knowing she would be there, I had not wanted to come, but could not refuse the invitation. The man on my right, a naval commander, was engaging me in conversation when I heard Avery's voice. "Excuse me, this is my seat." Of course it was not; the assignments were by table not by position, but Avery's manner was so confident that the commander obediently moved to another chair.

Avery sat down beside me, so close that I could feel the heat of his body. Remembering the last time I had been with him, my skin tingled. In his evening clothes he appeared darker than usual, sinister. His hands with their long, tapering fingers were on the table. Had I ever allowed—no, wanted—him to put those hands on me?

Pushing my chair back, I stood up. When I entered the ballroom, I had noticed Bucky Sheridan at one of the tables to the side. The woman beside him was slim and attractive, but much older than he; her hair was streaked with gray. They probably were not together, but were merely assigned to the same table. Bucky would make room for me. Avery put his hand on my arm. "Don't leave. Everyone is looking at us. They'll be trying to guess why you're afraid to sit next to me."

It was true. As a network television producer, he was one of the most famous men in the country. I sat down again, stiffly, as far away from him as the tight table setting would allow.

I expected him to be unpleasant, but his manner was the same as in the past—a mixture of flirtatiousness and aggression, coolness and a desire for intimacy. He was too skillful to pretend the unfortunate sexual encounter had never taken place. "That night in London," he whispered in my ear so softly that no one else at the table could hear,

". . . well, frustration makes one say and do things one shouldn't. We don't have to be enemies."

I remembered his playing the tape for me. In revenge. Of course we had to be enemies. But I had sufficient self-control to refrain from saying so. Avery possessed the tape and could use it on his program if he chose, making some disclaimer to protect himself legally, a disclaimer no one would believe or remember. I had to find a way of inducing him not to play the tape on his show. Bucky said Avery was taken with me. I had not believed it then, did not believe it now, but there was nothing to lose by behaving as if it were true. Yes, little as I liked the idea, I must respond to him, charm him if I could. So I moved a little closer, forced a smile.

"I once told you that you look like your great-grandmother, Beatrix. I think I was wrong about that. She was pretty, but you are beautiful. Your eyes are so big and your look is so soulful." I did not like his compliments or the way he was gazing at me. And I do resemble Hermine, pretty, but no more than that. I lack the style for beauty and I know it.

"You smile and flatter me, Avery, and say we don't have to be enemies. But . . ."

Skillful as ever, he broke in: "You're thinking about the tape. I shouldn't have played it for you. I was angry."

I might have believed him had I not known he was determined to fabricate a scandal about my great-grandfather. My abhorrence of what he was doing was so strong that it overrode my desire to make myself agreeable to him. "That tape. It has to be a fake."

Avery gave no sign of offense. He waited until the waiter put down the first course, a mousse made from the ballyhoo fish of Bahamian waters, before replying. "I haven't told you any lies, Beatrix. The man who spoke on the tape was on the Tremaine expedition. That can be proven."

"No, it can't." He was shaking his head, but I went on, certain I was right, explaining about the annual Explorers Club dinner honoring the survivors until the last one died.

The waiter had removed the uneaten appetizer without our noticing and was now serving the main course, Waoroni tapir with wild mushrooms from Bhutan. The natural gravy oozed out of the meat, brown against the white-and-gold plate, and a feeling of nausea welled up in my throat. I swallowed hard and forced back the sickness.

Avery gave one of those unamused half smiles I so thoroughly disliked. "This man didn't go to the Explorers Club. I'm sure he wasn't invited."

"What do you mean? All the expedition members were invited. They were lionized."

"Not all, Beatrix. Look around you at these stuffy people dressed in made-to-order evening clothes. To them, exploration is a gentleman's game. Those men who performed the menial tasks on an expedition didn't exist for them. Invite them to the dinner? Never. They wouldn't let such people stand in the back of the room. For that matter, could you name the carpenters and animal handlers who accompanied the expedition? I'll bet I'm the only person who ever went looking for them."

He was right, I thought with chagrin; I had committed the roster of expedition members to memory but barely glanced at the list of workers without whom the expedition would have foundered. All these years, and it had never occurred to me that a carpenter or dog handler might have something to tell me. How did I let these years slip by without tracking down every person connected with the Tremaine expedition, the crowning achievement of my great-grandfather's life?

"The man who spoke on the tape was named Wally Padgett. He was seventeen years old at the time of the Tremaine expedition and he worked as a dog handler. You see, Beatrix, I'm not hiding anything from you."

It was odd that I always doubted Avery after leaving him; in his presence, everything he said appeared plausible. Wally Padgett. A dog handler who might have felt he had been slighted, ignored by Tremaine. A grudge stored for a lifetime. And Avery had traced him and given him the opportunity to express himself at last. Now I had something to go on. There had been a misunderstanding. My great-grandfather was too good a man to commit an evil act. I must see old Padgett for myself and straighten it out.

"If you really are not hiding anything, then tell me where to find Padgett."

"I wish I could; I'd like to talk to him again myself. He's dead by now, was dying of emphysema and extreme old age when I went to see him. It wasn't easy to get anything coherent out of him." I understood how Avery had created the tape—recording a word here, a word there, and piecing them together.

For all his claims of openness, Avery was offering me nothing, a dead man. I forced a pleasant smile. "Well, what sort of a man was Padgett?"

"I expected to find a benign old character—I figured a man who cared for animals had to be like that—but nothing could have been further from the actuality. I don't think I ever saw a man so filled with hate. It was as if the wrong had been done him only yesterday, rather than in 1915 or 1916."

Seventeen years old when he went to the Antarctic with Tremaine. What of that boy had remained in the ancient man?

"What wrong did he claim was done him?"

"You heard the tape."

The words were ominous, the accusations vague. "And you believed a man like that?"

"I didn't say I believed him."

But neither did Avery say he did not. The hatred Padgett felt for Tremaine has been given new life by Avery. And it will not die with Padgett. Avery will see to that. A flicker of fear went through me. I had hoped to find Padgett and talk him into repudiating the tape. Now I saw no way of stopping Avery from using it. You can't libel the dead.

The waiter took away our plates. Avery's was also untouched; eating would have broken the intensity of the attention focused on me. He bent toward me with the air of intimacy he is so adept at creating. For an instant I was fascinated by him, drawn. Just an instant.

Glancing around the table, I became aware that the other diners were carefully looking away. I gazed up at the dais; Ronald's eyes were on us, his expression carefully blank.

The band struck up its opening number and the dancing began, led by the couples coming down from the dais. Avery turned his head. "Oh, there's the aging polar hero on the dance floor," he said nastily, almost as if he were a new lover, resenting the appearance of the old, when he was not a lover at all, but merely a mistake I once made. Ronald and his wife were an attractive couple, but I could not bear to see his deeply tanned hand, the top of one finger lost to frost-bite, against her bare skin, holding her tightly, while I was trapped at the table with Avery. Evening clothes did not become Ronald; he looked older than in his leather jacket and jeans. He danced only a few minutes and then left the floor, his lame knee obviously troubling him after the surgery.

Avery bent forward, looking suggestively down the bosom of my dress. I did not want to appear seductive to Avery; the low-cut neckline designed to make my breasts look fuller, give the impression of cleavage, had been intended for Ronald. But Ronald was returning to the dais, carefully not glancing in my direction as he went past my table. Instead, there was only Avery, whose proximity was disturbing to me. At least he did not ask me to dance, said he never danced. I caught sight of Bucky with the woman who had been seated beside him. Despite her lined face and graying hair, there was a connection between them. I wondered what had happened to the movie actress whose name was linked with his in the gossip columns. Bucky did not approach my table either. Avery's presence beside me walled me off from everyone else.

"You won't play that tape on the program, will you, Avery?" I glanced up at him from beneath my eyelashes; for the first time I was flirting.

My change in manner pleased him; his voice in response was smooth, honeyed. "I haven't decided yet."

"Why not?"

"I'm not sure. Maybe you have something to do with it." He put his hand on my bare arm, his long, thin fingers closing around it, and I was too taken aback to withdraw quickly. "There's something about you that appeals to me, Beatrix. I admire the way you stand up for your great-grandfather. Would you stand up for me if we were friends?"

I was annoyed with Avery for giving that air of intimacy, collusion. He was probably making fun of me. I had been allowing myself to forget that men like him are not charmed by me. "We'll never be friends, Avery." It is not my way to be so outspoken, but then I did not think Avery paid much attention to anything I had to say unless it was about Tremaine.

To my surprise, he drew back, biting his lip. When he spoke again, his manner was more aggressive. "Who would you say is your friend then, Beatrix? Besides the heroic Graham. Bucky Sheridan? I noticed your eyes on him and his elderly girlfriend on the dance floor. I'm not concerned with his private life, not even with his crazy wife." I gave a start; Avery noticed and responded with the smile that was no smile at all. "No, I'm interested in the phony expedition. You must admit I've proved my case against him with those photographs."

But had he proved his case? The truth was not necessarily what he said it was. Avery could easily have had photographs forged to make his point. Bucky's denials would only add drama to the program.

Unable to bear Avery's arrogance any longer, I rose from the table without a word and left the ballroom. Avery had no reason to assume I would not return, and did not follow me. Bucky, however, ran after me and caught up when I was taking my coat from the checkroom. "I'm sorry you're leaving so soon, Trixie. I wanted to introduce my mother to you, but definitely not to Avery."

"Your mother? That's your mother?"

"Sure. Who did you think she was? An aging lover?" He stopped short and we both flushed, thinking of Ronald.

"It means a lot to her, you know, to see me here," Bucky continued after just that little break. "I'm the embodiment of the American dream. Just two generations out of a shtetl in Galicia. My grandfather studied the Talmud and never did a day's work for pay though his family was in rags; my father was a salesman in a discount shoe store, and here I am, an Antarctic explorer."

"I'm touched, Bucky." And I was—a little envious, too, remembering how happy my mother had been when anything good happened to me. "I don't think any other explorer is here with his mother."

"I don't think there are many other Jewish explorers here either, Trixie. Jews are sentimental. I wanted her to have the pleasure of seeing me accepted as a member of the Explorers Club."

Looking at Bucky's open face, I was sure Avery had faked the photographs. But it would not matter. Once Avery got through with Bucky, the Explorers Club would ask him to resign.

"Don't look like that, Trixie. Do you think I don't know?" he asked gently. "That's the main reason I brought her tonight."

Now I felt I had to do whatever I could to help him. "Come to see me tomorrow, Bucky. I have some things to tell you, and I want to be out of here before Avery decides to look for me."

Once at home, though, the relief I expected to feel at having escaped Avery eluded me. *There's something about you that appeals to me.* As if he would change his program because of me—absurd even to imagine it.

I went to bed, but exhaustion did not bring sleep. I listened to Byron's old clock strike every hour. Just after three I heard the front door open. Ronald, though I had not expected him. No one else had a key. I felt the familiar lifting of the heart at the sound of his approaching footsteps, the characteristic hesitation of his limp a little more pronounced now. He came into the bedroom, still wearing his evening clothes, the tie off and the shirt collar open despite the cold of the night. I knew he had not worn a coat; he was always too hot in New York after his years on the ice. I sat up in bed and held out my arms to him, but then he turned on the bedside lamp and I saw his grim expression. After an evening of fencing with Avery, I felt too tired to face trouble and trouble there clearly was.

"So it was Avery in London." Ronald's voice and manner were chilling. He walked over to the side of the bed, and instinctively I moved away and pulled up the covers. His manner to me was always so courteous and conciliatory that I had forgotten there was another side to his nature. The leader of polar expeditions, he had been hard, known how to command.

"I knew there'd been someone. Little differences when we made love. You were trying too hard. You never tried too hard before. I kept wondering who the man had been. He had to be somebody you knew; you'd never take on a stranger. And then I settled on Bucky Sheridan; he's not much, but he's an explorer and that counts for a lot with you.

"I never suspected Avery. You've been so clever all along, pretending to dislike him. You certainly had me fooled. A man like that. His hands on your body."

As Ronald spoke, I could not help but remember how I had felt lying on the crumpled bed in the lavish London hotel room, Avery's hands on my breasts, his weight on my body, his breath coming in gasps. At the last, I had realized what I was doing, wanted him to stop. Too late.

Ronald pulled down the covers and looked at my body as if he were seeing Avery's long, tapering fingers caressing me. I felt hot, knew I must be flushing beneath the sheer nightgown, knew he would take it as a sign of guilt. As it was. My negligee was just within reach, so I put it on and got out of bed. There seemed no way to ameliorate the situation, no way to admit to the overpowering but momentary desire for Avery.

Ronald's face was lined and there were deep shadows under his eyes. The jagged scar on his forehead, perceptible only when he was excited or angry, was scarlet. When I left the hotel room in London, I had dreaded that Ronald would somehow learn the truth and leave me. Then as time passed and he did not and we were lovers again, I began to think the whole episode could be relegated to the past. I knew, of course, as I had from the beginning, that a love affair with an older man has its time. I have seen what happens. All at once, there is one small sign, a weakness too transient to appear to matter. But that does matter. It is as if just one more cell has died and with its death comes an end to a life of being a lover for a young woman. Yes, I had anticipated a moment of weakness, not of anger and jealousy. "Ronald, let me explain. You don't understand."

"I believe that's the classic line in these scenes." He laughed, a laugh as devoid of humor as Avery's smiles were of amusement. "What is it that I don't understand?"

"I haven't lied to you about Avery. The way I feel about him. The only reason I saw him in London was that I had to find out if he knew about Viola Lambert. Nothing of importance happened."

"I'd like to know how you define 'importance.' Your being with another man seems important to me."

"I don't want to be with him, Ronald. He . . . repels me."

"Repels you? When you couldn't take your eyes off him at the dinner tonight. I've been married three times and there have been many women in my life, but I don't think anyone has ever tried to sell me such a ridiculous story.

"Why, you might have been alone with him for all the attention you paid to anyone else. He put his hand on your arm—I didn't see you trying to shake it off—the hand that was above the table, I mean. I couldn't see where the other one was."

Ronald's hands were on me now, gripping me tightly. His hands, suntanned the year around, looked big, threatening. He let go of me so abruptly that I had to catch at the bedpost to keep from falling. "Many years ago, Beatrix, I had an affair with a woman who was much older than I, twenty years at least, but I never thought of her as old. After a while, though, there was another woman. Woman? That one was little more than a girl. My lover found out, and all she said was that she had never expected me to be faithful when I was so much younger.

"The night when we made love for the first time after you returned from England—you knew what I meant to ask when I spoke your name. You passed it off and I didn't insist. All I could think was that it was my turn now.

"But it doesn't work. Jealousy's a crazy emotion. I should know better. A lovely young woman like you, still in your twenties. With me."

With him. I loved Ronald more, not less, for being older than I, for having experienced so much more of life. The adventures he had known, the dangers he had faced, the courage he had displayed—he brought all this to me—the kind of life Byron Tremaine had lived. Through Ronald, it is mine. I would not have had him younger. I know younger men; Avery is younger.

He walked over to the bed and sat down on the edge, looking at the floor. Not at me. "But Avery. Of all people, Avery."

"You must believe me, Ronald, the reason Avery played that unspeakable tape was that he was so angry with me for not . . . wanting him, and was trying to get back at me."

"Not wanting him? And didn't you want him tonight?"

"No. I didn't, I don't want him. He was just making trouble. Don't let him. I wish I never had to see him again. You're the one I love."

Ronald's face was haggard, and he looked his age. Almost. "Do you love me or do you think you have to love me to protect your image of Byron Tremaine? You connect us, don't you?"

He had said that before. I had denied it and did so now, yet he makes Byron Tremaine live again for me. Better not to say that. Not tonight. Not ever. I sat down on the bed beside him, putting my arms around his shoulders, pressing his face to my breasts. "Believe in me."

He did not answer, but slowly began to caress me. His hands were so big and rough, the skin damaged by the many episodes of frost-bite, but no one had a gentler touch. I watched him then as he took off his clothes, neatly placing them on the bedside chair as was his way, and we lay down together. We made love, but there was a strain between us. I was trying too hard. He was trying too hard. A few minutes later, he got up and dressed. For once I was relieved he was not spending the night with me.

When the doorbell chimed early the following morning, my first reaction was fear that it must be Avery, but when I looked through the peephole, it was only Bucky, so I let him in. Odd that Bucky was the one Ronald had suspected of being my lover.

Bucky touched my arm; he was always touching me. "You look so worried, Trixie. Every emotion you feel shows on your face. What has the terrible television host been telling you about me?"

He was cheerful, not taking Avery seriously. If he were to protect himself against Avery's accusation, I had to make him understand how grave it was. "He says the photographs of you at the South Pole are faked. Of course it's not true, but he thinks he can get away with it. Why, he probably faked the pictures himself."

Bucky gave a rueful smile, quite different from his usual broad grin. "No. The photographs are fakes."

There stood Bucky with his clear eyes and all-American-boy face. And he was just what Avery insisted he was. I remembered that Ronald had said Bucky was not much, and I had thought he was speaking out of jealousy.

"Of course, if I'd known then what I know now, I'd have had them done on a computer, and then they'd really have been impossible to spot. But we were in a hurry with the television newscasters and the newsmagazines calling for the pictures and it didn't seem to matter. Unless someone is suspicious, you can get away with any kind of fake. I wonder who put Avery onto it."

"He said your photographer came to him."

Bucky appeared stunned. "George Carmody. We're friends; he was the one who suggested the whole thing."

"Why did you do it, Bucky? You must have known you were taking a chance."

"Everything was riding on the success of my expedition. I knew I'd be ruined, in debt for life, if we didn't make it to the Pole."

"Why would you be in debt? Don't you have backers?" Explorers risked their lives and backers their money. That was the way it was done. "My great-grandfather and all the other explorers I've known had supporters providing the money."

Bucky laughed. "Not me. I don't have the pedigree of a Tremaine or Ronald Graham. Who'd take me that seriously? I don't take myself that seriously; the expedition seemed a lark to me, like the other things I've done in my life. Then when I got into it, I was hooked. But no one would just hand me the money. Every dollar was advanced against the television documentary, the magazine and book rights, the endorsements. Ironclad contracts. Oh, no, Trixie, I had to reach the Pole—or make it look as if I had."

How open and honest he appeared; there was a kind of cleanness about him. All false. I wanted him out of my house, out of Tremaine's house. I did not wish to see that boyish smile again. He is not much taller than I and our eyes are almost on a level. His were as untroubled as if there were nothing on his conscience.

"I could have made it to the Pole, Trixie. Easy. Another seven days—maybe six and a half if the weather had held. I was still going strong."

Even knowing his deceit, I was struck by how sincere he sounded; Bucky is a natural for television. Easy. Had it been easy, he would not have needed to falsify. "If you could have made it to the Pole, why didn't you?" I asked, and waited for his lie.

"I told you, Trixie—Jews are sentimental. When it came down to it, I didn't have the heart."

"What do you mean?"

"Have you ever heard of a man named Ian Crosbie? Very few people recognize his name nowadays. But in the early years of the century he was a polar explorer almost as famous as Sharpe and Tremaine. I got interested in him when I was boning up on the great explorers, preparing for my expedition. He was referred to in glowing terms in the memoirs of the period. A giant of a man. Fearless. Everyone expected him to be leading an Antarctic expedition of his own one day."

"I don't understand. What does Crosbie have to do with you and your expedition?"

"I'll get to that. I'm going to tell you what really happened . . . to

Crosbie . . . and to me. Even if no one else ever knows the truth, I want you to know."

"Why should that matter to you?"

"You amaze me, Beatrix. What world are you in? The most courageous explorer of our time is in love with you; the king of television exposés is obviously fascinated by you. And you can't figure out why I might want your good opinion."

I was too startled to respond. I know myself—a pretty young woman with a good figure and a great family history, but hardly the glamorous seductress Bucky was presenting. Still, I could not help feeling flattered, and I did believe he wanted my good opinion. My curiosity was aroused, and I was eager to hear his story.

Ian Crosbie, he continued, was the second-in-command on Sharpe's doomed expedition. Sharpe's journals were filled with accounts of Crosbie's heroism; all the men depended on his strength and courage.

"Crosbie was the fifth man in the party that made the final assault on the Pole."

"Wait a minute, Bucky. There were only four men in Sharpe's Pole party. That's history."

"At the end there were four. But, according to Sharpe's journal, there were supposed to be five, and Ian Crosbie was the fifth. I assumed he died before making it to the Pole. But that's not the way it was."

Gradually, as the expedition made its way southward, a change in Crosbie became evident, Bucky went on with the story. It started with the dogs; Crosbie could not stand to be near them. He had killed a dog once with his bare hands, he said. No one knew whether to believe him. Taciturn heretofore, he began to speak wildly, describing episodes of violence. In Scotland. Crosbie had never spoken about Scotland. Sharpe came to suspect that something shady in Crosbie's past had been concealed. Mental illness of some sort. Crosbie was acting more strangely now, wandering away from the group to eat alone, fearing poison.

The weeks of travel over the harsh Antarctic icescape had taken their toll on all the other men, but he showed no signs of fatigue. Every day when they stopped, exhausted, to make camp, Crosbie was fresh enough to put up the tents by himself, allowing the others to rest. Still, Sharpe was uneasy; a lifelong navy man, he had no sympathy for psychological instability. What if Crosbie went mad on the final stages of the journey to the Pole? It could not be risked. Crosbie must return to the base camp with those who had not been chosen for the Pole party. The men who were to continue pleaded with Sharpe. Yes, they were sometimes afraid of Crosbie, but at the same time they did not think they could survive without him.

Sharpe would not be swayed. "We stood on the desolate summit of the glacier beaten by the brutal sleet-laden wind," Bucky quoted from Sharpe's journal, "and I told Ian that I could not depend on him, and he must return to the base camp. I think I broke his heart."

"What became of Crosbie?" I asked.

"Sharpe was right, you know, about breaking Crosbie's heart. He never recovered." Bucky spoke so movingly that I had tears in my eyes. "Crosbie's wife was an American and she took him back to New York and committed him to a mental institution in White Plains. Crosbie probably died there."

Bucky took my hand and held it then very tightly. "It's the saddest story," I said to him, "but it has nothing to do with you. Why do you care so much?"

"I told you I have a weakness for people with mental illness. And Crosbie does have something . . . everything really . . . to do with the way my expedition ended. Maybe it won't make sense to you; half the time it doesn't make sense to me. But that's here, in New York. When I was shivering in that brutal wind Sharpe wrote about high up on the glacier—maybe I was half-crazy myself, but it made perfect sense."

The Sheridan expedition was supposed to duplicate Tremaine's—and it did—but there was a parallel with Sharpe's expedition as well. Bucky's second-in-command, Joe Harney, like Ian Crosbie, had suffered a breakdown requiring hospitalization when he was very young. Unlike Crosbie, he made no secret of his psychiatric history, and insisted he had been perfectly well for several years before he volunteered to be the business manager for the Sheridan expedition. "He was a terrific manager, but I could see he was dying to be on the expedition. Every day, he'd ask if he couldn't go with me. Joe's a powerful guy, twice my size, an experienced mountain climber and champion skier. Anyway, I thought it wasn't fair to hold his history against him."

Joe Harney's story as it unfolded bore an uncanny resemblance to Ian Crosbie's, with the first signs of instability emerging as the expedition came closer to the Pole. His behavior became erratic, yet he was the strongest of the men, carrying the loads of those who were too exhausted to go on, able to function on the most limited rations. Soon another problem emerged—night after night, the men sharing the tent awakened to discover him gone. Cursing, they forced themselves to leave their sleeping bags, struggle into their many layers of clothing, and go out into temperatures thirty degrees below zero or colder. If they were lucky, Harney would be nearby. At other times, they had to traverse the bleak snowy surface for hours. Once found, he accompanied them docilely back to camp. The next day they were on the trail again as if they had not spent half the night searching.

The Tremaine expedition had journeyed to the Pole and back in 104 days and the Sheridan expedition was to maintain that schedule. Finally Bucky was forced to recognize that with Harney along, it could not be done. He must be left behind.

"Joe came out of the tent just then and walked up to me smiling. I told him about the change of plans as kindly as I could. 'You'd go on to the Pole without me?' I nodded. 'But I'm the strongest,' he said. 'Don't you trust me?' And then he broke down and cried. It was so goddamned cold that his tears froze going down his face."

The room was very quiet. At Bucky's words, I could see the two men, high up on the glacier, shivering, their bodies buffeted by the polar winds.

"At that moment, I remembered Ian Crosbie. I'd read his story just the way I told it to you, but I hadn't really understood it. Until then. Looking at those channels of ice down Harney's face, I knew he was feeling what Crosbie had felt all those years ago. Crosbie hadn't ever gotten over being turned down; his life was ruined. And here I was doing just what Sharpe did. Destroying a man. So I could be a hero.

"I couldn't, Trixie. I just didn't have the heart.

"The Pole was so close. So close. Standing there, half-crazy myself, on the glacier with a blizzard blotting out the sun, I knew how much I wanted to get there. You've no idea what it's like, day after day in the cold, blizzards locking you into your tent, soft snow making your feet slither, frostbite tormenting you. The agony of getting up in the morning to drag yourself up another icy hill. And none of that matters, Trixie. All you can see, like a vision in front of your eyes, is the Pole. You're going to make it and everything will be worthwhile. Not just the fame and the money—but to be there, to know you made it. I thought I couldn't bear to give that up. But I'd have to."

He had waited for another minute, hoping to find another way out. "But there wasn't any. So finally, I told Joe that I had just been using him as an excuse. We were all turning back from the Pole, because I didn't have the strength to go any farther. It was because of me."

*So I could be a hero.* I had not thought Bucky possessed that kind of selflessness. "But how did you get the other men—the ones who were supposed to go to the Pole with you—to agree?"

"I told them the same thing. And they had to agree, Trixie. I was the leader; they had to follow my orders. On the expedition anyway."

The next day he realized what he had done. The disappointment of losing the Pole was just the beginning. "Talk of a ruined life. Every manufacturer who had contributed to the expedition would demand the money back, and I didn't have it.

"I told George the truth; I was closer to him than anyone on the expedition, except for Joe. He thought for a while and then said there was an easy way out of the mess.

" 'I can fix it,' he said. 'As soon as we're back in New Zealand, I'll get copies of the photographs Tremaine had taken at the Pole and make some new prints. Then I'll superimpose photographs of us with our equipment, brand names and all, onto the Tremaine photographs. I'll keep in the shadows that prove the location.'

" 'It won't work,' I objected, 'everyone will recognize the pictures were doctored.'

" 'Why should they?' George came back coolly. 'People see what they want to, and they all want to see you at the Pole. They want you to be a hero.'

"The plan still was not feasible; the other men knew they had not reached the Pole and were bound to say so. George did not think so. 'If they go along with your story, they'll be heroes, too, and will get the benefits of the expedition's success. They've been counting on it.

" 'Besides, we're all in this together,' George told me. 'Friends.

Nobody will give you away.' Ironic, isn't it, that he was the one to say that?

"So now you see, Avery's right, and I'm not the hero your great-grandfather was."

I knew what Byron would have thought of Bucky's lie. Had the Tremaine expedition fallen short of the Pole, the world would have known it. According to my heritage, I should despise Bucky. But I did not. I wanted him to get away with his deception, to find a way of confounding Avery. My heart sank as I imagined Avery flashing the bogus photographs on the screen and bringing on a forensic photographer—or maybe George himself—to explain the forgery to the audience.

"Could you tell the story just as you told it to me, Bucky?"

He shook his head. "And give Harney away?

"Don't look so worried, Trixie—though I do like to see you worrying about me. But I've gotten out of tight places before. That's what I do best."

At his words, a feeling of uncertainty came over me. All the while Bucky had been talking, I was utterly convinced by the sincerity of his manner. *That's what I do best.* Perhaps the purpose of the whole story was to move me so that I would intercede for him with Avery. That thought had crossed my mind after hearing his affecting account of his wife's suicide, too. He held the unaccountable belief that I have influence with Avery. I thought of another possibility no more palatable—that this was a rehearsal of what he might say on Avery's program. If I, brought up to value courage, believed him, why not the television viewers?

These doubts made a kind of sense, but I could not accept them as valid. An opportunist—yes, that was Bucky. But *so I could be a hero*—that was Bucky, too. I knew he liked me enough to value my good opinion. Why seek for hidden motives in his words?

"So all this has happened because of something cruel that was done to a man named Ian Crosbie eighty years ago or more. A man forgotten by everyone but you."

"Now that I think of it, Trixie, it's odd that you never heard of Crosbie. He was married to a famous suffragette, the one you were talking about in London."

"Viola Lambert?"

"Yes. That's the one."

I wondered how I could have missed so important a piece of news. "When I was going through the British newspapers, I looked up every reference to Viola's name from the moment she arrived in England until her death. With all that was written about her, it's odd her marriage never made the newspapers."

"It doesn't seem possible, particularly as Sharpe was a witness. He wrote about the wedding in his diary. I remember the way he described her. She was so beautiful and had such personal magnetism that you saw no else in the room. He was so struck by her tremendous vitality, he wrote, that he was almost sorry he hadn't agreed to take her with him to the Antarctic as she'd asked him to do."

The Antarctic again. She had applied for the Sharpe expedition, married a polar explorer. Everything I learned about this woman fitted her for the all-women's Antarctic expedition Byron had so cryptically described. If only she had not died before the given dates.

"I wonder if she survived Crosbie," remarked Bucky.

"She couldn't have. The fire at Chessham Court in the last days of 1909 killed her."

"Did you say 1909? She couldn't have died then, Trixie. The Sharpe expedition took place in 1911 to 1912, and Viola was very much alive when she met Crosbie on his return and took him back to America."

I jumped up, too excited to sit still. Viola Lambert had not died in the fire. My search of the newspapers had ended too soon. I must start again and follow the events of her life—perhaps to the Antarctic.

"What is it?" asked Bucky.

In all my talks with Bucky, I had instinctively held back the baffling message about the Antarctic expedition, fearing that, backed into a corner by Avery, he might decide to tell that story as a diversion. Better to wait until I had the solution to the mystery. And so I gave him a vague answer and was relieved when he accepted it, smiled at me, pressed my hand, and went on his way.

The only person I would trust was Ronald. He was willing to help me in my search for Viola Lambert—Viola Crosbie as I now knew her to be. He was willing, but his heart was not in it. The change in him was still painful to me; somehow I must convince him of my love.

We went to the library together and began combing through the annual index volumes of the newspapers, beginning with 1910. References to Viola Crosbie were not as frequent as in the British press, but the marriage to Ian Crosbie was duly noted. Listings for the Sharpe expedition appeared in 1911 and 1912, followed by news of the Crosbies' return to New York and Viola's growing prominence in suffragette circles.

In 1913 Byron Tremaine made the formal announcement of his forthcoming expedition, and the newspaper reports for that year and the next described his plans and preparations. Promising to be the first American to reach the South Pole, he declared that his expedition was destined to be the greatest scientific voyage of all time, surpassing his first Greenland journey with its major finds. Scientists from the leading universities and museums were vying with one another for a chance to join the expedition. Even the clouds of war gathering over Europe did not displace the Tremaine expedition from the front pages.

Still hoping to find a link between Byron and Viola, a hint that she had been involved in his expedition, I turned to the *Suffrage Searchlight*. Her activities on behalf of the vote were recounted in detail, but this was hardly what I was looking for, and I was ready to give up when all at once, a headline caught my eye: AMAZONS WANTED. I had found it—the all-women's expedition to the Antarctic that had been expunged from the pages of history.

"It really happened." I felt exultant as I showed Ronald the recruitment advertisement. There it was, out in the open. But Tremaine had said that no word of the expedition ever got out. "Why was it concealed after that?"

"I'm afraid the likeliest explanation is that it didn't happen," replied Ronald. "I know from my own experience how hard it is to get financial support even when you have a name and reputation. My guess is that the women's expedition foundered because the money couldn't be raised. Or no 'Amazons' applied and the whole thing died right then and there."

But Byron's message implied the existence of such an expedition. I insisted on turning to subsequent issues of the *Searchlight* and then the daily newspapers. And gradually, the lost history of the expedition began to emerge. The truth was beyond anything I could have imagined.

In a bold challenge to Byron Tremaine, Viola Crosbie declared she would race him to the South Pole and win. The journalists repeated her boast, making a joke of it. The expedition was dubbed "Mrs. Crosbie's Folly" by the *New York Journal,* and the other newspaper columnists picked it up. Humorous references were made to the band of Amazons. In a more serious vein, the observation was made that Lieutenant Crosbie would surely have put a stop to his wife's poorly conceived plan were he not ill. I remembered Bucky's story then, and the tragedy of Crosbie's madness.

After the initial announcement, the women's expedition was relegated to brief mentions in articles inconspicuously placed on the back pages. The *Searchlight* gave more attention to the expedition, but the descriptions of it were disappointingly vague.

On June 1, 1914, newspaper headlines announced that Byron Tremaine's ship steamed out of New York Harbor, with the governor of the state, the mayor of the city, and crowds of cheering people on the dock. The marine band was playing. Newspapers from all over the world sent photographers and reporters. The photograph taken that day has been reproduced countless times; it shows my great-grandfather, handsome and resolute, standing on the deck of the ice-breaker, with Horace Graham beside him.

Where had "Mrs. Crosbie's Folly" gotten to? To my dismay, the *Suffrage Searchlight* suspended publication, leaving the newspapers as my only source for information. Viola had sworn to race Tremaine to the Pole, so her departure from New York must closely follow his. And it did. On the fourth of June, Viola Crosbie and her Amazons, fourteen in all, departed for New Zealand, en route to Antarctica. No cheering crowds came to see them off; the governor and the mayor remained in their offices; the marine band was playing somewhere else. Only suffragettes were on the dock that day waving their banners.

In the course of the next two years Byron Tremaine landed in New Zealand and set off again for Antarctica. The history books tell the rest of the story.

The Crosbie expedition, in marked contrast, disappeared from even the back pages of the newspapers. I searched for news of Viola Lambert Crosbie. The only references to the Lambert name were in connection with social events the family had given or attended, philanthropies supported. Mr. Lambert died and received a long obituary in keeping with his prominence. The two daughters and sons-in-law were listed.

*Thank God no word of that all-women's expedition to the South Pole in 1915–1916 ever got out! I still fear that it may.*

In the end there had been nothing for Byron Tremaine to fear. Not a word had gotten out. Not of the beautiful, magnetic Viola Crosbie, not of her band of Amazons.

The all-women's expedition had steamed out of New York Harbor in an ancient sealing ship, never to be heard from again.

# Chapter Twenty-three

HE FEARED THAT OUT OF his jealousy, he was sending her to her death. Until the last moment it had not occurred to Ian that he would not be accompanying Viola to the South Pole. This was the Crosbie expedition—and who was a Crosbie if not he? She had told him he would be left behind, but he did not believe she really meant that to happen. Why, he had planned every detail of the journey. For her, of course. But for him as well. This was how he would reinstate himself in her eyes, in the eyes of the world after the failure with Sharpe. An all-women's expedition—no one could possibly believe that Viola meant to observe this to the letter. One man, and he her husband, would be the logical exception.

Every mile of the route had been mapped. The course Ian worked out over days and weeks was ingenious, brilliant really. No one else had ever gone that way, but it was the best possible approach to the South Pole. The Crosbie expedition would arrive there ahead of Tremaine. He was sure of it. At least he had been sure of it as long as he had been sure of going along. Now that it was too late to alter the plan, he was tormented by second thoughts.

He would never have selected a promontory on the Bay of Whales for the base camp had he known the women would be there alone . . . without him. The decision was made when Viola told him Tremaine was planning to use Ross Island, as Sharpe had done. At that moment

Ian recalled the Bay of Whales, thought it an inspiration. The location would put the Crosbie expedition 60 miles closer to the Pole—760 miles, compared to 820. In terrain where every mile counts, the advantage would be incalculable.

Ian had learned about the Bay of Whales from Shackleton, who had seriously considered establishing his camp there in 1907. Night after night he had sat with Shackleton in the officers' messroom on the *Nimrod,* drinking brandy by gaslight and discussing whether they should abandon the known difficulties of Ross Island for the unknown of the bay. Ian had urged the more daring plan, but in the end Shackleton dismissed the location as too hazardous. They had no information about the condition of the ice sheet off the Bay of Whales, and were it unstable, huge chunks might break off and float away. Instead they started out from Ross Island and missed the Pole by a hairbreadth.

Originally they had intended to avoid climbing the icy cliffs of Beardmore Glacier, and selected an alternate route to the west going over the uncharted Axel Heiberg Glacier. Depots were laid along that route in the first summer season. But when the expedition returned the following year, a network of crevasses blocked the way to Heiberg and forced them back to Beardmore, where they were beaten to exhaustion by gale-force, ice-laden winds. Sharpe had done the same and met his doom.

He could not bear to think of Viola suffering the horrors of Beardmore. The Shackleton expedition had just been unlucky; crevasses appear and disappear from year to year. The route over Heiberg still seemed the best to Ian, and it was the shortest way to the Pole. No explorer had yet attempted to scale the heights of the glacier, but its dimensions appeared to be less formidable than those of Beardmore. At least he had thought so when drawing the route on the map laid out on the big table in the parlor at home on Washington Square. Here, in New Zealand, he was not so certain.

Ian was well aware that his determination to find an alternate route to the Pole had a dual motive from the start. Tremaine had told Viola he planned to cross Beardmore, and Ian could not endure the thought of their meeting on the approach to the glacier. Now he wondered whether it had been unconscionable to put her on an unknown path. He would never have done so had he not been certain that in the end she would agree to take him with her and equally certain that with his great strength, he could get the expedition through to the Pole and back no matter how treacherous the terrain.

Now he was afraid that out of his jealousy, he might be sending her to her death.

That morning they had been lying in bed, content, or so he thought. Since taking charge of the expedition, he felt as in the early days of their marriage when he made love to Viola without an instant's doubt. Now he was her lover again, bringing them both to a peak of fulfillment and joy. Caressing her breasts and then running his hands down her body—the elongated, slender waist and narrow, curving hips—he was gentle, so gentle, knowing how much his tenderness meant to her.

They kissed, and when she took her mouth away from his, she told him what was to be. The Crosbie expedition would be sailing for the Antarctic on the following day. Her voice was soft, but something about her tone alarmed him. He was not to accompany the group, not even to remain on board the *Explorer* when it deposited the women and their supplies at the Bay of Whales and then returned to New Zealand. Instead he was to go to Canada, to an uncle he barely knew. He could not remember having mentioned this relative to Viola, but he must have, as passage had been booked.

Taken by surprise, Ian lay there, feeling clumsy and helpless, unable to move or to speak. Viola got out of bed then, and he stared at her. Naked, her body gleamed in the dim light of the room just as on the night he had taken her for the first time in London. Then he had gone on the Sharpe expedition, and how terrible the years after that had been. Her conscience was clear, he supposed; she had stood by him for so long. But still it was wrong for her to abandon him now. Wrong. And foolish, too. Because they would not achieve the Pole without him. He sat up then, gasping for breath, feeling his throat close up. Only not with madness. He would have wished himself mad in that moment.

Day after day Viola had put off making the definite statement, telling herself he knew, he must know, while at the same time she was aware he was refusing the knowledge. All the while they had been making love, his tongue in her mouth, his body tight against hers, his hands so big, so gentle, stroking her, she was dreading the moment of telling him. This morning, knowing what must be said, her body was unable to warm to him, and she had pretended her response.

"But I told you this from the start."

He could only shake his head. She had told him, but surely they had both known that was not her intention. The women on the expedition had turned her against him. In the tight living quarters of the *Explorer,* its deck and hold crammed with supplies, equipment, and dogs, he could not help but hear them arguing with her as the long sea voyage neared its end.

On board ship, thinking herself indebted to him for his help, Viola had sometimes wavered. The expedition members began to doubt that she would leave him behind. "We've signed on for an all-women's voyage," Carla insisted. "You and me, Viola—we've been through so much for suffrage. Lesley died for it. That's got to count for something. You can't let one man spoil it all."

Carla liked few men and had disapproved of the marriage to Ian from the beginning, but her words could not be dismissed on those grounds.

Ian's misery was so acute that Viola could not look him in the face, and kept her eyes lowered onto his naked chest, which seemed strangely vulnerable. She remembered the giant heroic figure she had first seen in Sharpe's office and thought that he was still huge, still powerful, but somehow beaten. How could it have happened to this man who had brushed aside the line of police to run into the flames on Chessham Court? Never a thought of the risk to him. And then came Sharpe and his cruelty in denying Ian the Pole. Perhaps there had been an inevitability to Ian's breakdown; periods of madness had occurred earlier in his life after all.

What seemed particularly tragic now was that during the months when they were organizing the expedition together, he had been confident and resolute. This time she was the one who must be cruel, but the suffrage movement was supporting the expedition; she owed it to them and the Amazons who had joined her to make this gesture. Sending Ian to Canada was not the happiest arrangement for him, but not a terrible fate. She had originally planned to send him to Scotland to his brother, but while they were en route to New Zealand, the ship's wireless brought the stunning news that Archduke Francis Ferdinand had been assassinated at Sarajevo and Europe was plunged into war. The sea lanes to Europe would be unsafe and another haven for Ian must be found. It was fortunate indeed, she thought, that Ian once told her an uncle had emigrated to Canada. The modern wireless made it possible for her to arrange the whole thing. Perhaps there were cousins, too, whom Ian had known as a boy, though she could not recall his ever mentioning them. But then, Ian never spoke of his childhood.

She recognized all he had done to make the expedition possible, she told him, and would always be grateful to him, see that he received the credit he deserved.

Grateful. Her voice went on and on, low, throbbing, seductive, but not seducing him. Not now. He did not believe half of what she said. Why, she was not able to meet his eyes.

That day when she returned from seeing Tremaine, flushed and emotional, he had accused her of planning the expedition in order to meet Tremaine on the polar ice cap. He had been right. For all her bold talk about a competition, about votes for women, she intended to go to the Pole with Tremaine. That was the only way she could get there. Viola knew full well that an all-women's expedition could not reach the Pole without a man's strength behind it. His help had been refused. She did not need him, not with Tremaine standing by.

He had felt guilty about subjecting her to the unknown dangers of the new route. Absurd to have tormented himself. Her refusal to have him on board the ship for the final leg of the journey made sense to him, a terrible kind of sense. She did not intend to establish her base at the Bay of Whales, nor would she cross the Heiberg Glacier. Instead, the *Explorer* would set its metal-reinforced prow in the direction of Ross Island, where Tremaine was waiting for her, where the two expeditions would become one.

Looking back, it now seemed to him that the women had been arguing with Viola about Tremaine, rather than about him. Seeing her infatuated—surely Viola was not in love—with Tremaine, they thought he, not Ian, would destroy the gesture for suffrage. But Viola was the leader of the expedition, and if she insisted, she would have her way. No one crosses the leader.

After a while when he did not speak—how could he speak when she was betraying him?—her voice trailed off. Perhaps it did not seem betrayal to her, considering his history. But it was betrayal nonetheless. If it were not unmanly, he could have wept. Getting out of bed at last, he drew on his trousers and shirt, embarrassed at being unclothed in front of her. She was still naked, but that meant nothing, as she had no self-consciousness about nudity.

Her body, naked, panting in Tremaine's arms. Her cries of ecstasy. In the Antarctic summer, on days when the temperature rose to a few degrees below zero and the winds were still, it was warm inside a tent, warm for two bodies enclosed in a sleeping bag.

He wished he could hate her, find her undesirable, but that would never be. Putting out his hand, conscious of how big and how rough it was, he stroked her brilliant hair. She had cut it short in New York, for convenience, she said, but it had grown back even more luxuriant, with long strands of copper. He touched her skin. So hot. The dingy room in the Port Chalmers boardinghouse was damp and cold, and she was so hot. Could he sway her by making love to her again, have her forget Tremaine? But now, thinking back on the sex act just ended, he knew she had been pretending. There was a difference. She had not wanted him, was eager to be gone, to be away from him.

Whatever happened on the expedition, he knew with a terrible certainty that they would never be together again. Viola thought she had settled everything so neatly, arranging passage to Canada, where his uncle was to take charge of him. All done behind his back. But he would not go to his uncle or to anyone else in his family. They knew of his past; his memories, and theirs, were too ugly. Better to join an expedition. If not his own—there were others. Shackleton was planning another voyage to the Antarctic, intending to cross from the Weddell Sea to McMurdo Sound by boat. He had worked well for Shackleton, won medals and praise. Then he realized that Shackleton would not accept him now, nor would any other Antarctic explorer. He was not to set foot on the continent again, would never again see the ice glowing under the lemon yellow sky, never satisfy the hunger driving him to the Pole. Antarctic expeditions were too carefully planned to include a man with a questionable past; the Arctic, though, was still possible.

He would avoid his uncle, make his way northward from Canada and join . . . whom? Cook. That was the answer. Cook was not so fussy as the more respected explorers in choosing companions. He would remain in the Arctic, Ian thought. Change his name. Disappear there. Either he would die on the trail or settle in an Indian village. There was no place for him in the civilized world. For a time Viola had almost made him believe there was. She would wonder about him for a while, perhaps arrange for a search—but not too vigorously, as his absence would leave her free for Tremaine.

"I think I will never see you again," he said. *Think.* He meant *know.* And his voice broke when he thought that he would never hold her in his arms, feel the heat of her body, the smoothness of her skin against his, never kiss her throat, hear her call out his name in her throbbing voice, in rapture. He kissed her now, keeping his eyes open to see her face so close to his for one last time. She opened her mouth to him, but that meant nothing now.

He remembered the day she walked into Sharpe's office to volunteer for the expedition, and how dazzling she had been. How dazzling she was now, with the Antarctic ahead of her. And him behind her.

"Of course you will see me. I'll come back and we'll be together again." What could she say that would make him feel better? "There'll be another expedition." But her voice was shaking. "The Antarctic is vast; there is so much to explore. The next time it won't be just women." Even as she spoke, she was appalled by what she was saying. Like Tremaine, she was implying a promise she would not keep. Like Sharpe, she had seen his madness, would not trust him on the ice. Yet she could not bear to leave him in such despair.

Once he had promised her a place on an expedition in just this way, Ian was thinking. But the difference between the two promises was great. His had been sincere; hers was not.

Viola put her arms around him, slipped her hands under his shirt, but he kept his body stiff and she drew back. "Don't forget that I love you, Ian."

Perhaps she did. But not enough. It would be better to forget her. If he could.

Still, he did not say that. "I'll always love you" was what he said instead, while wishing it were not true.

Now he had to take her in his arms, knowing he was holding her for the last time. She was trembling; he wondered why. Her breasts were pressed against his chest. He would never look at them again, hold them in his hands.

Her face was wet with tears when he kissed her good-bye. At least she was weeping for him. *I know I will never see you again.*

# Chapter Twenty-four

꧁꧂

THE AIR WAS COLD AGAINST her face, bitter, but like a caress. The caress she had been waiting for. Viola stood on the ice, purple-white, glimmering with rose and golden sparks in the brief moments of sunshine breaking the long twilight of early spring in Antarctica. Looking southward toward the Pole, hundreds of miles away, yet so close. Soon it would be hers.

The first summer had been spent in laying depots, the winter in making repairs and preparations, and now another summer was to commence, a summer that would be the greatest of her life. Year after year of beating her head against the stone wall that was Byron, against the opposition of her parents, of society, against the burden of her sad husband—all that was behind her. Ahead was the journey across the unexplored glacier to her goal. January, she thought. On a January day in 1916, a day when the sun did not set, she would be at the South Pole.

Nothing would ever be the same again. For her. For women. Not just the women of the expedition, but all women.

The air was so clear that it seemed she might see as far as the base camp on Ross Island where Byron was preparing for his departure to the Pole. Sixty miles. That was the advantage she had over him. She was tempted to gain another by setting out in September, rather than waiting for more equable weather in October, but she could not chance losing even one pair of dogs or one sledge to the storms of early spring.

Tremaine would be leaving his base camp in October, too, with more men, more dogs, more food and fuel. She was not intimidated. At last she had the opportunity to best him. Her own supplies had been extended with meat and blubber taken from the seals and penguins captured by the women remaining at the base camp through the previous summer and with fish caught through holes in the ice. Life was abundant only in and around the polar seas; once on the ice plateau, the expedition would be dependent on the stores piled high in the depots.

Viola's confidence was bolstered by the success of the depot-laying expedition of the previous year. Ian's carefully marked maps kept them on the most direct route, and the weather was favorable. Had she not feared the oncoming blizzards of autumn, she would have stopped along the way, gathered more of the fossils that lay scattered amidst the moraine of the glaciers. These hinted at a prehistoric climate very different from that of today. On the return from the Pole, she thought, she would uncover evidence of the Antarctic's mysterious past.

Standing on the edge of the ice shelf, looking out at the icebergs looming like castles, like cathedrals over the bay, she remembered Greenland. Feeling the caribou fur soft against her body, she remembered his touch. Remembered touching him. That day in the hut on Disko Island when his skin had gleamed in the dim light and she had put her hand on him. Here on the desolate ice cap in a world without men, she was tormented by sexual desire, by her recollection of the time they were lovers. The way he had kissed, with his eyes open, green, blazing. The competition between them—when did it begin? On the day in New York when she refused to marry him? Perhaps he had fought her to make her fight him; perhaps she had fought him to make him fight her. Their rivalry had become an integral part of their lovemaking, brought it a greater intensity. No more. All that passion, that fire, was gone, lost when he refused to take her to the Pole, underhandedly sought to foil her expedition. Now she must hate him.

All the previous summer, as she skied ahead of the heavily laden sledges, she thought of him. Frostbitten, snow-blinded more than once, the desire to win over him gave her the strength to drive herself and her companions farther and farther on. One more depot and yet one more. Sharpe's final depot had been too far from the Pole; he had died eleven miles short of reaching it. The all-women's expedition dared not repeat the error.

But sometimes, as now, when she stood on her skis in the sunshine, seeing the shadows of the skua gulls on the ice, smelling the penguins in the nearby rookery, Viola was seized with the most terrible regret. The dream of the Antarctic—he had been a part of it. She had imagined being just here, just as she was now, with him beside her. Instead, miles away on Ross Island, right at this moment, Byron was preparing his assault on the Pole. He had taken over her discoveries, scorned her ambition, destroyed that dream. Still, she would arrive at the Pole ahead of him, leaving him to come upon the tracks of her skis, the paw prints of the dog teams, the imprints of sledge runners on the snow, as on the January day in 1912 when Sharpe stumbled across the proof that Carlsen had preempted the victory.

That sorry image of Sharpe reminded her of Ian. Even in his absence, he was a part of this expedition. Here were his maps; here was the hut built to his specifications. Two sets of boards separated by layers of rubberized fabric, felt, and dried seaweed formed the roof, walls, and floor and kept the room within warm and snug. The hut was located on top of the ice cliff, with a glorious view of the bay. Far to the west, the smoke was rising from the snowcapped summit of towering Mount Erebus, a still-active volcano. All was exactly as Ian had described it.

A sudden sharp ache came over her at the memory of his misery when she left him. If only she could have responded to Ian with passion that last morning in Port Chalmers. Now it was autumn in the Northern Hemisphere, and the snows come early in Canada. Perhaps Ian was looking with bitterness at the gleaming white surface, comparing it to the Antarctic. Every night after the journal entry was completed, Viola wrote to him, wording the letters carefully so as not to feed his envy. A hundred letters were in readiness by the time the *Explorer* arrived for its brief spring visit, bringing mail from home and picking up the mail to be posted upon its return to New Zealand.

When the heavy bags were unloaded and sorted, Viola was dismayed to discover that not a single letter from Canada was there. The likeliest explanation was that Ian was confined in a hospital for the insane and his uncle had not taken the trouble to write.

The likeliest explanation? Not at all. Not when she remembered the parting from Ian—*I think I will never see you again. Think.* He had spoken as if he knew. Until now she had rejected the finality of his words, but at last she recognized what they meant. He intended to disappear. To kill himself? She would not believe it, could not bear to believe it. But that he would hide himself in some place where she would never find him—that she could believe and did believe. The *Explorer* was scheduled to come again the following spring, but she expected no word from Ian. He would finish out his life in some desolate spot. Alone.

Could she have saved Ian by abandoning her vision of the Antarctic? She did not think so. His madness had destroyed his life, the madness concealed from her when they married. She had done all she could for him. And for years. What she felt now was regret rather than guilt.

Heavy at heart, she turned to the letters from home and found little comfort there. Her mother expressed concern about Viola's well-being, prayed for a safe return. But she could not understand why Viola put herself at such risk unnecessarily. Viola could hardly bear to read the account of Mr. Lambert's final illness. His disapproval of the life Viola had chosen never wavered, her mother wrote, but he had asked for her when on his deathbed. Viola did not see what she could have done differently, and yet was filled with regret over having failed her father at the end. When she returned to New York, she would do everything in her power to make her mother comprehend the vision that drove her and to achieve a reconciliation. Evelyn had written repeatedly, but her letters were sad. She had been pregnant, but lost the baby, and the doctors said she was too frail to bear a healthy child. Perhaps Bertram's view of her fragility was correct. Only the letters from Eileen and her suffragette friends were happy. The leaders were wild with enthusiasm, had the highest hopes— no, more than that, were confident—that the all-women's expedition would reach the Pole and return home in triumph. They were impatient to let the whole world know the truth about their sponsorship.

Here in the Antarctic the outside world seemed very distant; there was no reality beyond the ice cap. Yet all the while the war in Europe was being waged along the Western Front with devastating casualties and the Russians were fighting in the East. The women who had demonstrated with Viola in London were working in factories, on farms, and in hospitals; the suffrage movement was now centered in America.

Despite the attention concentrated on the war in Europe, the progress of the Tremaine expedition filled the newspaper columns. Feature articles about Tremaine described his adventures in Greenland and on Mount McKinley and presented him as a hero. Nothing was written about the women of the Crosbie expedition; they might have disappeared off the face of the earth.

In the final days before departing on the long southward journey to the Pole, Viola reviewed Ian's lists, remembering his warning that any miscalculation at the outset could seal their subsequent doom. They must carry the reindeer sleeping bags, the floor cloths, the tent poles and tenting fabric, the stove and the fuel, the food, the fur and woolen clothing, the meteorological instruments, the cameras and film and photographic plates, the medical kit. There should be just enough food and fuel to get them from one supply depot to the next, from the final cache to the Pole and back. The quantities must be calculated with exactitude; they would come to regret every excess pound. She recalled Byron's scornful remark that they would be weighed down with boxes of Lister's towels for the monthly bleeding. To their surprise, however, none of the women on the depot-laying journey needed them. It had not been so in Greenland where Viola had carried her own supplies, digging holes in the ice to dispose of the towels when used. Perhaps the more intense cold in the Antarctic, the ferocity of the winds, the extreme exertion were responsible for the cessation of bleeding. How could they tell, being the first women to undertake such a voyage of discovery?

The previous year, before setting out on the depot-laying journey, Viola had selected three women to accompany her to the South Pole: Carla, her companion in arms; Marcia, the expedition photographer; and Evadne, who had, without anything being said, become the second-in-command. On the depot-laying expedition, her slender dancer's body proved able to lift heavy cartons of supplies without

straining, drive tent poles deep into the snow. The women respected
Evadne, and more surprising, on shipboard, the seamen would do
anything she asked. Viola sometimes heard her talking with them,
telling jokes, cursing. Ian had disapproved; a navy man, he believed
a distance between expedition and crew members must be maintained: "I hear her laughing with them. A coarse laugh." Coarse?
Evadne with her flawless classical features and graceful figure?

A photographic record of the expedition was essential, so Marcia
had been guaranteed a place on the Pole party. But after the return
to the base camp, when the pictures of the first summer season were
developed, Viola was disappointed. The work was no more than
competent. A few days later a stack of photographs appeared on Viola's worktable. Just one look and she knew that Marcia was incapa-
ble of taking photographs like these. They were hauntingly beautiful,
revealed the wonder of exploration, the mythic fascination with the
unknown. The composition, the play of the light on the ice, the figures of the struggling women, their faces, the heavily laden sledges,
and the straining huskies—each scene possessed a quality of drama
that seized the imagination, caught at the heart.

Only once before had Viola seen photographs of such artistry. In
Greenland. Jim Corbett had been the photographer to make that expedition unforgettable. All at once she remembered a picture Corbett
had taken of her one day in the summer of 1905. Walking on the
rocky beach in Greenland, she had caught sight of Byron coming toward her. It was before the anger and bitterness, and she had been
filled with such overpowering joy that she ran to him, holding out
her arms. The passion of that moment was captured by the camera
so that it might live forever. Byron had been moved by the photograph, said he would never be parted from it. Even now, locked in
competition with him, the knowledge that it must long since be lost
was bitter to her. Hermine's was the photograph on the desk in his
office, Hermine's was the face he would see at the Pole. Horace had
told her this was the photograph to accompany him everywhere, the
first thing he unpacked when he made camp, the last he packed
when the camp was dismantled. Odd that the new photographs of
her should remind her so much of that earlier one. She looked almost
the same as in those days when she had first been in love with Byron.
The passion for life was as strong as then; only the love was gone.

Of course she knew who had taken the photographs—that strange woman, Araminta, who had signed the letter of application as Jane Scranton and later said she preferred the other name. When they were leaving on the depot-laying trip, Viola had been stunned to observe Araminta's photographic equipment: a Zeiss Triple Protar, Bausch & Lomb lenses, a field camera and tripod, an English Panro for speed photography, the best quality film. Could the woman have stolen them? She had thought to tell Araminta to leave the cameras behind. The photographic equipment filled almost an entire sledge as it was, and they already had an expedition photographer.

"You didn't say you were a photographer when you applied for the expedition."

Araminta had decided on this course as the only way to be certain her face would not appear on the photographs of the assault on the Pole. Those were the ones that would be published in newspapers, where they could be seen by members of the Tribe of the Greater God waiting to execute her. But she could hardly say that to Viola. "I . . . thought if I took good pictures, you'd need me at the Pole. So I went to a photographer and asked him to teach me and I'd clean his house and do the washing and ironing in the evenings after work."

"How did you get the cameras and the film and the rest of the photographic equipment?"

"He staked me. Said he'd never known nobody who got so good so fast. I told him I'd work it off when I got back."

Impressed by Araminta's determination, Viola allowed her to take the cameras. Now, seeing the photographs, Viola knew that Araminta, not Marcia, must make the record of the journey to the South Pole.

And then there was Carla. Halfway through the depot-laying expedition, Viola began to have doubts. Some days Carla seemed too fatigued to manage her backpack, and Araminta picked it up and carried it for her. But from the moment she placed the advertisement for Amazons, Viola had been waiting for a response from the one woman who must surely be with her climbing the great ice mountains, crossing the plateau, planting the suffragette banner at the Pole. The past bound them together, the days in England. Viola remembered Carla in her man's overcoat, grotesque but for the force of her personality. All the great moments—marching at the front of the demonstrations, taking on hecklers at the rallies, the hunger strikes at Hollowran—Carla was a part of them.

Evadne did not understand why Viola was hesitating. "Carla isn't up to the journey to the Pole, and if we have to drag her along, we won't get there.

"You know what some of the women are saying, Viola? That you don't want to win over Tremaine, that you're still in love with him."

"In love!" How could anyone believe that? Each night in her sleeping bag, her hatred for him kept her warm. She sustained it by recalling all the times he had made love to her in order to dominate, not to please her. She remembered Byron looking at her with his cold green eyes, mocking her, felt again the outrage of the day she had struck him with the paperweight.

"Oh, no, Evadne. He killed love long ago. I will be at the Pole ahead of him. That's what I live for."

Carla wept when Viola told her of the decision to leave her behind. "I guess I've really known I wasn't up to it from the beginning— when your advertisement was smuggled in to me at Hollowran. But I so desperately wanted to go to the Pole with you. It's just come too late." The police beatings, the imprisonments, and the hunger and thirst strikes had taken their toll. Even the depot-laying journey was beyond her strength. She did not know what she would have done if Araminta had not helped her. Without a word. Expecting nothing. And they had not even been lovers then. That had happened later, after they returned to the camp on the Bay of Whales, in the long night of winter. Araminta. Not her type at all. She had always favored small, intense women like Lesley, not like Araminta, who was big, rawboned, crude, powerful as Carla in the past. And she had never been with a woman before, did not know what women did with one another. But there was something about her. Before Carla, Araminta had no idea that a woman might take pleasure in sexual activity.

Viola felt like weeping herself. How could she go without Carla? But if she allowed sentimentality to take over, she would not reach the Pole ahead of Tremaine, make this gesture for suffrage. And yet.

"Who will you take instead of me?"

The decision was easily made. Claireve had been invaluable on the depot-laying expedition. No task was too heavy for her; nothing repelled her. She dug latrine pits and then covered them over, bathed the other women's hard, white, frostbitten toes, was uncomplaining about her own injuries. Placed in charge of the huskies, Claireve exercised them for hours each day of the winter, hitched them to sledges with light loads, then with heavier loads, trained them to pull in tandem.

Claireve could hardly believe what was happening to her. She had never before been chosen for anything other women wanted, was used to being relegated to the background—to taking care of bears, handling the dog teams, making love where no one could see. No, that was not true. Once she had been chosen, and by the most desirable of men. Claireve remembered that long-ago time when she saved Peter Graves from an assassin, when he came to her and changed everything . . . for a little while. He had kissed her on the mouth, not flinching at its deformity.

Afterward, she had returned to the life a handicapped woman must lead, returned to sexual encounters in the dark. On board the *Explorer,* the officers and sailors came to her cabin stealthily. To hers, and Evadne's. Once, lying in bed with the second mate, she heard Evadne laugh. "A whore's laugh," the second mate had said. Men think that about a woman who accepts love freely, as she did, as Evadne did. Claireve was quite sure Evadne did not guess that she, too, had lovers; many men saw her sexual potential, but no women.

At last she was accepted over other women, women of normal, even of beautiful appearance. Her disfigurement no longer mattered, only her strength and determination to achieve the South Pole.

Evadne, Araminta, and Claireve—these were the women who would stand with Viola at the South Pole. Four other expedition members were to go as far as the foot of the Axel Heiberg Glacier before turning back, and six would remain at the base camp.

By the first day of October the sledges were loaded and ready. All that was wanting was the first clear day, but though it was unseasonably warm, snow fell steadily that first week of October and the sunrise each morning was concealed by a gray cloud cover. If the weather did not improve by tomorrow, they must set out anyway, said Viola. It might be clear on Ross Island, sixty miles away, and she dared not allow the Tremaine expedition a head start.

The snow was still falling when Viola arose before dawn on the eighth of October. As she stepped outside the hut, a frigid blast of air made her pull the wool helmet worn under her fur parka down over her forehead all the way to her eyes. The temperature had dropped by twenty degrees during the night, but there was little wind, and the sky was clearer to the south, where they would be heading. It was not a good day, but not so bad that they could not set out as planned. She went back into the hut, where the expedition members soon joined her; no one was sleeping well. Viola had said her good-byes to the women who were to remain behind, but they were here, too, wanting to help. Marcia alone was sullen, having been certain of inclusion in the Pole party.

So close to the fulfillment of her dreams, Viola could hardly bear to wait while the cooks lit the Primus stove and prepared the breakfast of hot lemon juice sweetened with honey, oatmeal topped by raisins, crackers, and coffee. She choked down what food she could and then, followed by Carla, rushed outside to make a final check of the sledges.

The skis were in readiness beside the lead sledge, and as Viola bent down to put hers on, the snow surface quivered. She had never felt anything quite like it. There was a loud whirring of wings as flocks of gulls and petrels rose from their resting places to circle overhead. Taking off the skis, she ran to the edge of the ice cap to look over; Carla was beside her.

At that moment a loud roar filled the air, a sound like none ever heard before, as if the earth were being torn apart. Claireve's voice rang out, but what was she trying to say? The cleft palate made her words incomprehensible. And then the ice shelf at their feet shuddered, quaked, broke off, and in an instant Viola was hurtling down an abyss with ice walls, thrown violently into the frigid Bay of Whales.

Instinctively she held her breath as her head went under water, and then she came up choking and gasping. Her heavy clothes were pulling her down; she was drowning. With a tremendous effort, she came to the surface again. Carla had been right beside her. Where was Carla? Viola struggled to keep her head up and tread water; her boots were weighing her down, but there was no way to get them off. More loud crashes and groans alarmed her, as pieces of the ice shelf continued to break off. A small ice floe was nearby. If she could swim that far, she might be able to pull herself on top of it. One stroke. Then another. She could not do it; she had to do it. Twice she went under and thought she would not be able to bring herself to the surface again. And then the ice floe was right in front of her and she was reaching up and grasping at an unevenness in the slick surface, dragging her body with its waterlogged clothing onto the top. She was out of the water, freezing in the air, as ice formed on the fur hairs of her parka. Great bouts of shivering shook her body but did not warm it. Her teeth were chattering.

The sound of frantic barking was coming from behind her; the lead sledge must have gone over the top, too. Then she heard heavy breathing, and turning, saw Carla clinging to the sledge. The runners, designed to keep the sledge from sinking into the ice, were holding it afloat. The harnessed dogs were paddling desperately. Viola managed to signal with one stiffening hand to Carla to leave the sledge and get onto the ice floe. The sledge could not remain afloat much longer; it was already half submerged. The dogs were going under. Carla hesitated, clearly reluctant to leave them, but there was little enough she could do to save herself, nothing she could do for the dogs. She let go the sledge and swam the few feet to the ice floe. Viola stretched her arm into the water, but Carla ignored it and with a display of her old strength pulled herself onto the floe. The sledge, a few feet away, disappeared under the water.

And then Viola's throat constricted with terror as a whale's head emerged from the water close by, and then a second and a third. Viola knew that killer whales had been observed in Antarctic waters by earlier explorers, but the whales seen before this day belonged to less fearsome species. She staggered to her feet, followed by Carla. The whales were leaping above the water, coming nearer with every leap. Now they were diving under the ice. A crack appeared in the center of the floe, and before their horrified eyes, it broke in two. They were side by side, but with so little space to stand on the slippery surface that surely they must fall into the churning water. Carla was pointing to another ice floe separated from theirs by a foot or more of water. Just that much farther from the whales. Without a word, they leaped in tandem, not looking down at the dark, swirling water. Now they were on the second floe, a little closer to the margin of the cliff. In desperation they leaped again to yet another floe, a little closer still.

Half-frozen, their muscles stiffening, they jumped again. And once again. The whales had not followed. Not yet.

Viola looked up at the towering ice cliff and thought that nothing could be done to rescue them quickly enough. Even if the killer whales lost interest and swam away, she knew, as do all polar explorers, that no one can survive wet in below-freezing temperatures for long. While she could not blame herself for a natural disaster, she had been entrusted with Carla's life and felt the responsibility keenly.

*You can't change the world. Oh yes I can.* She had come so close to achieving that dream. Byron would win after all. It was strange that in this moment she remembered him as when they had been in love. Remembered and for that moment did not begrudge him his victory.

Carla was speaking; Viola did not have the energy to try to grasp the sense. But then she observed Carla's hand pointing up to the edge of the ice cliff. The snowfall had ceased, and she could just make out figures there. She thought she recognized Evadne's red helmet, Araminta's long yellow muffler. Araminta was on the unstable, broken edge of the ice cap. She would kill herself, thought Viola, in her desperate effort to save them. To save Carla. A rope was being thrown down. Carla grasped the rope, held it firmly, prepared to fasten it under Viola's arms. No. As leader, she must go last. That was the code. Accepting the order, Carla took hold of the rope. Viola had to remove her mittens, despite the sure knowledge of frostbite, so as to fasten the rope under Carla's arms and around the chest. The rope strained as Carla gripped it, and then she was up over the ice floe and swinging toward the side of the cliff, as the women at the summit struggled to lift her. With fascinated horror, Viola saw that the rope was fraying under Carla's weight. Faster, faster. Get her up. And then the rope broke, and Carla hurtled down into the water, breaking the surface with a terrible crash. Down. And did not come up. She had not cried out, but a piercing shriek was filling the air. Araminta's.

Black shadows appeared over Viola's head. No, they were not shadows, but skua gulls circling lower over the spot where Carla had sunk.

She looked up desperately; no one was in sight. And then Evadne and another woman—was it Claireve now?—were back with a second coil of rope. The ice floe was shaking in the turbulent water; in one more minute, Viola knew, she would be thrown off. Then the rope was hurled down. It dropped . . . just out of her reach. The women pulled it up and tried again. This time the rope was closer, and Viola was able to reach out and grasp it with stiffened fingers, then steady herself on the floe. Her eyelashes were frozen and she could barely see the dangling rope and she was alone, too numb to feel her hands and feet, too numb to grasp the rope and fasten it under her arms. What was the memory tantalizing her now? Surely she had done this before. And it was like that morning in MidValley in England, when her cold hands and feet had lost their hold on the rope and she had fallen to the floor of the great hall. She remembered that fall, felt as if she were falling still. The exploit for suffrage had failed then. She must not fall, must not fail now. In that instant she thought of Byron again and this time believed she would win over him. And then, without her knowing how it had been accomplished, the rope was tight around her, cutting into her breasts through the heavy furs.

Now she was up above the floe, dangling in the air over the water. Her slender body was so much lighter than Carla's, but her clothes were heavy, icy and waterlogged. Would the rope hold this time? And what if it did not? She looked down at the churning waters where Carla lay. No. Look up, not down. Up. And now she could see Evadne and Claireve straining as they pulled on the rope, and then another figure—Araminta's—joined them. Viola's arms were aching, but she must not allow herself to be dead weight.

The cliff was close now and the rope was swinging back and forth and she knew she was in danger of being hurled against the ice wall, her body shattered by the impact. But she was rising, rising. The summit was not so far now. All at once, with a terrible wrench that she thought would pull her arms from her body, she was at the top of the cliff, and falling now, but falling just the few feet onto the ice surface. For an instant she could not believe the ordeal was over, and then she lost consciousness.

When Viola came to herself minutes later, it seemed to her that the distinguished figure of Lord Hargreave was bending over her. Why, soon he would be telling her he was acquainted with Richard Everett Sharpe's second-in-command and could arrange an introduction. Then she recognized Evadne's face and knew all that was gone.

Viola's clothes had frozen so solidly that it was not possible to bend her arms or legs, and Evadne and Claireve carried her into the nearest hut as if she were a block of wood. There was no sensation in any part of her body. Without being able to turn her head, she heard the women running in and out. They must have gone to unpack the portable Primus stove lashed to one of the sledges. Soon the air of the shed was filled with smoke and warmth from the burning paraffin. Gradually the fur thawed enough to be bent, and Viola was eased out of the garments and wrapped in blankets. Now she was shivering violently. If she had despaired at feeling nothing before, now, as her body warmed, she was in agony. The pain of her frostbitten hands and feet became excruciating. Explorers in the past rubbed frostbitten skin with snow, but Ian had advised against this, saying it was better to rewarm frozen tissue as rapidly as possible no matter how great the suffering.

Gradually the worst of the pain subsided and the full horror of Carla's death returned. "What have I done? What have I done?" she cried out in misery. Risk is intrinsic to exploration and her advertisement had given full warning. Still, she felt sick at heart.

Araminta was sobbing in the corner. Well, she would get over it. Everything passes. Even love. At least Araminta did not have to watch love turn ugly and die.

After covering Viola's hands and feet with an antiseptic ointment and heavy bandages, Claireve carried her out of the hut and onto a sledge. The scene was one of chaos. Only half of the main cabin was still standing; the remainder had fallen into the bay when the ice broke off. Fortunately the women in the hut had managed to scramble to safety. Tables, chairs, desks, shelves, books, and equipment lay scattered on the snowy ground. The anemometer was smashed and one of the smaller huts had disappeared.

The dogs were howling. The best team of animals, fastened to the lead sledge at the time of the ice crash, was gone. One of the other sledges was missing, swept into the bay.

Standing on the edge of the ice cliff, looking down into the roiled water, Viola thought over the decision to locate the base camp at the Bay of Whales. Ian had told her Shackleton considered this location and then settled on Ross Island instead. That was one of the reasons he failed to achieve the Pole, Ian had declared. But why did

Shackleton reject this location? Ian had not told her that. She recalled how troubled he had been when he learned he would be left behind.

*I think I will never see you again.* When no letters from Ian arrived on the *Explorer,* she had been convinced he meant to disappear. Perhaps those words possessed yet another meaning, one that had not occurred to her until now. Perhaps he was referring to her fate as well as his own. Might he have known the location of the base camp was too risky, the route he had chosen—over the uncharted glacier—too dangerous? Had he believed that without his great strength and knowledge of the polar ice cap to guide them, they would fail? The concept was chilling. Ian had experience of the Antarctic; if he believed they could not get to the Pole and back, he might well be right. And the chances of success were poorer now with all that was lost.

No, nothing short of the death she had so narrowly escaped would stop her. Remembering Lesley, she thought of the weeks in Hollowran when they had faced death as a matter of course because it was for the cause they believed in. She believed in it now. In this expedition were combined the driving forces of her life—exploration and suffrage—and beyond that, the competition with Tremaine, the glory of being at the Pole ahead of him, of becoming the first scientist to solve the mystery of the frozen continent's past.

Viola called the expedition members to the largest of the remaining huts. The Pole party was resolute. Araminta was stoic now; she might never have screamed or sobbed. Claireve scribbled the words, "I'm not afraid." The desperate race with Tremaine was to begin.

In every other race, the teams of contestants are ruled by a common starting time, have an equal number of participants and amount of equipment. They follow the same route, face the same weather conditions, and traverse the same terrain. Not here. The two expeditions were going blindly into the icy wastes of Antarctica. Byron believed he would fulfill his destiny and prove his dominance over Viola once and for all. Viola believed she would raise the suffrage banner over the South Pole and prove him wrong.

# Chapter Twenty-five

BYRON, BATHED IN SUNLIGHT, WAS moving inexorably forward across the ice fields, up the steep glassy slope of Beardmore Glacier and then down, down toward the Pole. That image drove Viola to march fifteen miles in a day, then eighteen. By now only the members of the Pole party were advancing; the other group of women had been sent back with one of the sledges.

There was no longer a sunrise or a sunset. For a week or more, twilight had dimmed the sky for a few minutes each day. Now that was gone and a merciless, lemon yellow sun colored the transparent air. Yet it was cold, so cold that the condensation of breath froze eyelashes and formed ice over chins and noses. Lips, covered with cream and a thin strip of silk, were always sore nonetheless. Thirst was unending, barely relieved by the tiny slivers of ice chipped off to melt in the mouth. Any exposed skin became sunburned, and the Eskimo-style sealskin snow goggles with only the tiniest of slits for the eyes were not protection enough against the glare of light against snow. Worst were the bouts of snow blindness, which felt as if grains of sand or bits of glass were being hurled against the eyeballs.

Mirages forced unnecessary detours. Veering sharply eastward to avoid a huge iceberg, they would see it again on whatever alternate route was chosen. Were they then to decide another iceberg was but a vision and march resolutely forward, the trail would truly be blocked. Time after time, their spirits lifted at the sight of a rock cairn and suffrage banner marking a depot no more than a mile away. But an hour passed and a second and a third and they came no closer. One freezing afternoon they unpacked ice axes and ropes, prepared to climb an ice mountain looming ahead. As they approached, however, the mountain levitated and hung in the air above them. On this dread continent, unreality was just as real as reality.

Each evening it took two hours—three if the weather was bad—to unpack a sledge, put up the tent, get the Nansen cooker going, prepare a meal, stake and feed the dogs, and make the meteorological observations. Then Viola spent another hour entering the day's activities into her diary before going to sleep. In the morning, half an hour's effort was required for struggling into the woolen underwear, blouse, sweater, three pairs of socks lined with fur, leggings, gabardine and fur trousers, inner boots and fur outer boots, and over all that, the fur parka. Too much for the warm days, barely enough when the temperature plummeted. Then the better part of two hours went into taking down the tent, packing up, and getting back on the trail.

Oddly, Viola never thought that Byron must be enduring the same hardships. She saw him skiing forward effortlessly, the hood of his parka thrown back, handsome in the golden light, untouched by pain.

Still, no matter how extreme the misery of life on the trail, she was dazzled by the beauty of the Antarctic, caught in its spell, enchanted by the brilliance of the colors, the clarity of the air, and the silence— nowhere else on earth was there such perfect quiet. Sometimes, awed by the majesty of the ice mountains and the fantastical shapes of the icebergs, she could forget the desperate race with Tremaine. Now she understood why the great explorers of the past had returned to the icebound continent, forgetting past failure, past suffering. This vastness nurtured heroes; it was their natural habitat.

Except when a blizzard was raging, Viola would slip out of the stuffy tent each morning and, in the shelter of the overhanging canvas, strip off her nighttime clothing and bathe with chipped bits of ice. Naked, her skin glowed in the rays of the sun. A trifle leaner, stronger, her body was almost as it had been in the days when Byron was her lover, not her rival. She thought of his touch, as hot as the ice slivers were cold. Araminta followed her out of the tent one morning and took a photograph. Once she would have given the picture to Byron, knowing Hermine would not be so bold, had probably never shown herself to him naked.

After the ice bath she would return to the tent refreshed for the day's journey. Most often the women marched in silence. Claireve could not talk and Araminta would not. Occasionally Evadne was moved to speak of the dance. Only the dance. It was as if she had experienced nothing off stage. Yet her many love affairs had been chronicled in magazine and newspaper articles. Had none of these lovers meant anything to her? Or had they meant too much? Viola could not ask; in the Antarctic, no one need admit to a history.

Despite the physical misery that was integral to Antarctic exploration, the party was moving rapidly on the slick and slippery ice surface. Araminta was everywhere, in good weather and bad, capturing the expedition's progress with her camera. These photographs, the meteorological observations, compass readings, and Viola's diary entries would prove their conquest of the Pole. Evadne was keeping a journal, too. At first she tried to conceal it from the others, but there was no privacy in the small tent. Flushing, she murmured, "I want to keep a record for . . ." She broke off then, and added: "I wish I could write better, but I left school in the sixth grade." It was the most personal statement Evadne had ever made.

The women were advancing along the route established the previous year. At each depot they took half of the provisions that had been stored and left the remainder for the return journey. Viola was depending once again on Ian's carefully marked maps to direct them away from the greatest hazards, from the places where Sharpe had run into trouble. Every day, reading his handwriting on the maps, she was grateful to Ian. Grateful. But now that he had disappeared from her life, in the purity of the clear cold air, all self-delusion was gone and she saw her marriage as it had been. In the heartrending years since his return from the Sharpe expedition, Ian had become her burden. Somewhere along that hard road she had lost the hero with the great polar history, the hero who rushed into the flames at Chessham Court. Instead she was left with a broken man, calling forth compassion, pity, a sense of responsibility.

Why did she marry Ian when she was so determined to retain her freedom? It seemed to her that Byron had always been a partner to her marriage. She had desperately wanted to escape his domination. Even now, enough remained of the passion that had flared between them all those years ago on the Greenland expedition to fuel their deadly competition. The boldest of men, physically desirable, a kind and gentle lover—Ian would not have become her husband for those traits alone. Byron had thrown his own marriage in her face. His twisted love for a simpering doll, Hermine. *There is a kind of satisfaction in that mastery.* Only she had thrown him to this doll and was left with the bitter knowledge that it was Hermine's photograph he treasured, gazed at each night before falling asleep.

The expedition had been making good time, but now the weather took a turn for what seemed to be the better, but soon proved to be far worse. The temperature rose until the snow became soft and sticky, so that skis and sledge runners sank below the surface. The sledges were heavy with the food and fuel taken from the last of the depots along the trail. These supplies would have to support the women until they returned to this same depot on their way back from the Pole. It took all Claireve's coaxing to keep the dogs pulling the sledges. Every few minutes, she stopped to scrape the snow off the runners.

It was impossible to ski on that soft surface, but without skis the women sank to their knees in the snow, and every step became a struggle. On some days they covered no more than eight miles. Sweat poured from their bodies as they marched, and then, whenever they stopped to rest, the moisture trapped in their clothing froze, only to melt again in the warmth of the tent at night. Before getting into their sleeping bags, they would hang their clothing on a pole near the stove and lie there, smelling the wet wool and fur.

At last the women reached the limit of Ian's map and began the climb up the uncharted Axel Heiberg Glacier. The air was thin as they approached the towering summit. Their hearts pounded violently and breathing was painful when they swung their ice axes to cut steps into the sheer ice cliff and then broadened them to make a path for the sledges and dog teams. At such a height they were at the mercy of the strange katabatic winds that occur only in the Antarctic. Within seconds gusts reached velocities of two hundred miles an hour, blowing snow into their mouths and noses, so they would freeze and choke simultaneously. While the winds swept over the glacier, the women bent their bodies low against the icy surface, pulled

down their face masks, and waited. Araminta shielded the cameras
with her body. As abruptly as the winds arose, they were gone, and
the expedition was able to move on.

Upon reaching the summit, there was a moment of euphoria. A
moment and no more, for the most treacherous terrain they had ever
seen stretched before them. "A devil's playground," said Evadne,
pointing to the furrows, ridges, and waves of snow insanely criss-
crossed by crevasses. Only hairline cracks showed on the surface; the
deep holes were covered with a layer of snow too thin to support the
weight of a loaded sledge and dog team. Skiing was hazardous, so
they fastened iron crampons to their boots to grip the ice. Eyes on
the surface, leading the dogs, they struggled on, a foot at a time,
barely avoiding the crevasses. Knowing they must return the same
way, they built up mounds of snow to mark the location of the most
dangerous areas. After an entire day of ceaseless effort they had covered a distance of three miles.

When they made camp that night, they were too weary to do more
than melt snow to soak the frozen crackers, which were hard enough
to break a tooth. An hour later Araminta was up again, capturing the
drained faces of her companions, going outside to photograph the
crevasse-broken surface highlighted by the brilliant sunshine of
the night.

Three more days of inching across the ice, and they were over the
summit and starting down the slope leading to the South Pole. And
where was Byron Tremaine? His plan had been to approach the Pole
from another direction, but plans change under the rigors of Antarctic travel, so Viola kept looking for signs that the Tremaine expedition had preceded them. Was that a piece of rock, dark against the
snow, or a broken sledge runner? Were those merely the windblown
sastrugi markings on the snow or ski tracks and paw prints? The
competition was reaching its climax.

Sometimes, unbidden, however, came remembrance of the long-
ago time in London when, desperate, she had asked for Byron's help,
and he had crossed the sea to be with her. What if she had accepted
him? They would have married, not be locked in deadly rivalry now.
But would she be standing on the ice cap, with the South Pole within
her grasp? Obviously not. She would have been in Byron's power,
forced to do as he commanded. The demonstrations, appeals to pol-

iticians, imprisonment, and hunger strikes would have gone on without her. No. This was the only way for her to achieve her destiny and the destiny of the women's suffrage movement she had linked with hers.

When they made camp on the night of January 11, 1916, the sextant observations and compass readings put them within a few miles of the South Pole. Two hours of steady marching would bring them there. Then in the predawn hours, wakeful in anticipation, Viola heard the first roar of the wind rising and the sound of snow pelting against the canvas of the tent. The huskies were howling miserably. In consternation, she lifted the tent flap and could see nothing beyond a thick curtain of snow. In an instant, the force of the wind forced her to drop the flap. The Pole party would be trapped inside the tent until the blizzard wore itself out.

For two days the women remained miserably in the tent, days that might give Tremaine his victory. In the Antarctic, the weather can be quite different in areas no more than a few miles apart. The sun could be shining on the Tremaine expedition, the winds quiescent. At last the snowfall diminished and they set out again, though the wind was still so powerful as to blow them back one step for every two they progressed.

Toward midday the winds died down and the sun reappeared. In the startling clarity of the Antarctic air, free of dust or haze, they saw the two poles topped with the brilliantly colored British and Danish flags raised by Sharpe and Carlsen four years earlier. The South Pole was within their grasp. Evadne and Araminta were shouting with joy, but Viola stood quietly, trembling. Then she skied slowly forward, fearing that another flag might be flying from a third flagpole still out of sight. An American flag. Proof that Tremaine had after all preempted the Pole.

The competition was over. Within minutes she would know who had won. Viola went forward with hope and apprehension.

Now she was standing before the two flagpoles, and there was no other. *A woman cannot survive on the ice cap.* But she was here. And it was as she had imagined it would be to stand on her skis and look out over the fields of snow surrounding the Pole. She was dazed by the wonder of it. With shaking hands she took out of her backpack the American flag and the banner, Votes for Women.

*You can't change the world. Oh yes I can.* Standing here at the Pole, for an instant reality faded and she was back in an earlier time in London, in the flat, sitting with her friends at the oilcloth-covered table eating fish and chips out of twists of newspaper. Lesley, small, indomitable. Carla and Jeremy, big, strong. The commitment they had felt. Except for James. But she saw him more clearly than any of the others, could imagine him standing on the ice as he had stood in the doorway of her room with that smile. No one ever smiled like Jamie. She had disapproved of him. They all had, as they watched him go out for the night in his one good suit. And yet that smile. Even here in the Antarctic, she was warmed by the memory of Jamie's smile. He was with the suffragettes to have fun, yet he died trying to save the others when he could easily have escaped through the window. Oh, Jamie.

Before raising the flags, she must be certain this was the right place. The women made camp, and Viola unpacked the scientific instruments needed for the sun sighting. At any other latitude it would be possible to judge the altitude for this location by the sun's position in the sky, but in the Antarctic midsummer, the diurnal changes in the height of the sun were too slight to be seen by the naked eye. Instead she had to use a sextant and an artificial horizon created by capturing the sun's reflection on the mirrored surface of liquid mercury in a shallow pan. It was merely a formality, as the earlier explorers had done all that before and raised their flags at the bottom of the world—ninety degrees south latitude. To her amazement, the altitude calculations and compass readings did not confirm this location. Eighty-eight degrees, thirty minutes, eleven seconds south latitude.

Dazed, she turned to Evadne. "This isn't the South Pole. That means no one has reached the actual Pole. Neither Carlsen nor Sharpe."

"But everybody knows they did. Why else would they claim it, put up the flags?"

Why indeed—unless, incredible though it seemed, they had been mistaken—or even more incredible, had lied? How could she find out so long after the fact? Looking around the desolate landscape, she was surprised to see two small tents nearby and, followed by Evadne, ran across the barren icescape and into the nearest one. A document was lying on the table. Picking it up with shaking hands, she read, "We are so near to the South Pole that I do not hesitate to claim it for England, as Carlsen has, alas, made the claim for Denmark. No human being will ever come closer to the South Pole than we have done," Sharpe had written. "There is an abyss to the south that no man could cross. It prevents us, as it prevented Carlsen—and will prevent all future explorers—from traversing the last degree of latitude."

On the return journey from the Pole, he apparently decided that future explorers would be no more eager than he to reveal the unfortunate discrepancy. That would explain why not a word to indicate that he had fallen short was written in the diary found in the tent on the glacier where Sharpe and his men had waited for death.

"I wonder what Carlsen had to say." The report left in Carlsen's tent was in Danish, with a précis translated into English. Carlsen also lamented the impassable abyss, the unforeseen act of nature, robbing him of the South Pole. At that time, it appeared, he had intended to give an accurate account of his journey. After leaving the Antarctic continent, he must have thought better of it and claimed the South Pole outright. Despairingly, Viola thought that she too would be stopped by the abyss.

Coming out of the tent, the two women walked southward, seeking the abyss. They went farther and still farther, feeling their way carefully, yet the surface beneath their feet remained solid. At last they realized that the chasm was gone, filled in by the snowfall of the intervening years and the shifting of the ice cap.

Just then Viola saw what this could mean to her and was dazzled. She would not merely be the first American, or even the first woman to conquer the South Pole: She would be the first human being ever to set foot on the pristine ice at the southernmost point of the globe—unless Tremaine had been here ahead of her, found everything as she had and was already at the true Pole. There were no tracks in the snow, but the fierce Antarctic winds might have blown them away. The competition had not reached its conclusion.

Araminta and Claireve came up then, wondering why the flags were not flying.

"We're not at the Pole yet."

The women stopped only long enough to have a hot meal and feed the dogs before setting off on the final stage of the race. It was snowing again, more heavily this time, cutting the visibility to less than a foot. The party moved doggedly forward on skis, weighed down by the snow falling on their heads, settling on their shoulders. An hour passed, and another.

All at once the snowfall ceased and the clouds blanketing the sun lifted. Startled, they looked up and the sky was filled with an incredible brilliance made up of hundreds of millions of ice crystals as tiny as diamond dust, each surrounded with a sun halo. The sunlight refracting on the ice crystals created double and triple halos. The somber Antarctic had become a place of magic. The four women stood immobile; even the dogs were quiet. The ice was sparkling with red, orange, and green lights.

This time the instrument measurements confirmed their hopes—they were at the southernmost point of the globe. At Viola's signal, Araminta took the photographs that would prove their location. Then the clouds concealed the sun again and the crystals in the air dissipated, leaving them in the windswept desolation of the ice surrounding the Pole. Yet Viola, standing where no one had ever been before, could have wept at its beauty.

Everything she had dreamed of possessing was here, was here. She was at the South Pole and Tremaine was not. All the years of competition and she had won. The dream had become reality. Whatever followed, no one could take that away from her. Votes for Women. She was about to raise the banner she had followed for so long. The secrecy about the expedition would be ended and the suffragettes herald the news.

In that moment exhaustion left her, and she became oblivious to the pain of her strained muscles, her frostbitten hands and bleeding mouth. She felt like a girl. Light. Carefree. Reaching toward the Pole, she flung out her arms in joy. That was how Araminta captured her on film. The emptiness of the Antarctic was filled with her voice as she shouted her triumph. Evadne and Araminta were cheering in their joy, and a shriek rang out in Claireve's damaged voice.

The flagpoles were driven into the ice, the American and suffrage flags attached. Araminta moved from one location to the next, taking photographs.

"Let me have your camera for a minute, so that I can get your picture." Araminta shuddered at Viola's suggestion. "You deserve as much credit as the rest of us, Araminta; you've done as much."

*Deserve.* The Tribe of the Greater God thought she deserved to die. It was strange now for Araminta to remember that she had not applied for the expedition out of a desire to advance the cause of suffrage, nor had she possessed an interest in exploration. Rather, she had joined the expedition as a way to hide, to obtain a respite from her fears for a couple of years. The members of the Tribe of the Greater God were unforgiving. If they had so much as a clue to her whereabouts, she would be tracked down relentlessly. As soon as the expedition landed in New Zealand, she must disappear, travel on to Australia, find work in the vast outback.

Still, in selecting the expedition as a way of escape, Araminta had not imagined she would get so caught up in the grandeur of the Antarctic. These had been the greatest days of her sad life. She had loved and been loved by Carla. She had reached the South Pole, though no one besides these few women would ever know she had been here.

Viola meant to be kind, but she had to be stopped. "No. I'm the photographer, not the photograph." A shadow passed over her face and it troubled Viola, but no one has a history in the Antarctic.

Evadne was skiing, swooping and swirling around the flagpoles in great loops, dancing to the music playing in her head. With her limited education, Evadne had not even heard of the Antarctic until she was performing in London. Leafing through the newspaper pages to find the day's critique, she had read about the Sharpe expedition. It did not impress her. Nothing but dancing interested her, nothing but expressing the beauty of movement and of music, nothing but being a star. She did not seek out the suffragettes; they came to her, thinking the daring of her dancing made her one of them.

Had she not been convinced her career was about to plummet, she would not have applied for the expedition. But how could she have been so convinced? A career depends on many factors. An exploit like this, a victorious return to civilization—what might that not do for her? The newspapers would make much of her as they always did; her presence on the expedition was a good story. Why should she not have a comeback on the strength of that? It could all happen again. Swaying her graceful body as she stood on the densely packed snow, she imagined herself again leaping across the stage, the audience on its feet, applauding, cheering. Then she thought of the other triumph awaiting her when she placed her journal in her son's hands. Gerald would not have her stopped at the gate. A hero was not so easily dismissed.

*You should be a nun.* Here on the ice, Claireve laughed to remember her mother's advice. Her mother had meant well, certain that Claireve could not possibly have any other life. Well, she had made a life after all, from the days the boys threw gravel up at her window until this moment at the South Pole. Araminta was photographing her along with the others. Viola was giving her heart-stopping smile, Evadne her star's smile. Well, she was here, too. And a man had loved her. He had kissed her mouth. Remembering that, Claireve came as close as she ever could to a smile.

Viola took her diary out of her pack, pulled off her mittens, and with cold, shaking fingers wrote the entry that would make history. "Today—January 14, 1916—the all-women's expedition reached the South Pole." The culmination of her life. Yet all at once, the thought flashed through her mind: What was she doing here with these women? Why was she not with Byron Tremaine? The Crosbie expedition was her doing. And yet he had a part in it.

She thought again of the expedition she was leading. Odd, but it did not really fit her beliefs. She had not joined the suffrage movement to do without men. Equality had been her goal, not victory. The matching of equals. But somehow one action had followed inexorably on the last until the race became an inevitability.

Now she could pity Byron for the tragedy of coming to this awesome place and finding the evidence that she had been here. She looked northward, her eyes half-closed in the too brilliant sunshine, almost wishing she would see a dog team coming toward her, and Byron skiing alongside the sledge. And were it he, she thought, she would call the race a draw. What did she want with a competition? During the whole long journey, she had nurtured her anger toward him. It had helped her to endure and go forward. Now that she was here, the anger dissipated and she remembered how she had loved him, still loved him, and would have shared the Pole with him if she could.

The following day was spent in traversing the South Pole in ever widening circles, mapping the area. At first the landscape appeared devoid of landmarks, unbroken ice and snow, almost monotonous in its sameness. But gradually Viola became aware of the rare, haunting beauty of the polar ice field, of the subtle alterations in the surface, of patterns formed by waves and furrows, no two quite alike.

Toward evening the women built a small igloo with blocks of ice in the Eskimo style to contain another suffrage banner and the record of their achievement. The next day the long trek back to the Bay of Whales began.

After some hours of steady progress, the Pole party was brought to a halt when the dogs stopped in their tracks and refused to be prodded onward. Viola and Claireve looked at one another in consternation; the dogs were sensitive, able to smell out an imminent blizzard, the approach of katabatic winds. But the sky was cloudless. And then they felt the ice surface beneath their feet tremble once and again. A thunderous crash broke the stillness, and then another. An avalanche was Viola's first reaction, but the region was too flat. This could only be a snowquake, with snow collapsing under its own weight. They waited, fearing that any movement might bring mounds of snow down to crush them. Minutes passed and no more crashes could be heard; the ice surface beneath their feet was firm.

"The noise comes from the south," said Evadne.

The south. Then the snowquake must have shaken the area around the South Pole and the flags and igloo were in all likelihood buried beneath tons of ice. Viola longed to go back and make certain, raise the flagpoles again if need be, build yet another igloo, but she knew it was too dangerous. The surface at the epicenter might be unstable for days, and their movements could set off another quake. The photographs and measurements were evidence aplenty of their presence at the Pole; they must go on.

The skis and sledge runners moved swiftly over the hard, frozen surface, and they covered nineteen miles that day, eighteen the next. The crossing of the crevasse-broken summit of the glacier went more easily this time with the snow cairns to guide them. Coming down from the northern slope of the glacier onto the ice plateau, Viola thought with relief that they were on mapped territory again and would reach the first of the depots soon.

All at once, with no warning, the scene around them disappeared in a whiteout, an invisible world where surface blends into sky with no horizon. Companions just inches away were hidden in the whiteness. From then on it was a journey of fear, each woman knowing how easily she could be lost. Unable to make camp, they went on, calling to one another every minute or two, going down a gentle slope in what appeared to be a straight line. For a time it seemed that visibility would never return, but eventually, the whiteness mixed with gray and a golden, then an orange glow filled the air. The whiteout was over.

How far had they gone blindly? They should have been off the slope by now and on a flat surface, but there was still an incline. Viola took out her compass, hoping it would be pointing to the northeast, the direction they had been traveling. Instead they had veered off from the route during the whiteout and were heading west, away from the depot.

"Look!" cried Araminta, her voice filled with wonder.

Viola turned and just ahead the icy slope descended into a valley and there before her lay a mystical landscape, like no other in the world. It was as one might imagine a landscape on the moon—dry brown earth strewn with rocks, barren, desolate, but with a desolation quite different from the ice. Earth. Viola had not seen an expanse of naked ground in months. It could not be. This was a mirage, like so many others that had confused her in the past. The dry valley would remain the same distance away no matter how far she traveled. She skied forward a few feet, then a few more, and to her amazement, found herself on rough ground. Taking off her skis, Viola carefully put down one booted foot and then the other the dry valley was real.

Despite the barren nature of the scene, Viola felt a quickening of the senses. There at her feet lay lumps of black coal, formed from the vegetation of a prehistoric era. The ancient forms of life she had found previously in the moraines of glaciers had been paltry in number; most remains of the past had lain out of reach, trapped under the great weight of the Antarctic ice. But the ice had not advanced to this valley, and a wealth of fossils could lie on or close to the bare surface. Here in the arid, cold atmosphere, no rot, no mold ever touched them; they were preserved over the millennia.

The other women joined her then and they began to set up the camp for the night. The bamboo poles for the frame of the tent had just been forced into the hard soil when the dogs began to howl. Claireve rushed out and found them hurling themselves wildly against the ropes, trying to get at a seal lying on the ground nearby. The carcass was dried out, mummified, but in such perfect condition that the huskies were fooled. When had the seal met its death? A year ago? A hundred? Thousands? The dogs wanted to devour the dead beast immediately, and howled even more loudly when Claireve and Araminta dragged it away. Eventually, after a meal of penguin meat, they subsided.

The next morning Viola began her search for fossils and soon was overwhelmed by all she found. Coal was abundant, and imprints of organisms, both invertebrate animals and plants of aeons past, were etched on the rocks. The outlines of ancient fern fronds and stems were clearly discernible. The Antarctic continent, now frigid, barren, and hostile, had in millennia past been warm, hospitable, teeming with life. A temperate climatic zone had once extended nearly all the way to the South Pole.

*The history of the earth is written in fossils as if in a book.* Those were the words that had set her on a life of exploration. Here were the fossils. Here was the book.

As she sketched the fossils and wrote a full description in her daily journal, Viola was filled with the same elation she had known a decade earlier in Greenland when she looked through her microscope at organisms never before seen at that latitude.

On the morning of the fourth day in the valley, Evadne sought to convince Viola to get back on the trail. "The whiteout pushed us off course; we're not on the map. It may take us days to find our way back and reach the first of the depots, and we're running through our supplies."

Viola, in the grip of her obsession, would not give way. Evadne was being too cautious; food was sufficient for another few days, and the first depot could not be distant. Every instinct told Viola she was on the brink of a great discovery. She had wandered by accident into another world—the Antarctic, yet unlike every other place in the Antarctic—and must make the most of it. That very morning she had come upon a rock with the fossil imprint of a plant genus that had flourished in Australia 200 to 300 million years ago. She had studied specimens just like it in the Natural History Museum. As she stared at the rock, she realized that many of the other plant fossils discovered in the dry valley and earlier in the moraines of glaciers also appeared to be of Australian origin. In some ancient time a land bridge between Antarctica and Australia must have existed, making the two continents one.

Just then she observed a small, nondescript object lying in the hole left by the removal of the rock. Viola was never sure afterward why the sight affected her so strongly, but her heart began beating more rapidly and despite the cold, she felt hot, feverish. A piece of bone, she thought, but not skeletal bone. Crouching and taking off her mitten, she carefully brushed away the dirt with her bare hand. Why, it was a tooth—long, pointed, sharp, a canine, but slightly different in shape from any she had ever seen before. How old it looked, as old as teeth in the reconstructed jawbones of prehistoric reptiles in the Natural History Museum. But why should it not be that old? It lay in close proximity to the fossil of the ancient plant and could have belonged to some creature existing in the world at the same time. The tooth was not large enough for a brontosaurus nor small enough to have belonged to a lizard or ratlike animal. Perhaps it came from the jaw of a creature the size of a large dog.

Millions of years ago this desolate lifeless desert might have been a jungle where herds of strangely shaped animals lumbered clumsily through the underbrush. How could she reconstruct the creature on the basis of a single tooth? But it was unlikely that one and only one tooth should remain in this dry, isolated valley. There must be others within a fairly narrow radius, and probably skeletal bones as well.

Using her trowel with the utmost care, she began to scrape the hard, dry ground in widening circles around her. After a time her companions came to see what she was doing, but she waved them away, unwilling to allow anyone else to lift the soil, layer by layer, sift each grain of sand, each pebble to see what lay beneath. One moment's haste and a fossil that had survived the millennia could be damaged irretrievably. Her back ached from stooping, her eyes burned, and her hands became bruised from brushing the sand off the stones. The sun's movement across the sky was imperceptible and she was uncertain whether it was still the day she found the tooth. Evadne came and pleaded with her to stop, but she was unmoved.

At last a rock blocked the smooth movement of her trowel, and when she dug it out, there underneath lay the second tooth. She pushed aside the earth nearby and found a third tooth. Upon standing up, she staggered, and had to call for Araminta to help her back to the tent.

Three hours in her sleeping bag and she was up again to search the ground lit by the brilliance of the Antarctic night. As she discovered additional teeth, she was astounded to find them so different from one another in size and in form that it was hard to imagine what manner of creature had possessed them, or even to guess the shape of the jawbone. There were canine teeth, like the first she had found, as well as incisors and teeth for grinding, large and flat with the biting surface smoothed down.

As she studied them, she decided her first instinct had been correct and the teeth had belonged to a reptilian creature of 200 million, even 250 million years ago, possibly an ancestor of the dinosaur.

Soon afterward she came upon a skeletal bone and then a second and a third. Over the course of the day she uncovered more bones and bone fragments and was at last able to fit them together to form a jawbone that could contain the teeth. But now that she had the jaw lying in front of her on the sunbaked ground, the mystery deepened. The bones did not take on the appearance of a reptilian jaw; something was odd about it. The tooth-bearing bones of the dentary were larger than in the reptile, and there appeared to be traces of a secondary palate in the upper jaw.

Staring at the ancient bones, she was filled with awe by the theory that was emerging. The jaw came from an animal unknown heretofore. This was a protomammal, a cross between a mammal and a reptile, a major step in evolution.

She had made the scientific discovery she had dreamed of in Greenland and in all the years since then. This time her name would not appear as a footnote to the scientific papers.

When she returned to the tent, expecting the others to share her excitement, no one seemed much interested. The evening meal was being eaten, consisting of a few spoonfuls of hoosh, the sweet soup made of biscuits; three thin strips of pemmican; and a small piece of chocolate. Viola was startled by the meagerness of the portions. In her absorption in the fossils, she had paid no attention to food. Now it was clear why the others were not impressed by her discoveries.

They were hungry, and frightened by her staunch refusal to leave the dry valley. Over the last days she had been enthralled by her discoveries to the point of ignoring Evadne, ignoring what her own common sense should have told her. The search must be abandoned immediately. Someday she would return to the dry valley with another expedition, well financed and well supplied.

Viola spent most of the night, her last in the dry valley, carefully wrapping the jawbone and ancient teeth in woolen sweaters and packing them carefully on the sledge.

The following morning the women climbed out of the valley and back onto the ice cap. Within hours the temperature plummeted far below zero, to levels rarely experienced in the summer. Their energies were sapped by cold and hunger. At night they huddled around the stove, parkas and trousers laden with ice, the woolen helmets frozen tightly to their heads. Nearly an hour would pass before they could remove their clothing. The seal blubber was gone and the paraffin was too scarce for them to keep the stove burning all night, so that even in their sleeping bags, their rest was broken with fits of violent shivering. By morning the wet clothing had frozen again so that two women had to help a third push her arms into sleeves that would not bend.

After four days of marching, they were finally back on the route marked on the map, with the depot close by. They skied slowly now, fearing to miss the cairn built up of snow and rocks, topped by a flag. Soon they would feel warm again, with the Primus left burning all night. Soon their hunger would be satisfied by a hot meal of boiled seal meat and beans, a dessert of raisins and pudding, and coffee steaming in their tin mugs.

Claireve, in the lead, was calling hoarsely, pointing to the windswept, snowy surface ahead. The cairn was in plain view now, though the Votes for Women banner was not in evidence. It was blown away by the wind, thought Viola. Claireve rushed ahead, shovel in hand, to dig out the boxes, tins, and bags buried beneath a shallow layer of protective snow. Viola followed, faint with relief at having found the depot in time. In another few days, they would have been collapsing from starvation.

All at once what might have been a groan was heard from Claireve. A sound of despair in the Antarctic stillness.

Seized by a horrible fear, Viola raced across the slick surface, over the tracks of the sledge runners, the prints of the dogs' paws, the traces of skis. Now she could see beyond the cairn to the shallow pit in the snow.

The depot was empty.

# Chapter Twenty-six

"What do you know of a man named Ian Crosbie?"

Avery found me—by accident, he claimed, but I knew he did nothing by accident—in front of the store where I purchase my paints and canvases. Crosbie again. The man no one but Bucky remembered. Or so it had seemed.

This was the first time Avery and I had been together since the night of the Explorers Club dinner, but he spoke without preamble. "I came upon Crosbie by an odd coincidence when I was up north gathering material for a program about storing radioactive wastes in the Arctic. That could harm the Indians in the area, but no one else cares about them." I could hardly imagine that Avery cared about the Arctic Indians either, and started edging away. He was looming over me, so tall he blocked out the daylight and made me feel as if I were being crushed beneath his shadow.

Ignoring my movement of withdrawal, he went on talking. While seeking out folklore to use as human interest, he had learned of a legend concerning a huge white man, a polar explorer. Dishonored, accused of madness, he had, some eighty years before, hidden himself in a native village far to the north. The Indians believed that madness and wisdom are allied, so they made him a tribal shaman. He was greatly revered, and chiefs traveled for miles to seek his counsel.

Passersby were staring at us. I am not a conspicuous person, but

Avery commands every eye. He took my arm and propelled me into a coffee shop on the corner. People were waiting for seats, but Avery was immediately led to a booth. Instead of taking the place across from me, he sat beside me, close, too close, and ordered coffee for us both.

Who was the man behind the legend? he continued. The name given by the Indians was their word for giant. "I couldn't find any Arctic explorer of the period who fit the description. Then it occurred to me that polar did not necessarily mean North Polar. That sparked a vague recollection of something I'd heard about the Sharpe Antarctic expedition, so I took another look at Sharpe's journal, and there it was. His second-in-command, known for his great height and strength, was sent back from the Pole on the grounds of insanity. That's how I found Ian Crosbie."

As soon as he mentioned Sharpe, I guessed what was coming and was filled with amazement and trepidation. Could it possibly be true that Crosbie did not end his life in a mental hospital in White Plains, as Bucky believed?

I managed to speak in a fairly normal voice. "What makes you think that Crosbie ever went to the Arctic and was honored as a shaman, Avery? It's too far-fetched."

Avery's leg was pressing against mine under the table. Backed into the corner, I forced myself to remain immobile. How did I get into this position? But waiting nervously for an answer to my question, I did not ask him to let me out.

"It's more far-fetched to think there was a second polar explorer who fits the legend perfectly. Crosbie has to be it."

"You've come across an odd story, but why are you acting as if it's so important?"

For the first time he hesitated. "I have an instinct about Crosbie. I had it the moment I found out he was on the Sharpe expedition. The thought went through my mind that Crosbie has some connection with Byron Tremaine."

"Oh, come on, Avery. That's ridiculous."

"Is it? There is a connection, Beatrix, and you know it, too. Why did you go to London?"

My apprehensiveness increased. Avery's chance discovery put him on the same track I had been following. Which of us was running faster? "You figured out, just as I did, Beatrix, that there had been something between Byron Tremaine and that famous suffragette, Viola Lambert. She went with him to Greenland, the only woman he ever took on an expedition. They must have become lovers then."

*"Must?"* I interjected.

"He was the leader of the expedition and she was young and beautiful; it would have been the natural thing." He was looking at me in the intent way he had, observing my reaction. "I told a member of my staff to trace her movements after she arrived in London in 1907. No further connection with Byron Tremaine turned up. I had lost interest in her even before I learned she died in a fire late in 1909. So much for that, I thought.

"Until I heard about Ian Crosbie and had a researcher look into his background. You know what we found, don't you, Beatrix? The report on Viola's death was erroneous and she lived to marry Ian Crosbie shortly before he left on the Sharpe expedition. Later they went back to New York together and he was confined off and on in a mental hospital."

By now I was prepared for him and was able to reply coolly that I did not see what this had to do with Tremaine.

"Doesn't it seem strange to you, Beatrix? It does to me. Two polar explorers and one woman. What does that make you think of? Let's take this one step further—what did Viola Lambert Crosbie do when her husband came home from the Sharpe expedition insane? What would a woman do in such a case? I think she'd look up her old lover. It would have been the natural thing." He repeated those words with emphasis. "The Indians say Crosbie wanted to disappear in the Arctic because he was dishonored. They don't say why he was dishonored. By being sent back in disgrace from the Sharpe expedition? Or by having his wife taken in adultery by Byron Tremaine?"

I feared that he would go on to speak of the all-women's expedition, but his account was finished. Apparently he had not felt it necessary to continue tracing Ian and Viola Crosbie. Why should he devote more of his time and resources when he could wrest the information from me? Or so he believed. Avery picked up his cup and drank the cold coffee, looking over the rim, studying my expression.

"You're still searching for the illicit affair that will titillate the viewers of your program," I said coldly. "You're grasping at straws. Just because Viola and Tremaine were together in Greenland, you decide they were lovers. There's not a shred of evidence to prove it, and you said yourself that you couldn't find an association between them later. Ian Crosbie may add a nice touch of human interest to the program on the Indians, but he doesn't belong on the one you're doing about the Antarctic."

Avery was smiling again, the humorless smile I disliked. "You speak more firmly that you used to, Beatrix. I think I'm having a good effect on you." Angered by his assumption, I pulled farther away from him. "Just remember that often the truth does not leak out until I go searching for it."

I was ahead of him, I believed, in my knowledge of the Crosbie expedition, but I was still in ignorance of its fate. If Avery were to learn of the expedition and discover what had happened to it before I did, he would twist that information in such a way as to imply some dishonorable action by Tremaine.

"Why don't we work together, Beatrix. I want you on 'Avery Tells All.'" He moved his big body closer to mine and there was no room to retreat. His hand was on my arm and he bent over me to whisper: "Do it, Beatrix. You want to."

What was it he thought I wanted? Surely not the program. He was not talking about that anymore. I felt confused by the seductiveness he knows how to use. He acted as if I had not shown him in London how much I did not want him. His mouth was so close to mine I was not sure whether he meant to kiss me, was not sure in that moment how I felt about it. We might have been alone and not in the crowded coffee shop.

"Come home with me, Beatrix. It won't be the way it was in London. That was a mistake. This time it will be different. Just the way you want it. You'll see."

His personal magnetism was so strong that the offensiveness of the proposal did not strike me for an instant. I could almost believe him sincere. Just for an instant. Then I remembered what had happened with him before, and my mistrust returned. Nothing was done without a motive. He meant to trap me into telling him the story about the strange triangle of Ian Crosbie, Viola Lambert, and Byron Tremaine. I remembered the night in London when Avery had forced me to listen to the tape of Wally Padgett accusing Tremaine of foul deeds. Later, he claimed to have played it out of frustration and anger. But this was not a man who acted impulsively. He had known what he was doing, thought to shock me into revelations. Oh, he had felt desire for me. That I believed. And he was so close to me that I could feel the extent of his desire now. The sex had merely been an extra in London. It would be an extra now.

I drew back as far as I could in the cramped booth. "I won't appear on your program, Avery," I said, pretending that was all he had asked me.

There was a moment's hesitation as he took that in. Then he said merely, "Your great-grandfather never needed you so badly before."

I felt trapped, as if he would never let me out, but as soon as I said I wanted to go, he stood up and I brushed past him.

Shaken as I always was by an encounter with Avery, I was nonetheless hesitant to tell Ronald about it. Though he never referred to his accusations following the Explorers Club dinner, he obviously believed I had been an eager participant in the sexual adventure (misadventure surely) with Avery. And so I let several days go by before speaking of the Crosbie expedition.

"I think the women did get to the Antarctic, Ronald, even though there were no newspaper reports about them. Byron's message seems to prove that. But what happened to them then? Until I find that out, I'll always be afraid something will emerge that could be misconstrued and used to discredit my great-grandfather."

Ronald raised his eyebrows. "You've been with Avery, haven't you? He always gets you worked up." We both flushed at the suggestiveness of the remark. Unintentional?

A quarrel with Ronald was the last thing I wanted when I needed his help, so I forged on. "What if there's still some trace of the expedition left in the Antarctic?" I thought of the search party that found Sharpe's tent with his body, along with a treasure trove of journals, notes, and film. "Nothing rots or spoils in the cold; paper records don't disintegrate."

"Be practical, Beatrix; the continent is vast. In order to find something, you have to know where it's likely to be. Sharpe's tent was discovered quickly only because the search party had the map showing his exact route. A small tent somewhere, anywhere on the ice cap would almost certainly be missed. It has been missed for eighty years."

"No one ever looked for it before. What if we conducted a search by air?" Ronald had flown over the Antarctic several times and was frequently invited to return. He could arrange for the use of an airplane. "Let's go to the Antarctic together, Ronald, and if there are any remains of the Crosbie expedition, we'll be the ones to find them."

We were so close, closer than I had been to Avery in the coffee shop, but the closeness was only physical. Ronald took his hand away from mine and began to rub the finger with the missing joint, a nervous gesture he made only when tired. Still, I had been sure my suggestion would change his mood. He was in his element in Antarctica. Instead his response surprised me.

"Let's take one possible scenario—we'll assume the Crosbie expedition did reach the Antarctic at the same time as the Tremaine expedition and the race for the South Pole began. It's obvious the women never got there. Probably they died somewhere on the way. As a hero, shouldn't Tremaine have done something about it?"

Ronald's manner was just faintly hostile. I was taken aback by it. "What could he have done? He couldn't have saved them."

"He could have led a search party later or arranged for one, found their records and photographs, held a memorial service praising their effort. These are the things a hero would do. But he didn't do them. In fact, what he did do was conceal the expedition. There must be a reason for that."

Since first reading Byron's letter, I have spent countless hours imagining what tragedy might have been played out on the ice cap all those years ago. "I can believe something bad, even shameful, happened in connection with the Crosbie expedition. Maybe Tremaine's men raped the women before he could stop them, and he felt responsible. But I know Tremaine could not have done anything wrong. His whole life proves that."

"I find it hard to believe Tremaine ever lost control of his men. He was a born leader. Whatever happened, Beatrix, I think he made happen. That's the way he was. How can you be so certain the evidence will be favorable to your great-grandfather?"

"You sound like Avery." No sooner had I said that than I knew it was a mistake, for he flinched.

He recovered before I could say anything, and spoke softly but coldly: "Because for once I'm not blindly defending Tremaine."

"Is that how you see what you've been doing?"

"It's what I have been doing."

"Why?" But I knew why.

Ronald's eyes looked light against his ruddy skin. It was leathery, but not old, just weathered. "For you. That was the way to win you. And for a long time, it was the way to hold you. I always felt you loved Tremaine in me. I shouldn't have let it be that way. It was a mistake."

"I thought you admired him."

"I did. I do. And every time Avery has presented you with one of his rumors, I've gone to great lengths to help you prove him wrong. I thought that in defending Tremaine, I was defending myself. Only it hasn't worked out that way. Avery has not only been chipping away at Tremaine's life, but at mine.

" 'Let's go to the Antarctic together,' you say, with the naive certainty that only good things will emerge. And maybe they will. I could arrange a flight over the Antarctic and trace each possible route to the South Pole, and though it's like looking for a needle in a haystack, I just might find the tent and the bodies and the records. But I won't.

"I'm tired of Byron Tremaine."

*Tired of Byron Tremaine.* Did that mean he was tired of me? For a long time Ronald had *valued*—that was how he put it—my loving something of my great-grandfather in him. He concealed Byron's unhappy marriage from me out of the fear that it would make me love him less. Since then the association with Tremaine had become irksome. *I get tired of sharing my bed with him.*

I felt sick with apprehension at the possibility of losing Ronald. He appeared so desirable to me; I thought how it was to feel his body beside me. But sharing his bed with Tremaine—that was how he saw it. I put my arms around him and told him once again that I loved him for himself not for Tremaine in him. But I knew it was not enough. There was one way to hold him, and only one. "What if I were to give up Byron Tremaine?" Could I really do that? Just speaking the words made me feel as if I were cutting off a piece of myself.

Ronald leaned toward me, stroked my face very gently. "You touch me, Bibi." It was the first time he had used his nickname for me since I returned from London. "That you've been able to say it at all means a lot to me. Only you're not ready to make the break." I was torn by emotion, not certain whether I felt relief at his refusing my offer. "You'll never rest until you find out what really happened in Tremaine's life. It's Avery's doing; he spoils everything he touches." Ronald flinched again at the suggestiveness of those words.

Then he smiled, but sadly. "I know no one can pick his successor. But I do wish it weren't Avery."

He had no need to wish that, but protesting would only have made things worse. A few minutes earlier we had still been lovers. Now what were we? The love between an older man and a young woman is too fragile to last, its own destruction foreordained. I had been through love affairs with heroes, seen them end. But no one had captured my emotions as did Ronald. With him I had forgotten what was surely to come. The scene today caught me unaware. I wondered if it were true that Avery had spoiled everything. After Ronald left, I paced the living room, aching at the thought of life without him. Of love without him.

I walked over to the great photographs of Tremaine and Graham at the South Pole and considered whether some thought of the Crosbie expedition had darkened their mood.

Bucky dropped by to see me, as he does from time to time, unannounced. It never occurs to Bucky that he will not be welcome, and with his cheerful smile and manner, he always is. Though I had been plunged in gloom, my spirits rose. But they dropped again when he reported that Avery had been in touch with him and the program on polar exploration was scheduled for a date a couple of months away.

A couple of months was quite long enough to go to the Antarctic and back by air, but I would never go to the Antarctic, except on a luxurious cruise ship taking tourists to the penguin rookeries. If the record of the Crosbie expedition's fate was in the Antarctic, it was lost to me.

There was no need for concealment any longer. Avery or another would discover what had happened to the expedition. Not I. And so I told Bucky all I knew, all I did not know.

"That's a great story, Trixie." Bucky's eyes were shining with excitement. "If you really want to go to the Antarctic and search for traces of the expedition, I'll take you."

He could not really mean that. How impractical he was. Ronald, or Avery for that matter, might have the resources to arrange a search of the Antarctic; Bucky certainly did not.

"I'm not talking about an expedition like my last one. As you tell it, all I need to do is lease a plane and fly low over the Antarctic looking for the tent. I'll pilot the plane while you peer through the window with binoculars. I won't need a crew if I arrange with the people at a couple of the scientific stations to let me fly in, refuel, spend the night. Their mechanics will check over the plane."

"But why would they let you do that?"

"I made some friends when I was there with my expedition. And this time, I'll have a beautiful woman along—oh, I'll be welcome."

Bucky made everything sound so easy when it was not. "You haven't thought of the first thing, Bucky. How are you going to pay for leasing a plane and everything else you'll need."

"Who said I was going to pay for anything? I'll get a sponsor. It'll be great publicity for a news magazine publisher or an airplane manufacturer. Harney'll think of the right one and we'll go and sell him on it."

Bucky's casual assumption that a sponsor would be available to him whenever he wanted one was completely unrealistic. "Why would anyone sponsor you now?" I blushed at the tactlessness of my words, but Bucky was not offended.

"Why? On the strength of my scheduled appearance on 'Avery Tells All.' A television audience of millions."

"But Avery means to . . ." I could not bring myself to say what Avery meant to do to him.

"No one knows that now though, Trixie. Flying over the Pole and discovering a lost expedition would be the very thing to change Avery's approach. He'll probably present me as a hero after all." I will never get used to Bucky's optimism.

My native caution reasserted itself. "What if we don't find any remains? Or do find evidence that could be used in some way to raise questions about Tremaine? I doubt that would happen, but we should be prepared for anything."

"No one needs to know what we're looking for—until we're ready to tell them. I can sell this as a flight over an uncharted part of the Antarctic. Don't worry so much, Trixie. Just cancel your portrait sittings and get ready for the trip."

I had to put a stop to this. If it were Ronald, I would go without question, knowing there would be a plan for every contingency, a backup rescue party ready to set out from the nearest scientific station if the plane crashed, emergency supplies. But Bucky—I could just imagine how casually he would arrange the flight. "I wasn't serious, Bucky. I can't go to the Antarctic."

"Why not?" He seemed genuinely puzzled.

"I don't have the nerve for a trip like that, Bucky."

"Sure you do. Look at the way you stand up to Avery, and he frightens everybody. Think of what you'll have to say on his program if you come with me. You could end up a hero, too."

"I'm not going to be on his program."

"Of course you are, Trixie. It's been obvious from the start. He wants you too much to let you off." That was Bucky again with his odd idea that Avery was fascinated by me. "And you're too interested in him not to do it." A denial would only convince him, so I was silent.

He was smiling, and I could see he was sure I would agree to go with him. What gave him such confidence? People have always taken care of me. My parents. Ronald. They are all gone now. And here was Bucky, who could take care of no one. He said so himself. But it was clear that Byron's reputation now depended on me alone. Somehow I must have the courage to fly over the Antarctic and find the evidence that would dispel every doubt. Hardly believing I could be saying it, I told Bucky to proceed.

The day before our departure, I visited my great-aunt Susan to explain that I was going to search for the remains of the mysterious all-women's expedition. Only then would I understand what it had meant to her father.

"As soon as I get back from the Antarctic, I'll come to see you and tell you all about what I've found."

Aunt Susan became agitated and shook her head. I tried for a lighter note. "When I know the whole story, Aunt Susan, I'll be able to do just what you've always been telling me to do—get on with my life."

I expected her to smile at this, but instead she sighed.

"You don't know what you're doing, Beatrix. You mustn't go to the Antarctic. You . . . must . . . not."

# Chapter Twenty-seven

❧

THE CRASHING OF THE AVALANCHE awakened him. At first Byron did not know what it was, and then he recognized the sound and believed his last moment was at hand. Twice before, during the ascents of Mount McKinley, he had escaped the masses of snow and ice hurtling downward at breakneck speed. This time the noise seemed closer, and he thought with horror that he would be crushed, buried forever. Along with his men. They were stirring uneasily in their bunks, and he knew he must calm himself in order to calm them. He instructed them to remain where they were, and then forced himself to get up.

The floor was heaving and bucking beneath his feet as he staggered to the entrance, raised the tent flap, and looked out. The midnight sun was hidden by clouds, and a thin sleet was falling onto the snow, covering the furrows of névés and sastrugi. Byron took a few steps forward, and the moment he let go of the tent pole, was thrown to the ground. Two strong hands helped him up; he knew who was there. When was Horace absent in moments of danger?

After a few minutes the crashes of falling snow ceased and the snow surface was stable again. Byron made his way to the nearby tents, where the rest of the expedition was quartered, and ordered these men to join the others in the main tent. There he explained what had happened and gave reassurance that the worst was over. Table, chairs, scientific instruments, and books had been tossed around, but damage was minor, and beyond a few bruises, no one was harmed. A bad scare, he declared, that could be relegated to the past.

Just when he finished speaking, Byron had a presentiment of disaster. An avalanche is not set off on level ground, but on a mountain slope. "My God, Horace. It must have crashed off the Beardmore Glacier." They were but a half day's journey away, ready to begin the ascent that would take them over the glacier and on to the South Pole. Where could the masses of snow have landed?

He called to the orderly to bring ski boots and skis and quickly set off with Horace to reconnoiter. They advanced without too much difficulty for one mile, then for two, and were beginning to hope that all might yet be well when they were forced to halt, their way blocked by a steep, glassy ice mountain deposited by the avalanche.

This was an obstacle, and Byron's life was dedicated to overcoming obstacles. "We'll make a detour; we can afford to lose a couple of days." The arrival at the Pole would be delayed, but they must still get there ahead of Viola. The avalanche that was stopping him would stop her as well. All at once he felt a chill and wondered if she could somehow have been in the path of the avalanche. When would he get over the habit of caring what happened to her?

"A detour to where, Byron? We don't have any idea how far this barrier extends. We might lose not a couple of days but weeks, and the Antarctic summer is too short for that."

"We have to try. We can't let a little piece of bad luck force us to abandon the South Pole."

Back in the tent, Byron considered an alternate route to the Pole. Were he to turn to the west, he could travel between Beardmore and the Axel Heiberg Glacier. Part of the way was still uncharted and the journey would, therefore, be risky, but it was the shortest way to go. No woman would dare take the chance. Not even Viola. She would choose the detour.

"We have no depots laid along the new route," Horace demurred. "We'd have to travel all the way from here to the Pole without replenishing our supplies. And then, we'd still have to march for days before getting back to our depots."

Horace did not desire the Pole or indeed anything else badly enough to suffer for it, thought Byron. He was as devoid of passion as Hermine. What a perfect pair they would make, never touching one another.

It was not possible to dissuade Byron. The bleak realization came to Horace that he would never be with Hermine again, never see her face brighten when he approached, never again embrace her graceful, fragile body. He would have no part in rearing his son, watching Hermine's enchanting little daughter grow up. From the day Horace learned Viola had mounted her own expedition and declared a competition, he had known there would be trouble. That a group of women, poorly trained and ill supplied, could get within hundreds of miles of the South Pole was inconceivable. The effort was pathetic really. Yet Byron, while saying Viola must be far behind, clearly still feared she might overtake him. That woman was making him, would make them all, crazy, or kill them before they were done.

Byron was confident that his new plan would get them safely to the Pole. In order to extend the supplies, only four men were to make the final assault. The others would go back to the base camp, taking two of the sledges with them—quite enough for travel along the route where the depots were laid. The remaining five sledges, heavily loaded and drawn by the best dog teams, would accompany the Pole party, made up of Byron and Horace, Ed Pitman, the photographer, and Charlie Smithers, the camp cook and man of all work. Byron did not count Wally Padgett as a member of the Pole party, but of course he had to come along. He was little more than a boy, but no one else handled the dogs as well, and he could also serve as Byron's orderly.

Wally adored Byron and had willingly strained his still undeveloped body almost beyond endurance to complete the most unpleasant tasks; he rushed out to soothe the dogs' barking in the middle of the night, rose before dawn to feed them. Nothing Byron had asked of him was too much, but now he spoke up. "I don't wanna go to the Pole. I ain't strong enough. Lemme go back to the camp with the rest of them." Byron smiled at him, put his hand on Wally's shoulder. There, the matter was settled.

As they set off again, Byron's spirits were high; he was exhilarated by being on the trail again, pleased with the new route he had selected. Horace and Charlie went out hunting and killed a seal to add to their supply of fuel and food. The taste was foul, but needing fresh meat, they forced it down.

The thought of Viola drove Byron and caused him to drive his men and animals to the point of exhaustion and beyond, marching continuously for ten or twelve hours each day, covering twenty miles or better. Yet sometimes, even in his anger at her intransigence, he imagined that they would meet here on the ice cap, and Viola would yield the race, yield more than her body, yield her life to him. By now she must regret the marriage to Ian Crosbie, the years of carrying the burden of his madness. Yes, she must regret that.

Where was Crosbie now? Perhaps he was with Viola, the one male on the women's expedition. Byron's jealousy took over then, and he imagined them making love. On warm days in the Antarctic, as in the Arctic, they could lie naked out of doors, as he and Viola once had done. He thought of her body against another man's, her hands caressing. Why could he not accustom himself to the fact that she was married? Why should he accustom himself to the fact that she was married?

Once he had told her he would not marry her if she were free, if he were. The words had been spoken to hurt her, but were untrue. Here, in Antarctica, away from the conventions of the world, he knew that their marriages to other people, the wrong people, could be voided, the mistakes they had made rectified. In these modern times people were daring to do what earlier generations had thought sinful. Upon the return to New York, he would make a financial settlement on Hermine and arrange to continue seeing his children—he could not give up his son. Viola must find someone else to assume Crosbie's care.

Horace, as usual nearby, was looking at him quizzically, guessing his thoughts. What if Horace were to take Hermine off his hands? But Horace was much too proper, would be shocked were he to raise that issue.

To hide his emotion, Byron began to speak rapidly about the expedition. "According to my calculations, Horace, we'll be at the Pole only two weeks later than the date we set back at Cape Graham." He had given Horace's name to the base camp on Ross Island. "And we still have two-thirds of the supplies left. Even you have to admit we're in good shape."

Before Horace could answer, a cry rang out with a tone of desperation that horrified them both. As they ran forward, they saw Wally

Padgett in the distance frantically pulling the harness of a sledge tee-tering on the edge of a crevasse. As it went over, Wally let go of the straps to save himself. By now Ed and Charlie had seen what was happening and were rushing to the scene as well. Only two of the five sledges were in view. With horror, Byron realized the rest were gone. What kind of crevasse would take three sledges and dog teams?

Wally was standing at the edge of the crevasse, immobilized by ter-ror. "How did it happen?"

Wally was crying, the tears freezing on his face. "They was running ever so fast over the ice. There wasn't no crack on the surface. Noth-ing. And then it just opened up, and the first sledge went down and then behind that, the next. There wasn't no stopping them. I tried to hold them, honest I did, but they was too heavy. It wasn't my fault."

"You're the dog handler. You're responsible." But then looking down the gaping hole in front of him, Byron realized it was an abyss rather than a crevasse. The sledges were out of sight; he could hear the dogs barking desperately. The boy could not have stopped the precipitous fall, and Byron made haste to say so, but Wally was too dazed to take it in.

"Quick, a rope. I'll climb down and see how far the dogs and sledges have fallen. The other dog teams might be able to pull them up."

In an instant, Byron had fastened a rope under his arms and around his waist and, with Horace and Charlie holding the ends, had started to slither down the steep ice walls. Soon the opening widened so that he was unable to brace his feet against the other side, and he still could not see the sledges. The barking of the dogs was growing fainter. The abyss, it seemed, was bottomless, and the opening was so wide that dogs and sledges had fallen unchecked. There was noth-ing to be done; Byron pulled at the rope, and his companions drew him up.

Plunged in gloom, they made camp. Three loaded sledges were gone. Now even Byron would have to concede they must turn back to Cape Graham, thought Horace. However, Byron was not willing to do that. "We'll go on in the morning. The South Pole is not so dis-tant now. I've checked over the remaining supplies and they should be sufficient, provided we're careful. I think we'll be able to catch some penguins on our journey."

Horace looked around the desolate ice plateau. Emperor penguins? No other species was capable of existence so far from the sea. One look at Byron's face told him there was little point in arguing. Viola had bewitched Byron, he thought, as he had many times since the avalanche blocked their path.

After a few hours of troubled sleep, the men arose, broke camp, and set off on the march to the Pole. They went forward, each day more difficult than the one before. The food rations were reduced once, then again, and again. Growing steadily weaker, the members of the expedition soon were unable to traverse more than a few miles in a day. Slaughter the dogs, the men urged. Byron refused; without the dogs to pull the sledges, there was small chance of success. Then, too, eating the dogs had besmirched Carlsen's reputation; Byron wanted none of that.

Each night Horace forced himself out of the tent and, accompanied by a whining and surly Wally, went to hunt the emperor penguin. Nowhere did he find a trace of the huge, cold-hardy birds, but he kept trying. Anything was better than watching Byron and the other men starve, starving himself. At last, however, he had to tell Byron that this must be the last hunt; even his strength—surprising in view of his slender build—was giving way, and Wally could hardly stumble behind him.

As Byron watched them leave in the brilliant summer sunshine, he was stunned by the sudden realization of what he had done in his blind determination to reach the South Pole. The order to turn back should have been given days ago, when they still had sufficient supplies to carry them to one of the depots on the return trail, and sufficient strength to march that far. Now he was ready to give way on the dogs, but emaciated by now, they could provide little nourishment.

Lost in his dark reflections, Byron did not at first hear the men shouting. Cries of joy? That could not be. Rushing out of the tent, he was dazzled by a mirage, the figment of a mind disordered by hunger. Horace and Wally had harnessed themselves to the sledge to help the dogs drag the heavy load.

"Did you kill a penguin, Horace?" But it did not look like a penguin. "What do you have there?" He could hardly speak in his excitement, in his hope.

"Cartons of food, Byron, tins of paraffin and acetylene."

Coming closer to the sledge, Byron felt dizzy as he stared at the boxes of biscuits and dried fruits. A container of raisins was open. He was baffled, confused, feared he had taken leave of his senses. That happened to men in Antarctica; he had read of it often enough. But the food looked so real. "Where does all this come from? Have we somehow circled around to one of our depots, Horace?" He tried to calm himself, then searched for labels on the cartons, but there were none. These boxes of food did not come from one of his depots; each of those was clearly marked Tremaine Expedition.

"We found one of Shackleton's old depots," replied Horace. "A flag with his name on it was stuck on a pole wedged between the rocks above the cache, and the cartons were covered with another of his flags."

"Shackleton? But of course. He did set out in this direction. This is the route Shackleton planned to follow to the Pole. He must have laid the depots the previous year and then didn't get back to them. So Shackleton's misfortune is our good fortune. We are saved." In his gratitude, he threw his arms around Horace, and then reached for Wally, who drew back. Well, it really was not appropriate to embrace a dog handler.

An hour later, seated in a circle in the warm tent, they watched avidly as Charlie ladled out the thick hoosh, the first hot food they had eaten in days. Horace took one spoonful and then turned white and ran out of the tent. They could hear him retching outside. Food can be too much of a shock to a deprived system.

Byron knew he must never again allow the quantity of supplies to fall so low. Now he would be cautious enough to suit Horace. "Let's go forward for a week. Just a week, Horace, and see where we are. If the Pole is not within our grasp by then, we'll turn back." Of course the Pole would be within their grasp. If they traveled rapidly enough.

Twelve-hour marches soon were relegated to the past. The Pole was farther than Byron had thought. The territory was uncharted and the map did not show how they must twist and turn to avoid crevasses and strain their bodies to climb hills and descend into valleys.

They went fourteen, sometimes fifteen hours at a stretch. In his eagerness, Byron took the lead, refusing to concede exhaustion.

Late one afternoon he fell on an unevenness on the ice surface and could not rise. When Horace and Charlie pulled him to his feet, his ankle, badly sprained, buckled under him. Camp was made on the spot, and Byron took stock of the situation. He could not put on his ski boot, strap on his skis, or take a few steps unaided, and they dared not abandon any supplies to leave room for him to ride on one of the sledges. Several days must pass before he would be able to travel. The time limit was reached. This accident was the last of the series of misadventures that had bedeviled him since the avalanche had crashed. To go on was to court death. As leader, his paramount concern was the lives of his men.

But the South Pole. He had wanted it so badly. Why conquering the Pole had been taken for granted all his life; it was known to be his destiny. "After the Pole," he had said, people had said. A matter of course. It was small comfort to him to realize that if he had not reached the Pole, Viola could not have done so either. Now he would not return home in triumph, but as a failed explorer. No one would back another expedition. His son had admired him, spoken of following a career in exploration upon reaching adulthood. That was gone, too. This was the lowest moment of his life.

Nor had the scientific discoveries he had promised his backers come about, either. The paleontologists on the expedition, brilliant and acclaimed men all, did not have a grasp of what it takes to work in a polar environment. Only a small number of fossils had been gathered on the depot-laying expedition of the previous year, and when these were identified in the base camp laboratory, none proved unusual. He had hoped that many more prehistoric remains would turn up on the approach to the South Pole, but not one of the scientists was strong enough to be included in the Pole party. On his own, he came upon some rocks with fossil imprints and carried them along, but his discoveries were disappointingly sparse. Triple that amount had been collected by Viola on Disko Island and by the field party in Greenland. He could remember the pages and pages of drawings and descriptions in Viola's notebooks. She had been lucky in finding so much that was new.

As he thought of Viola, he was seized with apprehension. If the

Tremaine expedition was in a disastrous state, Viola and her Amazons were surely far worse off. No woman can survive on the ice cap. What had Viola done by creating this desperate competition? For what? Because she believed he sought to dominate her? When had he tried to do anything that was not best for her? He had warned her, done all he could to stop her. But when had he ever been able to have his way with Viola?

Three days later the return journey began. It was mid-January of 1916, and with Byron's injury reducing their speed, the men were not likely to complete the journey back to Ross Island before ice locked the ship in the harbor. In that case, they must spend yet another winter in the Antarctic. The men marched in almost complete silence; the disappointment of losing the Pole affected them all. They had endured so much to get here, would have to endure so much more before arriving back at Cape Graham to confront their companions and admit their defeat.

One bitterly cold morning in February, Byron, watching for landmarks, thought he saw a patch of darkness, startling against the whiteness of the snow. It was probably merely a grouping of rocks; the sun was blinding him, and after so many months in Antarctica, he had come to mistrust the evidence of his eyes.

Horace peered through his spectacles, protected as always with sun goggles. "It's a tent. A big green tent."

Like the depot, it must have been left by Shackleton, Byron thought, almost too weary to care. "Let's go take a look, Horace. Perhaps some things we could use have been left there."

He started limping toward the tent, surprised by the speed with which Horace was skiing. Why was Horace in such a hurry? And all at once, a wild hope came over him. How could it be that Horace had been the one to guess that this tent might belong to Viola? Hope mixed with dread as he went forward. His heart was racing and he found it hard to catch his breath. He did not know how he would stand the disappointment if he arrived at the tent and found only a few documents of the Shackleton expedition. No, even that was not the worst. He must face the possibility that Viola's dead body might be lying within the tent. Oh, that was beyond all endurance. The way was strewn with ice-covered boulders and he was stumbling, going so slowly, too slowly. He could not wait to be there; he could not bear to be there. Always sensitive, Horace doubled back on his tracks to be with Byron. Distances in the Antarctic are misleading, and the dark patch of the tent was farther off than they had thought; more than an hour elapsed before they were close enough to see the banner. Votes for Women.

The tent had been placed within a semicircle of boulders, out of the wind. The silence was complete. No wisp of smoke arose, nor any sound. A sledge stood beside the tent, but no dog team was tethered nearby. Byron's foreboding was stronger now.

"Let me go first."

"No, Horace. I must." He raised the tent flap and went in, Horace close behind him. The tent was very cold and the green canvas blocked the sunlight. Coming in from the brilliance outside, Byron could see nothing at first. Then, as his eyes became accustomed to the dimness, he saw what he most feared—two bunks side by side and two figures lying on them in sleeping bags, only their heads uncovered. A mass of curling blond hair. Not Viola. And then he saw the russet brown, the coppery strands gleaming in the gray-green light. She could not be lying there like that were she alive. The other woman, too, was still.

This was how the all-women's expedition had ended. Why had it been so important to Viola to defeat him? Why could she not have given way just once? It was over. All that life, that energy. He would never hold her again, feel her slender passionate body straining in his arms. Her husband was not there; forgetting his jealousy, Byron wished Crosbie with his great strength had been able to save her.

Byron put his hand on Viola's forehead and felt the icy cold. Just then she opened her eyes. Blue with a hint of violet. She was alive. Somehow, unbelievably, she had survived. He heard Horace gasp, while he, unable to cry out or speak, felt the tears start and run down his face. Nothing had ever mattered quite so much. Her gaze was unfocused. Did she know it was he?

Starving people have hallucinations; that is common knowledge. And in the Antarctic, mirage often seems more true than any truth. This hallucination had brought her Byron standing by the bunk, crying. And there was Horace, ashen-faced, behind him. They looked so real that were she to take her hand out of the sleeping bag to touch them, she would feel flesh where there was none. She must fight to retain her hold on reality. Viola closed her eyes again, willing the fantasy to leave her so that when she opened them, she would see the tent as it was.

"Viola." It was his voice. How far would this fantasy take her?

"Tremaine. You must be Tremaine. And who is the other one?" That was Evadne speaking in a faint, husky voice. But if Evadne saw the men, too, they must be here.

Viola opened her eyes and this time she believed, and the feeling that swept over her was one she had almost forgotten. Hunger was a thing of the past. It was a long time since she had wished for food. Cold—she no longer was aware of it. But love, physical desire, forgotten in the privations of the last weeks, seized her again upon seeing Byron, his dark green eyes bright with tears. She remembered passion; it lay in the brilliance of his face. With a tremendous effort, she unfastened the top of the sleeping bag to free her arms and took his hand.

Yes. She would lie with him once more, thought Byron. As in Greenland. In his office. In all the places they had made love with rapture, with anger. And just once she would yield to him completely. Just once she would admit she should have accepted his love, his care, when it was offered. How thin her arms were, and her cheekbones seemed about to push through the skin. What had she put herself through? How much had she endured? And he could have spared her all this. At least he had come in time to save her. "Oh, Viola." Wasted, exhausted, she still possessed the vital quality that always drew him to her. Byron's face filled with joy as he spoke her name, took her hands and kissed them, stroked her face. She was speaking to him, too, so softly no one else could hear.

"How did you find us?" It was the other woman again. Aware only of Viola, Byron did not think to answer her question. Horace spoke for them both, telling of the avalanche, the detour, and their discovery of the tent. Where had he seen that face before? Classically beautiful. She gave her name: Evadne. Just that. Why, it was the dancer whose performances were so scandalous they were often closed down by the police. Evadne was studying first his face and then Byron's; there was something vaguely hostile in her manner.

Horace was relieved to hear the sounds of the dogs and the sledge runners against the ice. The other members of their party had dismantled the camp, packed up, and come here. Horace ordered them to bring in the stove and the paraffin and food and to set about preparing a meal at once. Viola could barely raise her head to take the first sips of soup. Byron steadied her hand with the spoon, tenderly, speaking softly. He dipped one biscuit into the liquid and then another and gave them to her. Gradually a touch of color returned to her face. The competition between them might never have taken place. Perhaps they were comforting one another for their failure in reaching the Pole.

Ed Pitman rushed over to help Evadne. "Do you remember me?" he asked. "I took pictures of you dancing. You used them on your posters. I was mad about you and kept asking you to have supper with me." She smiled, but it was clear she did not remember.

No doubt she had so many suitors that one awestruck photographer made no impression. Horace wondered what had brought her to this desolate place. It was hard to understand why the newspapers had not made more of the presence of so famous or infamous a dancer on the Crosbie expedition.

Ed asked the same question, phrasing it more tactfully, and Evadne explained that she had not given out her name before. "We did not wish attention from the journalists too soon—in case we did not reach the South Pole."

At this Byron looked up. Evadne had caught his attention for the first time. A shadow seemed to have fallen over the tent; he could not tell why.

When Viola next spoke, it was no longer just for Byron's ear. Her thrilling voice was low and throbbing, giving the sense of excitement Horace remembered so well. The all-women's expedition had conquered the South Pole.

Byron recoiled; he could not control his reaction. From the moment he gave up hope of the Pole and turned back, he consoled himself with the certainty that if he had failed, so had she. With dismay, he heard her present the evidence of her success—the latest volume of her diary lying on the large boxes serving as a table, the compass readings, the calculations based on the sun sightings with the artificial horizon. There were boxes of film to be developed, proving the location by the shadows on the snow. Sharpe and Carlsen had fallen just short of the Pole, so the all-women's expedition was first. Now Byron could not doubt. His heart felt heavy and he feared he might be sick. He had thought the lowest moment of his life was reached when he fell on the ice and knew the Pole was lost to him. But this was the lowest moment of all, and he came close to hating her.

Seeing the expression on his face, Viola became silent, leaving it to Evadne to continue the account. The avalanche? They were not aware there had been an avalanche. Not on the route they were on. But then, they had never intended to cross Beardmore. The Axel Heiberg Glacier to the west was their approach to the Pole. Why had they chosen the uncharted route? Viola spoke then: "Ian Crosbie planned the journey."

With what affection she said that name, thought Byron bitterly. How could he have failed? A lifetime of planning for this expedition and he had been defeated by an avalanche, by the crevasse that stole his sledges and dogs, by an accident, by a madman. Yes, a madman—yet Ian Crosbie had been wiser than he.

After raising their flags at the Pole, they began the journey back, Viola took up the account. Perhaps she had spent too much time in a mysterious snow-free valley where she discovered fossils never seen before. Even so, all would have ended well, but for . . . Evadne gasped and Viola broke off at the sudden realization of what had happened.

It was Evadne who spoke then. "Look at them. I guessed as soon as they came in. How well they are, how strong."

"How could you do it?"

"Do what? Viola, don't look at me like that. Do what?"

"Don't pretend. You robbed us. You rifled our depot. You and your men ate the food and burned the fuel that would have carried us safely to the base camp and on to New Zealand."

"Your depot?" Byron was stunned by the accusation. "The supplies were taken from Shackleton's depot—one he had abandoned when he was forced to change his route. His flag was there." And seeing her expression of incredulity, he turned to Horace. "It was Shackleton's depot. Tell her, Horace."

Horace remembered the sun on the cairn of rocks marking the depot, thought of loading the supplies onto the sledge. And now here were the women starving in the freezing temperature of the tent, too weak to go any farther. "Yes," he answered hoarsely, "we were certain it was Shackleton's depot."

How could she possibly believe he would have taken anything from her had he known? Byron pleaded with her. A mistake had been made, a mistake terrible in its consequences, but a mistake nonetheless. He was an honorable man, would not knowingly commit such a crime.

"I would rather have died than subject you to this, Viola." It was true. He looked at her thin face and wasted body and thought that this was the woman he loved more than anyone else in the world— and he had all but killed her.

Viola listened to him with growing relief. He could not have done it; she had known that even while accusing him. "I believe you."

She did not hold him responsible, Byron thought, as indeed he was not. He had not known. Surely that exonerated him. Had he known, he would not have taken a . . . a single raisin. But still he was sickened by what he had done.

Viola was truly besotted, thought Evadne, and was forgetting that Byron would stick at nothing in his effort to win the competition. It was obvious to her that the men were lying. She had but to look at their faces to see the lie. Byron's smile was false, Horace's expression brooding, malevolent, the other men were embarrassed. Even the boy showed his guilty knowledge.

After finding the depot empty—Evadne repeated those words— they struggled on. There were four of them then in the Pole party. The dogs became ill, poisoned by food contaminated by the fuel. Only four dogs survived, pulling one sledge while the women dragged the other. They were exhausted when they found this sheltered spot and here they made a final, desperate plan. The rations remaining were too meager to sustain them all on the trail. Araminta and Claireve were the strongest; they must take the sledge and dog team and most of the food and journey to the next of their depots. After picking up supplies, they would return for Viola and Evadne. A three-day journey each way. They set off eight days ago, so surely they were lost.

"We conquered the Pole. Whatever happens, no one can take that away from us."

The confusion about the depot had distracted Byron for a little while from the immensity of his defeat. Now he felt spent yet keyed up, torn apart by conflicting emotions. Love, hate, regret, disappointment, resentment.

Looking from Byron to Viola, Evadne knew what was to happen in the tent. Byron would make up for his defeat by taking Viola, and she, deluded by love, would accept his body as she had accepted his excuses for the plunder of the depot.

Evadne recognized the slightly swollen look of desire. Lust. Strange she had never felt it for the men who came to her after her success. When making love with one of these clean, well-groomed, wealthy suitors, she was conscious of the need to be skillful, make the most of the opportunity. A whore long after the customer stopped putting his money on the dresser or slipping it between her buttocks. Even when in love with Gerald, the sex part of it hardly moved her. The only times she felt lust herself occurred when the man was crude, came from a background like her own. She was comfortable with men of that sort. The sailors on board the *Explorer* had aroused her interest, not the officers. None of these handsome explorers was sexually attractive to her. Except perhaps that dog handler—a boy, but she would not have had to teach him about sex. A product of the slums, he had probably taken a neighborhood girl, by force were she unwilling, before he was thirteen. She had known plenty of boys like that by the time she was ten.

Viola was gazing at Byron, drinking him in, capturing his soul. She wanted Byron. Horace closed his eyes and remembered Hermine putting her arms around his neck so shyly that first time. Now Viola was holding up her arms to Byron and they would make love, not caring that he, that everyone knew.

With a strangled exclamation, Horace left the tent. The others followed, exchanging glances. Collusion. The second woman, Evadne, soon came out, too, leaning on Ed's arm. She appeared indifferent. A dancer. Well, no better than a whore really. Everyone knew what was happening inside the tent. Like Greenland. The blood on the Eskimo blanket. Only it was not like Greenland, where they had both been free. *I have sinned. We have sinned,* Hermine had amended his words. And here was Hermine's husband breaking his marriage vows. Horace would have liked to put his hands over his ears. Did he hear or only imagine he heard their cries of ecstasy? Wally was licking his lips, taking his mittens off. Horace saw where the hands went. Re-volting. What were the other men doing? They had been without women for so long. That Byron's lovemaking should create dirty fantasies was not to be borne. The pictures in his own mind, desire mixed with disgust, could drive him mad.

Horace fought for calm. If he allowed himself to blame Byron, all he had done was for nothing. *My dreams are coming true.* He had given up those dreams. Viola was ensnaring Byron now as in the years gone by. All that vitality. She never lost it.

Byron had been startled by the manner of their departure, making clear that they were leaving him alone with Viola. Did they think he meant to make love to her? Why, he never wanted to touch her again. It seemed to him that Viola was in some way no longer human. No real woman could have crossed the glacier, the ice plateau, and arrived at the South Pole. He shuddered at what lay ahead. The return to New Zealand together, the announcement to the journalists, the entry into New York Harbor. He would be gracious, gentlemanly, the good loser. Gentlemanly, knowing her exploit was to become legendary. As was his failure. Defeated. By an all-women's expedition. Chapters in the history books would be devoted to her, while he would be a footnote. He wished he need never see her again.

"Byron." She said his name in the low, throbbing voice that always caught at his heart. "When I was at the Pole, I imagined you beside me. That was what I had always wanted. I wished to share that moment with you."

He did not believe her, and now she was putting out her arms to him. Reaching. He drew back, thinking he did not want her, thinking of the crowds waiting in New Zealand, the newspaper headlines. He would rather break her in two than make love to her. But even as that was going through his mind, he was moving to her, lifting the sleeping bag from the bunk and laying it on the floor. Then falling upon her body, he tore at the last fastenings of the sleeping bag, drew it back, pulled off her heavy woolen garments. She was shivering. From cold or desire—he did not know or care. He stood up just long enough to take off his clothing. His skin was burning as he fell upon her body again and began to kiss her, bruising her mouth with his teeth, gripping her painfully with his fingers. As if he could take revenge for her winning the Pole, for standing against him all these years. The scar on his forehead remained as evidence of the day she struck him with a paperweight because he refused her the Antarctic. The memory was so unpleasant that for a moment desire left him. He thought of the heartbreaking day in London when she told him she had lost his child, when she refused to be his wife. If anyone was responsible for his disastrous marriage to Hermine, it was she. His hands went around her neck and he felt he could choke out her life. Then he dropped his hands and stood up.

There in the strange gray-green light of the tent, she was moved by the whiteness of his naked body, the sharp contrast with his weather-beaten ruddy face and hands. That whiteness had dazzled her in the hut in Greenland long ago. And as she had done then, she put out her hand and touched him in the way nice women do not touch a man. With this gesture of love, she canceled, accepted, forgave the wrong he had unwittingly done her. And at this gesture of love, he accepted her as she was, and his anger dissipated.

Shuddering, he lay down on her body, and caressed her with hands roughened by frostbite. For once the conflict that had raged between them for years was forgotten. It did not matter then that she had won the Pole. Her breath was coming in short gasps and he could feel her heart beating so rapidly as she lay beneath him. Panting with desire in his arms. She moved on top of him, and he did not stop her. In her excitement, the weakness engendered by days of near starvation left her. Her knees gripped his sides, and her body leaned toward him, then away, toward him, then away. Only after the climax did her exhaustion return, and she lay down beside him, her eyes closed, quiet.

For all these months Byron had imagined they would come together on the ice plateau. Until today he had thought that when they met, she would yield the competition, her body, her life to him. The competition was lost, but she was yielding to him, her body, her life. "You are mine." And for once, she did not deny him. Then as if a cold wind swept over him, he shivered. Yielding? Yes, in the moment of passion. But not later. Never later. Then she would resume her life, find some reason to leave him. Inevitably she would return to suffrage, inevitably to her husband.

"What is it?"

"You will return to Ian Crosbie."

Byron was frowning, Viola observed, although he had no right to disapprove. Return to Ian? *I think I will never see you again.* But she did not want to say that to Byron. And what did it matter? "You will return to Hermine." She remembered the photograph of Hermine he treasured and felt betrayed by it. He made love to her, but afterward he was with that simpering doll in his thoughts. "Why pretend you don't love her, Byron? You enjoy having mastery over her shrinking flesh. You've said that, you know."

What had he not said to Viola when he wanted to hurt her?

He arose and melted snow in the pot left on the stove, helped her to wash and dress. "Let's call in the others to devise a plan." Viola and Evadne were still too weakened by hunger to travel, and the supplies were beginning to run short. Byron suggested that most of the remaining food and fuel be left here for the women while the men made a run for the first of their own depots. They were no more than two or three days' journey from the original route. By the time they returned to the tent with additional supplies, the women would be strong enough to accompany them to Cape Graham.

A good plan—only Viola refused to have it so. The group of women who remained at the base camp on the Bay of Whales must learn what had happened. Otherwise they would assume the Pole party dead and return to New Zealand. As was agreed, they would never speak of the failed expedition, would seek to conceal its very existence. How then could a claim be presented later? No one would believe it. There was only one thing to do—divide the supplies at the depot and separate. Byron and Charlie would make their way to the Bay of Whales to tell the women there to overwinter, and Horace, Ed, and Wally would come back for Viola and Evadne.

At first Byron insisted he must return for Viola, but Horace convinced him that was unwise. The leg injury was not fully healed, and Horace and Ed would be faster on the trail. Byron should not risk Viola's life out of his desire to be with her. That left only Wally objecting vehemently: "Lemme go with you, Cap'n Tremaine. I don't wanna go the long way to the depot and back. You're gonna kill me." Byron ignored him; Wally was only a dog handler and must do as he was told.

A mad scheme, Horace knew that all too well. Leaving directly from the depot, Byron and Charlie had a chance of reaching the Bay of Whales, but the rest of them were doomed. Too much time was already lost. He had believed all along that Viola would kill them with this competition. And he had been right. Better if they had never found the depot and died before this, saving themselves the agony of the final hopeless effort. He gloomily watched Charlie and Ed adding fuel to the stove, preparing a meal, filling pots with snow, and bringing in stores of food and paraffin from the sledge. Byron was insisting that everything possible be done to make the women comfortable.

Viola paid little attention to these efforts, concerned only that the world must learn the Crosbie expedition had achieved the South Pole. Should she and Evadne, weakened by weeks of hunger, collapse on the trail, then Byron or Horace must carry the news to New Zealand. Of course Byron knew that death lurked everywhere in the dangerous climate and hazardous terrain of Antarctica. He could bear that knowledge for himself, but not for Viola. What if it all failed and they were never to meet again?

Her gaze was intent, and he knew she was waiting for his promise. "You will present your claim yourself, Viola. I firmly believe that. Horace will return and bring you and Evadne safely to the Bay of Whales. But if it will put your mind at rest, you have my word that should anything happen, I will tell all that you have done." She was smiling now. "And if it turns out that Horace is the one to reach New Zealand, I know he'll do no less. Isn't that so, Horace?"

"Of course."

However, Viola still was not satisfied with the plan. The claim, undocumented, might not be believed. Perhaps some would say she had deceived Byron, and Horace, too. Neither had actually been witness to her conquest of the Pole. "Proof will be demanded—the evidence of my journal entries, the compass readings, meteorological reports, and photographs. And the fossils. Those must be presented as well." She thought with pride of the rocks with imprints of microorganisms and primitive plants extinct for millions of years, and the greatest discovery of all, the jawbone and teeth of a beast that had preceded the dinosaurs on the face of the earth.

The evidence should be divided between the men and travel with them. In treacherous Antarctica, that was the safest course. If Viola reached the Bay of Whales, she would reclaim her property. If not, it would speak for her through Byron or through Horace.

Their tasks within the tent completed, the men went out to reload the sledges carefully, making room for the two packages of documentary and fossil evidence Evadne had agreed to prepare.

"Let's go outside, Viola." There was a sheltered spot beside the tent where, hidden from the men loading the sledges, Byron could be alone with Viola for a last good-bye.

Evadne observed Byron's tenderness as he helped Viola on with her boots and parka, smoothed her hair, caressed her face. Perhaps he did love Viola. But love went only so far. It had not stopped him from robbing her depot.

Now at the moment of separation, Byron was overwhelmed by the thought of the wasted years. "Oh, why did you refuse me when I came to you in London, Viola? You were wrong. Admit it now." If only this once she could say that she regretted it all. Throwing away a life with him for the suffrage movement. For Ian Crosbie. Say she had made mistakes, that he had been her destiny all along. Say it just once.

But she could not say it. Wrong? She had not been wrong. Think of all that refusal had brought to her—a glorious part in the suffrage movement, the successful expedition to Antarctica. None of this would have happened had she accepted Byron on that long-ago day. Ian Crosbie had seemed a mistake, but he had brought her to the South Pole.

"Say it." Byron brushed the copper tendrils of hair away from her ear and whispered to her.

His breath was so warm against her face, like a caress, and she was conscious of his body, the body she loved so much, beneath the heavy fur. Why not tell him what he wanted to hear?

But the words would not come. The competition—that was his doing. She had wanted to go with the Tremaine Antarctic expedition, had all but begged him. If he had accepted her, they would have journeyed together and would not now be in such desperate straits. No, he was the one who had been wrong.

"I can't."

It was always this way. First the passion. Unchanging. Then the conflict. Unchanging, too.

A feeling of anger, familiar to him, a part of each encounter with her, came over him. Why could she not give way? Her body was so close to his, leaning upon his chest. She was too weak to stand unsupported, and still there was that splendor about her. It took him aback. From the day she had first walked into his office in the summer of 1904 through all the hard years since, she never wavered.

For the first time he wondered that he had ever thought to tame her, ever wanted to tame her. A mating of tigers. He had laughed at her a hundred times. But that was what making love with her had been. What it would always be.

She had been lucky in Greenland, lucky again in achieving the Pole. He could live with that. Other men—great explorers—had missed the Pole. Even Sharpe and Carlsen. He would return; of course he would return to the Antarctic, explore the vast uncharted polar wasteland, discover what no man had before, make history. Viola would be with him. At last he was ready to concede she had earned her place on the expedition.

When they finished making love, he had thought with bitterness that she would return to Ian Crosbie. Now he remembered that out on the ice cap he had decided they must both divorce. Viola was his. *You are mine.* He had said those words when she lay in his arms, and for once she had not rejected them.

Viola was speaking again—of love—that she had always loved him, despite the conflict, despite knowing he loved Hermine. The charge startled him. Loved Hermine—Hermine in her frilly white nightgown flinching from his touch? How could he love that simpering doll when he knew what love between a man and a woman could be? He had long ago realized he had married out of his anger at Viola's recalcitrance.

He could not deny his love for his wife, thought Viola. "The photograph of Hermine, Byron." That rankled the most. "Horace told me about it. Each time we make love—afterward, I remember. You're never without it—the first thing you unpack when you make camp, the last you pack when you leave. Each night you look at her face, the image for your dreams. Her face, not mine."

"You think it's because I love Hermine so much?"

"What else could it be?"

Without a word, he picked up his backpack lying nearby in readiness for his departure. The photograph, as she expected, was at the top, where he could get to it easily. Now he was taking out the photograph, bringing it to her, holding it out. Why was he tormenting her? She accepted it unwillingly, recoiling with distaste at the sight of Hermine's pretty smile. The top of the frame was loose and, hardly thinking what she was doing, she pulled, and it came apart, and there was the photograph in her hand. The cardboard was oddly thick. And in that moment, even before she turned it over, she knew.

Looking up at Byron, she saw the love on his face. They had fought so bitterly over the years. But the rivalry had not been able to destroy their passion for one another. The last climactic act of the competition between them was played out and it no longer mattered who had won. Standing at the South Pole, she had longed to share the moment with him. And in truth she had done so. Without him, without the spur of the Tremaine Antarctic expedition, she would never have been there.

Here, on the desolate ice cap, where only hours before she had been cold and starving, she felt warm and full of life.

Viola turned over the photograph and saw the picture pasted to the back. There was the beach on Disko Island as in those long-ago days when love began. Byron was walking toward her and she held out her arms to him. Then and in all the years since. Reaching.

# Chapter Twenty-eight

COULD A SMALL TENT ABANDONED eight decades ago in an unknown location on a vast icebound continent be discovered? Flying with Bucky over Antarctica, I believed it could. Evidence of lost, even forgotten, expeditions has been found in this part of the globe, where nothing changes over decades, over centuries. In that tent I would uncover the fate of the all-women's expedition and the reason for Byron's silence—tragic no doubt, but reflecting no discredit on him. Even if Avery did continue his research into Crosbie and Viola and came upon the newspaper reports about the departure of the women's expedition, I could disarm him by revealing the truth to his television audience. Without quite knowing how it happened, I was accepting Bucky's contention that I would appear on "Avery Tells All." Not because I was interested in Avery and he in me, as Bucky insisted, but to guard my great-grandfather's reputation—and my own.

Considering Bucky's insouciance, I had expected the venture to collapse, but a sponsor was quickly found. Before I could have second thoughts, we were on our way to Christchurch, New Zealand. Upon arriving, I discovered to my surprise that everything had been arranged in advance. A plane equipped with both wheels and skis for landing on ice was waiting for us. The sponsor's name had been painted in huge letters on the side; if there was one thing Bucky understood, it was the payoff.

We flew to McMurdo Sound, landing on the sea ice, thick and solid in the early springtime, and spent the night at the research station. I could tell that the scientific staff expected me to share quarters with Bucky. As did he. I pretended not to perceive what was going on. Though I was drawn to him, I am not impulsive. My one impulsive act had been out of character for me and disastrous.

"I'm not Avery," Bucky said with his open grin. "I don't have any hidden motives. I don't want to get anything out of you."

"That's disingenuous. You brought me here because you think finding the lost expedition will make you look good on 'Avery Tells All.' " I could say anything to Bucky.

He only laughed. "I keep forgetting you're used to a bona fide hero. I can't figure out why you need me, though. How come Graham isn't here? I thought he'd do anything you asked him to."

What could I say? I shook my head.

"Sorry. I spoke without thinking. I guess I've made you feel bad."

Bucky had been tactless and I must feel bad. But somehow—and I could not imagine why—I did not.

Bucky kissed me then and I opened my mouth to him and ran my tongue over his crooked front tooth. Then I remembered Avery and drew back. He was not Avery; he did not insist.

At dawn we took off for the interior. We would not waste time in searching the area near McMurdo Sound, the most populated region on the continent. Had the tent been there, it would have been discovered long ago.

"Let's fly directly to the South Pole, Trixie, stock up on fuel at the American research station, and start out again from there."

The women could not have crossed the entire continent, and I was about to object when I realized that Bucky had undoubtedly promised the South Pole to the sponsor. And sure enough, a photographer was waiting when the plane landed on the compacted snow at the Amundsen-Scott South Pole Base three hours later. At least we did not lose much time there, spending barely an hour on the skiway. The plane's engines were kept running all the while, as restarting would be a formidable task in cold of fifty-eight degrees below zero. I have been told that planes are not supposed to land and take off when it is below minus fifty, but no one, it seems, ever refuses Bucky.

"I'd like to fly with you forever," he said when we were in the air again.

"I didn't think you wanted to do anything forever."

"Only to have a good time. I want that forever. Why don't you, Trixie? I like your intensity, but you don't ever let up. That's what comes of spending your time with high-minded heroes. I'm not that kind of hero. Why don't you take me on? Not for my history, not because I'm like Byron Tremaine. But because it'll be fun."

"I can't jump from one relationship to another."

"Relationship. You use such serious words. We're already friends. That's a relationship."

"You know what I mean."

"Why not be better friends?"

I imagined making love with Bucky. It would be so different from Ronald. So different from Avery. Lighthearted. But I have lived the high drama of Byron Tremaine's life for too long to be content with lightheartedness.

While Avery's seductive chitchat made me uneasy, Bucky's did not. I enjoyed talking like this with him, but we were here for more important matters. He was right about my using serious words. Where Byron Tremaine is concerned, I am a serious person. "What's our course, Bucky? Don't you think we should follow Tremaine's route? The more I think about his message, the likelier it seems that he crossed paths with the women's expedition."

"I don't think we'll find the tent near there, Trixie. Tremaine didn't go that way—not for the whole journey. At some point on the return from the Pole, he veered off. You see, I was taking my expedition along the route Tremaine described in his journal and there were landmarks he didn't mention, distances that were off by several miles. After a while, I realized he hadn't followed the course he said he had, the one he'd marked on his map."

Because he had been to the tent and wanted to conceal its location? Once again I thought of rape or another act of violence. Perhaps a few of the men were sent ahead of the others to reconnoiter and found the tent and the women. There they were, with no leader on the scene. Long deprived of sex, safe in the isolation of the Antarctic, what might they not have done to the women? Somehow Byron found out later; one or another might have broken down and confessed. I imagined how he must have felt. Bloodstains, signs of a struggle, the broken bodies of the women remained in the tent. I could believe that in the stress of the moment, desperate to conceal what his men had done, he decided to falsify the map so that future explorers would not find it. And once having done so, he was bound by that lie, no matter how he regretted it. At least he did not lie for himself, only for his men. Byron would never have carried out a deception for any lesser motive, and I could not allow Avery to imply that he had.

"Don't look so worried, Trixie. I think we should search for the route Tremaine really did take. If we were on foot, it would be impossible, but we can easily fly over the fifty miles to the west and then the fifty miles to the east of the route he described. He can't have gone farther off the map than that and still have reached the Pole."

"You knew all this before we ever left New York."

"I wouldn't set out to fly over an entire continent without the faintest idea of where to start looking." Bucky was not so feckless as he appeared.

Though we were high up, the air was so clear that I was able to see the icy surface below. I could capture the sense of how it must have been to traverse the continent on foot. There was a grandeur about it, yet a terrible loneliness. Not a seal or penguin was in sight on the surface, not a skua gull or petrel in the air. The monotony of the scene was broken occasionally by icebergs, strange wind carvings on the ice, the deep cracks of crevasses.

"I do see something, Bucky." My eyes were aching from the sun's brilliance reflected on the ice, but I was sure a black patch was standing out against the whiteness of the snow. Bucky brought the plane down to a lower altitude and circled back over the area. The black patch was more in evidence, but I could not tell what it was. "Let's land here and take a look."

"The surface is too broken and the wind is gusting; a plane like this could crash on landing."

"But I must get there, Bucky. I must."

Anyone else would have told me this was probably just a rock; the women could not have come so close to the Pole. Not Bucky. He understood that as Tremaine's descendant and historian, I had to take this seriously. "I'll radio the South Pole station to have a helicopter ready. They're expecting to hear from me." Once again I had underrated Bucky's planning abilities.

Barely two hours later, Bucky was putting the helicopter down a few hundred yards away from the patch of blackness. I was nervous now and Bucky took my mittened hand in his to help me climb out of the helicopter. The instant we stepped onto the ice, great gusts of wind attacked us, whirling us this way and that. I am too light in weight to withstand the Antarctic winds and feared being knocked down. Bucky grasped my arm and held me firmly, resisting the wind so we could advance in a fairly straight line. Every few yards we had to pause for me to catch my breath.

All at once we were out of the wind, sheltered by a semicircle of huge snow-covered boulders. And the patch was not a rock, but a tent—dark green rather than black. We could hear the wind howling a little distance away, but in this place all was quiet. I held my breath as we approached, no longer certain that I wanted to discover whether the tent had belonged to Viola Crosbie or to some other explorer. Now I was afraid to find the tragic remains of the Crosbie expedition—the bodies, frozen, unaltered over the decades. Nonetheless, I moved forward, apprehensive, yet resolute.

Snow had drifted around the bottom of the tent, but it was soft, and Bucky was able to push it away easily. I took the last few steps and lifted the flap. Bucky's hand was on my arm and even through the thickness of the parka, I could feel the reassuring pressure. The cold was biting and I was shivering violently. "We'll go in together."

I stepped from brilliant sunlight into the dimness of the tent. What light filtered through the canvas was an odd greenish gray. Instead of switching on my flashlight, I waited until my eyes accustomed themselves to the gloom. Gradually shapes within the tent became evident. In front of me were two narrow bunks set side by side. I was so convinced bodies must be lying there that I thought I saw them, but a second glance revealed the beds to be flat and empty. Now I did switch on my flashlight and let the beam play over the tent. No bodies lay anywhere. I looked about for evidence of a struggle, such as bloodstains or overturned furniture. Nothing was disarranged. There were no signs to identify the possessors of the tent, whether Viola Crosbie and her Amazons or some other explorers. Whoever had used the tent was long gone, and I would never know who it had been.

Just then I caught sight of a strip of ribbon lying beside my foot on the gray floorcloth—a torn banner, bearing the remains of a slogan: . . . tes for Wom . . . The Crosbie expedition had been here. I bent down and picked up what was left of the banner, my excitement at such a pitch that I could not call out to Bucky. The achievement of these women was almost beyond belief. Though they had failed to reach the South Pole, they came closer than any but the greatest explorers—Tremaine, Sharpe, and Carlsen.

"Trixie, look here." Bucky's voice was filled with enthusiasm. He was standing beside a table of sorts, formed of stacks of cartons. "I think we've found the records of the Crosbie expedition."

I walked quickly to the table and stood there looking down. My heart was beating rapidly. Here lay stacks of loose papers, notebooks, boxes of film and glass photographic plates, rocks, and an oddly shaped package labeled Fragile. Handle with the <u>Greatest</u> Care. Here lay the evidence of the women's fate, evidence that must clear the shadow from Tremaine's reputation. Standing in the deserted tent, I thought of the women who had been here before me and left their records for a future explorer to find. Those long-dead women could not have imagined eight decades would pass before someone came. Before I came.

"What do you think happened to the Crosbie expedition?" I asked, hoping cheerful Bucky could think of a favorable response.

"There's no point in guessing," he replied, and my heart sank. "The diaries will tell us what the women planned to do when they left the tent."

I picked up the first stack of papers and turned the beam of my flashlight onto the page. The writing was small and the ink faded.

"Come on, Trixie. You can't read that now. We've got to get out of here. It's so cold you're shivering. And so am I. We'll need an hour or more to pack up this stuff and get it all back to the helicopter."

Although I was desperate with impatience to read every word about the course of the expedition, I knew he was right. Using infinite care, Bucky and I packed the documents and fossils and set off for the helicopter. With the wind buffeting us, we had to make two trips. Bucky suggested I stay put while he went back and forth. "This climate is too tough for you."

For once I did not agree, and accompanied him; somehow the wind did not seem so brutal anymore. "Tonight I'll read all the papers," I told Bucky as we flew back to the South Pole station.

"Do you think you should be alone when you read them?"

My mind was on the journals, on the package marked Fragile that I was holding on my lap, on the discovery of the lost expedition, and I did not respond to his flirtatious remark.

I asked to be excused from dinner with the research station staff and went immediately to the small room assigned me. Bucky had brought in the expedition records and piled them on the bunk. The stack of loose papers caught my eye and I picked up the top one. The handwriting was the same as in the letters Viola Lambert had sent Byron Tremaine.

"This evening we will leave the tent and go out on the ice. It is the best way, the only way possible for us now."

The words that spelled out the end of hope had been written so many years before; yet as I read them now, I could share the despair Viola must have been feeling.

Riffling through the stack of loose papers, I observed that each page was dated. Cut from Viola's diary. I could not imagine why she had removed those pages, nor why entries for many of the days were missing. Even so, I quickly learned that the Crosbie expedition had set off for the South Pole from the Bay of Whales at approximately the same time Tremaine had left Cape Graham. "We must get there ahead of him," she wrote. The competition with Byron Tremaine—he had not thought it of sufficient importance to mention in his diary.

On an impulse I turned to the summer's day in January when Tremaine and three companions arrived at the South Pole. Yes, this page was here.

"Today—January 14, 1916—the all-women's expedition reached the South Pole."

I read it again, and then again, rubbing my eyes to clear my vision. For a moment I wondered if the emotions of the day had pushed me to the point where I was not able to grasp reality, and saw what was not there. But no. The words were clearly written. Desperately I searched for a logical explanation. Byron had presented incontrovertible evidence to back his claim—the compass readings and altitude calculations were in his diary; the photographs showed him at the Pole. Two parties of explorers could have arrived at the Pole on the same day only if they had joined forces for the final assault. But Viola did not mention the Tremaine expedition, and Byron's journal contained no reference to her. Somebody was lying.

Just then, with a great sense of relief, I remembered the interview with Viola reported in the English suffrage publication. She claimed credit for the fossil theory that Tremaine had conceived. What did I really know of this woman? She had lied once. It seemed likely that she was lying again. That seemed more plausible than any other explanation. And indeed the pages for January 13 and January 15 were missing.

Still, my hands were shaking when I picked up the next stack of papers. As I read, I was stunned by the overwhelming number of details given in the meteorological observations, compass readings, maps of uncharted regions. There was more here than in Tremaine's journal. Much more. Drawings and descriptions of fossils abounded, too, with an interpretation of their classification.

"In the course of our journey," wrote Viola, "we stumbled upon a mysterious ice-free valley where I discovered fossils of unbelievable antiquity."

The rocks Bucky and I had taken from Viola's tent were lying on the bunk and I turned them over to study the fossil imprints. They bore an uncanny resemblance to those Tremaine had brought back from his Antarctic expedition, and to others, long since lost, depicted in his journals. Yet no description of the dry valleys of Antarctica appeared in Byron's diaries.

"The greatest discovery of all is the jawbone of a creature that I believe preceded the dinosaur, a link between reptile and mammal. No remains comparable to these have been dug up anywhere else on earth; no one else knows such a creature ever existed."

I unwrapped the oddly-shaped package with the care mandated by the label and found within it a collection of bones and teeth darkened by the ages.

"That find alone would make my reputation, even if I had not conquered the South Pole."

The newspapers sneered at "Mrs. Crosbie's Folly." Viola's ambition, her challenge to Tremaine, were ridiculed. Was it possible that she had led her band of "Amazons" to the Pole? In an era when women were supposed to stay quietly at home? If so, this was a story for the ages and I wondered that it had never been told. Then I remembered that Byron had not wanted it to be told, and I trembled.

What had really happened on January 14, the date both Viola and Byron claimed the Pole? What had happened after that day to send Viola to her death on the ice? I had finished with the loose pages, and turned to the bound notebooks, hoping to find the answers, fearing what the answers might be. The first of the notebooks was in a different handwriting, ill formed, little better than a scrawl. Oddly, however, once deciphered, the phrasing was sophisticated. The first page carried the message, "For my son, David . . ." and I could not make out the last name. Then in the center of the page was one word, "EVADNE." Instantly recognizable—the name of the legendary dancer in the early years of the century. A mystery surrounded Evadne, I recalled: She had disappeared at the peak of her career. Feature articles appeared from time to time in magazines and newspapers; there had been a movie, a fictionalized biography. "What ever happened to the incomparable Evadne?" The Antarctic had happened. None of the articles had mentioned her having a son; it did not fit the legend.

"The men are not coming back for us." And as I read that, I realized that the two expeditions had met, and a heavy weight settled in my chest. "Even Viola accepts this now, though she insists they tried."

Evadne felt the blackest despair when Viola offered the records of the Crosbie expedition to Byron Tremaine. Should she perish on the ice cap, Viola declared, she knew he would present their claim and document it with this evidence. Present the evidence of the Crosbie expedition's success? Evadne could imagine the scene at the depot where Byron would be telling Horace to leave the women to their fate and travel with him to the coast and thence to New Zealand.

"Viola is enraptured by Byron Tremaine. Let her make love with him while I stand outside and hear them, but not hand him the proof of our achievement."

It was all but certain she would die with Viola in the tent or nearby on the ice. Lacking the records, the all-women's expedition would be lost forever. The men could adopt the entries and readings as their own. The rolls of film showing the women at the Pole? How easily can photographs be altered. Evadne's own figure, photographed in a studio in New York, had been superimposed on a view of the Parthenon and so presented in theatrical posters. The fossil findings? She observed Byron's interest in them; he had made few discoveries of his own—these would be his.

Leave the evidence in the tent, she pleaded with Viola; nothing decomposes in the frozen Antarctic. If they failed to return to New Zealand themselves, the tent and its contents would be found at a later date by a search party or by subsequent explorers.

Viola would not consider doing so. As a suffragette, she was convinced the success of the expedition would help win women the vote. The evidence must be presented when the claim was made, she insisted. Did Byron and Horace look triumphant? It seemed so to Evadne. If only she could get the records in her hands. And then the opportunity was proffered her. Wishing to spend a last hour with Byron in the sheltered area beside the tent, Viola asked Evadne to prepare the packages.

Viola's diaries were lying on the table; Evadne picked up the last volume and turned to the entries about the arrival at the Pole and the descriptions and drawings of the fossils. "I took out my pocketknife and very carefully cut out half the pages. Araminta had labeled the boxes holding the rolls of film, and again I kept half of the ones showing us at the South Pole."

Next she divided the fossils, holding out those rocks with the clearest imprints. The jawbone and teeth were to remain in the tent; Tremaine must not profit by them.

When she finished, Evadne felt as triumphant, she wrote, as when she had leaped across the stage to the frenzied applause of the audience. No one was applauding now. Later. Later they would applaud. Her son would applaud. And what did it matter that she would not be there to hear him?

"I said to Viola, 'Did you ever think it would end like this?' 'I never thought it would end.' That was her weakness."

The handwriting on the next page wavered and was even harder to decipher than the rest; I wished I could not read any of it. "He stopped at nothing. Robbed our depot, ate our food, and burned our fuel—then left us here to die rather than admit he had lost the competition and failed to reach the South Pole. And Viola still believes in his honor. Viola believes, she actually still believes Tremaine will present our claim to the world. Tremaine, the hero."

Now I knew who had lied, and why. At last I understood Byron's cryptic message, knew what he had feared, knew why Wally Padgett hated him.

I had often said that the Antarctic in its golden or heroic age was my obsession. But my obsession had been with Byron Tremaine, and gripped by that passion, I never questioned the legend. Proud to be his historian, I did not look for the fabled photograph of Hermine or investigate the heroic death. Until the terrible knowledge was forced upon me, I had denied Avery's contention that a true hero might be false and Antarctic exploration be a confidence game after all.

Byron had accepted the acclaim for being first at the South Pole; no, more than that, had demanded it. His entire life was dedicated to maintaining that lie. Bitterly I thought that *my* life had also been dedicated to that lie. How was I to live with the realization that to make his great reputation, he had covered himself with his lover's blood? And I had helped him conceal it.

"Trixie." Bucky was standing in the doorway. "You've been at this since six o'clock last night and it's two o'clock in the morning. You can finish reading on the trip home. We'll be leaving for McMurdo at eight." Six more hours. I did not know how I would get through this night, or any night.

"I have finished reading."

He looked at me quizzically and, seeing my expression, for once he was not smiling. I had to tell him, get it over with as quickly as possible. "Tremaine didn't reach the South Pole. Viola Crosbie did. He was in the tent, Bucky, and he left her and the other woman to die. Then he took her records and altered them to look as if they were his. Only he didn't get them all. Here are the rest."

I felt Byron's betrayal as if I were one of the women he had wronged. Bucky sat down next to me on the edge of the bunk and put his arms around me. I hid my face on his shoulder, not wanting to see his pleasant, open expression. He smoothed my hair, stroked my face.

"I never suspected anything. Even with all the things Avery told me. Even after hearing Wally Padgett on the tape."

"It was selfish to bring you here, Trixie. I knew there was something wrong, something ugly. There had to be. But I put it out of my mind when I saw how this could work for me on Avery's program. The opportunity was too good to pass up. That's how I manage."

"How did he get away with it? People knew about the all-women's expedition. Certainly Horace and the other men in the Pole party knew."

"They couldn't go against the leader's orders, Trixie. I've told you that. And the other men didn't lift a finger to help the women either. I should think they'd have been ashamed of their part in the whole thing."

"But the families. The backers. Why did nobody follow up?"

"Maybe nobody wanted to, Trixie. A bunch of suffragettes going to the Antarctic—most people probably thought they were crazies. Maybe they had no families or had quarreled over joining the expedition, and Viola might have put up the money herself."

"The newspapers should have written about the expedition; they reported the departure from New York Harbor."

Even as I spoke, I knew what had happened. Communications were primitive in 1915–1916; no television cameras followed the expeditions. Tremaine was a prominent man, and his father was a senator. Newspapers in those days would bow to their demands not to print the story. Moreover, columns were filled with war news, and readers had little interest in a women's expedition. Byron Tremaine satisfied the public demand for a hero.

"Does Avery know?"

"There you go, thinking him omniscient again." Bucky looked at the stack of documents, the fossils lying on the bunk beside us. "How could he? You've got all the evidence."

"I wish we had left it in the tent." A terrible wish, but I could say anything to Bucky. "This is glorious really. A group of women marched and skied all the way across the Antarctic ice to reach the South Pole. They were the first human beings on earth to stand there. I should rejoice for them. Instead, I wish we never found those documents."

"Why should anyone know we did, Trixie? It's between you and me. Let's keep it that way."

I felt the most terrible conflict, knowing I could make Viola Crosbie famous, and at the same time knowing that to do so was to damn my great-grandfather. Like Bucky, I am not that kind of hero. As Tremaine's last living descendant, I could not endure the thought of being the one to destroy his reputation. The documents had been lost for eighty years. *Let's keep it that way.* I did not know what to do, and then I realized that this was not the time for making so significant a decision. I was overwrought, exhausted. Later, after my return to New York, I would think it all over quietly and rationally.

"You'll be under fire on Avery's program, Bucky. How will you answer his charges about your expedition?"

"Not by telling him about the Crosbie expedition, Trixie. Don't worry. I can handle Avery. I'll make a confession; viewers love the confessional." Bucky made everything sound so easy.

"But you told me you wouldn't give Harney away."

"I said a confession; I didn't say it would be a true confession. I'll think up another reason for having lied about reaching the Pole. Maybe I was out of my mind with snow blindness or a vitamin deficiency. Something will come to me."

"How could he do it? I can't understand."

Bucky said he could understand easily. "Just think that it all happened in the Antarctic, Trixie, and men go crazy here, not just Ian Crosbie and Joe Harney. Anyone." His arm tightened around me.

Perhaps I was crazy in the Antarctic, too, because when Bucky moved the documents and fossils onto the floor and pulled me down on the narrow bunk beside him, I did not draw away. When he took me in his arms and pressed his hard, compact body against mine, I could tell that he was holding back, not wanting to rush me. But I could not hold back and clutched at him desperately, wanting to lose myself in him. Strange that I did not think about that serious word *relationship* or consider whether I would ever lie with Bucky again. What I was doing with him seemed the only thing to do. I did not want another kind of hero that night; I could not have borne my kind of hero. For once I was glad not to be with Ronald. All along I had seen Tremaine in him, but Tremaine had been nothing like Ronald. Tremaine had not been my kind of hero after all. Bucky's skin was hot in the cold room, clean, his hands so expertly caressing that for a little while I went beyond thought, forgot the tragedy of Byron Tremaine and Viola Crosbie.

We did not speak while making love, but afterward I told him the one thing I had believed I would never be able to reveal to anyone. I could say anything to Bucky. One sentence in Evadne's journal haunted me. I could destroy the page, but it would be with me always.

"If Byron Tremaine has his way, no word of the all-women's expedition to the South Pole will ever get out."

# Chapter Twenty-nine

TO THIS, I HAD DEVOTED my life. To him. Coming back into the house that had belonged to Byron Tremaine, to the room that was in the nature of a shrine to him, I was repelled by the medals, the framed front page of *The New York Times,* the replicas of fossil-imprinted rocks, the spectacular photographs at the South Pole. I saw them all and shuddered. Now I could tell that the famed photographs had been falsified. As Bucky's photographer explained, I saw what I wanted to see. I had found excuses for the inconsistencies—the different camera used for these pictures, the greater skill displayed by the photographer.

Byron had treasured the woman's likeness but left her to die, had stolen her life, stolen her achievements and made them his. And no one ever knew. No one? Now I remembered my great-aunt Susan had warned me against going to the Antarctic. Now I understood why she separated herself from Byron Tremaine, refused to join in the celebrations. I knew why she always opposed my absorption in my great-grandfather, urged me to *get on with my life.* Instead, I had given so much of myself to Byron Tremaine that I could not think what I was to do in the years ahead. Using my small talent to paint portraits of pretty women had been just a sideline.

I was impatient to speak of all this to my great-aunt and hastened to make my way to the nursing home. "I had to go to the Antarctic to discover the truth about Byron Tremaine. You knew it all along, didn't you, Aunt Susan? And you despised him, despised your father."

"No. It wasn't like that. Byron Tremaine was a tragic figure, Beatrix," she replied softly, the pauses between her words longer now. "And I have not joined in the ceremonies, because . . . because I do not belong there."

"Of course you do. What are you talking about?"

She reached out her shaking hand and wiped away my tears. "Look at me, Beatrix. Really look at me."

And in that moment the elusive resemblance that had haunted me became clear. An idealized, unconsummated passion, Ronald told me; his grandfather never touched Hermine. Another distortion of history.

"Yet Horace and Byron went to Antarctica together as if they were still friends." And in Antarctica they crossed paths with Viola Crosbie, and the scene for tragedy was set.

"They were friends, Beatrix. . . . It was the best part of them. Oh, there's so much you don't know about the Tremaine expedition, Beatrix. So much."

I thought of the deserted tent, sheltered from the gusting winds, and the records of the women's expedition. "No, Aunt Susan. I know everything about it. Everything."

As I was leaving, a nurse's aide stopped me with a manila envelope. "Your aunt wants you to have this." Her final instructions for the disposition of her body, I thought; old people like to make their wishes known. But when, at home, I opened the envelope, I found a thick sheaf of heavy-grade stationery, stiff with age, and clipped to it a letter in my aunt's wavering script.

My dear Beatrix. The three people who played a part in those terrible happenings of long ago are dead, and many times I thought to destroy these pages. When I am gone, who is left to care? You? Until recently I did not think you wanted to know. You appeared content with maintaining your fantasy of Byron Tremaine's life. But when you left for the Antarctic, I feared what you might find, and I would not have despair and disillusionment spoil your life. There has always been something fragile about you, Beatrix, but over the past months, since that television producer opened the closed door to the past, you have been gaining strength. I would not have you slip back.

Gaining strength? Because of Avery? Because he forced me to defend Tremaine? It seemed absurd, yet I could not deny that because of Avery, I had gone to London alone, flown to the South Pole with feckless Bucky. I miss Ronald, but not because I need his care. Why, even Aimee comments that I seem more independent.

You think you discovered the truth in the Antarctic, know all there is to know about Byron Tremaine. What he did and felt, what manner of man he was, and what forces shaped his life and actions. You think you know, and are appalled by that knowledge. But there is much you do not know.

I put aside the letter and turned to the first sheet of the attached pages. The heavy paper was yellowed and the blue ink faded. The handwriting was small, with each letter formed perfectly, the lines straight, the margins even. Before reading the salutation, I guessed that Hermine was the author.

My dear daughter Susan. To know the truth and live a lie is a tragic fate. It is my fate, and by now I am convinced that the truth will never emerge of itself. We have been bound by our loyalty to one another to remain silent, a loyalty that has transcended Byron's death. Let it go. I struggle with myself and I cannot let it go. And so I bequeath the truth to you, my only surviving child. Tell it if you will—or continue the concealment that has been a part of my life.

Strange that of the three of us responsible for what happened on the polar ice cap in 1916, it was Byron—the least guilty—who could not live with it. But perhaps he could not bear to remain any longer in a world where Viola was not. It is hard for me to believe my cold, insensitive husband was capable of loving anyone so much. But his suffering is proof that he did. He never admitted that love to me. It was not Byron's custom to confide in me. We never knew what to say to one another.

The world believes Byron Tremaine was the first explorer to reach the South Pole, the first to discover the prehistory of the Antarctic continent. He was honored, decorated, idolized. How was it possible for the truth to be concealed, a lie to be taken as reality? I will tell you.

An apologia for Byron Tremaine. I could predict the tenor of the letter. Fearing the fraudulence of his claim would someday be revealed, Hermine had the defense ready. Well, she was his wife after all, had lived the pretense of a happy marriage to sustain his reputation. I did not want to read her excuses for him, but I could not toss the letter aside unread.

Sighing, I continued. Hermine wrote of passion in that small, neat handwriting. Yet passion there had been.

Horace Graham was the only wonderful thing that ever happened to me. The sweetness of those early times when he came to me is with me still. I did not feel guilty then, weighing his love against what I sometimes thought was Byron's dislike of me—not of me personally perhaps, just of my not being Viola. No, it did not seem like sin. But sin it was. And that sin was at the root of the tragedy that followed.

Horace was a good man, loyal to Byron and to me. He was too loyal. That has been my torment. I was to blame. It would have been different had I refused to let Horace touch me. And I could have. In these modern times, Susan, you think that love between a man and a woman must be consummated physically. It was not so when I was young. Had I declined to allow Horace to make love to me, he would have respected my virtue and the tragedy would not have been played out. My love! Of the three of us, I bear the greatest guilt.

The greatest guilt? I thought of the pages in Evadne's journal damning Tremaine.

Our love brought on the catastrophe that was inevitable, I sometimes think, from the moment Horace smiled at me—a man smiling at the woman he desires. I did not recognize the meaning of the smile at first. How could I? Byron never smiled at me in that manner, and there had been no other man in my life.

To understand what happened, you must understand how Horace came to hate Viola Lambert. It was because of me. Horace was convinced that Viola drained the life out of my marriage, out of me, believed she had bewitched Byron like a siren of mythology, stolen his love from me, that but for Viola, Byron would have been happy with me. But for Viola, he would have been the perfect husband as he was the perfect hero, and made me happy. Horace was selfless in that way, wanted what was best for me and for his closest friend, was willing to sacrifice himself for that. He hated Viola for making a travesty of that sacrifice, hated Viola far more than I ever did.

Byron's simpering doll, and Horace's great love.

Oddly, Byron and Viola had met—fallen in love, I must believe—long before I knew him. Horace told me Byron had proposed and she had refused, saying she would not marry a man who sought to dominate her. He did not believe her, saw it as part of the game she played to keep Byron under her spell. When she married someone else, an explorer from the Sharpe expedition, Horace thought Byron would be free of her. But even then, she did not let him go.

Once, I asked Horace to describe Viola to me. "She was like a picture painted in colors that were too bright," he answered. Too bright: If that were so, I have been like a picture drawn in pastels. I sometimes think of Viola and what I have been told of her vitality, her energy. I can imagine her rushing through her brief life with such desperate determination to succeed, so determined that no one—not even Byron Tremaine, whom I am convinced she loved—could stop her.

The rest of that page was blank, and then on the next, Hermine began her story with an account of the Tremaine expedition's triumphal return to New York Harbor on a summer's day in 1917:

The governor of the state and the mayor of the city were among the huge welcoming crowd. The children and I were placed right next to them. Horace's son, too, was there in the company of the aunt who had the care of him. He was a handsome boy, just a few years older than you were then, Susan. I had never seen the two of you together before and was impressed by the resemblance.

As Byron stepped onto the dock, all eyes were on him. Only I was not entranced, dreading the homecoming, as I had learned to dread earlier homecomings, when we would be together as husband and wife. I was glad the presence of the children distracted the attention of the journalists and photographers who might otherwise have seen how intently I was gazing not at Byron, but at Horace Graham. I was shocked at the change in him. He appeared drawn, exhausted, could barely summon a smile in greeting his son. I longed to comfort him, but weeks were to pass before I saw him alone.

During that time Byron was constantly feted for his conquest of the Pole, and I was always at his side, the admiring, adoring wife. I was not pretending admiration; I did respect his courage and achievement. The pretense lay in the adoration. He pretended, too. What a loving face Byron turned to me when others were watching. An idyll, people said, envying me. The newspapers and magazines were filled with articles about the expedition; publishing companies were competing for the rights to Byron's diaries. Only a dramatic, charismatic figure like Tremaine could take attention away from the war news. First at the South Pole, he was the quintessential hero. Everyone knew, marveled at the way he overcame the obstacles placed in his way in Antarctica. The avalanche might have fallen in the Adirondack Mountains, so frequently was it described. His scientific achievement was hailed, as the fossils he had gathered on the journey and carried across the ice with backbreaking effort were altering long-held perceptions of the prehistory of the world. The field of paleontology was forever changed.

Yet no sooner was he out of public view than Byron's mood became dark. I believed it was the aftermath of so hazardous a journey. As a father, he was not unkind to you, Susan, but distant. Sometimes I thought he had an instinct that you were not his child. I hoped that Horace's affection for you made up to some degree for this deprivation. Horace used to say he had to love you when you possessed my eyes and complexion, yet oddly—he thought it odd—the facial contours of his mother. Only your brother, in truth your half-brother, commanded Byron's attention, and he spent hours holding forth the lure of exploration, of heroism, inspiring our son to follow in his footsteps. It made me uneasy from the start. The child was not strong, never would be, was more suited to a scholarly life. But Byron never listened to me; nor did Junior. How could the boy resist so charming a father?

One evening when Byron appeared a trifle less preoccupied, I asked him what happened to the Crosbie expedition, recalling he had spoken of it before leaving for the Antarctic. I still marveled that any woman would have the courage to fling out a challenge to a man like him. Viola was a suffragette, that much I had learned from Byron, and was insisting that winning the race to the Pole would win women the vote. I did not believe that to be her motive. She was a woman who would not be dominated and her rivalry with Byron was behind the competition. It is to his credit that he tried to stop her from so insane a course, but she would not be deflected. Byron flushed at my question and muttered something, so I assumed the expedition came to grief. That was the likeliest, perhaps the only possible outcome. I knew—Horace was unable to keep it from me—that Byron had loved Viola Crosbie, and her death must be very painful to him. Still, the silence surrounding the fate of her expedition baffled me.

It was not until at last Horace and I were together, clasped in one another's arms, that the true story began to unfold. On that afternoon and many others to follow, he laid bare one horror after the other until I knew all. There were many times when I wished Horace had not told me, but of course he could not keep it from me.

Listening to Horace, I might myself have been on that all but unimaginable continent of ice, howling winds, and fierce cold. A world where the difference between life and death lies in a wind just a little too strong, a cold just a few degrees lower than can be borne, an injured foot, a few biscuits, a slab of chocolate, a cup of oil: So little to mean so much.

The ordeals endured by the Tremaine expedition were well known, and Horace did not trouble to repeat them, beginning his tale with Byron's decision to make the assault on the Pole accompanied by only three men—Horace, Edward Pitman, the photographer, Charles Smithers, the strongest of the expedition members, and a boy. Wally Padgett did not want to go on to the Pole; he was afraid. He had volunteered for the expedition to get away from home, had seen it as a lark. Now he begged to be allowed to return with the others to the base camp, which Byron had named Cape Graham in Horace's honor. But none of them handled the dogs as well. Byron smiled, put his hand on Wally's shoulder, said, "You'll go for me, my brave boy."

Horace thought the decision to continue was a mistake, but could not dissuade Byron. Soon food and fuel were all but gone, and Horace was venturing out each night with Wally to hunt the emperor penguin in vain. At last, his strength failing, Horace came upon a cairn of rocks, a flag planted firmly in its midst. Explorers mark their depots in that fashion, but neither Sharpe nor Carlsen had gone this way. Then he remembered Shackleton's expedition of 1907–1909. This had been the route taken in the first season, when the depots were laid. The following year Shackleton was forced to alter his course and never returned to the depot; the supplies must still be there.

With a burst of speed, Horace skied to the cairn, pushed aside the rocks, and saw the cartons—oil, paraffin, pemmican, biscuits, coffee, chocolate, lime juice, raisins, woolen socks, fur mittens. It was all he could do to keep from tearing the cartons apart with his hands then and there. A feeling of gratitude toward Shackleton came over Horace. He signaled to Wally to come up with the sledge to begin loading the supplies that would save their lives.

As the boy approached, eyes widening in wonder, Horace suddenly saw what Wally was seeing, what he had been too overwrought to observe before—a slogan on the flag almost but not quite obliterated by the snow: Votes for Women. A few cartons, he now noticed, were marked with crayon, 1914, and several bore the label Crosbie Expedition. Some of the fuel was of a kind that had come into use only two or three years previously; it was unknown in 1907. Horace was speaking so rapidly that I could hardly understand him, as if each word were painful to him.

A sense of the blackest despair came over Horace while he stood beside the cairn in the cold bright light, with the boy beside him. This was Viola Crosbie's depot, and now he saw that the depot was not untouched. Her expedition must have passed this way on the outward journey to the Pole, picked up a portion of the supplies, and left the remainder for the return trip. He could not take the food and fuel.

But surely Viola would never return here. No woman could survive on the ice cap. It was a miracle she had gotten this far, impossible that she should go all the way to the Pole and back to the depot. The supplies were his for the taking. Still, Horace was half inclined to pile up the rocks again and turn away. What if, against all odds, Viola did return to the depot and find it empty? Well, even then it was her life or Byron's. There was no question in Horace's mind as to whose life was of greater value. Byron was his closest friend, a man with a great destiny to fulfill. And he had betrayed Byron by making love to me. That was when I first realized the dreadful consequences of our passion.

Why should they die because of Viola, the woman who seduced Byron, made him withhold his love from me? Horace had never hated her so much.

"How can I make you understand how it was, Hermine? As I speak of it, my action appears heinous, inhuman. But then I was starving and starving men do frightful things. The history of Antarctic exploration is replete with such depravity. I could tell you of one man killing another for a handful of biscuits—worse than that, of cannibalism. And our situation was hopeless. Looking for the emperor penguin—I might as well have sought the bluebird.

"Terrible as it seems now, I do not think any man in those dread circumstances would have behaved differently." Horace paused then, and said softly, "Except for one man: Byron Tremaine. He would have died first. I knew that and knew, too, that Byron must never learn what I was doing."

I tried to understand what had driven Horace to commit such an act. Did he lose his moral sense to the hunger, cold, exhaustion, and unremitting fierceness of the Antarctic climate? Were these cause enough? I realized then that had he not hated Viola Crosbie because of me, he would not have taken her food and her fuel. I, too, was to blame as surely as if I had been standing beside him at the depot.

Wally opened one of the cartons, pulled out a box of raisins, and scooped them into his mouth. He looked like such a child, was a child. Horace knew he must make everything clear and ordered Wally not to tell Tremaine. Preparing to load the sledge, Horace took out his knife and cut off the part of each carton marked with the date or the name. Horace was never able to forget the way Wally had stared at him then. He pointed to the boy's full mouth. "Just a couple of raisins." Wally's voice trailed off; Horace was never able to forget that either. *Just a couple of raisins.* I have not eaten raisins since he told me of that.

"She's never coming back this way," Horace said firmly, and seeing Wally hesitate, told him that if he knew what was good for him, he would remain silent. What else could Horace do? Sullenly, Wally helped him cut off the labels, obliterate the markings, and load the sledge. It was too heavy for the dogs, so each of them took a harness and pulled as well.

That night, back in the tent, when Mr. Smithers ladled out bowls of thick hoosh, Horace retched and rushed outside. Just the smell of the rich food he had brought back from the depot made him ill. It might have been the smell of death.

Shackleton's depot: Byron accepted the falsehood without question. Why should he not have done so? He trusted Horace implicitly.

Some days later Byron fell and sustained a serious leg injury, forcing the decision to turn back. For a moment I did not comprehend what Horace was telling me, and then I knew and was shattered by that knowledge. Byron Tremaine had not been first at the South Pole; he had not reached it at all. Lies, all lies! The recognition of the scientific organizations and the adulation of the public were based on a false premise. His black moods were now explained; I had not suspected, could not possibly have suspected, their cause. My husband: I did not love him, but I had honored him as a hero. I waited, trembling, for the rest of the story.

Sorrowfully, the men began the long march back to Cape Graham. They had not been long under way when they caught sight of the dark canvas of a tent, startling against the whiteness of the snow. In great excitement, Byron rushed thither, and inside found Viola with a single companion, the famed dancer, Evadne. She was frail but alive. Horace could have wept with relief. However, later Byron told how he had dreamed of meeting Viola on the ice cap, thought of it from the moment she flung out her challenge. With what bitterness did Horace hear those words with their clearly stated indifference to me.

To his dismay, Viola was smiling at him as if they were friends as once in Greenland. Her body was wasted, but she was still so vivid. I could imagine how she looked: *Like a picture painted with colors that were too bright.* Her coppery hair gleamed in the dimness of the tent, her blue-violet eyes were deeply shadowed, but shining. He could not blame his friend. She had turned her eyes on Byron and he had been helpless against her.

Exposed on the ice cap, starving, battered by the wind, worn by the cold, convinced that Viola would never reach the depot, Horace did not foretell that his action was to cause such suffering. Seeing her now so weak, he was appalled.

Then came the triumphant disclosure that the women had reached the South Pole. I did not want to believe it. "She had the evidence, Hermine, the proofs that she had been there." Byron had turned back. Viola had been first at the South Pole, the first to raise the American flag.

Shock and horror seized me. That Byron lied about conquering the Pole had seemed intolerable to me, but this was a far greater deception. Viola's fame should have reached all four corners of the globe, even if she did not live to return to civilization. I knew why it had not.

Yet I could not help but feel compassion, too. Byron was the hero, had always been the hero, and conquering the Pole was his lifelong ambition. How terrible it must have been for him to learn Viola had outstripped him, garnered the victory. I wondered that he could have borne it. Then I realized he had not borne it. With Horace's collusion, he had lied and cheated, broken the code he claimed to live by. Even so, I ached for his misery on that day. He was my husband whatever he did. Still, I wondered how I was to face Byron that evening and on all the evenings to come, sitting across from him at dinner, lying beside him in bed, always pretending ignorance.

Horace's suffering as he spoke was so acute that I sought to conceal my agony at his disclosure. I wished I could put my hands over my ears to deafen myself to his words.

The other woman, Evadne, took up the tale of the journey back from the Pole, starting with the snowquake that must have buried the flagpoles and the igloo containing the record of their arrival at the exact location. Fortunately, the expedition photographer had filmed the scene so that the world would know the suffrage banner had flown beside the American flag at the Pole. All the while Horace waited, dreading the moment when she would reveal how they came upon the depot and found it empty. Byron was stunned when Viola then accused him of robbery, stunned and offended, too, at the suggestion that he could have been so corrupt.

"They were Shackleton's depots," Byron declared. "You saw that they were Shackleton's, did you not?" Horace nodded. What else could he do? Byron was able to convince Viola he had not known the supplies in the depot were hers. Indeed he had not, so his words rang true and she believed him.

Horace was hesitant about telling me what followed then, but I could guess and assured him it did not matter to me. Nor did it. There was no love between Byron and me. I felt no jealousy at learning that Viola sat up then, holding out her arms to Byron, ready to embrace him. Horace walked out of the tent and stood outside in the cold dry air, thinking she had mesmerized Byron once again. Horace believed her disingenuous, desirous of binding Byron to her again. She needed him now, and would use him. "I could not stand it," said Horace. "I had given you up for him. I had been without you for so long, and I thought that I would never see you again, never make love to you again. Every night in Antarctica, I imagined how it would be to return to you, to make my hands meet around your tiny waist, see your sweet smile." That was the loving way he spoke to me.

The plan devised by Viola and Byron appeared to Horace to be doomed from the outset, but he was guilty, so he remained silent. The women, too frail to travel as yet, would wait in the tent, strengthening themselves with the food left behind. The men were to go to the depot and separate there—Byron and Mr. Smithers to journey directly to the Bay of Whales, Horace and Mr. Pitman to return for Viola and her companion. Byron had objected, as he wanted to go back for Viola himself, but Horace convinced him of the unwisdom of that course. His leg injury was not healed and he could travel but slowly. Whoever reached New Zealand first would announce Viola's achievement. The journals, photographs, and fossils necessary to prove her claim would be divided between them for safety. Byron, recovered from his first shock, gave his promise as it was honorable to do, and Horace did the same. When I heard of this, a shiver shook my body, knowing of honor lost.

Wally pleaded to be allowed to go the shorter way with Byron, whining that the other was too dangerous.

Thus they departed the tent and a few days later arrived at the depot, where they divided the supplies and the evidence Viola had pressed upon them. The men clasped hands for the last time, and Byron and Mr. Smithers departed. Soon their figures were lost in the ice mist.

Mr. Pitman was quiet; he never talked much, but Horace could see he was calculating the number of cartons of supplies against the probable length of the journey. They were to go all the way back to the tent, set out once more, their pace slowed by the women. As this depot was now empty, they must continue to the next one, eighty miles farther on, for more supplies. This journey might well prove fatal, but Horace had given his promise.

Moving rapidly over the slick ice surface, they were taken by surprise when the dog team suddenly dropped out of sight into a crevasse. Three hours of desperate effort were spent pulling dogs and sledge back to the surface. The route they were following was broken with a chain of crevasses. They would have to make a detour, which would cost them at least a day.

Mr. Pitman spoke forcefully for the first time. "We'll die on the trail, Horace. We can't save the women either. Too many days have been lost. They won't still be alive by the time we get back to their tent. It's not possible for women to endure such privation. You saw how emaciated they were, and though we left as much food as we possibly could, it wasn't enough to make up for weeks of starvation. We should turn around and head for the base camp while there's still a chance of getting there."

At that moment, Wally interrupted. Throughout the journey he had been sniveling and complaining, but now he said they must go back. They had given their promise, and what if the women were not dead?

Wally was just a boy and did not understand that they must surely die themselves. In Byron's absence, Horace was responsible for his men, more responsible than for Viola and Evadne. Whatever his contribution to the women's plight, they should not have been in the Antarctic at all. Viola had been warned against it often enough; Byron had tried to dissuade her. Byron's son and daughter were eagerly anticipating his return, while no one was waiting for Viola and surely not for the dancer.

Horace had a momentous decision to make then. In the desolation of the Antarctic, that decision seemed justified—though even then, not morally right. Later what tormented him was that he had acted with certainty in a world where there is no certainty, on a continent where the bizarre is more common than the commonplace. He had not listened to Wally because he never listened to the boy before. This time, however, perhaps Wally had been right. Might Horace have found the women alive had he gone back? Might he have been able to bring them to the base camp? And saddest of all, might it not have been better for him to have died in the attempt? No, that he would not believe. It was necessary for him to go on living, to guarantee Tremaine a place in history, and he had done it.

Horace broke my heart when he told me that. I trembled at the thought of all the years I must live through, knowing of his guilt. It was my guilt, too. I was secretly glad he had abandoned the women. Had he not, he would have died himself, and that was not to be borne. Neither, however, could I bear the knowledge of Viola and Evadne waiting for him, dying in the tent. That would always be between us, holding us together, yet driving us apart. How could I look at him without thinking that somewhere on the desolate ice cap lay the bodies of the women, protected by the cold, unaltered by time, waiting to be found? And what then? It would have been easier had I not loved Horace so much.

As he turned north, the direction away from the tent, Horace realized that inevitably he must overtake Byron, who would be traveling slowly because of the leg injury. He would have to face Byron and confess he had not returned for Viola. That he could not, must not, do. Byron was so ensnared by the woman that he might make the insane gesture of turning back himself. The confrontation must be postponed until it was reasonable for Horace to say he had gone to the tent only to find the women dead. Before the episode at the depot, he had never lied to Byron, and now it seemed that lie must be piled on lie. Yet if he did not lie, Byron would never know a moment's peace of mind again.

This was Antarctica and no claim he made could be disproven. Mr. Pitman had as good reason as he to conceal the truth, and Wally would be ordered to keep quiet. All that was needed was time, which was easily arranged. Instead of following Byron's route to the Bay of

Whales, Horace would journey to Ross Island, to the Tremaine expedition's base camp that bore his name.

The sky had been lowering and heavy with snow to the south, but as they turned north, the direction leading them away from the tent, away from Viola, it was clear. In all his months in the Antarctic, Horace had never before experienced such beautiful weather. Glorious shades of reds and oranges and strange shades of green played over the sky as the daylight faded earlier each day and left them in a soft, gentle gray world. The pressure ridges of ice created fantastical sculptures resembling creatures of no form known on earth. The ice surface was slick and hard, and the skis and the sledge runners glided effortlessly. The temperature was low, but not so low that the breath condensing froze their eyelashes and the hairs of their beards. They marched nineteen miles on one day and twenty-one the next and the one after that. Horace went on, as if in a dream, disregarding the past and not thinking of the future.

Only as they approached Ross Island did Horace's spirit of euphoria fade. He would have hung back if he could. The men who had remained at Cape Graham greeted him with excitement, which dampened when they discovered Byron's absence. This was the moment to tell of Viola, but the knowledge that he had abandoned her weighed too heavily upon him and he could not bear to speak of her. There was time; his promise was to present the claim in New Zealand, and he would do so. Therefore, he merely said that Byron was injured and thus, with Charlie Smithers, had taken the shorter, easier route to the Bay of Whales. The two of them would overwinter there in a camp left some years earlier by the French explorer, Charcot. Thus began the deception. At the invocation of Charcot's name, Mr. Pitman looked up, startled but relieved. He felt no desire to reveal what had happened. Horace and Mr. Pitman were pressed for details. Horace was silent, but Mr. Pitman thought to tell that neither Carlsen nor Sharpe had reached the exact location of the South Pole. No one doubted that Tremaine was the first explorer to conquer the South Pole.

Horace had expected to overwinter at Cape Graham, but the return journey was accomplished with such rapidity that the harbor was not yet locked in ice and they were able to embark immediately for New Zealand on the *Polar King*. During the long, slow journey through the thickening ice pack, Horace had his first opportunity to read Viola's journals. They were so clearly written and well organized that he was able to skim rapidly to the days of late December, when the four women were close to the Pole, and then to early January, when they discovered that Sharpe and Carlsen had not preceded them and journeyed on to reach the goal. However, he was discomfited to find that the entries for the relevant time period were incomplete, jumping from one date to another two or three days later. The reason soon became evident; whole pages were missing, meticulously snipped out of the book. Byron must have the missing pages; yet Horace felt uneasy about the furtive nature of the act.

He had little interest in fossils, but now he was curious and took out the heavy rocks one by one and the bottles containing specimens. He remembered the rapt face Viola used to lift from her microscope in Greenland. Later he came to think her rapture over ancient organisms unwomanly, her desire to receive credit unreasonable. When Byron had been writing the scientific papers on the Greenland expedition, he remarked on the clarity of Viola's exposition. Each imprint, each organism was drawn with exactness on the page, accompanied by its classification and characteristics, the location of the find, and an analysis of what the discovery told of the prehistory of the area. But here again, a number of entries were lacking, and in some cases, the detailed descriptions applied to fossils that were not in the bundle. He remembered Viola speaking with passion about her greatest find, the remains of a creature she described as a protomammal living before the age of dinosaurs, but nothing about such a beast appeared in his part of the journal, and no ancient bones were in the package. Byron must have that specimen, too; there was no other place it could be.

When they had been at sea a few days, Mr. Pitman signaled Horace to follow him into the darkroom. At first, Horace could see virtually nothing, but then Mr. Pitman lit the acetylene gas burners and just enough light came through the shading screens to show a series of prints hung up to dry on a line over the porcelain, lead-lined sink. After the first glimpse, despite the dim light, Horace knew that never in his life had he seen photographs like these. They displayed an icy landscape, stark, harsh, desolate, yet radiant with a beauty unlike any other in the world. Captured in these scenes were the drama, courage, and adventure of exploration, captured here was the dream made reality. The joy on the women's faces was luminous.

Viola dominated the photographs, her vitality filling the bleakness around her. She was smiling and her arms were outstretched, reaching, reaching for the Pole, where the suffrage banner was hanging next to the American flag. Beside her was the dancer with her graceful figure and classic features, and a strange-looking creature with a horribly disfigured face twisted into a grin. Horace had thought Ed Pitman's photographs outstanding, but now he saw they lacked the artistry displayed by the unknown photographer.

As he gazed at another even more breathtakingly beautiful picture of Viola and Evadne, Horace said sadly, "I would sell my soul to have Byron standing at the Pole in place of Viola Crosbie, sell my soul to be beside him there."

The tedious journey continued, with little to break the monotony. One day the captain told Horace of an odd story circulating on ship board. The seamen were saying that Wally, down in the hold, insisted the expedition had never reached the Pole. He told some garbled story about women on the ice cap. No one believed him, of course, seeing him as merely a disgruntled boy trying to gain attention with fantastic imaginings.

Standing on the deck as the ship approached Port Chalmers, Horace could make out a crowd, a band, Welcome signs, and a throng of journalists waiting at the harbor. Everything had been planned in advance, two years in advance, by Horace to celebrate Tremaine's victory at the Pole. As he walked down the gangplank into the waiting crowd, Horace knew this was the moment to tell of the Crosbie expedition. Yet he did not see how he was to step off the boat into that cheering mass of people and admit failure. It would be seen as Byron's failure. The decision was made without his having fully perceived that he had made it. The celebration fell flat with Tremaine absent, and the crowd soon dispersed.

In his room in the boardinghouse that night, Horace could hardly believe he had let the false impression stand, and resolved to set the record straight. This decision made, he was able to sleep the night. The next day, however, he discovered the report that Byron was first at the South Pole had already gone out by wireless to newspapers in major cities throughout the world. How could he issue a denial now?

Still, that was what he would have to do. Why had he not spoken out in timely fashion?

While he was composing the announcement, Mr. Pitman came to his room. "Why should they ever find out, Horace? Viola is dead. Claiming the South Pole won't do her any good and it will ruin us—and Tremaine. His career as well as ours will be at an end." It was worse than that. The taking of supplies from the depot and leaving Viola and the famous dancer in the tent would be blamed on Byron. Horace's reputation must be destroyed, but no one would believe he had acted on his own. That was reason enough to persevere with the concealment. "But Ed, you're overlooking the fact that everything will come out when Byron returns next spring with the women who were left at the base camp on the Bay of Whales."

"If Viola were alive, of course he'd have to tell the whole story," Mr. Pitman responded. "But how do you know what Byron will do now that she's gone? I think he'll back us up. It's not just for himself, you know. But for us, all of us. A cloud would hang over Byron's son, too."

"And mine," added Horace in misery; he had almost forgotten how great the repercussions were to be.

"As for the survivors of the Crosbie expedition," continued Ed, "no one will believe them any more than they do Wally."

"The scientific organizations will be demanding evidence of our reaching the Pole, and that we cannot give, whereas the record of what Viola did exists. The entries in her journals, though my set is incomplete, give meteorological observations and compass readings establishing that the all-women's expedition arrived at the Pole. Why, the photographs are proof enough."

"Let me show you something, Horace." Mr. Pitman then took out a folder of photographs. There were the magnificent pictures of the Crosbie expedition at the South Pole—except that the figures in the most dramatic of them were unmistakably Byron and Horace, and the banner with its Votes for Women slogan was gone from its position beside the American flag.

"What have you done?"

"A little photographic magic. It came to me when you said you'd sell your soul to see Tremaine at the Pole and to stand beside him there."

Horace knew then that Tremaine's reputation might be saved, after all. Viola would not be benefited by the truth nor harmed by the deception. He could revise the entries in his own journals, adding whatever might be gleaned from Viola's writings and from the earlier diaries of Sharpe and Carlsen. Byron's journals would still be demanded, but these would serve for the present. By the time Byron returned, it would be too late for a denial. Horace believed Mr. Pitman: Now that Viola was gone, why should Byron deny anything?

The plot was laid. From then on, there could be no going back.

The following spring Horace returned to Antarctica on the *Polar King* and found Byron and Mr. Smithers in dire straits at the Bay of Whales. The two men had a fearsome story to tell; they had arrived in the autumn to be met by devastation. Little was left of the base camp, and the women were missing. After surveying the scene, they determined that the catastrophe had resulted when chunks of the ice cap sheared off and fell into the bay, carrying women and buildings with it. The women's ship, the *Explorer,* was nowhere in sight; perhaps it had come and gone. They must perforce overwinter and hope for rescue in the spring. Enough timber was left scattered about to allow construction of a crude hut, and several cartons of supplies had been spared.

Byron had expected to see Viola and, crushed with disappointment at her absence, feared she was still weakened by her ordeal. "Do you at least bring me letters from her?" Horace had carried the mail from New Zealand and there were letters from me. Byron did not ask about those. Horace was offended, but I could understand. My letters meant no more to Byron than his stiff, formal missives meant to me. I would not have them included among his collected correspondence and threw them away after a quick reading; I supposed he did the same with mine.

Horace was then forced to speak of Viola's death, to tell the prepared lie that he had gone back to the tent and found the two bodies. Byron accepted Horace's account. Why should he not have done so?

Devastated by Viola's loss, Byron remained in seclusion throughout the journey to New Zealand. Alone in his cabin, perhaps he revisited the past, wished he had not married me but made a life with Viola. In my heart, I wished that, too. We would all have been spared much grief. As the voyage drew toward its end, Horace was forced to intrude on Byron's solitude. Byron was stunned to learn Horace had not presented Viola's claim. It was the only time he expressed anger toward his friend. A promise broken: How could Horace have done it? Hers was the victory, and she had been convinced her exploit would help the suffrage movement. He would set the record straight immediately upon his arrival at Port Chalmers.

"Too late, Byron. What has been set in motion cannot be halted. It can't matter to Viola now, and it will destroy your future. Everyone will think you were involved in the deceit."

Byron declared himself indifferent to the consequences. He would reveal all and present the evidence entrusted to him and to Horace by Viola. Horace had never pushed himself forward, but now he made the one appeal that Byron could not reject. "Think what will happen to me if you do present Viola's claim, Byron. Everyone will know I lied. I will be disgraced. Henceforth, every word I speak will be disbelieved. Who will ever want to do business with me? Not only your career but mine will be over. This story will stick to me for the rest of my life. And whatever I did, I did for you, Byron."

He could see he had shaken Byron's resolve and despised himself, but once any part of the truth was revealed, the rest must inevitably follow. Eventually the abandonment of Viola would come out and break Byron's heart.

"How could our claim to the Pole have been accepted without proof?" Then Horace had to confess there had been proof, Viola's proof, altered to fit their claim. More would be needed to satisfy the august scientific organizations, but this had sufficed in the interim. He brought out the photographs, the most convincing part of all. Byron gazed at them in despair as he came to understand the extent of the duplicity. "Destroy them, Horace." The time for such action had passed; these photographs had already been reproduced in newspapers and magazines throughout the world.

"The last day we were together, Viola said that at the South Pole, she imagined me beside her. Had it been possible, she would have shared the victory with me. Think of that. I look at these pictures, and I am there and she is absent. Oh, Horace, how can I endure it?"

In the end, Byron agreed; his friendship with Horace was too deep. His own reputation at that moment, with Viola dead, meant little to him. Yet a confession that would salve his conscience and ruin his greatest friend was not a worthy act. "You risked your life to go back to save Viola. I will never forget that."

Byron walked off the ship into the cheering crowd, graciously responding to the acclaim, every inch the hero.

The next day Byron and Horace discussed what must be done to maintain the deception. Mr. Smithers was exhorted to remain silent. A loyal member of the expedition, he agreed without asking a single question, but surely his look was reproachful. Wally represented the greatest risk to their safety, had already talked too much. If he continued spreading rumors about the all-women's expedition and the lost race to the Pole, sooner or later someone would remember that such an expedition had left for the Antarctic. Byron sought him out and threatened dire consequences were he ever to say another word about Viola Crosbie. Tremaine was his leader, so Wally agreed sullenly.

Then Byron turned to the painful task of correcting the documentary evidence as Horace had done. His journals were the more important, for they would be studied, copied, published in book form, and preserved in the polar archives. They would have to be altered, with the pages revealing his failure omitted and new entries added delineating his success. He was sure he could garner sufficient information about the fossils to make a respectable show of scientific knowledge. With every sentence, he would be repudiating his word of honor. He imagined his son watching him at his work, the clear green eyes so like his own filling with dismay. The boy's future was being protected, too, but he might not see it that way. He must never learn the truth. Byron's hands shook and the ink blotted, making the entries appear authentic, prepared under the harsh conditions of the trail.

While looking for the relevant passages in Viola's journal, he made a heartrending discovery. He had assumed Horace held the journal pages and fossils missing from his share of Viola's legacy, but the two packages were now combined, and much was still lacking. Viola had not trusted him. It seemed they were so close, that the differences between them were resolved, the fearsome rivalry ended. He had been deceived. Evadne, indicating her mistrust, had urged that the evidence be left in the tent, but Viola had disagreed. No, he told Horace sadly, she had merely appeared to disagree.

Why should it hurt so much? If only he could assure her that when he left her in the tent, he had been ready to present her claim, give her the credit, the glory, whatever the cost to his pride. His was the shorter route; he should have been first in New Zealand. He could not have foreseen that he would be trapped at the Bay of Whales while events were being set in motion by Horace. Once the mendacious claim had been made, Byron was forced to accede out of loyalty to his friend. None of this would have happened had Viola survived. However, she and the others of the Crosbie expedition were all dead, and it was not his doing. His conscience was clear as to that. Both he and Horace had done their best to save the women. Yet, for the remainder of his life he would be bound to the lie, to the bitter knowledge that even in his arms, Viola had believed he would lie. Sadder yet was the knowledge that, as it turned out, she had been right to distrust him.

He had never felt so heartsick as when making up the false entries in his diary. At the same time he was filled with trepidation, knowing that Evadne had spoken truly: Nothing decays in Antarctica. The evidence giving him the lie was still in the tent where Viola lay. It was ironic, Byron remarked, that Horace had actually been back there, found the women dead, and left empty-handed when he could have taken away the missing pages and fossils. Miserable at being forced to underscore his deception, Horace replied that when he was in the tent, he did not know what it contained.

So long as the record of Viola's expedition remained hidden, Byron's version would be accepted. Should a search party find the tent, however, then all must be revealed. But would anyone be looking for the missing Crosbie expedition? Viola had told him about the pledge of secrecy made to the suffragettes. Her father was dead and the Amazons possessed no close ties.

There was the danger, though, that future explorers might trace the route of the Tremaine expedition and follow it to the tent. That must not happen. Byron altered his maps, omitting the area around the tent altogether.

Were it not for the world war, some enterprising journalist might have been curious enough to find out what happened to the Crosbie expedition after its departure from New York Harbor in 1914. In those years, however, no one had the time or the interest in an oddity of that type. Even after I learned the women's fate, it did not occur to me that Byron took part in silencing the press.

The geographical organizations of the United States and Europe accepted the evidence Byron presented. The fossil findings were hailed as landmarks in prehistory, surpassing those of the earlier Greenland expedition. Byron received awards and honors and was repeatedly offered financial backing to return to the Antarctic to continue his discoveries. In time he led new expeditions, though never again to Antarctica. On each one he deliberately exposed himself to the greatest hazards, performed acts of bravery, and returned home to receive accolades which he accepted with joy outwardly, misery within.

The years passed and the false was accepted as true. Other explorers arrived at the South Pole and found no sign of the Crosbie expedition that had preceded them; the flags lay buried by the snowquake. Of course there was no indication of the presence of the Tremaine expedition, and that was falsely attributed to the snowquake. The tent, too, was lost in the vastness of the Antarctic; no one knew to look for it. Yet the three of us were changed by the Tremaine expedition. Byron was silent, brooding, rousing himself in public, subsiding as soon as I alone was his audience. Was he thinking about Viola, mourning her death, though he never mentioned her name? I was in torment seeing Horace's unhappiness, knowing my love was the cause, knowing also that my love was his only pleasure now. In my arms and nowhere else could he find a few moments of relief from the anguish of what he had done.

Night after night, Horace told me, he dreamed he was standing on the ice plateau, turning away from the tent where Viola and Evadne were lying, tears of guilt freezing on his face. Sometimes in sleep, Byron tossing and turning beside me, I would dream Horace's dream, then awaken as he did to remind myself that the women had surely been dead and he had saved Byron's reputation and distinguished career.

Horace accompanied Byron on the expeditions and it was only when the two men were away that I knew peace, living quietly with you and Junior—Horace's daughter, Byron's son. Everyone thought you both fortunate to have so great a heritage; only I feared that heritage, and rightly so for my boy.

Day after day, year after year, I pretended to believe in the false claim to the South Pole, to admire Byron as a hero above all other men. He suffered, and the saddest part was that he was innocent of the greater wrong. Because of Horace, because of me, his life became a lie. Byron was not as guilty as I or as my lover, had not left Viola to die on the ice cap. Nonetheless, he was false. When finally he spoke openly to me on the last day we were together, he told me how often he thought to make a public avowal of the truth, take the humiliation as he had the praise. Each time, however, he realized that clearing his conscience would wreck Horace's life, implicate Mr. Pitman and Mr. Smithers in the collusion, and disgrace his children—and he was silent. I suppose I should be grateful to him for his generosity.

Each man, I came to see, though suffering, believed he was selflessly enduring because of the other. Their friendship sustained them. But what was to sustain me? My duty as a wife? To a husband who had loved and still mourned for another woman? My love for Horace? Yet was I not supporting him in a course I knew to be morally wrong? Another woman might have refused to go along with such mendacity. Viola almost surely would have done so.

For my children? I believed that for a long time, and I tried, insofar as it was possible, Susan, to make amends for your father's coldness, to temper my son's ambition. But I could not save him. A second Tremaine Antarctic expedition, led by his son: That was Byron's dream. It almost happened. Even after Byron's death, our son remained under his father's spell, or so I thought. Though he had not the physical strength, endurance, and athletic skill required for the Antarctic, nothing would stop him. He had married at twenty; his wife was pregnant, but still he went. Too young for his own expedition, he signed on with another. After just a few weeks in the Antarctic, he was lost in a blizzard. I remembered then that some months before he joined the expedition, I had come upon him in the parlor, standing in front of the enlarged photograph of Byron at the South Pole. "What are you doing?" "Nothing." However, he was staring at the picture and his manner was odd, and after his death I wondered what he had seen there.

That came later. I must tell you now of what happened on a day in August of 1925, just before Byron departed on his expedition to Mount McKinley. That was the day his lying to me ended, though my lying to him never did. Byron had been happy in the Arctic years before, and his mood was lighter than usual that summer. On this particular day, however, he returned home from his office grim-faced and shaken and paced the floor for hours in a mood of dark despondency. I did not know what to do. It was not our custom, as I have told you, to speak much to one another. Nonetheless, I could not see him so wretched, so I came close to him and rested my hand lightly on his arm. Usually he moved away when I touched him, but this time he did not, and only caught at my hand and held it so tightly that I thought he would crush my fingers. Yet it was an affectionate gesture, and so quite startled me. There was never affection in his manner toward me.

"What has happened?" I did not expect an honest answer. He never spoke openly to me; his lies and his love for Viola were always between us. This time he hesitated for a moment and then began to speak. "I must tell you how the Tremaine Antarctic expedition ended. I cannot go without telling the truth for once."

A sense of dread came over me as I waited for him to reveal to me the history I knew so well, yet could not admit without admitting my adulterous love for Horace Graham. But Byron said nothing about the ice cap, the depot, and the women waiting in the tent. Instead he told of an event that appeared quite trivial to me at first. Shortly after his return to New York in 1917, a suffragette, Eileen Lincoln by name, appeared unannounced in his office. She had moved through the reception room so rapidly that no one was able to stop her. There she stood, a small, thin woman with graying hair escaping from a bowl-shaped hat, and abruptly told him he must arrange a search party to go to Antarctica and find whatever remained of the Crosbie expedition.

She had already tried every other avenue. Viola's mother and sister expressed deep grief but were convinced she was dead. The expedition had been foolhardy; no one but she would have attempted it. They could not justifiably ask others to risk their lives, have those deaths on their conscience. The Lamberts had been embarrassed by the life Viola led, by the snide references to "Mrs. Crosbie's Folly." Relieved when talk about it died down, they did not object when Evelyn's husband, Bertram, asserted that the ship carrying the expedition had foundered soon after leaving New York Harbor.

Miss Lincoln thought then of Viola's husband, Ian Crosbie, who had planned the route and so was most likely to know where to search. Unfortunately, Ian was lost himself. There was a rumor that he had been seen in an Indian village far in the North. However, the description had been merely that of a large white man, and it might not have been he. Then she had gone to one Lord Hargreave. Byron recognized the name, and thought, My God! One more person to know the story, and wondered why Miss Lincoln had selected him. She had learned from the newspapers that Lord Hargreave was visiting New York, remembered that though he was an opponent of suffrage, he had been ardently in love with Viola and wanted to marry her. As he repeated Miss Lincoln's words, Byron flushed, and I thought that even after her death, he could not bear the thought of another man in love with Viola, and she perhaps responding physically to that ardent love. I could understand causeless jealousy; Horace's wife was dead before I knew him, yet I found it painful to think that he had lain with her, fathered her child.

Lord Hargreave had turned white on hearing Viola's name, Miss Lincoln reported with amazement. Oh, he remembered Viola; that much was clear. However, he would not help her, and he said in a choked voice that Viola deserved nothing from him, nothing.

Of course Miss Lincoln made an appeal to the suffragettes, but with little hope. They had known from the outset, as had Viola, that losing the race to Tremaine reflected badly on women, could damage the suffrage cause. It was essential to conceal the disaster of the Crosbie expedition. Men would joke about it as an example of women's refusal to accept their proper role in life. No one must know about that fiasco. Had there been a possibility the women were still alive, then they would consider breaking the oath of concealment. However, the harsh fact was that the Crosbie expedition could not possibly have survived a second winter on the ice. They were past helping, and the resources of the suffrage movement must be directed toward helping other women to the vote.

Miss Lincoln was unconvinced; she had been told of explorers who by seeming miracles survived periods as long as that. A search party must be mounted to rescue the women . . . or find their bodies. It would be better to know they had perished than to continue in this terrible suspense.

If only it were possible to tell her the truth, that Horace had seen Viola's body, Byron had thought; but he could merely reiterate that the women must be dead and there was no excuse for risking other lives in a vain search.

After Miss Lincoln left, Byron put his head in his hands and wept (he admitted having wept; I had never seen him shed tears) that Viola's body lay with no marker giving her name, the dates of her brief life, and a few words on her great achievement. It could not be helped; he must not allow a search party . . . ever. The tent with its burden of proof should forever be lost in the polar snows. Byron was obsessed with the fear that the all-women's expedition would yet come to light.

Miss Lincoln, however, did not give up so easily; she was a fighter, and thought to arouse public opinion and obtain enough contributions to pay for a search party. Rejecting the suffragettes' demand for secrecy, she went to a major newspaper bearing the meager bunch of newspaper clippings about "Mrs. Crosbie's Folly." The women had reached Antarctica, she insisted, and might still be alive somewhere close to the South Pole. The editor spoke with Byron and was convinced by him that Miss Lincoln was unreliable and her story false: The expedition had been lost at sea and had not come within thousands of miles of Antarctica.

From then on, Byron could not bear to have any association with the suffrage movement. Thenceforth each time he was called on for continuing support, he refused. I understood now why the Woman's party opposed Byron's candidacy for his father's seat in the Senate.

When he finished speaking of Eileen Lincoln's visit and its aftermath, he became silent, until at last I asked the obvious question: "What made you speak of that episode today when it is so long in the past?"

"I saw Wally Padgett by chance on the street today."

I was taken aback; Horace had told me that Wally was taken along for the assault on the Pole, but Byron appeared to have forgotten him. "I thought to cross the street and avoid him," said Byron. "I never liked the boy. A nasty, whining, dirty creature. But there was something about the way he was looking at me that made me uneasy, so I went over, put my hand on his shoulder as I used to, and spoke with him warmly, reminding him that I had called him a brave boy.

" 'Brave, I am,' he replied, 'and honest, too. More than can be said for others, ain't it?' He had this dreadful, ungrammatical speech. The insolence of his manner stunned me, but there was a threat in it that chilled my heart. 'What do you mean?' I asked. 'I remember things. Go hunt the penguin. What a damn fool idea that was. But anything you said, Mr. Graham jumped to. Like the depot.' 'What?' I asked. 'The women's depot where we took the food,' he replied. 'You knew all about it, gave the order, told Mr. Graham what he'd find and what to do about it.' 'But I didn't.' I couldn't believe I was defending myself against the lying words of an animal handler."

Observing the enmity in Wally's eyes, Byron suddenly understood what had happened. The boy knew it all. From the time of his return from the depot, he drew away from Byron, would not speak to Horace. Byron remembered then how strangely Horace had behaved, sickened by the food he had brought.

"I should have guessed, Hermine. I did not look closely enough. Still, I could not be angry with Horace, knowing how the brutal Antarctic can affect a man, knowing he had done it for me. 'None of that, Wally.' I forced him to look into my eyes. I had been his leader and he was afraid. But I was afraid, too. And he saw it and was encouraged to go on with his accusations. I had been indifferent to his fate, he said, had forced him to go by the most dangerous route. 'I didn't want to be with Mr. Graham, but I'd have kept our promise. Only you never meant us to save the women, did you? Mr. Graham just turned right around the way you told him to and went the other way. I said we had ought to go back to the tent. How could we leave them women to die like that? But if you didn't care, why should he?'

"Everything in me wanted to believe he was lying. A hateful boy. But I recognized the truth. Oh, Hermine, I should have known it all along. The plan to have Horace return for Viola from the depot was altogether wrong. That was for me to do. Instead I allowed him to talk me into taking the easier route, the safer route. That was how Horace thought. He must keep me safe. I should not have permitted it, particularly as I sensed Horace had a causeless dislike of Viola that might have influenced him in some manner." I was the cause, I thought with a heavy heart. Yet I remained silent. "Horace is a good man, a loyal friend. My life against Viola's. Mine was the most important. To him yes. But not to me. I had no right to send him and Ed and even Wally to face death for Viola's sake. For my sake. In my place. I should have died myself before I ever left her."

"It was not your fault. It was the Antarctic," I said.

"I used to think the Antarctic was in my soul."

After a long pause, he continued. "My betrayal did not end in Antarctica, but has gone on through all these years. If only I had it to do again, Hermine, how gladly I would tell the world of Viola Crosbie's victory over the Pole, over me. Hers should be the name in the history books, not mine. They call me a hero, but I took the coward's way."

The following morning he left for Mount McKinley. I knew he would not return. There is one matter concerning his death that troubles me, one thing I have never been able to understand: He had my photograph with him. It was returned with his body. I do not like to think he may have loved me all the while.

Later, after Byron's death, Horace wanted us to marry. But how could we marry with all that blood between us?

# Chapter Thirty

IT WAS QUIET IN THE tent after the men had gone. Viola remembered Byron's body in her arms, the feel of his skin. *You are mine.* During the act of love. Afterward the contest between them flared up again. For the last time.

Conflict had become basic to their love, so basic a part that she had refused him once and then again and again. Yet even now she knew she had not been wrong in the choice she had made. The possibilities were limitless. Horace would return from the depot within a few days and journey with her to the Bay of Whales and from there to New Zealand to a future in exploration, in science, a future with Byron Tremaine. In achieving the Antarctic, she had made a life with Byron possible. He would not force her into the doll-like existence his wife was leading. The matching of equals. He accepted that now.

In discovering the secret of the photograph, she had discovered the depth of his love. How vehemently she had fought him when all along it had been her picture, not Hermine's, that he unpacked upon arriving at his destination, packed when breaking camp.

She could almost pity Hermine, as she pitied Ian. In the silence of the tent, she thought once more of Ian. She had loved him, though not as he loved her, not as she loved Byron. Still, her feeling for him was deep and she was filled with regret for what was lost.

All at once she became aware that Evadne was walking purposefully about the tent, taking objects out of her sleeping bag and carrying them over to the crude table. Viola came closer and with dismay observed the neat stacks made up of pages cut out of journals, and next to them the boxes of film and glass plates, rocks with fossil imprints, bottles holding specimens of immensely ancient microorganisms, and the package containing the prehistoric jawbone. Fully half the evidence proving the Crosbie expedition's claim to the South Pole lay before her on the table.

Now Viola remembered that Evadne had pleaded with her to leave it in the tent. And how had she responded? By telling Evadne to make packages for the men to carry.

"Why have you done this?"

Why, thought Evadne. Because she could not bear to give it all to Tremaine, knowing he would adopt the evidence as his own. The record would not survive the inevitable betrayal. "I could not watch you throwing away our victory. It isn't yours alone, Viola; it belongs to all of us. To me. Someday my son must learn what I have done."

"Your son?" Who could have thought that beautiful, unmarked body had borne a son? Viola remembered the child she had lost in falling from the rope in the town hall of MidValley, and was seized by grief. Byron had children, sometimes spoke of his ambition for the boy. "I didn't know you had a son."

"Even my son doesn't know I had a son." Evadne's tone was bitter. "Gerald, his father, feels nothing but scorn for me. If my part in the expedition comes to light, then I think he must reveal the truth to David. It is my one hope."

"But I don't understand. Why would he want to conceal your existence from your son? You're a renowned dancer."

"A woman like me. That's what he said. A whore, Viola."

"He didn't mean it; surely he was just trying to hurt you." How often had she hurt herself in hurting Byron? How often had he hurt himself in hurting her? *In Greenland the men called you my whore.*

Not at all the same. Twelve years old and earning good money. "A couple of dollars was good money for us then. A whore. In my mama's apartment."

Viola remembered then that one night on board the *Explorer* she had noticed a seaman coming out of Evadne's cabin. The hallway was badly lit with a gas jet, and she decided she must have been mistaken.

Now she knew why Evadne had gotten along so easily with the ship's crew, why she had known their curses, laughed at their jokes. A coarse laugh, Ian had said.

"I gave the two men documents enough to prove our claim." But they would not do so. No one but Viola could possibly believe that would happen.

Evadne did not grasp what she had done, Viola thought resentfully. The members of the geographic societies were conservative men who would resist the knowledge that a women's expedition had conquered the South Pole unless it were proven beyond any doubt. The evidence Evadne had allowed Byron and Horace to take was insufficient for that purpose. Everything now depended on Viola's returning to New Zealand and presenting the claim herself. While she believed this was to happen, she knew the hazards of the Antarctic and had felt secure in the belief that Byron and Horace held the needed evidence.

"I wish you had at least given the prehistoric jawbone to Byron, Evadne. That discovery could make me famous, advance the position of women in science. That alone."

Make Viola famous? Hardly. Tremaine would seize the credit for the discovery of the ancient bones as he would for everything else.

"If the men come back for us, we'll be traveling together and can take the jawbone and the other fossils with us then, Viola."

" 'If'? Of course they'll come back for us."

"Of course."

Viola was perfectly aware that Horace did not like her; he had not responded to her last effort at friendliness, refused to return her smile. But his personal feelings would not weigh in the balance. Evadne did not understand the code of honor that ruled men like Graham and Tremaine. That was why she was certain Horace would come back from the depot even though the danger to him was great. That was why she was certain Byron would present her claim even though it was hard for him to admit defeat.

However she felt about Evadne's act of concealment, they must not quarrel in the close quarters of the tent, where there was little to do but maintain the diary entries and exercise to make their bodies strong again. Evadne spoke of the dance more often in these days. That was what she most missed in Antarctica. It was the greatest part of her life. "Better than the fame and the applause and the money. The joy of it. I could make everyone who saw me feel that joy, sway with it, sense the beauty of the body. Because for those few hours, I was the dance. And here in the Antarctic, I hear the music playing in my head, calling me to dance."

At least, Evadne was thinking, she was older than her mother had ever been. A whore aged quickly, died young. The girls who had been on the vaudeville circuit with her must be dead by now, too; that life was brutal. Only a few weeks had passed since the day at the South Pole when she had thought to return to the stage, once more a star. Perhaps it would have happened—were it not for the Tremaine expedition. Now all that was left was the diary, the record of her life. It was absurd, really, to believe that David would ever learn of her place on the Crosbie expedition and be proud of her, thought Evadne. Absurd. But was it any more absurd than for Viola to listen for the sound of the sledge runners on the ice, the dogs barking, and the men's voices?

The days passed until the last of the carefully husbanded food and fuel ran out. A few days more. Then Viola, too, accepted that Horace was not coming back. He would have done so were it humanly possible. Only the treacherous nature of the Antarctic weather and terrain could have forced him to retreat. Only that.

Well, she had always known the risk of exploration. So had Evadne and the other women. That was what made heroes.

One last day and she would go out on the ice with Evadne. They would ski as far as their strength allowed and stop there forever. It had been agreed between them.

As Viola completed the final diary entry, the silence was suddenly broken by the barking of dogs, a harsh voice shouting, sledge runners on the snow. The men of course. They were returning after all. But though it was hoarse, guttural, this was not a man's voice. She knew who made those sounds. Claireve. No one else. In an instant Viola and Evadne were on their feet and running to lift the tent flap. And there coming toward them in the brilliant sunshine were Claireve and Araminta followed by the dog team pulling the loaded sledge.

"We thought you were lost."

"Yeah. We was lost. It was awful."

Speaking slowly and laboriously as was her way, Araminta told the story. Every so often Claireve added something in the thick, raspy speech Viola had learned to decipher with some difficulty. They had been close to the depot when a whiteout had concealed the trail. Tying themselves to the sledge with rope, they went on, thinking they were following the direct route, but when the sky cleared and they could see again, they had missed the depot. Somehow they must reach another, so they marched on with food almost gone and no fuel to light the stove. Each night they dug a hole in the snow and huddled with the dogs, keeping just warm enough to stay alive.

"One morning when we knew we couldn't go on much more, we seen a pile of rocks and a depot with lots of boxes. Me and Claireve figured it was Tremaine's and we couldn't take nothing. We was going to leave when the dogs dug up a flag that had fallen down and it said Shackleton and the boxes were marked that way. We never heard of him, so we figured he was an old-timer and wouldn't be back no more, and we loaded up everything on the sledge. It took us three more days to get back to you."

Three days to return to the tent and another three merely to retrace their steps. Six days closer to the storms of autumn. Had Araminta and Claireve continued directly on the route, their chance of reaching the base camp would have been infinitely better.

"It was heroic for you to come back for us."

Heroic? Araminta and Claireve did not view their action in that light. They had promised to return.

While the two exhausted women took a brief rest, Viola made her final preparations for the journey. As she checked the map, she thought this was Ian's legacy. His last loving gesture. All the journals, photographic evidence, and fossils must be left behind, as the added weight might spell disaster. But the jawbone. Only that. Viola opened the package, and the remains of the mysterious ancient beast were in her hand, the bones darkened and hollowed, presenting their record of the past as clearly as if the creature still had life and could make the needed sounds. Take the jawbone with her? The risk of its coming to harm on so desperate a journey was too great. She would be wiser to replace the wrappings and leave it in the tent to be found by a search party the following spring.

She went outside, where Evadne was counting the cartons of supplies that would have to carry them all the way to the first of their own depots. "Not enough."

"I don't agree, Evadne. We will reach the next depot, and the one after that, and return to the Bay of Whales." Other voyagers to Antarctica had survived incredible hardships. She had heard of an explorer who marched for hundreds of miles across the continent alone after his companions died—and lived to tell of it. Why should they not do as well? Viola was never stopped by the insurmountable. Escape from the blizzard on Disko Island and the fire at Chessham Court had been impossible. For women to reach the South Pole had been impossible. Even the suffragettes were prepared for their failure.

If the weather held, she could reach the Bay of Whales before the ship departed and find Byron waiting there. They would return to New Zealand together to proclaim the conquest of the Pole and to announce a new expedition greater than any in the past. They would yet traverse the vast uncharted Antarctic, forcing it to give up its mysteries.

Viola was dazzled by the splendor of the life she foresaw. A glittering future with Byron Tremaine. Two tigers mating.

It was night, but the sun was still high and the sky overhead and the ice beneath her feet glowed in a golden brilliance. As Viola moved forward on her skis, it seemed to her that Byron's figure was ahead of her on the trail, radiant in the same golden light. A feeling of rapture came over her, as it had when she looked out on the shimmering ice surrounding the South Pole in the culmination of her life's dream. As it had when Byron placed the photograph in her hand and she knew he was hers. The contest between them had ended and she was going to him.

When at last she crossed the gleaming fields of ice, Byron would be waiting for her. As soon as she came into view, he would run toward her with his arms outstretched. Reaching.

# Chapter Thirty-one

UNTIL AVERY SPOKE, I THOUGHT the choice was mine—whether to reveal Viola's triumph or go on with the concealment Byron had maintained throughout his life. Now the decision was taken out of my hands.

"Viola Crosbie conquered the South Pole and Byron Tremaine failed." Avery must have felt exultant, yet his face was impassive, his voice without inflection.

When I first learned of Byron's lies, the knowledge had broken my heart. After reading Hermine's letter, I did not judge him quite so harshly. A tragic figure, my great-aunt had said. Avery, however, would be merciless in his exposé.

How had he found out when I held all the evidence? And how much did he know? I could believe he had come upon references to the Crosbie expedition. There were articles about it in the newspapers of the period after all. But the last report described the embarkation from New York Harbor. After that the expedition disappeared from view.

"So you have the program you wanted, Avery."

"It could be one of my best programs, Beatrix, a sure bet for the forthcoming retrospective, 'Great Moments from Avery Tells All.' " Still, he appeared somber.

"What led you to Viola Crosbie?"

Avery looked away, as if deciding how much to tell me. We were in the living room of the house on Gramercy Park that had belonged to Byron Tremaine, sitting with the small table between us as on the day Avery first came to see me. It seemed a very long time ago. Ronald was my lover then. That seemed a long time ago, too. I miss him, but I would not go back; he reminds me too much of Byron Tremaine—my false image of Byron Tremaine.

When Avery did not answer my question, I tried another approach. "How long have you known? How many times have you come to me pretending you needed information?"

"You were disingenuous, too, Beatrix, looking at me with those enormous melting gray eyes and defending your great-grandfather. It did not occur to me that you actually knew about the Crosbie expedition until I heard you'd gone off to the Antarctic with Bucky Sheridan. Then I realized I'd been had."

"I don't understand. I knew hardly anything before that."

"Then why did you go?" Avery had a theory that explained everything to his satisfaction: Bucky did not reach the Pole, and instead wandered far enough off the route to stumble on a hut or tent, evidence of some kind.

"He was probably saving the information to use on my program when I showed him up as a fraud, but then he couldn't go through with it and confessed to you. He cares too much about you, Beatrix; I can tell." My face was hot, remembering the night with Bucky in the cramped quarters of the South Pole station. "You talked him out of using it, didn't you? When it comes to protecting your great-grandfather, you're inspired. Then the two of you waited for him to get the financial backing to go back to the Antarctic and pick up the evidence. He probably couldn't risk carrying the extra weight with him the first time."

"That's not the way it happened."

Avery shook his head. "I had thought of going to the Antarctic myself, taking you along, Beatrix. You remember I suggested we join forces. But the costs for the program were already way out of line. More to the point, I didn't have the faintest idea where to look. No one had come upon the remains of the Crosbie expedition in eighty years. Sheridan just got lucky."

"I wouldn't have gone with you, Avery."

"You don't trust me. You trust Sheridan, but not me."

It was an odd thing for him to say, as if my friendship with Bucky had anything to do with him. And he was glossing over the fact that he was the one who threatened me.

"Why should I trust anything you say, Avery? You spoke so touchingly of how Tremaine was to be the true hero on your program, and you were resolved to make him your 'bad guy.' From the very beginning."

"You may find it hard to believe, Beatrix, but I did intend him to be the true hero on 'Avery Tells All.' I hadn't the faintest idea there was anything false about Byron Tremaine. It came as a shock to me. Not as big a shock as to you. But a shock, nonetheless."

"Oh, come on, Avery." I was not going to let his lies go unchallenged. "That first time you came here, sitting right where you are now, you had the cassette in your pocket. You were waiting for the right moment to play it for me."

"I was just trying to get some color. Tremaine was too perfect; I didn't think the viewers would buy him. A love affair was what was needed. Only no one else had found any hint of one. You were my only hope."

"Who was that woman on the tape, Avery? With all I've found out, I still have no idea."

"Oh, Beatrix, the tape was what you thought it was. A fake. I wrote a few lines that sounded interesting and asked one of the actresses in the studio to read. There was a chance it would startle you enough to get you to reveal a family secret about a hidden romance. That was all I wanted. I never planned the tape for my show. You were the only audience it was intended for."

He had duped me. I had done everything he wanted, run around trying to disprove the accusations.

Avery was watching me in his intent way. I wished I could hide my face. "Actually I was slow to catch on that Tremaine hadn't reached the South Pole. With all I knew about polar deceptions, I didn't give it a thought. The photographs should have tipped me off that something about the Tremaine expedition was phony. Here I was so pleased with myself for learning that Bucky Sheridan had faked his photographs, and I never even studied Tremaine's.

"I was as mesmerized as everyone else by the aura you cast about them, Beatrix, and about him. You're good at that, convincing. The photographs were not only masterpieces; they were sacrosanct. Without you guarding Tremaine's memory, I think the truth would have come out long ago." It was painful to hear this, knowing that though diffident, I have been bold in maintaining the fiction of his heroism. "You are so sincere, so earnest that when you said he was the true hero, why, who could refuse to believe you?"

"Only you."

"No, I believed you, too." He stood up then and went over to the wall where the photographs were hanging. I would have to take them down. "It's impossible to say why, but one day when I was visiting you, Beatrix, I saw the obvious—they were like Sheridan's photographs, with new figures superimposed on earlier ones. Tremaine and Graham in place of whom? Sharpe and a member of his Pole party? Carlsen?"

He quickly realized that was impossible; the photographs had been widely reproduced and experts declared they were taken at the actual Pole, and contrary to their claims, Sharpe and Carlsen had fallen short.

"Didn't the newspaper reports about 'Mrs. Crosbie's Folly' make you suspicious, Avery?"

"Is that what they called it? A nasty touch. But I didn't know about the expedition then. It isn't possible to do open-ended research and go through every newspaper and publication for years on end in the hope that something will turn up; you'd never finish. You have to find a starting point, and I didn't have one.

"For a long time I couldn't figure out whose figures these could possibly have been. No one else, to my knowledge, had conquered the South Pole before Tremaine."

"How did you learn you were wrong about that?"

"Wally Padgett. He put me onto the women's expedition."

I thought I held all the evidence. Instead, here was the witness. I wished I could believe this tape, too, was bogus, but Padgett was a real person and the meeting with him had precipitated Tremaine's suicide.

"Padgett was in pretty bad shape and when I asked him for the name of the expedition's leader, he mumbled something that sounded like 'Viola.' The only Viola I knew about was Viola Lambert, but at the time I believed her to be dead. I'd called off my London researcher too soon. So I figured that either there was another woman with the same first name, or I hadn't understood Padgett."

By chance the research for the program on the Arctic Indians brought him to Ian Crosbie, then to Viola, and at last to the long-lost Crosbie expedition.

There was something wrong here, though I could not think what it was. "You played the tape for me," I said, feeling a chill at the memory of the night in London when Avery held me in his hotel room listening to words I did not want to hear and could not forget. Now I realized what was troubling me about Avery's account. The tape did not reveal what he said it did. "Padgett didn't say anything about a women's expedition."

For once, Avery was embarrassed. "Not on that tape. To be honest, Padgett wasn't dead when we talked about him at the Explorers Club dinner. It was clear from what he said the first time—the part you heard—that he knew a lot more. I went back and talked to him again, and he gave me the whole story."

*The whole story.* My hands were cold and my throat was constricted. To conceal my consternation, I stood up and started pacing the room, but everywhere I turned, I came upon another memento of the Tremaine expedition. At last I managed to speak. "Why did you tell me he was dead?"

Again Avery seemed ill at ease. "I didn't want you going to see him. You're so winning, standing up for Byron Tremaine the way you do. I thought you'd get him to make another tape denying what he'd told me." And Avery wondered that I mistrusted him; I felt lost in his lies.

"What did he tell you?" I wanted to hear the exact words.

"The women reached the South Pole but didn't survive the journey back. Padgett described how Tremaine and his party came upon the dead bodies and took as many of the records and as much of the film as they could carry. These were later used to support their own claim."

I was taken aback. Padgett could not have said that. He knew the men had not returned to the tent and found the bodies. And he held Byron responsible for leaving the women to die. At first I could not think why Avery was lying about this, and then I knew. His program. Everything centered on that.

"You thought I'd appear on 'Avery Tells All.' 'Your great-grandfather never needed you so much.' You said that to me the last time we met. Then you were going to spring it on me—what Wally really told you—confident I'd respond with sufficient horror to impress your millions of viewers. That's the kind of drama you look for." My voice sounded hoarse, unfamiliar to me.

Avery appeared astounded by my accusation, though it was perfectly reasonable, considering the nature of "Avery Tells All." He actually stammered as he responded; I could not imagine why he was reacting so strongly. "I never intended to do anything like that."

"Then why are you lying about what Padgett said?" I was too angry to speak in a temperate manner.

"Because I didn't want you to know, Beatrix. I don't see how you could have found out, unless Padgett told someone else. You wouldn't have learned it from me—on my program or anywhere.

"When I left Padgett, I was horrified by what he had said to me, by what it would mean to you, Beatrix. I never wanted to be the one to tell you."

I did not believe him, and asked coldly, "Why not?"

"I couldn't bear to have you hate me."

So great was his personal magnetism that for a moment he convinced me; then the truth intervened. "I don't think you care about being hated by one person, Avery. It's your millions of viewers who have to love you. Your ratings. That's all you care about. It's why you came back to see me again and again."

"Again and again. You're quite right about that, Beatrix. If I spent this amount of time on every program, I'd be doing one a year, not one a week." Bucky said that to me once; I had not believed him.

I was outraged that while meaning to be charming, Avery was ignoring how much this program would hurt me. And he believed I would be flattered by his spending so much time with me. "I think the world would be a better place if you did one program a year."

He looked as if I had struck him. If only I could. "You say you found Crosbie when you were looking into radioactive wastes to help the Indians—is that a real program, Avery, or just something you thought up to impress me with the importance of your exposés?"

"It's a real program. You're wrong to distrust me; each of my programs has a purpose, a mission." This was how he glorified what he did. "I could review them for you one by one and show you how many people's lives have been changed for the better. Of course I look for the sensational. If I didn't, no one would turn to the channel. But it's not just for sensation's sake. Listen to me, Beatrix." He leaned toward me, and I was surprised to realize he was almost pleading. "The exposé on child prostitution has saved thousands from abuse and degradation. My investigation of corruption in government led to fact-finding commissions. The shocking interviews with disfigured victims of drive-by shootings were instrumental in passing gun-control legislation. My programs have brought about needed reforms. Exposing indifference and fraud is useful; it's television journalism at its best."

He was impassioned, and I could remember the programs he described, but I would not allow him to affect my judgment with his lofty talk. That is how he will explain the harsh exposé of Tremaine. Yet he did not know what had led to the tragedy. The account given him was twisted. Padgett believed Tremaine had issued the orders for the most heinous actions—the removal of the supplies from the depot, the abandonment of the women in the tent. How could I convince Avery that Horace had acted on his own?

"Tremaine behaved badly, but not as badly as you think he did, Avery. He was not entirely to blame for what happened to the Crosbie expedition."

Avery gave the humorless half smile that had become familiar to me. "I might have known it. Of course you'd find a defense for Byron Tremaine. Don't bother. You don't need to use it with me."

"Don't I? All along you've been deceiving me, trying to trick me into giving you information. I suppose you rationalize that on the grounds that it's television journalism at its best," I said bitterly.

"I just kept on looking for things to bring you, Beatrix, flaws in the Tremaine legend. But not to trick you. In the beginning I enjoyed baiting you; your loyalty to Tremaine was so touching, like something out of another era. You seemed like someone out of another era yourself. I was fascinated with the idea of bringing you to life. Maybe that's why I goaded you. Such a timid girl, not too different from your great-grandmother. I thought I could shock you out of your timidity—hiding behind Byron Tremaine, having an affair with a man who is so much older than you.

"I believed the relationship with Graham had to end. How long can these old explorers keep going? How long would it be before he'd get tired of your fascination with Tremaine? Before you'd be ready for a younger man? I never imagined you'd take up with Bucky Sheridan. I underrated him. But there it is, one always underrates these devil-may-care Boy Scout types, thinks they're too uninteresting to be competition. I guess you shared a room with him at McMurdo and the South Pole. A bunk probably. Tight quarters at the research stations, no doubt."

I knew I must be flushing beneath Avery's piercing gaze. There is some truth in what he said about Ronald, and I am not sure how I feel about Bucky. I thought of Bucky holding me that heartbreaking night at the South Pole station. Looking back, it seems that we both stepped out of character, I to make love so carelessly, he to make love so carefully. In New York, he reverted to his lighthearted manner, I to grieving over Tremaine. Bucky is planning a new venture, to Tibet or the Amazon, the choice depending on the sponsor. He wants us to make love again—between his voyages, I assume—but such serious words as *relationship* are not for him, and those are the words I know best.

I wondered what lay behind Avery's pretense of jealousy. Perhaps he thought it a necessary part of the seductiveness he practiced, a useful component of the interviewer's art.

"I know you don't trust me, Beatrix. But I've done more for you than Graham ever did. I've brought you to life. Give me credit for that at least."

"Your arrogance sickens me."

"Does it? I don't think so. In London, for a little while, I thought all the passion I know you're capable of would be given to me. The passion Graham never aroused in you and Sheridan never can. It will still happen."

"Your arrogance sickens me."

My chilling response appeared if anything to please him. "Something has changed about you in these months, Beatrix. I've had something to do with it." I was astounded by his effrontery in assuming his attention could affect me. Yet I feel myself quite a different person now, though I am not certain in what way. And when he put his hand with its long, tapering fingers on my arm, I did not shake him off.

I had to know what he planned. "How are you going to handle Padgett's story on 'Avery Tells All'? What are you going to say about Viola, about Tremaine?"

His response was totally unexpected. "That depends on you."

"What do you mean?"

"What do you think I mean, Beatrix?"

I shook my head, baffled.

"Once, and only once, I dropped a program that would have been outstanding, because I was asked to do so."

Had it been anyone else, I would have thought he was offering to drop this program, too, but I knew Avery too well. He was merely playing a game. "Who had that much influence on you?"

"My wife," he replied.

It made sense. She had been a top executive at the network when they married and had given him his big chance. This was the payback.

"Some people think I used her, Beatrix. But I didn't; she used me. I saved her job. She was on the way out because she hadn't produced a hit series in a year. 'Avery Tells All' was a sure thing; the other networks were after me.

"We'd been married about five years when I got inside information for a program about unethical business practices. The main subject of the exposé turned out to be a friend of hers. That's what she said. A lover, I learned later. But I didn't know it then. Anything she asked, I would do. I loved her."

Love. The word sounded peculiar coming from him, and was no doubt untrue. In his highly publicized divorce proceedings, his affair with a public relations executive who did wonders for his career had been disclosed. I did not say anything, but he answered as if I had. "My marriage was falling apart by then and the woman came along at the right moment. The network hired her firm because it was the best. She had to help my career; that was her job. She's the kind of person I meet, Beatrix. Aggressive, pushing. Except for you."

His manner was enticing; he knew how to make me feel important.

It meant nothing. "What are you planning to do, Avery? Why don't you come right out and tell me?"

"I've told you already," he replied. "It depends on you. I'll leave Tremaine out of my program if you ask me to."

I could not believe he meant what he was saying. I needed time to think. "Then the program will focus on Bucky Sheridan?"

Avery pulled away from me and frowned; he seemed harsher, older. "You worry about him. Don't bother. He'll be all right. I can tell you exactly what he'll do. He'll look wide-eyed into the camera and confess everything. Television viewers love confessions. He'll offer a reason for his actions that everyone can accept. Temporary insanity perhaps. The Antarctic drives men mad. Or loyalty to his men, whose future livelihood depended on success. Men like Sheridan always have an answer ready."

I tried not to show my surprise at his prescience. That is exactly what Bucky plans to do.

"I thought the polar program was a certainty for 'Great Moments from Avery Tells All.' "

"It is. And without the Tremaine segment, it won't be. But I'll cancel that if you ask me to." His voice was soft, caressing.

"But why? I can understand your canceling a program for your wife at a time when you still loved her. But why me?"

I had always avoided looking at him directly, but now I did, and his dark brown eyes were not hard or merciless. I might even have described them as melting. "You have no sense of yourself, Beatrix. Any other woman would know why."

Incredibly, I did know why. Men like this are not attracted to me. I had thought that all along; I did not think so now. I am not attracted to them. I had thought that all along; I did not think so now. Avery was bending toward me in the seductive way that had offended me before. I was not offended now. His face was pale and when he reached out and took my hand, his was trembling. Oddly, so was mine. The whole world seemed to be spinning and I was not certain where I would be standing when it became still.

I do have a sense of myself; I knew Ronald desired me when he first saw me, know Bucky wants to be my lover. Only Avery, with his seeming coldness and relentless pursuit of scandal, confused me. I had believed Avery would stick at nothing to create a sensational television exposé. Regardless of who was hurt. He had seemed impervious to human emotions. It had never crossed my mind that he might care enough to do this for me.

*I just want to have a good time,* Bucky had said in an airplane flying over the Antarctic snows. I want more. In that sense, Avery with his dark intensity is a more suitable lover. A lover? But making love with him had been disastrous. I thought of that night in London, only this time I remembered the beginning not the end of it. Going in the elevator with him, holding on to the wall because my knees would not hold me up for wanting him. Wanting him. Nothing would have happened otherwise. The image I had of myself did not fit that woman in the elevator, that woman on the bed, and I had been appalled. *It could be different,* he said the last time we were together. *The way you like it.* I had not believed him then, but what if it could?

When I first met Avery, I had described him to myself as the kind of man one instinctively imagines in the sexual act. *One?* Or was that was how *I* imagined him?

I had not accepted Avery's sincerity. Until just now. A tremendous sense of relief swept over me as I realized I had won. Just a few words from me and Byron Tremaine was safe.

Here was the last threat to my great-grandfather. If I silenced Avery, it was not likely that anyone else would ever come upon the truth. Who else would look for it? Viola's journals and fossil discoveries were in my possession, along with Hermine's letter. If I wished, I could destroy every piece of evidence. Did I not owe that to Byron? As his chief apologist, how could I be the one to bring him down? Were all his truly great achievements as an explorer to count for nothing? It was in my power to protect him because Avery had fallen in love with me.

Love had not saved Viola. One more betrayal. Considering the stakes, could that matter now?

Like a picture painted with colors that were too bright. The low throbbing voice that could inflame the heart. All at once Viola Lambert came to me unbidden. A personality so vivid, so entrancing, that its aura remained after her death. She had been destined to make her mark in exploration and in scientific discovery, and by so doing to improve the lot of women. Nothing stopped her from pursuing her goal. Not even her love for Byron Tremaine. The competition for the

South Pole had seemed an act of madness, doomed from the start. Yet she went forward, overcame the horrors of the Antarctic, only to be foiled at the last by the man she loved—the man who loved her, yet left her to the mercy of the friend who hated her. All her achievements had been seized, her memory obliterated. Hers was the victory. And no one knew.

No one? But *I* knew.

*If Byron Tremaine has his way, no word of the all-women's expedition to the South Pole will ever get out.* Byron did have his way throughout his life and for the seventy years that followed. He might have it for all time. Were I to ask Avery to cut the Tremaine segment from the program, the all-women's expedition would be lost forever.

Avery was watching me, waiting for my answer, and I thought that during all these years I had drawn courage from Byron Tremaine, only to discover at last that he took the coward's way. *If only I had it to do again,* he had said. He did not have it to do again. But I do. I could do it for him.

The choice was mine after all. And now my doubts left me. Continue the concealment that robbed Viola of her place in history, the concealment that ruled Byron's life and eventually ended it, the concealment that destroyed the happiness Horace and Hermine might have known? No, it was over.

"Shall I drop the Tremaine segment, Beatrix?" For the first time since I had met him, Avery's manner was uncertain.

I thought of the gesture he had made and why he had made it. For me. I could wonder now that I had mistrusted him, thought nothing but his program mattered to him.

When I shook my head, his face fell. "You want nothing from me then."

"I don't need you to protect me or Tremaine, Avery. But there's more than nothing between us." I pressed his hand and he smiled and this time it was not the humorless half-smile that had always troubled me.

"I'll appear on 'Avery Tells All.' "

I imagined how it would be to face the cameras and microphones, to raise my voice and proclaim the glory of the all-women's expedition to the South Pole and reveal the tragedy that followed. This will be my final act as Byron's historian and afterward I will be free of him, free to get on with my life.

"You asked me for photographs never shown before, Avery. I have them now—the true pictures of the women raising the suffrage banner over the South Pole."

"I asked you for a love affair, Beatrix."

"I have found that, too." It was a love so powerful that all the years of bitter rivalry could not destroy it.

I opened the drawer of the desk that had belonged to Byron Tremaine and took out the photograph he cherished. Holding it in my hand, I remembered how I had felt when I first discovered the image of a beautiful, unknown woman hidden behind the portrait of Hermine.

As I gazed at the photograph, I was touched once more by the vitality and eagerness, so strong, so strong that even now, generations later, they arouse the senses.

Viola's face is filled with joy. Her arms are outstretched. Reaching. For Byron Tremaine? Or across the years to her final victory?